aise for Caitlín

W9-BPJ-883

New York T

NOVELS BY CAITLÍN R. KIERNAN

Silk

Threshold

Low Red Moon

Murder of Angels

Daughter of Hounds

The Red Tree

The Drowning Girl: A Memoir

THE
DROWNING
GIRL

A Memoir

ᕗᘻᕐ

CAITLÍN R. KIERNAN

RoC

A ROC BOOK

ROC
Published by New American Library,
a division of Penguin Group (USA) Inc.,
375 Hudson Street, New York, New York 10014, USA
Penguin Group (Canada), 90 Eglinton Avenue East, Suite 700, Toronto,
Ontario M4P 2Y3, Canada (a division of Pearson Penguin Canada Inc.)
Penguin Books Ltd., 80 Strand, London WC2R 0RL, England
Penguin Ireland, 25 St. Stephen's Green, Dublin 2,
Ireland (a division of Penguin Books Ltd.)
Penguin Group (Australia), 250 Camberwell Road, Camberwell,
Victoria 3124, Australia (a division of Pearson Australia Group Pty. Ltd.)
Penguin Books India Pvt. Ltd., 11 Community Centre,
Panchsheel Park, New Delhi - 110 017, India
Penguin Group (NZ), 67 Apollo Drive, Rosedale, Auckland 0632,
New Zealand (a division of Pearson New Zealand Ltd.)
Penguin Books (South Africa) (Pty.) Ltd., 24 Sturdee Avenue,
Rosebank, Johannesburg 2196, South Africa

Penguin Books Ltd., Registered Offices:
80 Strand, London WC2R 0RL, England

First published by Roc, an imprint of New American Library,
a division of Penguin Group (USA) Inc.

First Printing, March 2012
1 3 5 7 9 10 8 6 4 2

Copyright © Caitlín R. Kiernan, 2012
All rights reserved

ROC REGISTERED TRADEMARK—MARCA REGISTRADA

LIBRARY OF CONGRESS CATALOGING-IN-PUBLICATION DATA:
Kiernan, Caitlín R.
The drowning girl: a memoir/Caitlín R. Kiernan.
p. cm.
ISBN 978-0-451-46416-3
1. Schizophrenics—Fiction. 2. Self-actualization (Psychology) in women—Fiction. I. Title.
PS3561.I358D76 2012
813'.54—dc23   2011044675

Set in Sabon • Designed by Elke Sigal

Printed in the United States of America

For Peter Straub, master of the ghost story.
And for Imp.

In Memory of Elizabeth Tillman Aldridge
(1970–1995)

This is the book it is,
which means it may not be the book
you expect it to be.

CRK

There's always a siren,
Singing you to shipwreck.

"THERE THERE (THE BONEY KING OF NOWHERE),"
RADIOHEAD

In the forest is a monster.
It has done terrible things.
So in the wood it's hiding,
And this is the song it sings.

"WHO WILL LOVE ME NOW?" PHILIP RIDLEY

Stories shift their shape.

"PRETTY MONSTERS," KELLY LINK

THE DROWNING GIRL

A Memoir

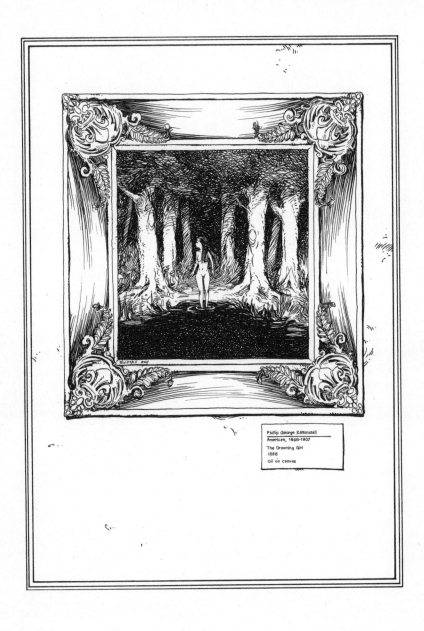

Phillip George Saltonstall
American, 1668-1907

The Drowning Girl
1898
Oil on canvas

1

❦

"**I**'m going to write a ghost story now," she typed.

"A ghost story with a mermaid and a wolf," she also typed.

I also typed.

My name is India Morgan Phelps, though almost everyone I know calls me Imp. I live in Providence, Rhode Island, and when I was seventeen, my mother died in Butler Hospital, which is located at 345 Blackstone Boulevard, right next to Swan Point Cemetery, where many notable people are buried. The hospital used to be called the Butler Hospital for the Insane, but somewhere along the way "for the Insane" was dropped. Maybe it was bad for business. Maybe the doctors or trustees or board of directors or whoever makes decisions about such things felt crazy people would rather not be put away in an insane asylum that dares to admit it's an insane asylum, that truth in advertising is a detriment. I don't know, but my mother, Rosemary Anne, was committed to Butler Hospital *because* she was insane. She died there, at the age of fifty-six, instead of dying somewhere else, because she was insane. It's not like she didn't know she was insane, and it's not like I didn't know, too, and if anyone were to ask me, dropping "for the Insane" is like dropping "burger" from Burger King because hamburgers aren't as healthy as salads. Or dropping "donuts" from Dunkin' Donuts because doughnuts cause cavities and make you fat.

My grandmother Caroline—my mother's mother, who was born in 1914, and lost her husband in World War II—she was also a crazy woman, but she died in her own bed in her own house down in Wakefield. No one put her away in a hospital, or tried to pretend she wasn't crazy. Maybe people don't notice it so much, once you get old, or only older. Caroline turned on the gas and shut all the windows and doors and went to sleep, and in her suicide note she thanked my mother and my aunts for not sending her away to a hospital for the mentally insane, where she'd have been forced to live even after she couldn't stand it anymore. Being alive, I mean. Or being crazy. Whichever, or both.

It's sort of ironic that my aunts are the ones who had my mother committed. I suppose my father would have done it, but he left when I was ten, and no one's sure where he went. He left my mother because she was insane, so I like to think he didn't live very long after he left us. When I was a girl, I used to lie awake in bed at night, imagining awful ways my father might have met his demise, all manner of just deserts for having dumped us and run away because he was too much of a coward to stick around for me and my mother. At one point, I even made a list of various unpleasant ends that may have befallen my father. I kept it in a stenographer's pad, and I kept the pad in an old suitcase under my bed, because I didn't want my mother to see it. "I hope my father died of venereal disease, after his dick rotted off" was at the top of the list, and was followed by lots of obvious stuff—car accidents, food poisoning, cancer—but I grew more imaginative as time went by, and the very last thing I put on the list (#316) was "I hope my father lost his mind and died alone and frightened." I still have that notebook, but now it's on a shelf, not hidden away in an old suitcase.

So, yeah. My mother, Rosemary Anne, died in Butler Hospital. She committed suicide in Butler Hospital, though she was on suicide watch at the time. She was in bed, in restraints, and there was a video camera in her room. But she still pulled it off. She was able to swallow her tongue and choke to death before any of the nurses or orderlies noticed what was happening. The death certificate says she died of a seizure, but I know that's not what happened. Too many times when I visited her, she'd tell me she wanted to die, and usually I told her I'd rather she lived and get better and come home, but that I wouldn't be angry if that's really what she had to do, if she had to die. If there came a day or night when she just couldn't stand it any longer. She said she was sorry, but that she was glad I understood, that she was grateful that I understood. I'd take her candy and cigarettes and books, and we'd have conversations about Anne Sexton and Diane Arbus and about Virginia Woolf filling her pockets with stones and walking into the River Ouse. I never told Rosemary's doctors about any of these conversations. I also didn't tell them about the day, a month before she choked on her tongue, that she gave me a letter quoting Virginia Woolf's suicide note: "What I want to say is I owe all the happiness of my life to you. You have been entirely patient with me and incredibly good. I want to say that—everybody knows it. If anybody could have saved me it would have been you. Everything has gone from me but the certainty of your goodness." I keep that thumbtacked to the wall in the room where I paint, which I guess is my studio, though I usually just think of it as the room where I paint.

I didn't realize I was also insane, and that I'd probably always been insane, until a couple of years after Rosemary died. It's a myth that crazy people don't know they're crazy. Many of us are surely as capable of epiphany and introspection as anyone else, maybe more so. I suspect we spend far more time thinking about our thoughts than do sane people. Still, it simply hadn't occurred to me, that the way I saw the world meant that I had inherited "the Phelps Family Curse" (to quote my aunt Elaine, who has a penchant for melodramatic turns of phrase). Anyway, when it finally occurred to me that I wasn't sane, I went to see a therapist at Rhode Island Hospital. I paid her a lot of money, and we talked (mostly I talked while she listened), and the hospital did some tests. When all was said and done, the psychiatrist told me I suffered from disorganized schizophrenia, which is also called hebephrenia, for Hēbē, the Greek goddess of youth. She—the psychiatrist—didn't tell me that last part; I looked it up myself. Hebephrenia is named after the Greek goddess of youth because it tends to manifest at puberty. I didn't bother to point out that if the way I thought and saw the world meant I was schizophrenic, the crazy had started well before puberty. Anyway, later, after more tests, the diagnosis was changed to paranoid schizophrenia, which isn't named after a Greek god, or any god that I'm aware of.

The psychiatrist, a women from Boston named Magdalene Ogilvy—a name that always puts me in mind of Edward Gorey or a P. G. Wodehouse novel—found the Phelps Family Curse very interesting, because, she said, there was evidence to suggest that schizophrenia might be hereditary, at least in some cases. So there you go. I'm crazy because Rosemary was crazy and had a kid, and Rosemary was crazy because my grandmother was crazy and had a kid (well, several, but only Rosemary lucked out and got the curse). I told Dr. Ogilvy the stories my grandmother used to tell about her mother's sister, whose name was also Caroline. According to my grandmother, Caroline kept dead birds and mice in stoppered glass jars lined up on all her windowsills. She labeled each jar with a passage from the Bible. I told the psychiatrist I'd suspect that my great-aunt Caroline might have only suffered from a keen interest in natural history, if not for the thing with the Bible verses. Then again, I said, it might have been she was trying to create a sort of concordance, correlating specific species with scripture, but Dr. Ogilvy said, no, she was likely also schizophrenic. I didn't argue. Rarely do I feel like arguing with anyone.

So, I have my amber bottles of pills, my mostly reliable pharmacopeia of antipsychotics and sedatives, which are not half so interesting as my great-aunt's bottles of mice and sparrows. I have Risperdal, Depakene, and Valium, and so far I've stayed out of Butler Hospital, and I've only *tried* to kill myself. And only once. Or twice. Maybe I have the drugs to thank for this, or maybe I have my painting to thank, or maybe it's my paintings and the fact that my girlfriend puts up with my weird shit and makes sure I take the pills and is great in the sack. Maybe my mother would have stuck around a little longer if she'd gotten laid now and then. As far as I know, no one has ever proposed sex therapy as a treatment for schizophrenia. But at least fucking doesn't make me constipated or make my hands shake—thank you, Mr. Risperdal—or cause weight gain, fatigue, and acne—thank you so much, Mr. Depakene. I think of all my pills as male, a fact I have not yet disclosed to my psychiatrist. I have a feeling she might feel compelled to make something troublesome of it, especially since she already knows about my "how Daddy should die" list.

My family's lunacy lines up tidy as boxcars: grandmother, daughter, the daughter's daughter, and, thrown in for good measure, the great-aunt. Maybe the Curse goes even farther back than that, but I'm not much for genealogy. Whatever secrets my great-grandmothers and great-great-grandmothers might have harbored and taken to their graves, I'll let them be. I'm already sort of sorry I haven't done the same for Rosemary Anne and Caroline. But they're too much a part of *my* story, and I need recourse to them to tell it. Probably, I could be writing fabricated versions of them, fictional avatars to stand in for the women they actually were, but I knew both well enough to know neither would have wanted that. I can't tell my story, or the parts of my story that I'm going to try to tell, without also telling parts of their stories. There's too much overlap, too many occurrences one or the other of them set in motion, intentionally or unintentionally, and there's no point doing this thing if all I can manage is a lie.

Which is not to say every word will be factual. Only that every word will be true. Or as true as I can manage.

Here's something I scribbled on both sides of a coffeehouse napkin a few days back: "No story has a beginning, and no story has an end. Beginnings and endings may be conceived to serve a purpose, to serve a momentary and transient intent, but they are, in their fundamental nature, arbitrary and exist solely as a convenient construct in the mind of man. Lives are messy, and when we set out to relate them, or parts of them, we cannot ever discern precise and objective moments when any given event began. All beginnings are arbitrary."

Before I wrote that and decided it was true, I would come into this room (which isn't the room where I paint, but the room with too many bookshelves) and sit down in front of the manual typewriter that used to be Grandmother Caroline's. The walls of this room are a shade of blue so pale that sometimes, in bright sunlight, they seem almost white. I would sit here and stare at the blue-white walls, or out the window at the other old houses lined up neatly along Willow Street, the Victorian homes and the autumn trees and the gray sidewalks and the occasional passing automobile. I would sit here and try to settle on a place to begin this story. I would sit here in this chair for hours, and never write a single word. But now I've made my beginning, arbitrary though it may be, and it feels about as right as I think any beginning ever will. It seemed only fair to get the part about being crazy out up front, like a disclaimer, so if anyone ever reads this they'll know to take it with a grain of salt.

Now, also arbitrarily, I'm going to write about the first time I saw *The Drowning Girl*.

For my eleventh birthday, my mother took me to the museum at the Rhode Island School of Design. I'd told her I wanted to be a painter, so that year for my birthday she bought me a set of acrylics, brushes, a wooden palette, and a couple of canvases, and she took me to the RISD Museum. And, like I said, that day was the first time I saw the painting. Today, *The Drowning Girl* hangs much nearer the Benefit Street entrance than it did when I was a kid. The canvas is held within an ornately carved, gilded frame—same as all the others in that part of the museum, a small gallery devoted to nineteenth-century American painters. *The Drowning Girl* measures about nineteen by twenty-four inches. It hangs between William Bradford's *Arctic Sunset* (1874) and Winslow Homer's *On a Lee Shore* (1900). The gallery's walls are a uniform loden green, which, I think, makes the antique golden frames seem somewhat less garish than they might otherwise.

The Drowning Girl was painted in 1898 by a Boston artist named Phillip George Saltonstall. Hardly anyone's written about Saltonstall. He tends to get lumped in with the Symbolists, though one article called him a "late American disciple of the Pre-Raphaelite Brotherhood." He rarely sold, or even showed, his paintings, and in the last year of his life burned as many as fifty in a single night. Most of the few that survive can be found scattered about New England, in private collections and art museums. Also, one hangs in the Los Angeles County Museum of Art, and another in Atlanta's High Museum. Saltonstall suffered from seizures, insomnia, and chronic depression, and he died in 1907, at the age of thirty-nine, after falling from a horse. No one I've read says whether or not it was an accident, that fall, but probably it was. I could say he was a suicide, but I'm biased, and it would only be speculation.

As for the painting itself, *The Drowning Girl* was done mostly in somber shades of green and gray (and so seems right at home hanging on those loden walls), but with a few contrasting counter-points—muted yellows, dirty-white shimmers, regions where the greens and grays sink into blackness. It depicts a young girl, entirely naked, possibly in her early twenties, but maybe younger. She's standing ankle deep in a forest pool almost as smooth as glass. The trees press in close behind her, and her head is turned away from us, as she glances back over her right shoulder, into the forest, towards the shadows gathered below and between those trees. Her long hair is almost the same shade of green as the water, and her skin has been rendered so that it seems paradoxically jaundiced and imbued with some inner light. She's very near the shore, and there are ripples in the water at her feet, which I take to mean she's only just stepped into the pool.

I typed *pool*, but, as it turns out, the painting was inspired by a visit Saltonstall made to the Blackstone River in southern Massachu-setts during the late summer of 1894. He had family in nearby Ux-bridge, including a paternal first cousin, Mary Farnum, with whom he appears to have been in love (there's no evidence the feelings were reciprocal). There's been some conjecture that the girl in the paint-ing is meant to be Mary, but if that's the case, the artist never said so, or if he did, we have no record of it. But he did say the painting began as a series of landscape studies he made at Rolling Dam (also known as Roaring Dam, built in 1886). Above the dam, the river forms a reservoir that once served the mills of the Blackstone Manu-facturing Company. The water is calm and deep, in sharp contrast to the rapids below the dam, flowing between the steep granite walls of the Blackstone Gorge, which are more than eighty feet high in some places.

The title of the painting has often seemed strange to me. After all, the girl isn't drowning, but merely wading a little ways into the water. Still, Saltonstall has invested the painting with an undeniable sense of threat or dread. This may arise from the shadowy forest looming up behind the girl, and/or from the suggestion that something there has drawn her attention back to the trees. The snapping of a twig, maybe, or footsteps crunching in fallen leaves. Or a voice. Or almost anything else at all.

More and more, I've come to understand how the story of Saltonstall and *The Drowning Girl* is an integral part of my story—same as Rosemary Anne and Caroline are integral to my story—even if I won't claim that it's truly the beginning of the things that have happened. Not in any objective sense. If I did, I'd only be begging the question. Would the start be my first sight of the painting on my eleventh birthday, or Saltonstall's creation of it in 1898? Or might it be better to start with the dam's construction in 1886? Instinctively, I keep looking for that sort of beginning, even though I know better. Even though I know full well I can only arrive at useless and essentially infinite regressions.

That day in August, all those years ago, *The Drowning Girl* was hanging in another gallery, a room devoted to local painters and sculptors, mostly—but not exclusively—artists from Rhode Island. My mother's feet were sore, and we were sitting on a bench at the center of the room when I noticed the painting. I can recall this all very clearly, though most of that day has faded away. While Rosemary sat on the bench, resting her aching feet, I stood gazing at Saltonstall's canvas. Only, it seemed like I was staring *into* the canvas, almost the same as if it were a tiny window looking out on a soft-focus gray-green world. I'm pretty sure that was the first time a painting (or any other sort of two-dimensional image) struck me that way. The illusion of depth was so strong that I raised my right hand and pressed my fingers against the canvas. I believe I honestly expected them to pass right on through, to the day and the place in the painting. Then Rosemary saw me touching it and told me to stop, that what I was doing was against the museum's rules, so I pulled my hand back.

"Why?" I asked her, and she said there were corrosive oils and acids on human hands that could damage an old painting. She said that whenever the people who worked in the museum needed to handle them, they wore white cotton gloves to protect the canvases. I looked at my fingers, wondering what else I could hurt just by touching it, wondering if the acids and oils seeping from my skin had done all sorts of harm to all sorts of things without my knowing.

"Anyway, Imp, what were you doing, touching it like that?"

I told her how it had seemed like a window, and she laughed and wanted to know the name of the painting, the name of the artist, and the year it was done. All those things were printed on a card mounted on the wall beside the frame, and I read them off to her. She made notes on an envelope she pulled out of her bag. Rosemary always carried huge, shapeless cloth bags she'd sewn herself, and they bulged with everything from paperbacks to cosmetics to utility bills to grocery store receipts (which she never threw away). When she died, I kept a couple of those bags, and I still use them, though I don't think I kept the one she was carrying that particular day. It was made from denim, and I've never much liked denim. I hardly even wear blue jeans.

"Why are you writing that stuff down?"

"You might want to remember it someday," she replied. "When something makes a strong impression on us, we should do our best not to forget about it. So, it's a good idea to make notes."

"But how am I supposed to know what I might want to remember and what I won't ever want to remember?"

"Ah, now, that's the hard part," Rosemary told me, and chewed her thumbnail a moment. "That's the most difficult part of all. Because, obviously, we can't waste all our time making notes about everything, can we?"

"Of course not," I said, stepping back from the painting, but not taking my eyes off it. It was no less beautiful or remarkable for having turned out not to be a window. "That would be silly, now, wouldn't it."

"That would be very silly, Imp. We'd waste so much time trying not to forget anything that nothing worth remembering would ever happen to us."

"So you have to be careful," I said.

"Exactly," she agreed.

I don't recall much else about that birthday. Just my gifts and the trip to RISD, Rosemary saying I should write down what might turn out to be important to me someday. After the museum, we must have gone home. There would have been a cake with ice cream, because there always was, right up to the year she was committed. There wouldn't have been a party, because I never got a birthday party. I never wanted one. We left the museum, and the day rolled on, and midnight came, and it wasn't my birthday again until I turned twelve. Yesterday, I checked a calendar online, and it informed me that the *next* day, the third of August, would have been a Sunday, but that doesn't tell me much. We never went to church, because my mother was a lapsed Roman Catholic, and always said I'd be better off steering clear of Catholicism, if only because it meant I'd never have to go to the trouble of eventually lapsing.

"We don't believe in God?" I might have asked her at some point.

"*I* don't believe in God, Imp. What *you're* going to believe, that's up to you. You have to pay attention and figure these things out for yourself. I won't do it for you."

That is, if this exchange ever actually occurred. It almost seems that it did, almost, but a lot of my memories are false memories, so I can't ever be certain, one way or the other. A lot of my most interesting memories seem never to have taken place. I began keeping diaries after they locked Rosemary up at Butler and I went to live with Aunt Elaine in Cranston until I was eighteen, but even the diaries can't be trusted. For instance, there's a series of entries describing a trip to New Brunswick that I'm pretty sure I never took. It used to scare me, those recollections of things that never took place, but I've gotten used to it. And it doesn't happen as much as it once did.

"I'm going to write a ghost story now," she typed, and that's what I'm writing. I've already written about the ghosts of my grandmother, my mother, and my great-grandmother's sister, the one who kept dead animals in jars labeled with scripture. Those women are all only ghosts now, and they haunt me, just the same as the other ghosts I'm going to write about. Same as I'm haunted by the specter of Butler Hospital, there beside Swan Point Cemetery. Same as my vanished father haunts me. But, more than any of these, I'm haunted by Phillip George Saltonstall's *The Drowning Girl*, which I'd have eventually remembered even if my mother hadn't taken the time that day to make notes on an envelope.

Ghosts are those memories that are too strong to be forgotten for good, echoing across the years and refusing to be obliterated by time. I don't imagine that when Saltonstall painted *The Drowning Girl*, almost a hundred years before I saw it for the first time, he paused to consider all the people it might haunt. That's another thing about ghosts, a very important thing—you have to be careful, because hauntings are contagious. Hauntings are *memes*, especially pernicious thought contagions, *social* contagions that need no viral or bacterial host and are transmitted in a thousand different ways. A book, a poem, a song, a bedtime story, a grandmother's suicide, the choreography of a dance, a few frames of film, a diagnosis of schizophrenia, a deadly tumble from a horse, a faded photograph, or a story you tell your daughter.

Or a painting hanging on a wall.

I'm pretty sure that Saltonstall was, in fact, only trying to exorcise his own ghosts when he painted the nude woman standing in the water with the forest at her back. Too often, people make the mistake of trying to use their art to capture a ghost, but only end up spreading their haunting to countless other people. So, Saltonstall went to the Blackstone River, and he saw something there, something happened there, and it haunted him. Then, later on, he tried to make it go away the only way he knew how, by painting it. It wasn't a malicious act, the propagation of that meme. It was an act of desperation. Sometimes, haunted people reach a point where they either manage to drive away the ghosts or the ghosts destroy them. What makes all this even worse is that it usually doesn't work, trying to drag the ghosts out and seal them up tight where they can't hurt us anymore. I think, mostly, we only spread them, when we try to do that. You make a copy, or transmit some infinitesimal part of the phantom, but most of it stays dug so deeply into your mind it's never going anywhere.

Rosemary never tried to teach me to believe in a god or sin, in Heaven or Hell, and my own experiences have never led me there. I don't think I even believe in souls. But that doesn't matter. I *do* believe in ghosts. I do, I do, I do, I *do* believe in ghosts, just like the Cowardly Lion said. Sure, I'm a crazy woman, and I have to take pills I can't really afford to stay out of hospitals, but I still see ghosts everywhere I look, when I look, because once you start seeing them, you can't ever *stop* seeing them. But the worst part is, you accidentally or on purpose start seeing them, you make that gestalt shift that permits you to recognize them for what they are, and they start to see you, too. You look at a painting hanging on a wall, and all at once it seems like a window. It seems so much like a window that an eleven-year-old girl tries to reach through it to the other side. But the unfortunate thing about windows is most of them work both ways. They allow you to look *out*, but they also allow anything else that happens past to look *in*.

I've gotten ahead of myself. Which means I need to stop, and go back, and set aside all this folderol about memes and ghosts and windows, at least for now. I need to go back to that night in July, driving alongside the Blackstone River not far from the spot that inspired Saltonstall to paint *The Drowning Girl*. Back to the night I met the mermaid named Eva Canning. But, also, back to that *other* night, the snowy night in November, in Connecticut, when I was driving through the woods on a narrow chip-and-tar road, and I came across the girl who was actually a wolf, and who may have been the same ghost as Eva Canning, and who'd inspired another artist, another dead man, a dead man whose name was Albert Perrault, to try and capture her likeness in his work.

And what I said earlier about the girlfriend who puts up with all my weird shit . . . that was sort of a lie, because she left me not long after Eva Canning showed up. Because, finally, the weird shit just got too weird. I don't blame her for leaving, though I miss her and wish she were still here. Regardless, the point is, it was a lie, pretending she's still with me. I said there's no reason doing this thing if all I can manage is a lie.

So I have to watch for that.

And I have to choose my words carefully.

In fact, I find that I'm quickly, unexpectedly coming to realize that I'm trying to tell myself a story in a language that I'm having to invent as I go along. If I'm lazy, if I rely too heavily on the way anyone else would tell this story—anyone else at all—it'll look ridiculous. I'll be horrified or embarrassed by the sight of it, the sound of it. Or I'll be horrified *and* embarrassed, and I'll give it up. I'll stash it away in a disused suitcase beneath my bed and never reach the place that will, arbitrarily, turn out to be the end. No, not even the end, but just the last page that I'll write before I can stop telling this story.

I have to be careful, just like Rosemary said. I have to stop, and take a step back.

———

It wasn't raining the day I met Abalyn, but the sky was overcast with the deceitful sort of violet clouds that roil and rush by and keep you thinking that it *might* rain. It was windy, and there was definitely the *smell* of rain. So I was wearing my galoshes and my raincoat and carrying my umbrella that afternoon, which was two years and four months ago. I was walking home from the bus stop after work. It was one of those last cool days in June, before the weather turns hot and nasty. Below the clouds, the air was sweet, and the trees seemed almost too green to be real. Not too green in any gaudy way, mind you, not as if they were artificial, but as if they had achieved a greenness that was so very green, so lush, it couldn't possibly exist in nature. Or if it did, human eyes probably weren't meant to perceive it. I got off the bus on Westminster and followed Parade Street, flanked on either side by those great green whispering chestnut and oak trees. On my left lay the open expanse of Dexter Training Grounds, which is only a park now, despite the name. Ahead of me, at the southern edge of the Training Grounds, the Cranston Street Armory rose up like a fairy-tale castle, its high crenellated turrets and glazed yellow bricks sharply delineated against the clouds. The Armory, from which my neighborhood takes its name, isn't actually an armory anymore. It occurs to me that a lot of things in Providence aren't what they used to be, but no one's ever bothered to give them new names, and names can mislead and confound you.

I passed my street, because I felt more like walking than going straight home. I walked another two blocks, then turned right on Wood Street. I left most of the big trees behind, trading them for the high narrow houses with their mansard roofs and bay windows, gingerbread trim and stingy, weedy yards. I hadn't gone far when I came upon a disorderly mound of cardboard boxes heaped near the curb. There were DVDs, books, a few pieces of vinyl, and some kitchen utensils. There was clothing (mostly T-shirts, jeans, and women's underwear) stuffed haphazardly into still more boxes.

There were two wooden kitchen chairs, a coffeemaker, a dinged-up nightstand, a floor lamp missing its shade, and, well, other things. I guessed someone had been evicted and their belongings tossed out on the street. It happens, though not as much on this side of town as over on College Hill. I was surprised there wasn't a mattress, because there's almost always a mattress and box springs. I propped my umbrella against a telephone pole and began picking through the boxes. A good thing it *hadn't* rained, because then everything would have been ruined.

I'd long since learned that it pays to scavenge the castaway belongings of people who haven't paid their rent, who've left everything behind and moved on. Half my apartment is furnished with castoffs, and I once found a first edition of *The Great Gatsby* and a stack of 1940s *Superman* comics tucked inside the drawer of an old chifforobe. A used bookstore downtown paid me almost enough for the lot to cover a month's rent. Anyway, I'd just started sorting through the books—mostly science fiction and fantasy—when I heard footsteps and looked up. A tall girl was crossing Wood Street, her black boots clopping loudly against the asphalt. The first thing I noticed was how pretty she was, in an androgynous Tilda Swinton sort of way. The second thing I noticed was that she looked really, really pissed off.

"Hey!" she shouted when she was still only halfway across the road. "What the fuck do you think you're doing?"

She was looming over me before I was able to think of an answer. Abalyn is close to six feet tall, which means she has a good five inches on me.

"Is this stuff yours?" I asked, wondering if her short hair was really that black or if she dyed it.

"Hell yeah, it's mine," she said, and snatched a paperback out of my hands. I would say that she growled, but that might be misleading, like Dexter Training Grounds and the Armory. "What makes you think you can come along and start rummaging through some-one else's shit?"

"I thought it was abandoned," I said.

"Well, it's not."

"I thought it was just junk," I added.

"If it was just junk, what the hell would you want with it?" she demanded, and I realized that her eyes were green. Not green like the trees along Parade Street, but green like shallow seawater in winter rushing over granite cobbles, like waves on the floating, shapeless oceans, or green like the polished lumps of beach glass that used to be Coca-Cola or 7Up bottles. A green that was almost, but not quite, blue.

"Well, if it's not junk, then why's it piled out here on the curb like it *is* junk?"

"Oh, my fucking god," she said, and rolled her eyes. "Where does that get to be any of your business?"

She glared at me, and I thought for a second or two that she would either punch me in the face or turn around and walk away. Instead, she just dropped the paperback into a different box than the one I'd taken it from and dragged her fingers through that black, black hair, which I'd decided had to be dyed. Also, I'd decided maybe she was a few years older than me.

"Honestly, I didn't know it was yours. I didn't know it was still anybody's. I'm not a thief." Then I pointed up at the cloudy sky. "You know, it might start raining any minute, so you should prob-ably take all this inside somewhere before it gets wet and ruined."

She made that face again, like maybe she was going to punch me after all.

"I'm waiting on someone," she said. "A friend of mine, he has a truck, and he promised me he'd be here two and a half hours ago." She scowled and glanced down Wood Street towards the park. "I'm going to store everything in his garage."

"So, where do you think he is?" I asked, even though she was right, and none of this was my business. I think it was the hair that kept me talking. The hair and the eyes together.

"Fuck all if I know. He's not answering, and I've texted him like ten times already. Probably lost his phone again. He loses phones a lot, or they get stolen."

"If it rains," I said again, thinking maybe I'd spoken too softly the first time and she hadn't heard, but she ignored me. So I asked what all her stuff was doing piled out by the curb on a cloudy day, if she still wanted it. She pointed across the street at one of the more run-down houses, one of the ones no one's yet bothered to fix up and gentrify and rent to people who wouldn't have wanted to live in the Armory just ten years ago. The paint job made me think of cottage cheese, except the trim, which made me think of boiled cabbage.

"You used to live there?" I asked. "Did you get evicted?"

"Yeah, in a manner of speaking," she said (again, I would say she growled, but . . .) and sighed and stared down at her books and CDs and everything else. "Bitch whore of a girlfriend kicked me out, which I guess amounts to pretty much the same thing as an eviction. The lease is in her name, since my credit's lousy, because I defaulted on my student loans."

"I didn't go to college," I said. "My apartment's only a couple of blocks over," and I pointed off towards Willow Street.

"Yeah, and?"

"Well, it's not very big, my apartment. But it *is* mostly empty, because I don't have much furniture, and I don't have a roommate. I have a car, though. It's a tiny little Honda, so it might take us two or three trips, but we could get your stuff off the street. Well, the chairs might not fit."

"Screw the chairs," she said, smiling for the first time. "They're junk. The nightstand and the lamp, that's junk, too. You're serious?

I mean, if I wait here another few hours, he might actually show up. I don't want to impose on you or be a bother."

"It wouldn't be an imposition," I told her, trying to sound like I didn't care one way or another whether she took me up on the offer. I wanted her to say yes so badly I probably had my fingers crossed. "I didn't have any plans for the evening, anyway, and it would suck if it rained and all your things got wet."

"This isn't even all of it," she said. "The TV and computer and my gaming stuff, it's still sitting in the downstairs hallway," and she pointed at the cottage-cheese-and-cabbage-colored house again. "I wasn't about to drag it out on the street, I don't care how loud she screams."

"I'll go get my car," I said. "You wait here, in case anyone else comes along and assumes it's just junk." And I handed her my umbrella. She stared at it a moment, as if she'd never seen an umbrella before and had no idea what it was for.

"Just in case it does start to rain," I said. "Might at least help keep the books dry."

She nodded, though she still looked kind of confused. "You're absolutely sure about this?" she asked. "I don't even know your name."

"I'm India," I told her. "Like the country, or India ink, but mostly people call me Imp. So you can call me Imp, or India. Either's fine."

"Okay, Imp. Well, this is wicked nice of you. And I promise, I'll get everything out of your way by tomorrow night at the latest. And my name's Abalyn, which is what everybody calls me. Just don't call me Abby. I hate that."

"Okay, Abalyn. Wait here. I'll be right back."

She looked worriedly at that low, worrisome sky and opened the umbrella. I hurried home and got my car. It wound up taking us four trips, because of the computer and the television and all her gaming stuff, but I didn't care. She said she liked my galoshes, which were blue with yellow ducklings, and if black hair and green eyes hadn't already gotten me, that would've done the trick.

And that's the day I met Abalyn Armitage.

"I think I've been telling lies," Imp types.

Not that I didn't meet my ex-lover on a not-quite-rainy day in June when the trees were very green. All that part's true, and so is the part about her belongings being heaped by the curb. And me almost unintentionally stealing books. But I have no idea what we said to each other. I don't think anyone could write that scene and *not* lie, recollections of a conversation that happened two and a half years ago. Still, I didn't set out to lie, trying to write about how Abalyn and I met. Then again, I didn't set out *not* to lie, either. That's some sort of fine line I'm walking, isn't it? Maybe I should cut myself some slack. How I wrote about Abalyn is true, just not especially factual, like a movie "based on" or "inspired by" actual events. I'm having to fill in all the gaps so this is a story, and not just a bunch of snapshots laid out in words instead of photographs. My memory's not very good, which is why I was never able to learn the multiplication and periodic tables, or all the state capitals, or how to play the alto saxophone. And why I decided not to go to college. I felt like I was lucky to have graduated high school, what with this lousy memory of mine. Besides, I couldn't really afford college, and at least I'm not in debt now, like Abalyn. Yes, that part's both true *and* factual. And none of the names have been changed to protect the innocent.

Of course, I've never actually met an innocent person. Everyone hurts someone eventually, no matter how hard they try not to be hurtful. My mother, she hurt me by getting knocked up by my ass-hole father (who never even had the courtesy to marry her, though he hung around for ten years), but I'm sure that she had no intention, at the time, of hurting a daughter who didn't even exist yet. I guess that makes it a crime of passion, what she did, or only a lack of foresight. I'm sure Grandmother Caroline had no idea, when she got pregnant, that her daughter would inherit her insanity and then pass it along to an illegitimate granddaughter. When I almost stole books from Abalyn that day, books I wasn't *trying* to steal, I had no intention of causing her harm just by talking to her, but the way things worked out, the way that conversation led to our relationship, I did. I did cause her harm. I don't believe in sin, original or otherwise, but I do believe people cause other people harm, and that to imagine it can be any way else is only asking for disappointment. I believe this is true, just like my inaccurate recounting of that first talk with Abalyn, even though I would be hard-pressed to suggest any sort of factual foundation or causal agent for *why* it's true.

All this said, I feel as if I should write something factual, now. Telling this ghost story, I'm beginning to think of facts and truth like bricks and mortar, only I'm not sure which is which. The facts are probably the bricks, with truth being the mortar that holds it all together. I like the sound of that, so I'll consider it a provisional truth. By the way, all this business about truth and fact, I can't take credit for that. It comes from an essay in defense of fairy tales, written by Ursula K. Le Guin, titled "Why Are Americans Afraid of Dragons?" She might just as well have asked, "Why Are Americans Afraid of Ghosts, Werewolves, and Mermaids?" Anyway, she writes, "For fantasy is true, of course. It isn't factual, but it is true. And that is precisely why many of them [Americans] are afraid of fantasy." That's another quotation I keep thumbtacked to the wall in the room where I paint, right next to the quote from Virginia Woolf's suicide note.

Imp stared a moment at what she'd written, then added, "Stop stalling, India Morgan Phelps. It's annoying."

My favorite fairy tale when I was a child was "The Little Mermaid," and I was especially fond of having it read aloud to me by Grandmother Caroline. She had a tattered old copy of *Stories from Hans Christian Andersen*, which had been printed in 1911, three years before she was born. She said her mother had purchased it at the Brattle Book Shop in Boston, while she was still pregnant with Caroline. My grandmother's book of fairy tales is illustrated with twenty-eight beautiful watercolor paintings by a French artist named Edmund Dulac, who was born in 1882 and died in 1953. When Caroline killed herself, this book was one of the few things she left to me, and it's yet another thing I keep in the room where I paint. The pages have turned yellow and brittle, and the illustrations are beginning to fade. I imagine they were much more vivid ninety-seven years ago, when my great-grandmother bought the book so that she'd have fairy tales to read to her child. Sure, I also liked some of the other stories, especially "The Snow Queen" and "The Wind's Tale," but none of them half as much as I liked "The Little Mermaid." I'm sure Caroline must have known the story by heart, I asked to hear it so many times. But she always pretended she was actually reading it, and would pause to show me the illustrations by Edmund Dulac. I've seen two film adaptations of the story—*Splash*, which came out two years before I was born, and the animated Disney version, which was released when I was three, so I saw both on VHS. The way Disney changed the ending made me angry. Sure, *Splash* changed the ending, too, but it wasn't filled with insipid music, and at least Daryl Hannah didn't have to stop being a mermaid.

To me, the ending of the Disney film took a true (though not factual) story, and turned it into a lie.

My least favorite fairy tale when I was a child was "Little Red Riding Hood." It wasn't in the book my great-grandmother bought in Boston, of course, because it wasn't written by Hans Christian Andersen, but by Charles Perrault (not to be confused with Albert Perrault). And it wasn't published in 1911, but in 1697. That's the first time it appeared in print, but the story existed in many forms long before Perrault put it down on paper. I have a file on "Little Red Riding Hood" with versions that go back as far as the eleventh century. Most people know the story the way that the Brothers Grimm wrote it, and most children are told that tamed and toned-down variant, in which a huntsman saves the girl from the wolf. But Caroline told me the story the way that it was published in *Histoires ou contes du temps passé, avec des moralités: Contes de ma mère l'oye* in 1697. Little Red Riding Hood and her grandmother are both eaten by the wolf, and no one comes to save her, and there's no happy ending. This is, I think, the truer incarnation of the story, though, even as an adult, I really don't care for either.

Anyway, even with the happy ending, the story terrified me. For one thing, I never pictured the wolf as a real wolf, but as something that walked upright on two legs, and looked a lot more like a man than a wolf. So, I suppose I saw it as a werewolf. When I was older, and read a book about wolves and saw a National Geographic documentary, I realized that the way I'd seen the wolf, in my mind's eye, made the story truer, because men are much more dangerous than wolves. Especially if you're a wolf, or a little girl.

My mother never read me fairy tales, and she never told them to me from memory. Rosemary Anne wasn't a bad mother, she just didn't do fairy tales.

Imp typed: "I think this is what you call prolegomena, what I've written so far, which is a word I've never before had a reason to use." And then she got up and went to the bathroom, because she'd needed to pee since that part about Daryl Hannah. She also got a handful of Lorna Doones and an apple, because she'd skipped dinner again. Then she sat back down at the typewriter and typed, "The importance of fairy tales, and her love for 'The Little Mermaid,' as well as her aversion to 'Little Red Riding Hood,' is very much at the heart of the ghost story she's writing."

Which means that wasn't a digression.

A couple of months after Abalyn moved in with me, we went to an exhibit at the Bell Gallery at Brown. Going was her idea, not mine. The exhibit, which was called The Voyeur of Utter Destruction (in Hindsight), was a retrospective of the work of an artist who'd died in a motorcycle accident a few years before, a man who called himself Albert Perrault (though that wasn't the name he was given at birth). I'd heard of him, but not much. Abalyn had read an article about Perrault somewhere online, and I went because she wanted to go. The exhibit consisted of an assortment of oil paintings, sculptures, and mixed-media pieces, almost all of it inspired, in part, by fairy tales, and mostly by "Little Red Riding Hood." Had I known that beforehand, I might have let Abalyn go alone. I probably would have insisted. As it was, I held her hand almost the whole time we were in the gallery.

We signed the guest book at a table near the door, and Abalyn took a copy of a glossy brochure about the exhibit. The first painting had a Latin name, *Fecunda ratis*. The canvas was executed mostly in shades of gray, though there were a few highlights of green and alabaster, and a single striking crimson smudge floating near the center. A card on the wall beside the painting explained that Perrault borrowed the title from a book by an eleventh-century pedagogue named Egbert of Liège, a book that had included "De puella a lupellis seruata," an account of a lost girl found living with a pack of wolves. In the story, she's wearing a red wool tunic, given to her by her grandfather on the day of her baptism. Someone spots the red tunic, and she's rescued, which I suppose makes it a morality tale. Baptize your children, or they'll go live with wolves.

I didn't like the painting. It made me uncomfortable. And not only because it went straight back to my old hang-up about "Little Red Riding Hood." There was something awful about it, something that made it hard for me to look directly at for more than a few seconds at a time. I suppose this should have impressed me, that the artist had so effectively managed to imbue his work with such a sense of dread. My impression of it was formed piecemeal. I'd glance at the painting, then turn away again. I don't think Abalyn noticed I was doing this; I'm not sure she had any idea how the exhibit was affecting me until I asked if we could please leave, which was about twenty minutes and several paintings and sculptures later.

Before I sat down to write this, I googled *Fecunda ratis* and looked at some images on the web, because I didn't want to rely on my unreliable memories. The painting doesn't upset me the way it did that August day at the Bell Gallery. Too much has happened, and the sculptures and paintings of Albert Perrault, for all their dreadfulness, pale by comparison. But, like I've said, mostly all in gray, and then the red smudge near the center. The smudge forms a sort of still point, or a nexus, or a fulcrum. It's the child's wool baptismal tunic, and it's the only thing she's wearing. She's on her hands and knees, her head bowed so that her face is hidden from view. There's nothing but a wild snarl of matted hair and the red tunic, which, when the painting is considered as a whole, seems to me cruel and incongruent. The girl is surrounded by a circle of dark, hulking forms—the wolves—and the wolves, in turn, are sitting within an outer circle of standing stones, a looming megalithic ring.

The wolves are rendered so indistinctly that I might have mistaken them for something else, if I hadn't first read the card on the wall. I might have looked at those great, shaggy things squatting there on their haunches, lewdly, hungrily watching over the girl. And I might have mistaken them for bears. Bears or even, I don't know, oxen. You can't tell from the painting if the wolves are about to eat the girl, or if they're keeping her safe. You can't tell if they're marveling at what a strange wolf she is, or thinking about how they've never made love to a human woman and maybe that would be an interesting change of pace.

But the very worst part of the painting was a strip of rice paper worked into the lower left-hand corner of canvas. Printed on the paper were the words *Nobody's ever coming for you.*

I had it in my head, when I sat down with my apple and my Lorna Doones, that I would be able to write in detail about all the pieces that made up The Voyeur of Utter Destruction (in Hindsight), or at least those I saw before I started feeling sick and we had to leave the gallery. *Night in the Forest*, which was very much like *Fecunda ratis*, only more so. And *1893* and *Sudden Fear in Crowded Spaces*. A series of rusty metal cages collectively titled *Breadcrumbs*, each cage holding a single cobble inside, each stone engraved with a single word. And the grotesque pinwheel spread out at the center of it all, *Phases 1–5*, a series of sculptures portraying a woman's transformation into a wolf. Not just any woman, but the murdered and dismembered corpse of Elizabeth Short, known to most of the world as "the Black Dahlia." I had nightmares about those sculptures for weeks. Sometimes, I still do. I was going to describe all of this to the best of my abilities. But now I think it's better if I don't. Maybe later into the story I will, when doing so might become unavoidable, but not now.

"So," Imp typed, "I've made my beginning, however arbitrary and disjointed it may be. I've begun my ghost story, and I'm going to pretend there's no turning back now."

It's a lie, but I'm going to pretend, regardless.

In the end, it may or may not all add up to something coherent. I won't know until I've *found* the end.

Me. Rosemary Anne. Caroline. Three crazy women, all in a row. My mother's suicide and my grandmother's suicide. Taking away words so that scary things are less scary, and leaving behind words that no longer mean what they once did. "The Little Mermaid." The cloudy day I met Abalyn. Dead sparrows and mice trapped inside stoppered bottles. *The Drowning Girl*, painted by a man who fell off a horse and died. *Fecunda ratis*, painted by a man who fell off a motorcycle and died. A man who took the surname of the Frenchman who is often credited with having first written down the tale of "Little Red Riding Hood," and then proceeded to create horrific works of art based on that same fairy tale. Which happens to be my least favorite fairy tale of all. Jacova Angevine and the Open Door of Night, which I'll come to later. Contagious hauntings and pernicious memes. The harm we do without meaning to do any harm at all.

A dark country road in eastern Connecticut. Another dark road beside a river in Massachusetts. A woman who called herself Eva Canning, who might have been a ghost, or a wolf, or maybe a mermaid, or possibly, most likely, nothing that will ever have a name.

These are the sum of the notes my mother told me I should make, so I won't forget that which has made a strong impression upon me. This is my apology to Abalyn, even though I know she's never going to read it.

This might be my pocket full of stones.

"That's enough for now," Imp typed. "Get some rest. It'll still be here when you come back."

2

"And what about this business with chapters?" Imp typed. "If I'm not writing this to be read—which I'm most emphatically not—and if it's not a book, as such, then why is it that I'm bothering with chapters? Why does anyone bother with chapters? Is it just so the reader knows where to stop and pee, or have a snack, or turn off the light and go to sleep? Aren't chapters a bit like beginnings and endings? Arbitrary and convenient constructs?" Nonetheless, she typed the Arabic numeral two precisely seventeen single-spaced lines down a fresh sheet of typing paper.

October is slipping away around me. I've spent several days now, days filled with work and not much else, trying to decide when and how to continue the ghost story. Or *whether* I should continue the ghost story. Obviously, I decided that I would. That's another sort of being haunted: starting something and never finishing it. I don't leave paintings unfinished. If I start reading a book, I have to finish it, even if I hate it. I don't waste food. When I decide to go for a walk, and I've planned the route I'm going to take, I insist upon taking the entire walk, even if it starts snowing or raining. Otherwise, I have to contend with that unfinished thing haunting me.

Before I met Abalyn Armitage, I'd never played a video game. I didn't even own a computer. I also didn't know much about transsexuals. But I'll get back to that later. I'll write about the video games now, because it was one of the very first subjects that she and I talked about that night. We managed to get all her things from the place on Wood Street where she no longer lived, because her exgirlfriend had evicted her when they broke up, to my place on Willow Street before it started raining. It did start raining, which proved I'd been sensible after all, if somewhat premature, bringing the umbrella along and wearing my galoshes. We got her stuff back to my place, and up the stairs to my apartment. Most of it we piled in my front parlor, which was pretty much empty anyway.

"You're the first person I've ever heard describe a room in their house as a parlor," Abalyn said. She was sitting on the floor, sorting through her CDs, as if to be sure something hadn't been left back at her old apartment.

"Am I?"

She watched me a moment, then said, "If you weren't, I'd never have said you were."

"Fair enough," I replied, and then asked if she'd like a cup of tea.

"I'd really prefer coffee," she said, and I told her that I didn't drink coffee, so I couldn't make her any. She sighed and shrugged. "Never mind," she said, then added, "I'll have to rectify that *tout de suite*. I can't live without coffee. But thanks, anyway."

I was only in the kitchen maybe ten minutes, but by the time I got back she'd already plugged in her television and was busy hooking up one of the gaming consoles. I sat on the sofa and watched her and sipped my tea. It was sweet, but there was no lemon, because I hadn't thought to buy one the last time I'd gone to the market.

"Did you love her?" I asked, and Abalyn looked over her shoulder and frowned at me.

"That's a hell of a thing to ask," she said.

"Right. But . . . did you?"

She turned back to the wires and black plastic boxes, and I thought for a moment she was going to ignore me, so that I'd have to think of another question.

"I wanted to," Abalyn said. "Maybe I thought I did, at first. I wanted to think I did."

"Did she love you?"

"She loved the person she thought I was, or the person she'd thought I was when we met. But no, I don't think she ever loved me. I'm not even sure she ever knew me. I don't think I ever knew her."

"Do you miss her?"

"It's only been a couple of hours." Abalyn was starting to sound annoyed, so I changed the subject. I asked instead about the black boxes and the television. She explained that one was an Xbox 360 and the other was a PS3, then had to explain that PS was an acronym for PlayStation. She also had a Nintendo Wii, which she pronounced "we." I sat and listened, though I wasn't particularly interested. I'd started to feel bad for having asked the question I'd asked, about her girlfriend, having belatedly realized how personal it was, so listening seemed like the least I could do. I figured talking would take her mind off her ex and suddenly not having a place to live and all.

"I get paid to write game reviews," she said, when I asked why she spent so much time playing video games. "I write for websites, mostly. A few print magazines, now and then, but mostly for websites."

"People read reviews of video games?"

"Do you think I'd get paid to write them if they didn't?"

"Right. But . . . I never thought about it, I suppose." And I told

her I'd never played a video game. She wanted to know if I was jok-
ing, and I told her that I wasn't.

"I don't especially like games," I said. "I've never much seen the
point. I'm pretty good at checkers, and gin, and backgammon isn't
so bad. But it's been years . . ." I trailed off, and she looked over her
shoulder at me again.

"Have you always lived alone?"

"Since I was nineteen," I told her, and I suspected she was thinking something along the lines of, *So that's why you're so strange.*
"But I do okay," I said.

"Doesn't it get lonely?"

"Not especially," I replied, which was a lie, but I didn't want to
come across as pathetic or maudlin or something. "I have my painting, and I have work. I read a lot, and sometimes I write stories."

"You're a painter and a writer?" By this time, she was untan-
gling a snarl of black cables she'd pulled from one of the boxes.

"No, just a painter. But I write stories sometimes."

"Does anyone ever publish them?"

"I've sold a few, but that doesn't make me a real writer. Not an
author, I mean."

She glared at the snarl of black cables, and, for a moment, it
seemed like she might put them back in the box or hurl them across
the parlor.

"Have you ever sold a painting?" she asked.

"No," I replied. "Not really. Not my real paintings. Only my
summer-people paintings."

Abalyn didn't ask what I meant. By "summer-people paintings,"
I mean.

"But you think of yourself as a painter, and not a writer. You
know that doesn't make a lot of sense, right?"

"I also work at an art supply store, and I get paid for that. Still,
I don't ever think of myself as a clerk or a cashier. The point is, I

think of myself as a painter, because painting is what I love to do, what I'm passionate about. So, I'm a painter."

"Imp, you don't mind me setting all this stuff up, do you? I guess I should have asked before I started. I just want to be sure nothing's broken." She finally managed to untangle the cables, connected the consoles to the television, and then pulled a power strip from the cardboard box.

"I don't mind," I said, and sipped at my tea. "It's actually sort of interesting."

"Should have asked before I started, I know."

"I don't mind," I said again.

I considered the big flat-screen television a moment. She'd propped it against the wall. I'd seen them in shop windows and at the mall, but I'd never owned any sort of TV. "I don't have cable," I said.

"Oh, I'd already figured that part out."

So, it rained, and we talked, and Abalyn was relieved that nothing had been broken. She told me that her girlfriend—who was named Jodie, by the way (I suppose she still is)—had set most of it out in the hallway rather roughly while they were still arguing. Abalyn hadn't tried to stop her. Anyway, she showed me how to play a couple of games. In one, you were an alien soldier fighting an alien invasion, and there was a blue holographic girl. In another, you played a soldier who was trying to stop terrorists from using nuclear weapons.

"Are they all this violent?" I asked. "Are all the central characters male? Are they all about war?"

"No . . . and no, and no. Maybe I'll show you some *Final Fantasy* tomorrow, and maybe *Kingdom Hearts*. That stuff might be more your speed. Though, there's still sorta combat. It's just not as graphic, the violence, if you know what I mean. Cartoon violence."

I didn't know what she meant, but I didn't tell her that. Eventually it stopped raining. We ordered Chinese takeout, and my fortune cookie said, "Don't stop now." It really did. I'm not making that up.

Abalyn said, "That's an odd thing to put in a fortune cookie."

"I like it," I replied, and I still have that fortune, tacked to the wall with the Virginia Woolf and Ursula K. Le Guin quotes. I always save fortunes from fortune cookies, though usually I put them in an antique candy tin in the kitchen. I probably have at least a hundred.

"Where is all this headed?" Imp typed, because it was beginning to seem a bit ramblesome. Then she answered herself by typing, "It really happened. It's one of the things I'm sure really happened."

"How can you be so sure?"

And Imp typed, "Because I still have the fortune from that cookie," though that hardly seemed like a satisfactory answer. "Fine," she said aloud. "Just so long as you don't lose sight of why you're doing this, don't forget."

I haven't forgotten at all.

Isn't that why I'm writing this down, because I haven't forgotten, because I haven't figured out how to forget? Abalyn is one of the ghosts, same as my mother and grandmother, and Phillip George Saltonstall and Albert Perrault, same as Eva Canning. No one ever said you have to be dead and buried to be a ghost. Or if they did, they were wrong. People who believe that have probably never been haunted. Or they've only had very limited experience with ghosts, so they simply don't know any better.

Abalyn slept on the sofa that night, and I slept in my bed. I lay awake a long time, thinking about her.

If I let her read this, Dr. Ogilvy would probably tell me that I'm exhibiting "avoidant behavior," the way I'm going about writing this ghost story.

But it's mine, isn't it? Yes, and so it's mine to tell however I wish.

It's mine with which to tarry and stall and get to any particular point in my own sweet time. There is no Constant Reader to appease, only me and me alone. That said, I want to try to write about the road. And about the night I met Eva Canning. However, for the moment, it makes no difference whether it's 122 winding along the Blackstone River, just past Millville, Massachusetts, or whether it's Wolf Den Road in northeastern Connecticut. Which means it also doesn't matter whether this night on this road is during the summer or the autumn, respectively. For now, the road is archetypal, abstract. It might be any road or any night. Specificity wouldn't make it any truer, only more factual.

I need to put all this down. All of it. I need to be both true *and* factual, but I also must start off by looking at that night (or those nights) indirectly. Out of the corner of my eye. Or the corner of my memory, as it were. Out of the corner of my *mind's* eye. To do otherwise is to risk bolting. Blinding myself and walking away from these pages and never coming back again. I don't have to stare *at* the sun to see the light it radiates. That would be awfully foolish, wouldn't it? Staring at the sun. Of course it would.

So, I'm driving in my Honda along a road, and it could be Massachusetts or Connecticut, and it could be summer or November. This is the month after I met Abalyn, or almost four months farther along. Either way, I'm alone, and it's a very dark night. The moon is new, and the only illumination comes from the headlights and from the stars, which, this far out, you can see much better than in the city and the suburbs, where there's so much light pollution. There's also light from the Honda's dashboard, a soft but sickly green light that puts me in mind of a science fiction movie, or absinthe, which I've never tasted.

This is something I do sometimes, when I can't sleep. When my head is too full of thoughts, voices, the past. I'll get in the Honda and drive nowhere in particular. Just drive to be driving. Usually, I go west or north, away from Providence, away from places where there are so many people. I go to places where I can be alone with my thoughts, and work through them enough that when I finally get back home I can rest (and sometimes that's after dawn, so I'm half-asleep all day at work or, on days off, sleep until late afternoon). I try to lose myself out there in the dark, but never become so lost I can't find my way back again.

"Journeys end in lovers meeting." I used to think that was Shirley Jackson, because it goes through Eleanor's head again and again in *The Haunting of Hill House*, but, turns out, it comes from Shakespeare and *Twelfth Night*.

> *Journeys end in lovers meeting,*
> *Every wise man's son doth know.*

> *Sons and daughters.*
> *Because death could not stop for me, I kindly stopped for*
> *him.*

Where were we, Imp? Oh, we were right here, on the road, on a night of the new moon, and it's November, unless it's July. There's snow heaped at the side of the road, or it's warm enough that I have the windows down and cool air is blowing into my crappy little car. I'm rushing through the dark (I admit, I often drive too fast on these nocturnal expeditions, because there's an urgency when trying to outrun myself). And one moment she isn't there, and the next moment, there she is. It's just like that. Not so much like I came upon her. It's more like she just appeared. Never mind. I know exactly what I mean. If it's November in Connecticut, she has her back to me, walking away, the forest on her right. If it's July, she's standing still in the breakdown lane, staring south at the black place where the river is hiding. Either way, she's naked. There's a surprising amount of precision here, despite my need to be indirect. That should at least earn me a silver star beside my name.

I'm driving fast, and given the way she appeared so suddenly, so all at once, I'm already past her before I'm even quite sure what I saw. But then I slow down. I slow down and pull over into the breakdown lane, if it's July. If it's November, I just stop, because there isn't a breakdown lane, and there's no other traffic on the chip-and-tar of Wolf Den Road. Besides, the snow's heaped so high that I'd probably have gotten stuck had I tried to pull over.

I stare at the rearview mirror, and the brake lights have turned everything behind me red. I can see her, though, just barely. Standing naked at the side of the road, though she doesn't appear to have seen me. What would a sane woman do in a situation like this? Would she keep driving, and think it's better not to get involved? Would she call for help? Would she get out of the car, as I did? I can only know what I decided to do, though I don't recall actually making a decision. So, I should say, instead, I only know what I did. I shifted the Honda into neutral, pulled up the parking brake, and opened the car door.

She doesn't turn towards me, if she's seen me. She doesn't acknowledge me. She's walking towards me, or she's standing perfectly still.

"Are you okay?" I call out. She's far enough away that I shout, even though, if it's November, the night is very quiet. If it's July, there are crickets and katydids and maybe cicadas. "Do you need help? Do you need a ride someplace?"

She turns towards me, glancing past her right shoulder, or she stops walking and looks at me.

"Are you okay?" I ask her again.

It'll sound silly if I say her appearance was unearthly, but she was unearthly. Worse, it's presumptuous, right? It presupposes I know everything that is earthly, and so would recognize anything that isn't. I don't, of course. But that's the way she struck me, standing there on whichever road on whichever night, my breath fogging or the air smelling like tar and wild grapevines. That's the word that first popped into my head, *unearthly.*

She narrowed her eyes, as though the light from the car was too bright. I guess it would have been, after all that darkness. Her pupils would have suddenly contracted, and her eyes would have hurt. She would have squinted, maybe shielded her eyes with one hand. Later, I'll see that her eyes are blue, a shade of blue that Rosemary Anne used to call "bottle-blue." Except, if this is November, I'll see that her eyes are a strange shade of brown, a brown that almost seems golden. Regardless, she narrowed her eyes, and they flash iridescent eyeshine, and she blinks at me. I think *feral,* which is much more appropriate and far less presumptuous than was *unearthly.* She smiles very, very slightly, so slightly, in fact, that I may have imagined it. She takes a step towards me, and I ask, a third time, if she's okay.

"You must be freezing to death out here. You'll get pneumonia." Or.

"The mosquitoes must be eating you alive."

She takes one step and stops. If she was smiling, she isn't anymore.

"You can't keep having it both ways, Imp. You can have it one way or the other, but not both." Her voice isn't remarkable. Not the way her eyes are. It might be any woman's voice. "I never meant it both ways."

"But that's how I remember it," I protest. "That's how it happened, twice, both ways."

"You often distrust your memories. That trip to New Brunswick, for instance. Or finding a seventy-five-dollar bill on Thayer Street."

"There's no such thing as a seventy-five-dollar bill."

"My point precisely. But, regardless, you remember finding one, don't you?"

"If you only wanted me to remember it one way, you shouldn't have let it happen twice."

"Hasn't it occurred to you that you're supposed to make a choice? You can't have it both ways. You create a paradox, if you try."

"Like particle-wave duality," I reply, and think to myself, *Checkmate.* "Matter exhibits the properties of waves and the properties of particles, depending how one examines it. There's the EPR Paradox. I have a book on quantum physics, and I understand more of it than I thought I would when I bought it at a yard sale on Chapin Avenue."

Eva Canning frowns and says, "Imp, you're putting words into my mouth. You're talking to yourself. This is you and you, not you and me."

Right.

Also, I didn't buy the book at the yard sale. I just stood there reading it, until the old woman who was selling stuff asked me if I *wanted* to buy it. I got embarrassed and told her no, I was just browsing, and put it back down. I did all my best to smile. Still, this *is* what I remember, that I met Eva Canning twice, once in July and again in November, and that both times were the *first* time we met. I'm going to proceed as if these are not false memories, though it'll surely make telling my ghost story much, much more difficult. It does create a paradox, and, offhand, I don't see how to resolve it and make a single narrative out of these conflicting recollections. Eva could not have come to stay with me in July and in November— not for the first time—could she? Because I only remember Abalyn leaving once, and that was definitely in August, and it was definitely *because* of Eva. I have multiple lines of physical evidence to corroborate this.

The scales seem to tilt in favor of July, and Highway 122, and mermaids. Away from Albert Perrault and towards Phillip George Saltonstall. But . . . I have this sickening feeling that next time I sit down to write more of this, the scales will somehow manage to tilt the other way, in favor of November, and Connecticut, and wolves. That's not just a turn of phrase, either—this sickening feeling. Knowing that may happen makes me queasy. Not quite full-on nauseous, but definitely queasy.

I'm going to go put the kettle on for a pot of tea, and maybe eat some toast or a crumpet with blueberry jam. And I need to get dressed, because I have to be at work in an hour. There isn't time for a shower, though I need one, because I've been sitting here writing this ever since I woke up from a dream about Abalyn and Eva. Hopefully, if I use deodorant and wear clean underwear, no one will notice I need a shower.

My kitchen is the main reason that I rented the apartment at the east end of Willow Street. It gets the morning sunlight. The walls are painted a cheery sort of yellow, and in the morning the room is bright and, in autumn and winter and late spring, seems warmer than it actually ever is, which is nice. The kitchen puts me at ease after sleep. Sleep usually leaves me disoriented, my nerves jangling; I have dreams that are as bright, as vivid, as the eight o'clock sunshine off those kitchen walls, but there's rarely anything cheery about the dreams. I didn't used to have such bad nightmares—the dreams started after Eva. Grandmother Caroline always said that the kitchen is the most important room in any house (or apartment), and her advices have hardly ever steered me wrong.

The morning after the first night that Abalyn came to stay with me, we sat together at the kitchen table. I was having tea, a banana, and a crumpet—my usual—and she was eating Nilla Wafers with peanut butter. My tea was pale with milk, and hers was not. She was wearing a black T-shirt and black boxer shorts. I had on my gingham nightgown, the one with blue and white checks. It had stopped raining and the sun was out, so the yellow kitchen was very, very yellow. These details are so clear to me, which strikes me odd, since so many far more important details are hazy or have been altogether lost.

My memory is almost like Caroline and Rosemary never died. It plays surrogate and tries to keep me safe. It selects and omits, saves and sorts and wipes clean. Often, I think it smothers. Not intentionally, of course.

"Do you always have Saturdays off?" Abalyn asked, using a spoon to spread a thick glob of peanut butter onto a cookie.

"Mostly," I replied, sipping my tea. "But I wish I could get more hours than I do. I wouldn't much mind working weekends. Do you have a job?"

"I told you. I write reviews of video games."

"I mean besides that."

She chewed and stared at me a moment or two. "No, not besides that."

"It pays enough you don't need another job?"

"Not exactly," she muttered around Nilla Wafer and peanut butter. "That's one of the things busted up me and Jodie. She kept nagging at me to get a *real* job." When Abalyn said "real job," she used her fingers to make sarcastic quotation marks. "You get paid enough at the art supply place for the rent on this apartment?"

"Mostly," I said again. "And I have some money put away, some money that my grandmother left me. So, I make ends meet."

"So you're sort of a trustafarian," she said, and laughed.

"No," I said, and I think I said it a little angrily. "I just have a little money Grandmother Caroline left me and my mother. It's a trust fund, but I work. If I didn't, it wouldn't have lasted half this long."

"Lucky you," Abalyn sighed.

"I've never thought of it that way."

"Maybe you should start."

Neither of us said anything for a while then. Abalyn wasn't the first person who'd made a snide remark about my inheritance (my aunt Elaine is the trustee). It happens sometimes, and sometimes I explain there's not all that much of it left. That it'll run out in a few more years, and who knows how I'll manage then, what with rent and my meds and all? But I didn't go into that with Abalyn, not that morning. We talked about it at some point later on.

"Sorry," she said. "I'm just a little prickly on the subject of money right now."

"No. It's okay."

She told me about Jodie, how they'd fought a lot, usually about the finances. Jodie had a nine-to-five office-job-type job, and Abalyn said Jodie resented the fact that her girlfriend spent all day sitting at home playing video games. Abalyn said they'd get into arguments because Jodie would see something in an Ikea catalog, for instance, and remark how they could have nicer things if Abalyn was making more money. She also talked about how they met, out on the Cape, at a bar in Provincetown.

"I know. Terribly cliché. She was a little drunk, but I bought her another beer and we got to talking. She didn't even realize I was a tranny until we were leaving to go back to my hotel room."

"I haven't said anything about Abalyn being a transsexual," Imp typed. "She wouldn't have wanted me to make a big deal out of it, and it never mattered to me. That's why I haven't really brought it up before now.

"It's just part of who she was," Imp typed.

"Did she get pissed? When she found out, I mean?" And I was thinking about that scene in *The Crying Game*, when Stephen Rea first sees Dil naked, then goes to the toilet and pukes. I didn't tell Abalyn that's what was running through my mind.

"As a matter of fact, she did. So, we didn't go back to my room, after all. But I'd given her my card—"

"You have cards?"

Abalyn smiled. "Started out sort of like a joke. But they come in handy. Anyway, she had my card, which has my email and Facebook and everything, and she got in touch with me about a week later. Wanted to meet up again."

"And you did? Even after the way she'd acted?"

"You will find I can be a very forgiving soul, especially when pretty women are involved."

We talked a little more about her being a transsexual then. Not a lot, just a little. I didn't tell her how I'd known right away, when she'd caught me rummaging through her stuff the day before. I thought it would have been rude to tell her that. She told me about going to a clinic in Bangkok for her surgery, and the guy she'd been living with at the time. She said, "He paid for almost all of it, but then we broke up right after. Turned out he didn't like me afterwards. I've met a lot of guys like that. They have hard-ons for preops, but they're really just gay men with a fetish, so post-ops are a complete turnoff."

"Did you love him?" I asked, though, in retrospect, I think it was an indelicate question.

Abalyn ate another cookie with peanut butter, and frowned slightly, as if it was hard thinking of the answer, or hard putting the answer into words.

"I believed that I did. At the time. But I got over it. I was grateful for what he'd done for me, and it was an amicable split. We still talk, every now and then. He calls me. I call him. Email. He's a good guy, but he really ought to stick to straight-up cock."

"This is more relevant than it may at first glance appear," typed Imp. The keys jammed, and she had to stop to get them unstuck, staining the fingers of both hands with ink. "Duality. The mutability of the flesh. Transition. Having to hide one's true self away. Masks. Secrecy. Mermaids, werewolves, gender. The reactions we may have to the truth of things, to someone's most honest face, to facts that run counter to our expectations and preconceptions. Confessions. Metaphors. Transformation. So, it's very relevant. Not just a random breakfast conversation. Don't leave out anything relevant, no matter how mundane it might feel."

Hemingway said to write about the weather.

Imp stopped and stared at what she'd written.

"You're a very beautiful woman," I told Abalyn. Then I said, quickly, because it immediately occurred to me how that could be taken the wrong way, "Not that beauty matters. Not that it has anything to do with whether or not—"

"It's okay. I know what you meant," Abalyn said, holding up her left hand and interrupting me.

"You do?"

"Probably. Close enough."

"Have you ever regretted it?" I asked, knowing I shouldn't, but the words tumbling out before I could stop them from coming.

Abalyn sighed loudly and turned her head, looking out the window instead of at me. "Only once or twice," she said very softly, almost whispering. "Not often, and not for very long. I doubt I've ever made a decision I didn't regret somewhere down the line, but it was the right thing to do. It was the only thing to do."

I don't want to write any more about this. At least, not right now. I'll probably have to come back to it later, even though I'd prefer not to. I don't like thinking of Abalyn this way. I dislike remembering how self-conscious and awkward she could be at times, and the expression she'd get whenever we'd be out and some asshole would say something hateful or inconsiderate. Or called her *sir*. I don't like remembering the way that hurt her. Hurts her. I'm sure it still does; I'm just not around to see, and I don't like dwelling on that, either. That's only normal. Missing people you still love, and not wanting to see them in pain and angry and humiliated.

I wish I could be merciful, and leave Abalyn out of the ghost story entirely.

But just like Rosemary and Caroline, Phillip George Saltonstall and Albert Perrault, she's part of the tapestry, and I can't tell my story without telling part of hers. She's part of mine. If Abalyn ever writes her own ghost story, I'll have to be part of it, and I'm pretty certain she knows that. I wouldn't hold it against her.

We drank our tea and ate our breakfast, and the conversation turned to video games, and how I'd never owned a computer. When the kitchen began to get too warm (no air-conditioning), we moved to the sofa. She lectured me on MMORPGs and the pros and cons of various consoles, and the relative merits of PCs and Macs. She patiently explained glitches and gigabytes and how she regretted having been too young in the eighties to have been in on the Golden Age of the Video Arcade. It went on like that for hours. I kept up, for the most part. And I began to understand why Abalyn lived the way she did, writing reviews for video games, avoiding conventional workspace. She felt safe cloistered in front of her monitor or television screen, with no prying, uninvited eyes studying her, drawing unwelcome, uninformed conclusions. I would never begrudge her that privacy. Not ever.

Back to Phillip George Saltonstall.

Back to *The Drowning Girl*.

My ghost story is filled with significant moments that I would only become aware were significant moments in hindsight. Perhaps this is always the way of it. I can't say, because I've only ever lived my *one* haunting. I have a single data point. Still, I would stress mine's not a simple haunting, obviously. The sort you usually read about or hear around a campfire. I didn't merely feel a sudden and inexplicable chill in a dark room. I didn't wake to the sound of rattling chains or moaning. I was not shocked at an ectoplasmic woman drifting down a corridor. Those are only cartoons, caricatures of phantoms, invented by people who've never suffered (or been graced by) an actual, true, factual haunting. Of that I'm very certain.

So, this, then, is a significant event, and, in time, its significance would be made plain to me. But first it was only an anecdote or an interesting story that my grandmother told me.

L'Inconnue de la Seine.

I don't speak French. I had a year of it in high school, but I wasn't very good at it (as with so many other subjects), and I've forgotten almost all I did manage to learn. But Caroline, she spoke French. When she was a young woman, she'd gone to Paris and Mont Saint-Michel, Orléans and Marseille. She had photographs and picture postcards. She had a box of souvenirs. Sometimes she'd take them out and show them to me. She had stories of France. She told me one when I was nine years old.

I treasure her stories of France, as I seriously doubt I'll ever be able to go there myself. Travel isn't as cheap or easy as it once was, and I don't like the idea of being on an airplane (I've never flown).

I was in Girl Scouts, working on my first-aid merit badge. One day, a woman came to our scout troop, from a hospital in Providence, and she taught us CPR with a rubber dummy she called Resusci Anne. We learned how to properly administer chest compressions, and how to press our lips to the dummy's lips and breathe our breath into it. How we would breathe into the mouth of someone who'd stopped breathing after a heart attack. Rosemary was busy that day—I don't recall why—and Grandmother Caroline picked me up after the meeting.

Caroline drove this huge car, a Dresden blue 1956 Pontiac Star Chief, and I loved riding in the wide backseat. That car was the antithesis of my crappy little Honda. The speedometer went all the way to something like 120 miles per hour. It glided so smoothly along the road that you hardly ever felt a bump or a pothole. Rosemary sold it to a collector in Wakefield right after my grandmother committed suicide, and I've often wished she hadn't, that it had been passed to me. Of course, gas is so expensive now, and I'm sure the Star Chief got lousy mileage, so I probably couldn't have afforded to drive it. I can't afford to go to Paris, or to drive Caroline's lost Star Chief.

We went back to her house, and while I was trying to make sense of my math homework, after I'd told her about Resusci Anne, she told me about *l'Inconnue de la Seine*.

"The dummy had a very distinctive face, didn't it?" she asked me, and I had to think about the question for a moment. "Not just any old generic face," Caroline added. "Not like a face someone made up, but a face that must have been the face of a real human being." In hindsight, I realized that she was right, and I told her so.

"Well, that's because it wasn't a made-up face," she said. And then she told me the story of a drowned girl who'd been found floating in the river Seine in the 1880s or 1890s. The body was discovered near the quai du Louvre, and taken to the Paris Morgue.

"The woman was very pretty," Caroline said. "She was beautiful. Even after all that time in the river, she was still beautiful. One of the morgue assistants was so smitten with her that he made a death mask. Copies of the beautiful girl's face were sold, hundreds and hundreds of them. Almost everyone in Europe knew that face, even though no one ever did learn who she'd been. She might have been anyone. Maybe a girl who sold flowers, or a seamstress, or a beggar, but her identity is still a mystery. No one came forward to claim the corpse."

By this time, I'd completely forgotten about the confusing tedium of my homework, and was listening with rapt attention to my grandmother. She said she'd seen a copy of the mask when she was in Paris in the 1930s. Stories and poems and even a novel were written about *l'Inconnue de la Seine* (which she translated as "the unknown woman of the Seine," although Babel Fish tells me it should be translated as "the unknown factor of the Seine." It also tells me that "the unknown woman of the Seine" in French is *Le femme inconnu du Seine*. Maybe it's right, but I don't trust a computer program as much as my dead grandmother). She said one story had been written from the point of view of the dead girl, as she floated down the river. In the story she doesn't remember who she was when she was alive. She can't even remember her name. She's become a new sort of being, one that must live always at the bottom of the river, or in the sea. But she doesn't want to live like that, so she lets herself rise to the surface, where she quickly drowns on air.

Grandmother Caroline didn't tell me the name of the story or its author, or if she did, I forgot. I found it many years later. The story was written by a poet named Jules Supervielle, who was born in 1884 and died in 1960. First published in 1929, the story is titled simply "L'Inconnue de la Seine." I found it in a library at Brown University, in a collection of Supervielle's work called *L'Enfant de la haute mer*. I brought it home, though like I said, I can't read French. I copied the story down by hand. I still have it somewhere. And I've found other poems and stories about the drowned girl. Vladimir Nabokov wrote a poem about her, a poem that was also about the Slavic *rusalki*. Man Ray took photographs of that face.

One thing I have come to comprehend about true ghost stories is that we rarely know they're happening to us until after the fact, when we're haunted, but the events of the story proper are over and done with. This is a perfect example of what I mean. The first woman I ever kissed was *l'Inconnue de la Seine*, the likeness of an unidentified suicide who was born over a hundred years before me. That day, I pressed my lips gently to hers, again and again, breathing gently into her lifeless mouth. And I felt a peculiar tingle in my belly.

I know now, in hindsight, this was one of my earliest sexual experiences, even though it would be several years yet before I fully admitted to myself that I would only ever want to make love to women. My lips brushing those silicone lips, and there was a . . . a what? A frisson, I think. A shudder of pleasure that came and went so fast I was hardly even consciously aware of it.

I've sat staring at photographs of the death mask. I have a book on sculpture with two black-and-white photographs of it. She doesn't look dead. She hardly even looks like she's sleeping. There's a wry sort of a smile (which is why she's sometimes called the "drowned Mona Lisa"). Her hair is parted in the middle. You can see her eyelashes clearly.

It's all a perfect circle, in hindsight. A mandala of moments that are possessed of great significance, in hindsight. I only *say* that now, state it as a fact, but maybe it will become clearer farther along in my ghost story. Or maybe it won't, and I'll have failed.

Two years later, on my eleventh birthday, I would see Phillip George Saltonstall's painting *The Drowning Girl*, hanging at RISD. Eleven years later, I would take a drive one night in July and find Eva Canning waiting for me near the banks of the Blackstone River. Beautiful, terrible, lost Eva. My ghost who was a mermaid. Unless she wasn't. She would kiss me, and her lips were no different from those of the CPR dummy, or the lips of *l'Inconnue de la Seine*. And so I would fall in love with her, even though I was already very much in love with Abalyn. Did the morgue attendant kiss those dead lips, either before or after he made his mask?

In my head, this all makes a perfect circle, an elegant and inescapable circuit. But seeing it on paper, it comes across confusing. I'm afraid it isn't clear at all, what I mean. What I want to take from my mind and put someplace outside of me. I don't know the right words, and maybe that's because there are no right words to pull a haunting out into the light and trap it in ink and paper.

In his painting, Saltonstall hid the face of *The Drowning Girl* from view, by having her look over her shoulder, back towards the forest. But the painting was done in 1898, right? So . . . he might well have seen *l'Inconnue de la Seine*. He was in love with his first cousin, and if Mary Farnum is the girl he painted, it could be that's why he hid her face. But also maybe not. Eva Canning didn't ever wear the face of *l'Inconnue de la Seine*, though she wore at least two faces that I know of.

I could never stand to be a writer. Not a real writer. It's entirely too awful, having thoughts that refuse to become sentences.

The drugstore closes in half an hour, and I have to pick up a refill.

Am I repeating myself? Bah. Dah. Ba-ba.

I don't mean, when I ask this, repeating myself in a useful sense that underscores and makes manifest the ways in which all these occurrences and lives are bound inextricably together to create the ghost story that I've lived and am now trying to write down. I mean, am I *repeating myself* (Bah. Dah. Ba-ba.), and I also mean to ask, am I doing it to avoid moving forwards towards the terrifying, sad truth of it all? Am I dragging my feet because I'm a crazy woman who knows damn well she's crazy, but who doesn't want to be reminded just *how* crazy she is by having to tell two stories that are true, when only one can be *factual*? I feel as though I'm doing just exactly that. That I'm acting out Rosemary's old joke about a man in a rowboat with only one oar, rowing in endless circles and never, ever reaching shore. But how can I do otherwise, when the story is a spiral, or spirals set within spirals? Am I panicking because I think I need or I wish to force a straight, sane line, a narrative that begins *here* and proceeds to *there* by a conventional, coherent route? Am I too busy second-guessing myself and pulling my insecurities up over my head—like the blankets when I was five and afraid of the dark, afraid of what might be in the dark, *afraid of wolves*—to stop procrastinating and relate these events straightforwardly?

Am I a crazy woman only transferring her delusions and disordered consciousness into the written word?

Dr. Ogilvy dislikes the word "crazy," and she dislikes "insane," as well. She probably approves of the way Butler Hospital changed its name. But I tell her these are honest words. Fuck the political or negative connotations, they're *honest* words, and I need them. Maybe I'm frightened at the thought of being committed, of the antiseptic sterility of hospitals and the way they rob people of their dignity, but I'm not frightened by these words. Nor am I ashamed of them. But I *am* frightened by the thought that I'm caught in a loop and am incapable (or so unwilling I may as well be incapable) of communicating in a straightforward manner. And I would feel shame if I couldn't muster the courage to tell the truth.

"Nothing is ever straightforward," Imp typed, "though we lose a lot of the truth by pretending it's so."

Stop the questions. Just stop it. It makes me angry when I'm afraid. It makes me almost indescribably angry. I can't possibly finish this if it makes me angry to try, and the only thing that makes me more angry than my fear is my failures. So, I have to do this, and I won't stop me.

Abalyn and I didn't really ever discuss her moving in. She just did. I had the space, and she needed someplace to live. Almost right from the start, I wanted her to be near me. I wanted to be in love with her, or it was the beginning of love. It never felt like a crush. I wasn't a virgin. I'd had lots and lots of crushes, and it didn't feel like that. It wasn't that . . . what? Insistent? But I wanted her to stay, and she did stay, and I was glad of it. I do *remember* how she slept on the sofa the first few nights, out there with all her video game stuff, before I finally convinced her that was foolish when there was so much room in my bed. I wanted her in my bed. I wanted her close to me, and it was a relief when she accepted the invitation. The first time we made love, which was the first night she slept in my bed, that was a magnificent relief.

The Thursday after we met, I got off work early, and we walked together down Willow Street to the park, to Dexter Training Grounds, which, as I've said, isn't a military training grounds anymore, though it's still called that. On Thursdays, every week from early June until October, there's a farmers' market. Even if I don't buy anything, I enjoy going and seeing all the produce heaped in colorful, fresh piles, arranged in woven wooden baskets, and in those little cardboard cartons, waiting to be purchased. Early in the summer, there are sugarsnap peas, green beans, cucumbers, many varieties of peppers (hot, mild, sweet; scarlet and yellow and green), apples, strawberries, kale, turnips, crisp lettuce, spicy radishes, heirloom tomatoes, and big jugs of cider. In June, it's too early for good corn, and the blueberries aren't ripe yet. But there's bread from local bakeries. Sometimes, there's fresh sausage and bacon sold from coolers by the same men who raised and killed the pigs. All of this is arranged on long folding tables beneath the chestnut trees.

That day I bought apples and tomatoes, and when I had, Abalyn and I sat on a bench beneath the trees and each ate one of the apples, which were just the right blend of tart and sweet. The next day, I used the rest to bake a pie.

"Want to hear something creepy?" I asked, when I was done with my apple and had tossed the core away for the squirrels and birds.

"Depends," she said. "Is this where you tell me you're an axe murderer or into furries or that sort of creepy?"

I had to ask her what furries were.

"No. It's something I saw about a year back, something I saw here in the park."

"Then sure," she said. "Tell me something creepy." She was eating her apple much more slowly than I had (I often eat too fast), and she took another bite.

"I was driving home from work one night. Usually, I take the bus, right? But that day, I drove because, well, I don't know, I just felt like driving. On my way home that evening, passing by the park, I saw four people walking along together. They were away from the streetlamps and under the trees, where it was the darkest, but I still saw them pretty clearly. When I first spotted them, I thought they were nuns, which was strange enough. You never see nuns around here. But then they didn't seem like nuns anymore."

"Nuns are creepy enough," Abalyn muttered around a bite of her apple. "Nuns freak me out."

"I saw that they weren't wearing habits, but long black cloaks, with hoods that covered their heads. Suddenly, I wasn't even sure they were women. They might just as well have been men, from all I could make out of them. And then—and yeah, I know how this sounds—and then I fancied they weren't even people."

"You *fancied*? No one actually says they *fancied*."

"Language is a poor enough means of communication as it is," I told her. "So we should use all the words we have." It wasn't really an original thought; I was paraphrasing Spencer Tracy from *Inherit the Wind*.

She shrugged, said, "So the nuns who weren't nuns might not even have been people. Go on," and took another bite of her apple.

"I didn't say for sure that they weren't people. But for a moment they seemed more like ravens trying very hard to *look* like people. Maybe trying too hard, and because they were so self-conscious, I could see that they were actually ravens."

Abalyn chewed her apple and watched me. By then, she already knew why I take the pills I take. She'd seen all the prescription bottles on my nightstand, and I'd told her some stuff. Not everything.

Not anything about Caroline or my mother, but I'd told her enough that she understood about the state of my mental health (a phrase Dr. Ogilvy does approve of). Still, that day, she didn't say she thought I was nuts. I'd expected her to, but she didn't. She just ate her apple and considered me with those blue-green beach-glass eyes of hers.

"Sure, I know they weren't ravens, of course. I don't know why it seemed that way. I think they might have been Wiccans. There are a few witches around here, I suspect. Maybe they were on their way to a ritual or witches' sabbat or potluck or whatever it is Wiccans do when they get together."

"Frankly, it's a lot more interesting to imagine they were ravens trying too hard to pass themselves off as human beings," Abalyn said. "It's a lot creepier than if they're just Wiccans. I've met witches, and, unlike nuns, they're never creepy. They tend to be rather humdrum, in fact." She finished her apple and tossed the core so that it landed in the grass near mine.

"Whatever they were, they gave me the willies."

"Gave you the *willies*?" she asked, smiling. "No one actually says that, you know."

"I do," I replied, and flicked her lightly, playfully, on the left shoulder, as I was sitting on her left. She pretended that it had hurt and made faces. I continued, "They gave me the willies, and I went home and locked my doors and slept with all the lights burning that night. But I didn't have bad dreams. I looked for them again the next night, and the night after that, but I haven't ever seen them again."

"Were you homeschooled?" she asked me, which annoyed me since it had nothing to do with what I'd seen that night in the park.

"Why?"

"If you were, it might explain why you use old-fashioned words like *fancied* and *willies*."

"I wasn't," I said. "I went to public schools, here in Providence

and in Cranston. I hated it, usually, and I wasn't a very good student. I barely made it through my senior year, and it's a miracle I
graduated."

Abalyn said, "I hated high school, for reasons that ought to be
obvious, but was a pretty good student. Had it not been for most of
the other students, I might have loved it. But I did well. I aced my
SATs, even got a partial scholarship to MIT."

"You went to MIT?"

"No. I went to the University of Rhode Island, down in Kingston—"

"I know where URI is."

"—because the scholarship was only a partial scholarship, and
my folks didn't have the rest of the money."

She shrugged again. It used to irritate me, the way Abalyn was
always shrugging. Like she was indifferent, or stuff didn't get to her,
when I knew damned well it did. She'd wanted to attend MIT and
study computer science and artificial intelligence, but instead she'd
gone to URI and studied bioinformatics, which she explained was a
new branch of information technology (she said "IT") that tries to
visually analyze very large sets of biological data—she gave DNA
microarrays and sequences as examples. I was never any good with
biology, but I looked this stuff up. Bioinformatics, I mean.

I stared at the ground a moment, at my feet. "There must be
good money in that," I said. "But, instead, you write reviews of
video games for not much money at all."

"I do something I'm passionate about, like you and painting. I
was never passionate about bioinformatics. It was just something to
do, so I could say I went to college. It meant a lot to me, and more to
my parents, because neither of them had."

Katharine Hepburn said something like, "Do what interests
you, and at least one person is happy."

There was a breeze then, a warm breeze that smelled like freshly mowed lawns and hot asphalt, and I suggested we should head back. Abalyn caught me peering at the place beneath the chestnuts and oaks where I'd seen the not-nuns, not-raven people, and she leaned over and kissed me on the right temple. It was confusing, because the kiss made me feel safe, but letting my eyes linger at the spot below the trees, that sent a shudder through me.

"Hey, Imp," she said. "Now I owe you one."

"How do you mean?" I said, standing, straightening my shirt, smoothing out the wrinkles. "What do you owe me?"

"Tit for tat. You told me a creepy story, now I owe you one. Not right now, but later. I'll tell you about the time me and some friends got stoned and broke into the old railroad tunnel beneath College Hill."

"You don't have to do that. You don't owe me anything. It was just a story I've never told anyone else."

"All the same," she said, and then we walked back up Willow Street to the apartment. Just now, I almost typed "*my* apartment," but it was fast becoming *our* apartment. While I made dinner in the comfort of the butter-yellow kitchen, she played something noisy with lots of gunfire and car crashes.

If there are going to be chapters, this one ends here. I've been neglecting a painting, and I've got extra hours at work this week, so I may not get back to it—the ghost story—for a while, and the thought of leaving a chapter unfinished makes me uncomfortable.

3

⚬⚬⚬

Returning, briefly, to the subject of Phillip George Saltonstall and *The Drowning Girl*, before returning to Eva Canning and that maybe-night in July. I've written that I first saw the painting on the occasion of my eleventh birthday, which is both true and factual. I was born in 1986, and am now twenty-four years old, so that year was 1997. So, that August, the painting was ninety-nine years old. Which makes it 112 at the present, and means that it was 110 the summer I first met Eva Canning. It's odd how numbers have always comforted me, despite my being terrible at mathematics. I've already filled these pages with a plethora of numbers (mostly dates): 1914, 1898, #316, 1874, 1900, 1907, 1894, 1886, & etc. Perhaps there's some secret I've unconsciously hidden in all these numbers, but, if so, I've lost or never had the codex to riddle it out.

Dr. Ogilvy suspects that my fondness of dates may be an expression of *arithmomania*. And, in fairness to her, I should add that during my teens and early twenties, when my insanity included a great many symptoms attributable to obsessive-compulsive disorder, I had dozens upon dozens of elaborate counting rituals. I could not get through a day without keeping careful track of all my footsteps, or the number of times I chewed and swallowed. Often, it was necessary for me to dress and undress some precise number of times (the number was usually, but not always, thirty) before leaving the house. In order to take a shower, I would have to turn the water on and off seventeen times, step in and out of the tub or shower stall seventeen times, pick up the soap and put it down again seventeen times. And so forth. I did my best to keep these rituals a secret, and I was deeply, privately ashamed of them. I can't say why, why I was ashamed, but I was afraid, and I lived in constant dread that Aunt Elaine or someone else would discover them. For that matter, if I had been asked at the time to explain why I found them necessary, I would've been hard-pressed to come up with an answer. I could only have said that I was convinced that unless I did these things, something truly horrible would happen.

Always it has seemed to me that arithmomania is simply (no, not simply, but still) the normal human propensity for superstition to run amok in the mind. A phenomenon that might seem only backwards or silly when expressed at a social level becomes madness at the individual level. The Japanese fear of the number four, for example. Or the widespread belief that thirteen is unlucky, sinister, evil. Christians who find special significance in the number twelve, because there were twelve apostles. And so forth.

On my eleventh birthday, the painting was ninety-nine years old, and I wouldn't begin any serious research into it until I was sixteen, at which point it had aged to one hundred and four (11. 99. 16. 104). I'd hardly thought about *The Drowning Girl* in the years since I first set eyes on it. Hardly at all. And when it reentered my life, it did so—seemingly—by nothing more than happenstance. It seemed so then. I'm not sure if it seems so any longer. The arrival of Eva may have changed coincidence to something else. I begin to imagine orchestration where before I heard only the cacophony of randomness. Crazy people do that all the time, unless you buy into the notion that we have the ability to perceive order and connotation in ways closed off to the minds of "sane" people. I don't. Subscribe to that notion, I mean. We are not gifted. We are not magical. We are slightly or profoundly broken. Of course, that's not what Eva said.

All my life, I have loved visiting the Athenaeum on Benefit Street. Rosemary and Caroline took me there more often than the central branch of the Providence Public Library downtown (150 Empire Street). The Athenaeum, like so much of Providence, exists out of time, preservationists having seen that it slipped through the cracks while progress steamrolled so much of the city into sleek modernity. Today, the Athenaeum isn't so very different than in the days when Edgar Allan Poe and Sarah Helen Whitman courted among the stacks. Built in the manner of the Greek Revival, the library's present edifice was finished in 1838 (sixty years before Saltonstall painted *The Drowning Girl*), though the Athenaeum was founded in 1753. (Note the repetition of *eight*—at *eight*een or twenty-two I would have been helpless to do otherwise—1 + 7 equaling 8; 5 + 3 equaling 8; 8 + 8 equaling 16, which divided by 2 equals 8; full circle.) I couldn't begin to imagine how many hours I've spent wandering between those tall shelves and narrow aisles, or lost in some volume or another in the reading room on the lowermost floor. Housed there within its protective shell of pale stone, the library seems as precious and frail as a nonagenarian. Its smell is the musty commingling fragrance of yellowing pages and dust and ancient wood. To me, the smells of comfort and safety. It smells sacred.

On a rainy day in the eighth month of 2002, on the twenty-eighth day of August, I pulled from the shelves in the Athenaeum a book published in 1958, written by an art historian named Dolores Evelyn Smithfield—*A Concise History of New England Painters and Illustrators* (1958 + a name with eight syllables + I was 16 = 2 x 8).

Somehow, I'd never before noticed the book. I took it back to one of the long tables, and was only flipping casually through the pages when I happened across eight paragraphs about Saltonstall and a black-and-white reproduction of *The Drowning Girl*. I sat and stared at it for a very long time, listening to the rain against the roof and windows, to thunder far away, the footsteps overhead. I noted that the painting appeared on page 88. I used to carry loose-leaf notebooks with me everywhere I went, and an assortment of pens and pencils in a pink plastic box, and that afternoon I wrote down everything Smithfield had written about *The Drowning Girl*. It doesn't amount to much. Here's the most interesting part:

> Though best remembered, when he is remembered at all, for his landscapes, one of Saltonstall's best-known works is *The Drowning Girl* (1898), which may have been inspired by a certain piece of folklore encountered in northwestern Rhode Island and southern Massachusetts, along a short stretch of the Black Stone [*sic*] River. A common local yarn involves the murder of a mill owner's daughter at the hands of a jealous fiancé, who then attempted to dispose of her body by tying stones about the corpse and sinking it in the narrow granite channel of the old Millville Lock. Some accounts have the murderer dropping the dead girl from the Triad Bridge, where the river is especially deep and wide. Tradition has it that the girl's ghost haunts the river from Millville to Uxbridge, and possibly as far south as Woonsocket, Rhode Island. She is said to have been heard singing to herself along the banks and in the neighboring woods, and some claim she's responsible for a number of drownings.
>
> We can be quite certain that the artist was well enough aware of the legend, as he notes in a letter to Mary Farnum, "Perhaps I will catch sight of her myself on some evening, as

I sit sketching my studies. Sadly, I've not yet encountered anything more exciting than a deer and a blacksnake." While this is hardly irrefutable evidence that he named his painting for the grisly tale, it appears too much to dismiss as coincidence. Could it be that Saltonstall meant to capture a careless swimmer moments before a fateful encounter with the ghost of "the drowning girl"? It seems a reasonable enough conclusion, and one that settles the question for this author.

That same day . . . well, that night, I managed (much to my surprise!) to find the envelope that Rosemary Anne had made notes on all those years before, on my eleventh birthday, in the presence of the painting that had seemed like a window to me. The next day, I returned to the Athenaeum and prowled through volume after volume of Massachusetts and Rhode Island folklore, hoping to come across anything more about the story of "the drowning girl." For hours, I found nothing at all, and was about to give up, when I finally discovered an account of the legend in *A Treasury of New England Folklore* by Benjamin A. Botkin (New York: Bonanza Books, 1965). Here is an excerpt, and an excerpt I found later, in another book:

A far more malevolent spirit is said to haunt the Blackstone River near the village of Millville. Ask almost anyone in the area, and you may be regaled with the tragic story of a young woman saddled with the good Puritan name of Perishable Shippen. Murdered by her father and tossed into the river, the restless, vengeful ghost of Perishable is said to wander the riverbed, often seizing the feet and legs of unwary bathers and pulling them down to their doom in the murky green waters. Others claim that you can hear the ghost singing to herself on summer evenings, and that her voice is beautiful, but has been known to lure melancholic souls to commit suicide by jumping from railroad and highway bridges, or even flinging themselves from the steep walls of the gorge just upriver of Millville. The story appears to date back at least to the 1830s, a thriving "protoindustrial" time when Millville was the site of grist, fulling, corn, and sawmills, along with a scythe manufacturer. To this day, teenage boys looking to spook their girlfriends often visit the old railroad trestle over the river on the night of the full moon hoping to catch sight of the "Siren of Millville."

Also, I found:

There's a folk tradition among some residents of the towns along the Blackstone that many years ago, something from the sea became trapped in the river. The tale usually involves a hurricane and/or a flood, though the details often vary wildly from one teller to the next. Few seem to agree on which disaster was responsible, or how far in the past the event occurred. Variously, the tale invokes the Great Hurricane of 1938, the Saxby Gale of 1869, the Norfolk and Long Island Hurricane of 1821, flooding in February 1886, and again in 1955. But most followed more familiar folktale conventions and would only agree it happened many decades ago, or when they were young or before they were born, or when their great-grandparents were young.

As to what entered the river and remains there to this day, accounts can be divided into the prosaic and the fantastic. The former category includes a shark or several sharks, a sea turtle, a seal, a giant squid, a huge eel, and a dolphin.

The latter includes a mermaid, the ghost of a woman (usually a suicide) who drowned in Narragansett Bay, a sea serpent, and, in one instance, a wayward selkie whose sealskin
was stolen by a whaler. Yet all agree on two points: the creature or being has caused injury, mishap, and death, and that
it originated in the sea. The man who insisted the impris-
oned thing was a conger eel claimed that it had been caught
and killed when he was a child. He consistently mispro-
nounced *conger* as *conjure*.

(from *Weird Massachusetts* by William Linblad
[Worcester: Grey Gull Press, 1986])

As with my file on "Little Red Riding Hood," I have a thick file
on the haunting of the Blackstone River containing almost everything I've been able to learn about it over the last eight years. Before
and after I met Eva Canning—both times, if, indeed, there were two
meetings. The file tab was originally labeled "Perishable Shippen,"
though Botkin's is the only account of the legend that grants the
murdered woman that name. I've never shown the file to Abalyn,
though I think now that I should have. That's one more mistake I
made, keeping that history to myself (though, of course, Abalyn
believed she'd uncovered her own "history" of Eva). I could make a
lengthy roster of those mistakes, things I did that only drove us farther apart. I will say, "If I'd have done *this* or *that* differently, we
might still be together." That's another, more insidious sort of fairy
tale. That's another facet to my haunting—having driven her away—
another vicious wrinkle in the meme.

I'll come back to my file and its contents, after I force myself to
spit up one version of the truth.

"A woman in a field—something grabbed her."

A line from Charles Fort's *Lo!* (1931) that I've been carrying around in my head for days. It was incorporated into one of Albert Perrault's paintings. I wanted to get it down here so that I wouldn't forget it. All the same, this is not where it belongs, not in the first version of the coming of Eva Canning, but in the second. But now I won't forget it.

July, two years and three months ago and the spare change of a few days (one way or the other). That night alone on the highway in Massachusetts, passing by the river. That night I left Providence alone, but didn't return alone. I think maybe now I'm ready to try to write it out in some semblance of a *story*, what I recall of the first version of my meeting with Eva. A story is, by necessity, a sort of necessary fiction, right? If it's meant to be a true story, then it becomes a synoptic history. I read that phrase someplace, but I can't for the life of me recall when or where. But I mean, a "true" story, or what we call history, can only ever bear a passing resemblance to the facts, as history is far too complex to ever reduce to anything as clear-cut as a conventional narrative. My history, the history of a city or a nation, the history of a planet or the universe. We can only approximate. So, now that's what I'll do. I'll write an approximation of that night, July 8, the most straightforward I can manage.

But I'll also keep in mind that history is a slave to reductionism.

Telling this story, I diminish it. I reduce it. I make of it a *synodic* history.

I *render* it. That night. This night.

Begin here:

I work until ten o'clock, so I've driven the Honda because I dislike walking home from the bus stop after dark. The Armory is a much tamer neighborhood than it used to be, but better safe than sorry, et cetera. I drive home to Willow Street, and Abalyn is sitting on the sofa with her laptop, writing. I go to the kitchen and pour myself a glass of milk and make a fluffernutter sandwich, plenty enough dinner. I rarely eat very much at a time. I snack, I suppose. I bring the milk and my saucer with the sandwich back to the parlor and sit down on the sofa with Abalyn.

"It's a beautiful night," I say. "We should go for a drive. It's a beautiful night for a drive."

"Is it?" Abalyn asks, briefly glancing up from the screen of the laptop. "I haven't been outside today."

"You shouldn't do that," I reply. "You shouldn't stay cooped up in here all day." I take another bite and watch her while I chew. After I swallow, and have a sip of milk, I ask her what she's writing.

"A review," which is what I would have guessed, so it doesn't seem like much of an answer.

For a few moments, maybe for a few minutes, I eat my sticky sandwich and she types. I almost don't ask about the drive again, because there's something so peaceful about the rhythm of the evening as it's playing out. But then I do ask the question, and from *that* everything else follows.

"No, Imp," she says, looking up at me again. "I'm sorry, but I've got a deadline. I need to have this piece finished in the next couple of hours. I should have finished it yesterday." She tells me the name of the game, and it's one I'd watched her play, but I've entirely forgotten what it was. "I'm sorry," she says again.

"No, that's okay. No problem." I try not to sound disappointed, but I've never been very good at hiding disappointment. It almost always shows, so I will assume she heard it that night.

"Know what?" she says. "Why don't you go, anyway? No reason you shouldn't, just because I've got to work. Might even be better without me along. More quiet and all."

"It won't be better without you."

I finish my sandwich and my milk and set the saucer and the empty glass on the floor beside the sofa.

"I still say you shouldn't let me keep you from going. It's supposed to rain the rest of the week."

"You're sure? It's all right if I go without you, I mean."

"Positive. I'll probably still be up when you get back, this one's turning out to be such a bitch."

I tell her that I won't be gone more than a couple of hours at the most, and she says, "Well, then I'll definitely still be up when you get back."

Regardless, I almost don't go. There's a wash of apprehension, or dread. Some brand of misgiving. It isn't so very different from what I felt back when the arithmomania was so bad, or the night I saw the raven-nuns in the park, or on innumerable other occasions when the crazy kicks into overdrive. Dr. Ogilvy has said repeatedly that whenever this happens, I should make a concerted effort to go ahead and do the thing that I'd meant to do, but was suddenly afraid of doing. Within reason, she's said, I shouldn't let the delusions and magical thinking and neuroses prevent me from living a normal life. Which means not locking up.

Normal is a bitter pill that we rail against.

Imp isn't sure what that means. It just occurred to her, and she didn't want to lose it.

I dislike this language, the detached argot of psychiatry and psychology. Words like *codependent* and *normal*, phrases like *magical thinking*. They disturb me far more than *crazy* and *insane*. Let it be enough to say, *There's a wash of apprehension, or dread.*

Even so, I almost decide not to go alone. I almost reach for the book I've been reading, or go to my studio to work on the painting I've been trying to finish.

"I think it would be good for you," Abalyn says, not looking away from the screen, her fingers still tapping away at the keyboard. "I don't want to become a ball and chain."

And this calls to mind another warning from Dr. Ogilvy, that if

I ever should find myself in a relationship, not to allow my illness to let it drift into codependence. Not to risk losing my self-sufficiency.

"If you're sure."

"I'm totally sure, Imp. Go. Get out. It's an order," and she laughs. "If it's not too late when you get home, we'll watch a movie."

"I have work tomorrow," I say. "I can't stay up that late."

"Go," she tells me again, and she stops typing long enough to make a shooing motion with her left hand. "I'll still be here when you get home."

So I got my keys, and a summer sweater just in case the night was chillier than it had seemed coming home from work. I kiss her, and say I won't be gone long.

"Be careful," she says. "Don't drive so fast. One of these nights, you're gonna get a ticket. Or hit a deer." I reply that I'm always careful. I sound more defensive than I meant to, but Abalyn doesn't appear to have noticed.

"You have your phone?" she asks.

It's almost eleven thirty when I leave the house, but I don't have to be at work until eleven the next morning. I pull back out onto Willow, turn onto Parade Street, then right on Westminster. I hardly think about where I might be headed. I hardly ever do on these drives. Any forethought or planning seems to defeat the purpose. Their therapeutic value seems to lie in their spontaneity, in the particular routes and destinations always being accidental. From Westminster, I cross the interstate and drive through downtown, with all its bright lights and unlit alleyways. I turn left, north, onto North Main Street, and pass Old North Burial Ground.

I don't play the radio. I never play the radio on my night drives.

So, past North Burial Ground, and I continue on through Pawtucket, North Main becoming Highway 122. There's more traffic than I would like, but then there's almost always more traffic than I'd like. It's long after midnight by the time I get to Woonsocket, with its decaying, deserted mills and the roaring cacophony of Thunder Mist Falls, there where the Blackstone River slips over the weirs of the Woonsocket Falls Dam. I pull into the parking lot on the eastern side of the dam. When I get out of the car, I look up and see that there's a ring around the moon, reminding me of Abalyn's warning that rain was on the way. But rain tomorrow, not tonight. Tonight the sky is clear and specked with stars. I lock the Honda's doors and cross the otherwise empty parking lot and stand at the railing; I try hard to concentrate on nothing but the violent noise of the water crashing down onto the ragged granite island below the dam.

"Wouldn't it be interesting," Imp typed, "if there were a third version of the truth, one in which you met Eva at this dam? It would be poetic, wouldn't it?"

No. Things are quite complicated enough already, thank you very much. Let's not make it worse with obvious lies, no matter how pretty they may be.

I'm standing there, wanting only to hear the wild torrent against those water- and timeworn Devonian rocks. But, instead, my head's filling up with distracting trivia about the dam's history, minute clots of fact that intrude and push their way unbidden up and into my consciousness. It was completed in 1960, this present dam, after the terrible floods of 1955. But there were dams before *this* dam, and as long ago as 1660—before there was any dam and only the natural course of the falls—a mill stood on this spot. The mood is broken, and I turn away from the dam and the falls and the roar, crossing the street back to the parking lot and the car.

I continue north, leaving Rhode Island behind me and crossing into Massachusetts. I ford the river on Bridge Street, just east of the rusty railway trestle from which the lifeless body of Perishable Shippen might have been dropped, if those stories are true. I slow down in Millville, recalling what Abalyn said about speeding tickets. I've never gotten a speeding ticket. I've never even gotten a parking ticket. Millville is small, and I think of it as a village or hamlet, not a town. But still there are so many sodium-arc or mercury-vapor streetlights that they blot out the stars. Who needs all this light? What are they afraid of? There's no point to being out in the night, beneath the night sky, if I can't see the stars. But Millville is small, and soon I'm on the far side of it, heading northwest on 122. Soon, I can make out a few twinkling stars again.

Imp—nervous, fretting, skittish little Imp—typed, "Are you sure you want to do this? It's not too late to stop, you know? You can stop right here, or say that you turned around and drove home to Willow Street. Or, if you insist, that you drove on to Uxbridge or wherever most suits you, but that nothing out of the ordinary whatsoever happened that night or any other. Not in July and certainly not in November."

And I could never use the word *insane* again, and also I would pretend that Rosemary Anne died of a seizure, that she didn't commit suicide. I could go through all the rest of my life in denial, always evading what makes me uncomfortable for fear of triggering uncomfortable, disturbing, appalling thoughts. I could do that, right? I could always call something one thing when, in fact, it's the exact opposite. Lots of people do it, and it seems to work for them, so why the hell not me?

Hesitantly, Imp typed, "But we both know better, don't we?" The persistent clack of the keys against the paper rolled into the carriage was pregnant with resignation.

But point taken.

I know better.

Stop.

Yesterday, I honestly did try to make it through that all at once. I wanted to spit it out and be done with it, put it at my back, that first version of the night on the road. I wanted to follow Dr. Ogilvy's advice and proceed despite my anxiety. But then I was talking to myself, talking at myself, questioning myself, heaping aspersions upon my resolve and casting those aspersions into the cold, hard default Courier black-and-white of this typewriter. And, even though I immediately called myself on it, that was that. I had to step away. I find today that I'm still not ready to return to the events of that night, what occurred after I left the parking lot in Woonsocket, after I drove through Millville. But I also need to write, so I'll write *this*, instead. Before sleep last night, I was thinking again about the night I saw the raven-nuns, and about relating that story to Abalyn, and I remembered what Caroline once told me about the meaning of ravens, and those birds closely related to ravens.

· Maybe I was six or seven. I'm not sure. Rosemary had left me with my grandmother while she went shopping (she often did this, as I had a peculiar aversion to grocery stores and such). Caroline was sewing, and I was watching her sew. She had an antique Singer sewing machine, the sort you work with a foot pedal. I loved the rhythm of it. The sound of my grandmother's sewing put me at ease; it was a soothing sound. We were in her bedroom, because that's where she kept her sewing machine, and she was making a shirt from calico printed with a bright floral pattern.

What happened might seem strange, if you're not me, or Caroline, or Rosemary. If you're not someone or something like Eva Canning was, for that matter. It's never seemed odd to me, but, then, I'm keenly aware how my perceptions are so often at odds with those of most other people I've met in my life. Maybe it wouldn't seem strange, but only quaint or foolish. I don't mean charmingly odd when I say quaint. I mean strange.

I was sitting on Caroline's bed, which smelled of fresh laundry and tea rose perfume and very slightly of the Ben-Gay ointment she used when her bad shoulder was hurting her. Comfortable smells, all of those, in perfect harmony with the *chuga-chuga-chuga* of the old Singer. And I was telling her about Rosemary taking me down to Scarborough Beach just the week before. It was autumn, so there weren't a lot of people at the beach, no tourists, no summer people, and we'd walked back and forth for a couple of hours, filling a plastic pail with shells and a few unusually shaped cobbles. And, sitting on the bed, telling my grandmother about that day by the bay, I said:

"And then Rosemary looked out across the water, and she said, 'Oh, baby, look. Do you see it?' She was awfully excited, and she pointed at the water. I tried very hard to see what she was seeing, but I didn't, not at first.

"'You can't see it, because the sun's reflecting off the water,' and she told me to shade my eyes with my hand and try again."

"Did that work?" Caroline asked, stopping to fiddle with the machine's bobbin. "Could you see what she was pointing at?"

"Yes," I replied.

"And what was it you saw?"

And, thinking that I'd delivered the yarn without a trace of guile and that she'd believe every single word, I said, "I saw a great sea serpent slithering about in the waves. It was the color of kelp. It looked smooth and rubbery like kelp. I thought that if I could touch it, it would even feel the way kelp feels."

"You're sure it wasn't kelp?" Caroline asked me. "Sometimes there are pretty big tangles of kelp in the bay. I've seen them myself. At a distance, they can look like all sorts of things besides kelp."

"Oh, absolutely sure," I told her. "Kelp doesn't have a head like a snake and red eyes and a tongue that flicks out the way a snake's tongue flicks out. Kelp doesn't turn and stare back at you and open its mouth to show how many teeth it has, so you'll know it could eat you if it wanted to, if it decided to swim towards you and you weren't fast enough to get out of its way. Kelp doesn't slap at the water with its tail like a whale does, now, does it?"

"Not in my experience," she said, and went back to working the Singer's pedal and feeding the bright calico beneath the needle. "Doesn't sound much like kelp."

"It must have been at least as long as a school bus, however many feet that is. Mother was afraid, but I told her it wouldn't hurt us. I told her how I'd read about a sea serpent that was in Gloucester Harbor in 1817—"

"You remember the date?" Caroline wanted to know.

"I most certainly do, and it's rude to interrupt." She apologized, and I continued. "I told Rosemary that lots of people saw that sea serpent in 1917, and it didn't attack any of them."

"You said before that it was *1817*, didn't you?"

"Does it make any difference? Either way, it didn't attack anyone, and that's what I told Mother. We stood there and watched the sea serpent swimming around, and it watched us back, and we even saw it stretch out its long neck and try to snatch a seagull out of the air."

No sooner had I mentioned the gull than a large crow appeared at the bedroom window and perched there, gazing in at us with its beady black eyes. Caroline stopped sewing, and I stopped telling my story about the sea serpent off Scarborough Beach. The crow pecked once at the window screen, cawed once, then flew away again. My grandmother stared at the window for a moment, then turned and looked at me.

"Imp, now I *know* you made up the story about the sea serpent."

"How?" I asked, still watching the window, as if I expected the crow to return.

"It's something that crows can do," she said. "Tell whenever someone's lying. If you're listening to a story, and a crow shows up like that, you can bet the storyteller is making the whole thing up."

"I've never heard that before," I protested, though I think by that time I'd decided it was wise not to press the issue of my fabulous sea serpent.

"Imp, there's lots of stuff you've never heard before. You're just a kid, and you've got a lot to learn. Anyhow, it's not just crows. Same goes for ravens, too, and also rooks, magpies, and pretty much any sort of corvid, even blue jays and nutcrackers. They're damn smart beasts, and it's their special ability, to know a lie when they hear one. And what with their troublesome dispositions, they have an annoying tendency to show up and remind someone when they've strayed from the facts."

"You're not just making this up?"

Caroline nodded towards the window. "Did you see a crow?" she asked.

"What's a corvid, anyway?" I wanted to know, as it was a word I'd never heard before.

"The family Corvidae, into which ornithologists place ravens and crows and all their close relatives."

"You read that in a book?"

"I most certainly did," she said, and started sewing again.

"And you also read the part about blackbirds showing up when people are making stuff up?"

"Strictly speaking, Imp, blackbirds aren't corvids, though most corvids are birds that are black."

By this time I'm sure I must have been quite entirely confused. Caroline had this habit of talking in circles, so maybe that's where I got it from. The circles almost always made sense, which is why they were so frustrating, especially to a six- or seven-year-old girl who'd not yet learned for herself the trick of talking in meaningful circles, conversational mandalas that resist scrutiny and refutation.

"You didn't answer my question, Caroline. Did you read it in a book, that part about corvids showing up whenever people tell lies?"

"I don't remember, Imp, but it doesn't make any difference. Lots of things are true, but no one's ever bothered writing them down in books. Lives are filled with true things, things that really happened, and hardly any of it ever shows up in books. Or newspapers. Or what have you. Maybe my mother told me about crows and ravens. But I might have read it somewhere."

"I really did read about the Gloucester sea serpent," I told her, somewhat sheepishly, I expect.

"I don't think that's what the crow was objecting to, India Morgan." Grandmother Caroline rarely ever called me by my first and middle name like that, but when she did, it got my attention. And then she said:

"*I have fled in the shape of a raven of prophetic speech.* That's something I read. It's from a Welsh poet named Taliesin. You ought to look him up next time you're at the library."

And then she recited, rather dramatically:

> *Crow, crow, crow God,*
> *Send Thee a black thraw!*
> *I was a crow just now,*
> *But I shall be in a woman's likeness even now*
> *Crow, crow, crow God!*
> *Send Thee a black thraw!*

Then she laughed and jiggled the bobbin again.

"More Taliesin?" I asked.

"Nope. *That's* something I read in a book, an invocation Scottish witches used when they wanted to turn back into women, after having turned themselves into crows."

I asked what *thraw* meant, because I'd never heard the word before.

"To throw," she replied. "To twist, turn, distort, and so forth. It's an old Scottish word, if I'm not mistaken." I still didn't quite understand what it meant in the context of the incantation, but I didn't say so. I already felt foolish enough over the sea serpent.

"Oh," she said, "here's one more, from Shakespeare, from *Cymbeline*."

"At least I've heard of him."

"I should hope so," she scowled, and then recited:

> *Swift, swift, you dragons of the night, that dawning*
> *May bare the raven's eye! I lodge in fear;*
> *Though this a heavenly angel, hell is here.*

"Another poem?" And she said, "No, a play."

So, Grandmother Caroline, the night I was driving home from work and saw the four raven-nuns walking there beneath the trees, what lie had I told that day? What truth were they trying to remind me of that evening?

There were no ravens, or crows, or (to the best of my recollection) even blue jays the day before the night I found Eva. Or the day after. And I've never seen a crow or a raven at night, so that goes without saying. There was an owl, and whip-poor-wills, but that's hardly anything out of the ordinary.

Yesterday, when I was typing out the story of that night in July, no crow or raven appeared at my window. If one had, I'd have been relieved, and I might have been able to finish.

I had an appointment today with Dr. Ogilvy. I've not mentioned to her that I'm writing all these things down, though we have spoken several times now of Eva Canning, both the July Eva and the November Eva, just as we've talked about Phillip George Saltonstall and *The Drowning Girl* (painting and folklore) and "The Little Mermaid." Just as we've talked about Albert Perrault and The Voyeur of Utter Destruction (in Hindsight) and "Little Red Riding

Hood." I have no idea yet if I'm going to tell her I'm writing this ghost story. She might ask to read it, and I'd have to say no. She might ask if I'm being literal when I say "ghost story," or if I'm being metaphorical, and I'd have to say I'm being very literal. These things would worry her. I think that I know her well enough to know they would. Worry her, I mean. For someone who doesn't like to cause other people consternation, I've surely done more than my fair share.

There's no point to being out in the night, beneath the night sky, if I can't see the stars. But Millville is small, as I've said, and soon I'm on the far side of it, heading northwest on Route 122. Before long, I can make out a few twinkling stars through the windshield. I have the driver's-side window down, and the air is fresh and plant scented. There's the faint musky, muddy odor of the river, which is no more than fifty feet away on my left (or southwest, along this short stretch of road). I have often thought that rivers and lakes and the ocean smell like sex. So, the summer night has about it the not disagreeable bouquet of sex. I've just checked the speedometer, and see that I'm only doing forty or forty-five miles per hour, which I don't think Abalyn would think of as speeding. Though, I don't know what the speed limit is; there are signs, no doubt, but I've never noticed them. If I have, I've forgotten.

There's absolutely no sense of foreboding, none of the apprehension I felt before leaving Providence. All of that has passed away. The drive is relaxing me. I'm glad I didn't stay home.

I think I'll even go as far as Worcester before turning back. And then . . . I've written this part down before. I just stopped, went back through the pages, and found it:

And one moment she isn't there, and the next moment, there she is. It's just like that. Not so much like I came upon her. It's more like she just appeared.

Yes. Exactly like that. Or I only blinked at an inopportune moment, and it *seemed* like that. Does it matter which? No, not at all.

A nude woman standing in the breakdown lane, gazing out into the dark towards the Blackstone River, caught in the low beam of the Honda's headlights. Later, Abalyn will want to know why I stopped. Eva will ask me, as well. And I'll say, "What else would I have done? What would you have done?" And I'll say, "I don't know why I stopped."

Because she could not stop for me, I kindly stopped for death.

I don't "hit the brakes," but I do slow down pretty quickly. I surely haven't gone more than a hundred yards before I pull over. I sit there with the Honda's engine idling, my eyes fixed on the rearview mirror. I linger there in the car for a couple of minutes, maybe, at the most. When I cut the engine, the night becomes all at once enormously, profoundly, oppressively silent—but just for the space of a few heartbeats, a handful of breaths—and then there are insect trills and clicks and the throaty songs of frogs. I leave the lights on and get out of the Honda. There's a high granite wall on the right side of the northbound lane, a rocky wound sliced into the earth however long ago the road was made. Once upon a time, a wooded hillside sloped gently down to the river, but men and their gelignite made short work of that and all the stone and soil and all those trees were carted away, and now there is but this wall of granite.

I turn from it and look both ways before crossing the road. My shoes crunch in the gravel as I walk cautiously towards the woman. I can't see her right off, of course. I've gone too far and the taillights don't reach that far. I even consider I might have imagined it all. I've imagined lots and lots of things over the years, and I consider that I might have hallucinated the woman. Or, instead of making an appeal to my insanity, it might only have been a disquieting optical illusion that any driver could have experienced. I'm not running, or even walking at a fast pace. I'm wishing the moon were full, or at least first quarter, because then there would be so much more light. But then my eyes begin to adjust, and I can see her (there actually is a small bit of reflected reddish glow from the taillights, and that helps). If she's noticed me, she doesn't act like she has.

"Are you okay?" I call out. She doesn't reply, or give any sign that she's heard. I stop walking and call out to her a second time. "Do you need help? Has something happened? Were you in an accident? Did your car break down?" In retrospect, the last two questions will strike me as very absurd, but there you go. What part of this doesn't strike me as absurd?

Now I can see well enough that I realize her hair's wet, and I glance towards the river, hidden in the darkness, but smelling much stronger than it smelled when I was only driving past. I look back to the woman and notice that she's standing near the beginning of a dirt path that leads down towards the water. *Fishermen made that path,* I think. *Fishermen and people with canoes and kayaks.*

"Were you swimming?" I ask, and finally she turns her head in my direction.

What happened next, I've written it down already, back on page 66, and what's the point of trying to reword it, reward it, rewind it? This is what I wrote days and days ago, more or less:

"Are you okay?" I ask her again.

It'll sound silly if I say that she's unearthly, but she *is* unearthly. Worse, it's presumptuous, right? It presupposes I know everything that *is* earthly, and so would recognize anything that *isn't*. I don't, of course. Know unearthly from earthly, or vice versa. But that's the way she strikes me, standing by Route 122. That's the word that first pops into my head—*unearthly.*

She narrows her eyes, as though the faint red light from the car is too bright for her. I guess it would have been, after all that darkness. Her pupils would have suddenly contracted, and her eyes would have hurt. Later, I'll see that her eyes are blue, a shade of blue that Rosemary Anne used to call "bottle-blue." (If this were November, and not July, I'd see that her eyes are an unusual shade of brown, a brown that almost seems golden.) Regardless, she narrows her eyes, and they flash iridescent eyeshine, and she blinks at me. I think *feral*, which is much more appropriate and far less presumptuous than was *unearthly*. She smiles very, very slightly, so slightly, in fact, that I may be mistaken. She might *not* be smiling. She takes a step towards me, and I ask, a third time, if she's okay.

(Rewrote more of that than I thought I would.)

I add, "Do you need me to call for help?"

Her lank, wet hair hangs down about her shoulders, clinging to her skin in dark tendrils. She licks at her thin lips, and her skin glistens. In passing, it reminds me of the skin of an amphibian, a frog or a salamander, the way it glistens. And in passing, I have the impression that when I touch her (and I know now that I *will* touch her), her skin will be slimy.

She takes another step towards me, and now there can't be more than ten feet remaining between us.

"Imp?" she asks, and that should startle me, but it doesn't. Not in the least.

"Do I know you?" I ask her, and she frowns and looks confused.

"No," she says, almost whispering, "not yet."

A pickup truck rushes past then, *roars* past, going much faster than forty-five miles an hour. It's heading towards Millville, and so it passes so near to us that if I'd held out my left arm, the car might have hit me. Might well have taken my hand off, broken my arm, whatever happens. We're washed in the brilliance of the headlights. The driver doesn't even slow down, and I'll always wonder what, if anything, she or he might have glimpsed.

The headlights leave me half-blind for a few seconds, and I stand there cursing and blinking at the afterimages.

"It's not safe, just standing here," I say, sounding annoyed. "A wonder that truck didn't hit us both. You know that, right? Where are your clothes? Did you leave them down by the water?" And I point at the darkness concealing the Blackstone River.

In the quiet after the car, the quiet that is punctuated only by katydids and crickets and frogs and an owl, she says, "I have dreamed it again." I have no doubt this is what she says, and, too, "Till your singing eyes and fingers."

"It's not safe here," I tell her once more. "And the mosquitoes must be eating you alive."

And she asks, "Who are hearsed that die on the sea?" She asks as if I haven't spoken, as if it's perfectly safe to stand naked at the side of Route 122 in the middle of the night with trucks racing by.

I'm as sure she said that as I am that she wasn't wearing any clothes. It's from "The Whale Watch," chapter 117 of *Moby-Dick*. I don't know that yet, of course. I've never even read *Moby-Dick*, not this summer evening.

I've stood there asking questions long enough, and I walk up to her and say, "Come on," holding out my hand. She takes it. I'm relieved that her skin isn't slimy at all, just chilled from having been wet. "If I can't get you to make sense, I can at least get you someplace safe," and she doesn't resist or say anything else as I lead her back across the road to the Honda.

I give her the light cotton sweater I brought with me, but she just stands there holding it, so I put it on her myself. I button it up, covering her small breasts and her flat belly. There's a flannel blanket in the backseat, from a trip to the beach, and I wrap it about her waist. "It's not much," I say, "but it's better than before."

When I suggest that she get into the Honda, she only hesitates a moment. On the drive back to Providence and Willow Street she doesn't say another word. I repeat questions she already hasn't bothered to answer. I ask new questions, such as "Where do you live?" and "Do you need to go to a hospital?" and "Is there anyone you'd like me to call for you?" She doesn't answer any of them, either, and I start to wonder if she's deaf. She switches on the radio, but doesn't seem content with any of the stations, roaming restlessly up and down the dial. I don't tell her to stop. I figure it's something to keep her occupied while I try to think what I ought to do with her. And then I'm home, pulling into my driveway, wondering why I can't recall most of the trip back from Massachusetts; wondering, too, why I've brought the woman home with me; wondering, finally, what Abalyn is going to say.

And so this is the night I meet Eva Canning. The first night I meet her for the first time, I mean.

It's as true as I can manage. It's almost factual.

I was in the kitchen eating a cucumber and cream-cheese sandwich with black pepper, and it suddenly occurred to me that if I *were* writing a novel, or even a short story, or novella, or novelette—if I were writing any of those things, I'd have neglected to say very much at all about Abalyn. Or about our relationship during that late June and July, the short time we were together, before she left. A critic might fairly say that I've neglected to include enough character-ization. If this were a story by Beatrix Potter or A. A. Milne or Lewis Carroll, I might pause here and say something like, "Oh dear me!" and then apologize and promptly rectify the omission.

But whatever I'm writing, it isn't any of those things, and *I* know who Abalyn Armitage was and is, as much as I will ever know her. It also occurs to me that maybe I've not, so far, said more about her or about us because in this first version of my ghost story, we weren't together very long before Eva came and Abalyn went away. So, in *this* rendition, I really didn't have the chance to get to know her very well, and there's not much to say about us. So, perhaps in the other version, the November and wolf version, when it seems that we were together much longer than a few weeks. I might just be waiting until

I tell the story that way round to write about Abalyn in greater detail. From here, though, it's all supposition and not much else, these thoughts of why I might have proceeded this way and how I might proceed another way farther along.

I'm afraid you've made an awful, stupid mistake, India Morgan Phelps, choosing to relate this ghost story as you remember it, as two separate narratives, as a particle and a wave, the devil *and* the deep blue sea, instead of boiling it down to a single narrative free of paradox and contradiction. I'm very afraid frustration will win out before much longer, and you'll give up, never finish this. It's difficult enough to hold both versions in my head, though both strike me as equally true (though, as I've said, the first has more evidence to support its factualness), much less translate these competing, parallel histories into prose.

Live and learn, or at least that's what I keep hearing people say. I've heard them say that all my life. Even Caroline and Rosemary said, "Live and learn." Why can I only turn half that trick?

When I got back to Willow Street, a little more than two hours after I left, Abalyn was still awake. She'd said she would be, so I shouldn't have been surprised, but I was. She'd finished her article and was watching a movie on her television. Abalyn watched a lot of movies when she was here, but I hardly ever watched them with her. I don't like movies much more than I like games.

I led the woman up the stairs to my front door. I still didn't know that her name was Eva Canning, because she hadn't said anything more to me since asking "Who are hearsed that die on the sea?" I unlocked the door and asked her in. She hesitated, not immediately accepting the invitation. She stood there in the hallway, her hair almost dry now. She squinted her cornflower blue eyes at me, then looked back over her shoulder at the stairs leading back down to the foyer.

"What's wrong?" I wanted to know.

She began to take a step forwards, then hesitated, and asked me, "You're sure?"

"Yeah, I'm sure. Come on. You can't just stand out there in the hall all night."

She stepped across the threshold, and behind me, Abalyn asked, "Who is it, Imp?" Abalyn hadn't met many of my friends, in part because I didn't have many. She'd met Jonathan, who used to be a barista at White Electric Coffee on Westminster, and I'm pretty sure she'd met Ellen, who worked downtown at Cellar Stories, but has since moved away to be with her boyfriend.

"We have a guest," I replied, trying to sound casual, just, slowly, beginning to realize what a peculiar thing I'd done, bringing Eva home. Or how it might seem that way to Abalyn, who's a surprisingly practical person for someone who makes her living writing reviews of video games.

I shut the door, and Abalyn got up from the sofa. She had the remote in her hand, and she paused the DVD. Then she stood there, smiling uncertainly at Eva Canning, and Eva Canning said, "Hello, Abalyn."

I'd not told her my girlfriend's name (or that I had a girlfriend, for that matter). But it seemed perfectly natural to me that she would know Abalyn's name; after all, hadn't she known mine without being told?

"Hi," Abalyn replied, and glanced questioningly at me.

"Abalyn, this is . . ." But I trailed off, only realizing then that I didn't know the woman's name, despite her knowing ours.

"My name is Eva," she said. She spoke so softly it was almost hard to make out her words. "Eva Canning."

"Imp, why is she dressed like that?" Abalyn wanted to know. I thought it was rude, her bringing up the fact that Eva was only wearing my sweater and a blanket cinched about her waist, but I didn't say so. I was beginning to feel confused and jittery. I tried to remember if I'd forgotten my eight o'clock meds.

"Imp, do you mind if I take a hot shower?" Eva Canning asked. "If it's not an imposition."

It wasn't, and I told her so, since it seemed like a reasonable request. I warned her to be careful, as the cast-iron tub was a little on the slippery side, and the showerhead mounted too low, so it was necessary to bend over a bit if you were as tall as Eva or Abalyn. She said she was sure it would be fine, and I told her I'd find her something better to wear. She thanked me, and I pointed her towards the bathroom door. And then she was gone, and Abalyn and I were alone in the parlor.

"Who *is* she?" Abalyn asked. No, it would be more accurate to say that she *demanded*.

"Not so loud," I said. "She might hear you."

Abalyn furrowed her brow, and she repeated the question in a hushed tone.

"I don't know," I confessed, and I told her how I'd been driving along Route 122 and found Eva Canning standing naked by the side of the river. I said she'd seemed disoriented, and I hadn't known what else to do, that Eva hadn't asked to go to the hospital or police or volunteered an address.

Abalyn's expression, which before had been suspicious, grew incredulous. "So you brought her *home* with you?"

"I didn't know what else to do," I said.

"Imp," Abalyn said, turning her head towards the bathroom door, towards Eva Canning on the other side of that door, which had been opened and was now closed again. Abalyn ran her long fingers through her black hair and chewed at her lower lip. "Do you make a habit of bringing strangers you find by the side of the road home with you?"

"Isn't that how I found you?" I countered, growing indignant. "Isn't it?"

Abalyn looked back at me, that expression of incredulity increasing. I believe she was almost speechless, but only almost, because then she said, "You really think it's comparable?"

"No," I admitted. "Not exactly. But I didn't know what else to do. I couldn't leave her standing there."

"Standing naked, at the side of the road," Abalyn said, as if checking to be sure she'd heard me correctly. "Jesus, Imp. She's probably on something. No telling what's wrong with her."

"You might have been a serial killer," I said, unhelpfully, understanding I was making the situation worse, but unable to keep shut up. "I didn't know you weren't, now, did I? I didn't know you weren't a crack addict. I didn't know anything about you, but I brought you home with me."

Abalyn shook her head, and laughed—a dry, hollow, exasperated sort of laugh. She said, "I need a smoke. I'm going for a walk." When we met, Abalyn had almost given up smoking, and when she did want a cigarette, she always went outside. I never asked her to; Caroline and Rosemary Anne, and even my aunt Elaine had been smokers, and it hadn't much bothered me.

"Will you be gone long?" I asked.

"I don't know," she replied, then jabbed a thumb at the bathroom door. I could hear the sound of the shower. "Is she staying?"

"Honestly, I haven't thought about that. I don't know if she has anywhere else to go."

"For fuck's sake, Imp. Didn't she tell you anything at all? She must have said something."

"Not much. She said, 'Who are hearsed that die on the sea?'" I told Abalyn. "It's from 'The Rime of the Ancient Mariner,' right?"

Abalyn went to the coat hook and reached into a pocket for her cigarettes and lighter. "No, Imp. It's not. It's *Moby-Dick*."

"It is?"

"I'm going for a walk," she said again. "Unless you'd rather I didn't," and here she glanced at the bathroom door again.

"No, I'm fine. I wish you wouldn't get angry. I didn't know what else I was supposed to do."

"I'm not angry," Abalyn said, but I could tell she was lying. Whenever she lied, the corners of her mouth twitched. "I need a cigarette, that's all."

"Be careful," I told her, and she laughed again, that same laugh devoid of any trace of humor. She didn't slam the door, but her footsteps as she descended the stairs sounded heavier than usual. And I was alone in my apartment with the mystery woman who said her name was Eva Canning, and, belatedly, the weirdness of it all was starting to sink in. I sat down on the sofa and stared at the image on the television screen. It was some sort of big Japanese monster frozen in the act of stomping a toy army. I tried to find the remote control, but couldn't, and wondered if maybe Abalyn had taken it with her, and if so, whether or not she'd done so on purpose. When I heard Eva shut off the shower, I stood up again and switched off the television. I went to my bedroom and got her a T-shirt, underwear, and a pair of pants that were a little too big for me. And some socks. Eva was taller than me. Not as tall as Abalyn, but taller than me. I figured the clothes would fit her.

I didn't know what to do about shoes.

When I came back from the bedroom, she was sitting naked on the floor near a window, drying her long hair with a towel. I hadn't realized, until that moment, how very pale she was. Her skin was almost like milk, it was so pale. That probably comes across like an exaggeration, and possibly it is. My memory could easily be exaggerating her paleness, as it exaggerates so many things so often. It would probably be more factual to say that there was about the *whole* of Eva Canning a peculiar, arresting *paleness*. I might mean a paleness of soul, if I believed in souls. Regardless, I might indeed mean that, but since it's easier to remember someone's skin than the hue of her soul, I can't rule out having unconsciously misattributed the milky complexion to her skin.

"I have some clothes for you to wear," I said, and she thanked me. This was the first time I comprehended how musical her voice was. I don't mean it was lilting or singsong or . . . never mind. I'll come up with the right word later. I hope I will, because it's important. Also, whereas back by the river, Eva's voice had been sleepy, almost slurred—the unfocused voice of a somnambulist who's just been rudely awakened—now she spoke with a quiet, alert confidence.

"It's all been very kind of you," she said. "I don't mean to put you out."

"You'll sleep here tonight, okay? We'll figure it out in the morning."

She silently watched me for a few seconds, then replied, "No. I have friends nearby. They'll be glad to see me. You've done too much already."

Ten minutes later, she was gone. She went barefoot; she left the socks behind. And I was standing by the window looking down at Willow Street splashed with sallow pools of dim street light. But I can't say it felt like none of it had happened, even though people in ghost stories say that sort of thing all the time, right? It felt very much like it had *all* happened, every bit of that night, even if the long drive and finding Eva and bringing her home with me made less and less sense the more I played the events over in my head.

I stood at the window, trying to puzzle it all out, until I saw Abalyn. She had her hands stuffed into the pockets of her jeans and her head was down, as if the sidewalk were far more interesting than it had any right to be. I went to the kitchen and poured milk into a pot, then set it on the stove, hoping Abalyn would want a cup of hot cocoa. Hoping she wasn't still angry.

That was also the night the dreams began.

4

I suppose, before Eva, *and* before Eva, I never had anything more than the usual number of nightmares. It was infrequent that I remembered my dreams, before Eva. When I did, they mostly seemed silly and inconsequential. Sometimes I've even felt I was letting down this or that therapist or Dr. Ogilvy by not giving them more to work with in that department. No ready, accommodating window into my subconscious mind. That sort of thing. Sometimes, they've turned to my art, in lieu of dreams. But yeah, Eva Canning changed all that. She brought me bad dreams. She taught me insomnia. Or maybe both are a sort of intangible disease, bereft of conventional vectors. Which brings me back around to memes, and hauntings. In a moment, a few more lines, it will bring me back around to both.

Last night, I lay awake, thinking about what I've been writing, how there's a story here, but how I've taken very little care to fashion a coherent narrative. Or, if there *is* a coherent narrative, how it might be getting lost between other things: exposition, memories, rumination, digressions, and what have you. It's not that all these things aren't equally valid, and not as if they're not an essential component to what I'm trying to *get out of me*. They are. It's more like, in ten or twenty years, I might look back at these pages, digging them out from wherever I've hidden them away, and be disappointed that I didn't take greater care with the story of Eva and Abalyn and me. Because, by then, when I'm in my forties or fifties, I probably will remember so much less of the details. And I'll see how I missed an opportunity. I'll feel as though the me of now cheated the me of then.

Last night, I couldn't shake the feeling that Abalyn was standing at the foot of my bed. She wasn't, of course. It wasn't even what I'd call a proper hallucination. I think most people fail to see how little difference there is between *imagination* and *hallucination*. Sometimes, to me, the two seem divided only by a hairsbreadth. But I listened, and it was easier to listen knowing that Abalyn was probably sound asleep in her apartment in Olneyville. Or maybe she was sitting up playing a video game, or writing a review. Regardless, she wasn't standing at the foot of my bed, talking to me.

She mostly asked questions, like "If you ever do show this to someone, or if you die and they find it, aren't you just as bad as anyone who ever created a haunting? This manuscript, isn't it an infected document, just waiting to spread its load of plague?"

I didn't answer her, because I knew it *wasn't* her. But I did lie there, not sleeping, unable to stop thinking about her questions, and I remembered something I wish I'd written about back in the first "chapter," because it's such an excellent example of what I mean by: Hauntings are *memes*, especially pernicious thought contagions, *social* contagions that need no viral or bacterial host and are transmitted in a thousand different ways. A book . . .

The Suicide Forest. I have a file here on the table next to me with several articles about the Suicide Forest of Japan. At the base of Mount Fuji, on the shores of Lake Sai, there's a three-thousand-hectare forest called Aokigahara Jukai, which is also known as the Sea of Trees. The forest is thought of as a national treasure and popular with hikers and tourists; it's home to two hundred species of birds, and forty species of mammals. The trees are mostly Japanese red pines, Japanese oaks, tiger-tail spruce, boxwoods, beech, bamboo, and *himeshara* (*Stewartia monadelpha*: a medium-sized deciduous tree with shiny reddish bark and broad leaves and pretty white flowers). The forest is very dense and dark. In fact, the trees are so dense that they block the winds rushing down the slopes of the volcano, and, in the absence of the wind, the forest is said to be eerily silent. There are more than two hundred caves. There are claims that the soil and stone below Aokigahara is so rich in iron that it renders compasses useless, so it's easy to get lost inside that maze of trees. That part might be true, and it might not. I don't know, but it's probably not important here.

What's important is that the Sea of Trees is also known as the Suicide Forest. People go there to kill themselves. Lots of people. I have a February 7, 2003, article from the *Japan Times* (a Japanese newspaper published in English). It reports that in 2002 alone police recovered from Aokigahara the bodies of seventy-eight "apparent" suicides, and that they stopped another eighty-three people intent upon taking their lives who were found in the forest and placed in "protective custody." In 1978, seventy-three men and women (mostly men) committed suicide there in the gloom of Aokigahara. There were one hundred in 2003. Every year has its own grisly tally, and only the Golden Gate Bridge is a more popular suicide destination. Signs have been placed in the forest imploring the people who travel there in order to kill themselves not to do so, to reconsider their decision. There are stories told by Buddhist monks that the forest *lures* suicides into its perpetual twilight, that it calls out to them. The woods are said to be haunted by ghosts called *yurei*, the spirits of the suicides, who are lonely and howl at night.

The woods are said to be haunted. That's the important part. At least, to me that's the important part. Importance is always conditional, relative, variable from person to person. But what's more important (to me) than the tales of the *yurei* is the fact that all this trouble in the Sea of Trees didn't begin until Seichō Matsumoto, a Japanese detective and mystery writer, published a novel, *Kuroi Jukai* (The Black Forest, 1960). In Matsumoto's book, two lovers choose Aokigahara as the most appropriate place to commit suicide. And people read the book. And people began going to the forest to kill themselves.

I haven't read *Kuroi Jukai*. I don't even know if it's been translated into English.

A book. A pernicious meme that created a haunting, a sort of focal point for people who don't want to live anymore. Same as with Phillip George Saltonstall and *The Drowning Girl*, I find it hard to believe that Matsumoto meant anyone harm. I doubt he consciously set out to trigger the haunting of the Sea of Trees. But do his intentions enter into this? Do Saltonstall's, or Albert Perrault's? Are they innocent, or do we hold them accountable?

"What makes you any different?" I imagined Abalyn asking from the foot of my bed last night.

If I had answered, maybe I'd have said, "Nothing." Maybe I'd have said, "I'm still trying to figure that out." Possibly, I would have pointed out that those three, the novelist and the two painters, created something that was *meant to be seen*, whereas I'm not doing that at all.

"Write about Eva," Abalyn told me. "What you brought home that night. Write about what happened to us because of what you brought home that night."

I wanted to say, *I still love you, Abalyn. I'm never going to stop loving you.* I didn't say that, because I didn't say anything, but if I had replied to my imagination, I believe Abalyn would have turned away, angry, bitter, lonely as any *yurei*, but not howling. Determined I wouldn't *see* her loneliness.

Walking through the woods, I have faced it. . . .

"You need to get dressed and go to work," Imp typed.

I know. I just glanced at the clock. But I needed to get this down first. If I hadn't, I might have forgotten that I meant to, because I forget so much.

I have to tell *the story*, because I forget so much.

The next morning—the morning after I found Eva Canning by the Blackstone River—I awoke to find that Abalyn was already up and about. That was sort of unusual. She tended to stay up later than me, and sleep later. Sometimes, she slept until two or three in the afternoon, after staying up until dawn. But not that morning. That morning I put on my robe, brushed my teeth, and went out into the parlor to find her flipping through my records.

"Good morning," I said, and she probably said "Good morning," too. Or something of the sort.

"You're up early," I said, and she shrugged.

"Don't you have anything recorded *after* 1979?" Abalyn asked me, frowning. "And you have heard about CDs, right?"

"Those were Rosemary's records."

"Rosemary? An ex?"

"No, no. Rosemary my mother."

"So, where is your music?" she wanted to know. All this time, she hadn't looked at me, she just kept flipping through the records. She pulled out *Rumours* and stared at Mick Fleetwood and Stevie Nicks on the cover.

"Those are my records, Abalyn. They're the only ones that I have."

"You're shitting me," she said, and laughed.

"No, I'm not. I don't listen to music a lot, and when I do, I listen to Rosemary's records. I grew up hearing them, and they make me feel safe."

She looked at me then, over her shoulder. She made that face she used to make when she was trying to figure me out. Or when she was having trouble with one of her video games. It was pretty much the same expression, in either case. "Okay," she said, "I guess that makes sense," then turned back to the bookshelf (which is where I keep all Rosemary's records, which are now my records). She slid *Rumours* back onto the shelf and pulled out Jackson Browne's *Late for the Sky*.

"I especially like that one," I told her.

"You have a turntable?"

"Yeah. It was also my mother's."

"Jodie has a turntable. She collects this stuff. Me, I stick to CDs. Vinyl just gets scratched up, and it's too much trouble to lug around whenever you move."

I yawned, thinking about hot tea and toasted crumpets and strawberry jam. "I don't know much about music," I said. "Not about the newer stuff, I mean. Just Rosemary's records."

"We gotta remedy that, Imp. You need a crash course."

I asked her what she liked, and her answer didn't make much sense to me. EBM, synthpop, trance, shoegaze, Japanoise, acid house.

"I've never heard of any of those bands," I said, and she laughed. It wasn't a mean-spirited laugh. I don't remember Abalyn ever making fun of me, or laughing at me the way you laugh at someone when you're making fun of them.

"They're not bands, Imp. They're genres."

"Oh," I said. "I didn't know that."

"Seriously, we must begin the musical education of India Phelps ASAP." She did play a lot of her music for me later, and I listened, trying to listen with an open mind, but I didn't really like any of it. Well, except for a few songs by a British band named Radiohead. One of their songs had something about a siren in it, and shipwrecks. But in most of what she played for me, the lyrics, when there *were* lyrics, didn't seem very important.

She was looking at the back cover of *Late for the Sky*, and I asked if she'd had breakfast. She said that she had, and that she'd made a pot of coffee. I reminded her I didn't drink coffee. And really, I know I'm trying to get back to the story, and maybe this doesn't *seem* like part of the story of Eva Canning, but it is. And, anyway, I'm just sort of in the mood to write about Abalyn. I'm missing her more than usual tonight. I even thought about calling her, but chickened out. Verily, I'm an invertebrate. Spineless.

I pointed at the album cover she was holding and said, "I really do love that one. I always thought Jackson Browne was so cool."

"Imp, Jackson Browne doesn't have a cool bone in his body. Not so much as a goddamned cool mitochondrion. That's how uncool Jackson Browne is."

It felt like an insult—like she was insulting me, I mean—but I knew she hadn't *meant* it that way. Obviously she was insulting Jackson Browne.

"Have you ever listened to that album?" I asked.

"Nope," she said. "Intend to keep it that way."

"Then how can you possibly know?"

She didn't answer the question. Instead she asked one of her own. "You're evening shift today, right?" And I told her yeah, that I didn't go in until four.

"Then get dressed. I'm taking you out for lunch."

"I haven't even had breakfast."

"Fine. I'm taking you out for breakfast, brunch, whatever. You'll have to drive, though."

So, I got dressed, and we went over to Wayland Square, to a coffee shop she liked that I'd never been to, a place called the Edge, because coffee makes you edgy, I guess. There were big wooden tables and mismatched chairs and lots of people reading newspapers and working on their laptops. Lots of Brown students, I suppose. I thought about ordering a sandwich, but got something called a Cowboy Cookie, instead, and a cup of scalding-hot Darjeeling. Abalyn got an egg-and-cheese sandwich and a huge latte. The tea and coffee were served in great ceramic cups, green cups with red coffee beans painted on them. I told Abalyn I thought the coffee beans looked more like ladybugs.

We sat down at a table in the back, a corner table, and neither of us said anything for a few minutes. We ate and sipped our drinks. I watched people with their laptops and iPhones. I didn't see many people having conversations or even reading books or newspapers. Almost all of them were too absorbed with their gadgets to talk to one another. I wondered if they even noticed anything going on around them. I thought how strange it must be, to live like that. Maybe it's no different from always having your nose in a book, but it feels different to me. It feels somehow colder, more distant. No, I don't know why it strikes me that way.

Finally, Abalyn put down her sandwich, chewed, swallowed, and said to me, "I don't want you to think I'm pissed or anything. I'm not. But what happened last night, Imp, maybe we ought to talk about it."

"Last night you sounded angry," I said, not meeting her eyes, stirring at my tea with a spoon.

"Last night, well . . ." And she trailed off for a moment, and she glanced over her shoulder, and I thought maybe she was checking to see if anyone was eavesdropping. They weren't. They were all too busy with their gadgets. "Last night I was sort of freaked-out, I admit. You brought a stranger home, a woman you'd found standing naked and soaking wet by the side of the road in the middle of nowhere."

"She left," I said, wishing I didn't sound so defensive. "I'll probably never see her again."

"That's not the point. It was dangerous."

"She didn't hurt me, Abalyn. She just played with the radio."

Abalyn frowned and picked at her sandwich.

"I like you," she said. "I think I like you a lot."

I replied, "I like you a lot, too."

"You can't do stuff like that, Imp. Sooner or later, you keep picking people up, doing shit like that, something bad's gonna happen. Someone's not gonna be harmless. Someone will hurt you, sooner or later."

"I haven't ever done it before. It's not like a habit or anything."

"You're too trusting," Abalyn sighed. "You never know about people, what they'll do."

I sipped at my tea and nibbled at my cookie. Turned out, a Cowboy Cookie was oatmeal and chocolate chips with cinnamon and pecans. Sometimes, I still go back and have them. I always hope that I'll see Abalyn, but I never have, so maybe she doesn't go to the Edge anymore.

"She was helpless," I told Abalyn.

"You don't know that. You shouldn't ever assume stuff like that."

"I don't want to argue about her."

"We're not arguing, Imp. We're just talking. That's all." But she sounded the way people sound when they're arguing. I didn't tell her that, though. By then, I was wishing I were back at home, in my own kitchen, eating a breakfast I'd made myself.

"She might have been hurt," I said.

"Then you should have called the police and told them about her. That's what police are for."

"Please don't talk to me like that. It's condescending. Don't talk to me like I'm a child. I'm not a child."

Abalyn looked over her shoulder again, then back to me. Part of me knew she was right, but I didn't want to admit it.

"No, you're not a child. It just freaked me out, that's all, okay? It was seriously weird. Imp, *she* was seriously weird."

"Lots of people say that about me," I told Abalyn. "Lots of people might say that about you."

I think maybe I was baiting her, and I know I shouldn't have been. My face felt flushed. But she stayed calm and didn't bite.

"Just promise me you won't do anything like that again, please."

"She might have been hurt," I told her for the second time. "She could have been in trouble."

"Come on, India. Please."

I chewed a corner of my Cowboy Cookie. And then I promised her, all right, I wouldn't ever do anything like that again. I meant it. But I would. In November, the second time I met Eva Canning, I'd do exactly the same thing all over again.

After the coffee shop, we walked to a used bookstore around the corner. Neither of us bought anything.

"Only write what you saw," Imp typed. "Don't interpret. Only describe."

That's what I would like to do, but I already know exactly how I'll fail. I already see that I'll draw attention to parallels that I wouldn't realize existed until long after the July day that Abalyn and I had our little brunch at Wayland Square. I'm too impatient to allow these events to unfold in a truly linear fashion. The present of that afternoon has become the *past* of my *present* moment, the precipice from which I survey the convoluted landscape of all the moments leading from then to now.

We left the used bookstore, and briefly thought about ducking into the little junk shop in the basement next door. It's called What Cheer, as in "What Cheer, Netop?" *Netop* is supposedly a Narragansett Indian word meaning "friend," and is supposedly the greeting Indians shouted out to Roger Williams (who founded Rhode

Island) and his cohorts as he crossed the Seekonk River in seventeen thirty-whatever and such and such. "What Cheer" are magical words in Rhode Island, which is pretty ironic when you pause to consider just how bad things would go for the Narragansetts not too long after they welcomed white men into their lands. No, I wasn't thinking any of this as we stood there on the hot sidewalk trying to decide if we wanted to go down the stairs into the junk shop. They have antique postcards, vintage clothes, and huge antique apothecary cabinets. The drawers are filled with countless random, inconsequential treasures, from doorknobs to chess pieces to old political-campaign buttons. What Cheer also sells a lot of vinyl, by the way.

I still visit the shop sometimes, though I never buy any of those records. Or much of anything else. Mostly, I just like to browse through the records and try to figure out why Rosemary bought the albums she did, instead of this one or that one. We never really talked about music, though she played her records a lot. I love the way What Cheer smells, like dust and aging paper.

But we didn't go in that day. Abalyn needed to get back to the apartment, because that night she had a deadline on a review she'd not even started writing. And I'd forgotten to bring my one o'clock meds with us. It was still a couple of hours before I had to be at work. I remember how it was an especially hot day, up in the nineties, and we stood together in the shade of a green canvas awning, sheltered but sweating, anyhow.

Abalyn turned back to the Honda, and that's when I saw her watching us from the other side of Angell Street. Eva Canning, I mean. It took me a few seconds to recognize her, and at first it was just this blonde woman. (Have I said Eva had blonde hair that first time she came? Well, she did, even if I haven't said it already.) She wasn't wearing the clothes I'd given her. She was wearing a long red dress with spaghetti straps, and sunglasses, and a straw hat that kept her safe from the sun the way an umbrella protects you from rain. It was one of those cone-shaped Asian hats, tied at her chin with a blue silk ribbon. In Vietnam, those hats are called *Nón lá*, and in Japan they're called *sugegasa*. Japan has now made three appearances in this "chapter," and maybe that means something, and maybe it's just my arithmomania rearing its ugly head. My grandmother called those hats coolie hats, but also told me I couldn't call them that, because it was racist.

So, Eva in a red dress, sunglasses, the straw hat with a blue silk ribbon. And she was barefoot. One, two, three, four, five, and I suddenly knew it was her. It was her, and she was watching us. I don't know how long she'd been standing there, but when I realized who she was, at the same instant I recognized her, she smiled. I reached out to take Abalyn's arm, to tell her. I also started to wave to Eva Canning. But I didn't actually do either of those things. Abalyn was already walking away towards the car, and Eva had turned her back on me. Just as quickly as I'd recognized her, I thought maybe it wasn't really her after all. Whoever it was, I lost sight of her, and then I followed Abalyn back to the Honda. It was so hot inside the car (black upholstery) that we had to stand with the doors open for a while before we got in.

I wish I were a writer, a real writer, because if I were, I expect I wouldn't be making such a goddamn mess of this story. Rambling, tripping over my own feet. I wish I were sane enough to always distinguish fact from fancy, but, like Caroline used to say, if wishes were horses, beggars would ride. Rosemary, she used to tell my grandmother . . .

"Cut the crap and tell the story, Imp," Imp typed. I typed. "Tell the story or don't, but stop stalling. Stop procrastinating. It's annoying."

It is. I know it is.

I know it is.

I know.

On the July afternoon after the night I found Eva Canning the first time, and brought her back to my apartment, I saw her watching us at Wayland Square. She didn't wave or call out to me or try to get my attention in any way. She saw me, and when she was sure I knew it was her, she turned away. I never told Abalyn.

In a letter Phillip George Saltonstall wrote to Mary Farnum, in December of 1896, he mentions "a most curious and absurd dream." He describes waking late at night, or thinking that he'd awakened. He eventually decided that he'd only gone from one nightmare to another, the illusion of having woken up acting as a sort of "dreaming transition." He crossed his bedroom and stood at the window, gazing down on Prince Street. This was in Boston, of course, because he lived in Boston. He looked out the window and saw that it was snowing very hard, and "on the street below there was a tall woman in a red coat and a red bonnet. She wore no shoes. I thought how cold she must be, and wondered to what end she was tarrying below my windowsill in such a storm. It happened that she glanced up at me then, and I beheld her eyes. Even now, dear Mary, writing you by the cheerful light of a bright winter's day, I am chilled at the memory of her face. I cannot place my finger on how that face was rendered so demonic, for it was a fair face. A beautiful face, but it was a beautiful face that filled me with a singular dread. It was a face almost as blanched as the fresh snow, and she smiled at me before turning and strolling slowly away. She left no footprints, and I thought she must surely be a phantom."

My fairy tales are beginning to blur together here. I can see that, yes. Eva's red dress, a barefoot woman in a red coat with a red bonnet, *Le Petit Chaperon Rouge*. But I never said there wasn't overlap, even if I forgot to say there was. There was. There is. This may be one of those places where I should draw a distinction between the truth of my story and its facts. I don't know. Eva who was a mermaid and Eva who was a wolf are blurring together, even though I wish it were all more cut-and-dried.

I don't think hauntings care one whit for my need to keep things neat and tidy. I think they have a disdain for shoe boxes.

In an interview that I have in my manila folder on Albert Perrault, he talks about a dream he had not long before he began painting *Fecunda ratis*, that hideous image of the child surrounded by wolves, the wolves surrounded by ancient standing stones. I've highlighted what he said with a yellow marker. "Oh no, no. Never suppose there's but one source of inspiration. I might just as well claim that I had a mother and no father, or a father without having a mother. True, I had already conceived the painting, that's true, after visiting the Castlerigg Stone Circle just outside Keswick. But a dream played a significant role, as well. I was staying with a friend in Ireland, in Shannon, and one night I dreamed I was back in California. I was on the beach in Santa Monica, within sight of the pier, and on the sand was a young woman in a crimson cape and a crimson cloche. There were black dogs walking in a circle around her, nose to tail. I say dogs, but maybe I ought to say beasts, instead. They seemed like dogs at the time. The woman was gazing out to sea and seemed not to notice the beasts, the dogs. I don't know what she saw in the water, or what she was trying to see.

"Sure, sure. You may conclude it was my obsession with the painting I'd not yet started, but which was congealing in my mind's eye, that inspired the dream. You may conclude it was not the other way round. But I do not think of it that way."

Wolves or beasts walking nose to tail in a circle. But snow is crystallized water, right? And the woman in the cloche was watching the ocean.

So, it all bleeds together. It gets messy.

I try to force it not to, and it gets messy nonetheless. I'm sure stories don't care what I want from them.

Stories do not serve me. Even my own stories.

If I owned a laptop, if I could afford to buy one, I would. Then I'd sit in a coffeehouse or a library and write my ghost story, safely surrounded by other people. It's too easy to scare myself in this room with its blue-white walls. Especially when I write after dark, like I'm doing now. If I could call Abalyn and borrow one of her laptops, that's what I'd do. I don't think ghost stories should be written in solitude.

The house is so quiet tonight.

I've never liked quiet houses. They always seem to be waiting for something.

The forest became a siren. Matsumoto wrote his book, and when he did that, Aokigahara on the shores of Lake Sai became the Suicide Forest. Matsumoto sounded the first note in a song that is still singing out to people, still drawing broken, hurting people to take their own lives in that Sea of Trees. And the world is filled with sirens. There's always a siren, singing you to shipwreck. Some of us may be more susceptible than others are, but there's always a siren. It may be with us all our lives, or it may be many years or decades before we find it or it finds us. But when it does *find* us, if we're lucky we're Odysseus tied up to the ship's mast, hearing the song with perfect clarity, but ferried to safety by a crew whose ears have been plugged with beeswax. If we're not at all lucky, we're another sort of sailor stepping off the deck to drown in the sea. Or a girl wading into the Blackstone River.

Dr. Ogilvy and the pills she prescribes are my beeswax and the ropes that hold me fast to the mainmast, just as my insanity has always been my siren. As it was Caroline's siren and Rosemary's siren before me. Caroline listened and chose to drown. Rosemary drowned, even though there were people who tried to stuff her ears and did tie her down.

I don't think it much matters what shape the siren assumes. No, I believe that doesn't matter at all. It may as well be a woman with the wings and talons of birds, or a mermaid, a *rusalka* in her river, or a kelpie drifting in a weedy pool. All those patient, hungry things. A siren may be as commonplace as greed, grief, desire, or passion. A painting hung on a wall. A woman found standing naked at the side of a dark road, who knows your name before you divulge it to her.

The first time I went to see Dr. Ogilvy, she asked me to describe the one symptom that caused me the most difficulty, that seemed to lie at the root of everything that shut me down and made it hard to be alive. She admitted it's not that simple, that there might be a lot of symptoms like that, but it's a place to start, she said. She asked me to tell her what it was and then to describe it as accurately as I could. She told me to take my time. So I sat on the sofa in her office. I shut my eyes and didn't open them again or say anything for ten minutes or so. Not because I hadn't known right off what the answer was, but because I hadn't known right off how to describe it to her.

When I opened my eyes again, she asked, "Can you tell me now, India?"

"Maybe," I said.

"It's okay if you don't get it right the first time. I only want you to try, okay?"

I've always been very good with metaphors and similes. All my life, metaphors and similes have come to me effortlessly. I used a simile that day, to try and explain to Dr. Ogilvy what that one worst thing in my head was, or one of the worst things. I wasn't trying to be clever. I've never thought of myself as especially clever.

I explained to her that, "It's like I put on a pair of headphones, and at first there's no sound at all coming through them. No music. No voices. Nothing."

(I do *have* a set of headphones. They came with Rosemary's stereo and records. They're big and padded and nothing at all like the tiny white earbuds that Abalyn used with her shiny pink iPod. I don't use them much. I prefer to have a room filled with music, instead of silence all around me and only music in my ears.)

"But then," I said, "way in the background, so soft maybe you only think you're hearing it, there's static. White noise. Or someone whispering. And slowly that sound gets louder and louder. At first, it's easy to ignore. It's hardly even there. But, eventually, it grows so loud you can't hear anything else. In the end, the sound swallows the whole world. Even if you take the headphones off, that noise won't stop."

She nodded, and smiled, and told me I'd eloquently described what are called *intrusive thoughts*. Involuntary and unwelcome thoughts that can't be shut out no matter how hard someone tries. Later, we'd spend a lot of time talking about exactly what sorts of intrusive thoughts I have. That day, she told me I was clever, to have described it the way I did. She said my description was apt. But, like I said, I've never imagined myself to be a clever woman. I took it as a compliment, even though I happened to be of the opinion it was a mistaken compliment.

Sirens are intrusive thoughts that even sane men and women have. You can call them sirens, or you can call them hauntings. Doesn't matter. Once Odysseus heard the sirens, I doubt he ever forgot their song. He would have been haunted by it all the rest of his life. Even after his terrible twenty-year journey, the archery competition, even after he gets Penelope back and the story has a happy "ending," he must still have been haunted by their song, in his dreams and when he was awake. Every time he saw the sea or the sky.

After that afternoon at Wayland Square, Abalyn and I went home. And everything seemed okay for a few days. But all that time the white noise through the headphones was getting louder and louder, and eventually it was all I could hear. Eventually, all I could see was Eva, barefoot and in her red dress and straw hat, watching us from across the street.

And it's not as if I could have told Abalyn. I was too amazed that she was there, and too afraid she'd leave. I had every reason to suppose it was just me being crazy little Imp, daughter of crazy Rosemary Anne, granddaughter of mad Caroline. I assumed exactly that, and I wouldn't risk Abalyn going away and never coming back again over a bout of white noise that, sooner or later, would get bored of humming, crackling, sizzling, popping in my ears, and stop. It always stops. Dr. Ogilvy had taught me ways to turn the volume down. And I had my pills, my beeswax.

I'm not clever. Clever women don't pick up naked strangers late at night. Clever women are honest with themselves and their lovers, and they do something before it's too late to do something.

I wasn't a virgin. I lost my virginity in high school, before I thought better of sleeping with boys. Before I started listening to my libido and set aside my misgivings and stopped listening to the expectations of my peers. Anyway, even though I wasn't a virgin, every time I made love to Abalyn, she handled me as if I *were* a virgin. As though I were a china doll that might crack and shatter unless she was always, always mindful of frailty, an imagined brittleness. It seemed to me she thought you have to fuck crazy women with kid gloves. But it's not as if I took any of this as an insult. I suppose it amused and flattered me. In our bed (for the short time it was *our* bed). Lying in her arms, or grasping the headboard while her long arms encircled my waist and her tongue gently probed the most intimate recesses of my body, it was difficult for me to imagine this beautiful woman had ever been a boy. I mean, that she'd ever been caught inside the body of a boy, of a man. I'm not being sexist. Sure, men can be considerate, easy lovers. At least, I'm sure I'd be a chauvinist if I allowed my own more or less unfortunate and unremarkable experiences with them to lead me to conclude otherwise. What I'm trying to say is, the way she made love to me, it was clear that Abalyn understood my body, what it needed. She grasped the nuances and attended to my most minute longings. I would say she played me like a musical instrument, but she probably played me more like a video game. My clit and labia, my mouth and nipples, my mind and my ass, the nape of my neck, the space between my shoulder blades, all 1.5 square meters of my skin—perhaps, had I asked, she might have said my body was the controller with which she manipulated the game of my flesh.

I hope I'm not sounding like one of those trashy paperbacks you see on the racks at a Shaw's or Stop & Shop. If I am, I've not done Abalyn justice. It's not as though I've never written about sex before, in those odd bits of fiction I sometimes feel compelled to write. But that's different, even if I don't feel like taking the time just now required to explain *how* it's different.

On a morning almost a week after I thought I saw Eva Canning watching me in Wayland Square, Abalyn and I lay on top of sweaty sheets, sheets left sweaty from fucking. Our best sex was usually in the morning, as though it were some natural bridge between dreaming and wakefulness. We lay together, the sun through my bedroom window splashed across our breasts and bellies. It was one of my days off, and we pretended we'd just stay in bed all day. We both knew we wouldn't, that we'd eventually get bored and do other stuff, but it was nice to tread the boards, as Caroline used to say when she meant someone was putting on an act.

"Am I better than she was?" I asked, tangling my fingers in coal-black hair. Blonde roots were starting to show, but I did my best not to notice, not wishing to spoil the effect.

"Better than who was?" Abalyn replied.

"You know. Better than her. Better than Jodie."

"Is there a contest?"

"No, there's not a contest. I'm just curious about how I measure up, that's all."

She turned her head and looked at me and sort of scowled, making me wish I hadn't asked. It was a dumb, insecure question, and I wanted to steal it back. Erase it from the space between us.

"Jodie's Jodie," Abalyn said. "You're you. I don't have to like oranges better than I like apples, do I?"

"No," I whispered, and kissed her forehead.

"Jodie's into all sorts of kinky shit, which is cool. But sometimes it gets tiresome."

"You mean like spankings and being tied up?"

"Something along those lines," Abalyn sighed. "I'm hungry. I'm going to make a peanut butter and jelly sandwich. You want one?"

"No," I told her. "I should take a shower. I want to spend the day painting. I've been negligent."

"What's the rush?" she asked me. "Do you have deadlines?"

"Sort of. I mean, I have my paintings, the ones that I really love and care about, the ones that are just for me. And with those I can take as long as I need, right? But then there are my Mystic and Newport paintings." She asked me what I meant, and so I explained how I did seascapes that I sold to the summer people, the tourists. Sometimes I sit out on the hot sidewalk and sell them myself. Other times, I let galleries sell them, but then they take a commission. They're pretty cheesy, my summer-people paintings, and I think of them as my paint-by-number pictures. But they bring in enough money to cover the cost of my paints and brushes and canvas and what have you for the rest of the year. I hardly ever sell the paintings that are just for me, which means I have an awful lot of them hung on the walls and leaning against the walls of the apartment.

So, Abalyn went to make her sandwich. I took my shower, then had a cup of tea and a bowl of Maypo with sliced banana. Abalyn parked herself on the sofa, her laptop already open and signed into one of her MMORPGs (I'd picked up the lingo pretty quickly), the one with orcs and two sorts of elves and space goats with Russian accents.

That day, the canvas on my easel was one I'd been working on for a month or so. The paintings that are just for me, they always take a long time. Almost always, coming in their own sweet time, like Abalyn said they needed to do. So far, it was hardly more than a mottled interplay of ebony and reds so deep they were almost the color of currents. I wasn't even sure yet what I meant it to be. I put on my smock and sat and stared at it. I sat and breathed the comforting aroma of linseed oil and paints, turpentine and gesso. The smells that are always present in the room where I paint, and that I imagine will remain long after I've moved somewhere else (assuming I ever do move somewhere else). I sat and stared, listening to the muted sounds from the parlor, Abalyn killing pixel monsters. Abalyn tends to curse a lot when she plays her games. So, the muted sounds of her game and her cursing.

At some point, I picked up a pad and began sketching in charcoal. At first, I must have meant the sketches to be studies for where the canvas might be headed. I'm almost certain that's what I meant to do. Down on the street, I could hear a car stereo, Mexican pop music blaring from a car stereo. You hear that a lot in the Armory. It doesn't annoy me the way it did when I first moved here. I sat and listened to Abalyn and the music and filled page after page after page with my hasty sketches. Down on the street, men shouted in Spanish. I licked my lips and tasted sweat and thought how I ought to get up and open a window, switch on the old box fan sitting on the floor.

I sketched until Abalyn knocked at the door to tell me that she was going out for a smoke.

"Yeah," I said. "Okay," I said, speaking so quietly I'm surprised she heard me. Maybe she didn't.

"Won't be gone long," she said. "Might walk down to the corner store. Anything you need?"

"No," I told her. "Thanks, but I don't need anything."

Then she was gone, and I sat staring at the drawing pad open in my lap. I'd torn each page out once I was done with it, and the floor around my stool was littered with paper. It made me think of fallen leaves. I saw then what I was sketching, what I'd sketched again and again and again for almost two hours. Eva Canning's face. There was no mistaking it for anyone else. I sat for a long time, just staring at those sketches. It was Eva, but it was also the wryly smiling face of *l'Inconnue de la Seine*. In every one of the sketches her eyelids were shut.

And each and every one of them was so alike each and every other they might almost have been photocopies. I'd gotten her face right the first time, and then I'd repeated myself twenty or twenty-five times.

"Is that what you saw on those pages, Imp? Are you absolutely certain that's what you saw?"

I am. Later, Abalyn saw them, too.

There were water stains on some of the sketches, splotches made by sweat dripping from my face onto the paper. There were the careless smudges left by my fingers and the heel of my right palm.

"You tried to hide them from Abalyn."

No, no, I didn't. But I gathered them all up before she got back. I rolled them into a tight bundle and put a rubber band around them before placing them on the top of a shelf. My head felt fuzzy and my stomach was sour, but that might have been the heat. I'd let the room get hot, let it fill up with the afternoon sunlight without even having opened a window.

After I put the sketches away, I took off my smock and went to the kitchen sink to wash the charcoal from my hands. I wasn't hiding anything from anyone, or I wasn't aware that I was. But I felt guilt just the same, as sharply as I've ever felt guilt, like when Aunt Elaine walked into the bathroom and I was masturbating to pictures in a *Penthouse* magazine. Like that. I was still washing my hands (though they were clean) when Abalyn got back from the store.

Thirty-four pages back, I said that the dreams began the night I brought Eva Canning back with me to Willow Street. But I've said nothing since then about the dreams. No, wait, I see now that on page 136 I wrote, "I suppose, before Eva, *and* before Eva, I never had anything more than the usual number of nightmares. It was infrequent that I remembered my dreams, before Eva." And also, ". . . Eva Canning changed all that. She brought me bad dreams. She taught me insomnia." So, there. I haven't neglected the matter as badly as I was afraid I had. The matter of my own dreams, I mean. I've talked about Saltonstall's dream, and Albert Perrault's, but I haven't taken the time to describe any of my own. More evasion, and I'd be lying if I said it wasn't at least half-conscious.

I've never liked talking about my dreams. It never seemed to me that different than if I were to talk to people about my bowel movements. Okay, that was, admittedly, a weird analogy. I can't help but wonder what Dr. Ogilvy would make of it. A mountain from a molehill, I suppose, especially the way it's followed by the word "analogy," which I can readily break into [anal]ogy.

That first night, and every night between that first night and the day I repeatedly sketched her face, the dreams came. They came like camera-bright flashes in my sleep. After I woke up each morning, they left afterimages that I spent the days trying to blink away. I didn't talk to anyone about them, though anyone would have pretty much amounted to Abalyn. I didn't see much of anyone else that week, none of my very few friends. Not Jonathan at the coffee shop on Westminster, or Ellen from Cellar Stories (though I did talk with Johnny on the phone that Thursday). I knew that the next time I saw

Dr. Ogilvy, I wouldn't talk to her about them, either. They felt like such private things, messages meant for no one else but me, and messages that would be diminished if I dared to share them with other people. There's also my continuing—what?—my continuing insistence that one may perpetuate a haunting simply by speaking certain words aloud, even when all you want to do is get rid of them. But I'm alone now. No one's listening. No one's reading these pages over my shoulder.

The dreams were not all the same, so I guess it wouldn't be accurate to call them recurring dreams. Not the way people usually mean *recurring*. But there was a sameness about them. Those dreams, they had the same mothers: Eva and I. The union of her touch and my insanity. It's like Poe said. Well, sort of like that. *Passions from a common spring*, if dreams may be called passions. I see no reason not to call them passions. Certainly, the dreams that Eva brought me were as ardent as passion, as intense. I awoke from each one breathless, sometimes sweating, disoriented, always afraid I would also startle Abalyn awake (but I never did, as she's a very deep sleeper).

Tuesday night and early Wednesday morning—after my drive to the Blackstone River—I began keeping a written record of my dreams for the first time in my life. I was thinking of what Rosemary had said to me on my eleventh birthday: "You might want to remember it someday. When something makes an impression on us, we should do our best not to forget about it. So, it's a good idea to make notes."

This is a haunting within a haunting, the advice of my suicide mother still reaching out to me after thirteen years.

Dead people and dead thoughts and supposedly dead moments are never, ever truly dead, and they shape every moment of our lives. We discount them, and that makes them mighty.

Here is my record of the dreams, which I wrote with a ballpoint

pen on several blank endpapers in the back of the novel I was reading, Jane Austen's *Mansfield Park* (I've always had a thing for Jane
Austen, and I've read every one of her novels over and over again).
This is the first time I've copied them from the book, and the first
time I've looked at them in almost two years:

Wednesday (July 9th): Dreamed me and Abalyn arguing about
Moby-Dick. Her telling me how Vishnu first appeared to mankind
in the guise of a gigantic fish that saves all creation from a flood, like
Noah and his ark. Said it was the Matsya Avatar. She said that.
Outside it was raining hard, very hard. Cats and dogs. And she kept
pinting [*sic*] at a window. It wasn't a window in my apartment.
Don't know where we were. And then I knew I wasn't hearing rain,
only Eva Canning taking her shower. Told Abalyn repeatedly how I
didn't want to talk about this, and that I haven't read *Moby-Dick*,
but she wouldn't let up. She kept telling me how stupid I was, picking up stray dogs and cats and women at the side of the road like
that. All so vivid, all of this. All so vivid my head almost hurts.

Note: I don't know all that much about Hinduism. Didn't then,
still don't. But this is a quote from Wikipedia, regarding Matsya:
". . . the king of pre-ancient Dravida and a devotee of Vishnu, Saty-
avrata who later was known as Manu was washing his hands in a
river when a little fish swam into his hands and pleaded with him to
save its life. He put it in a jar, which it soon outgrew. He then moved
it to a tank, a river and then finally the ocean but to no avail." Farther along, this will seem almost prescient. No, I don't believe in
prescience, clairvoyance, ESP, precognitive people, whatever. It'll
only *seem* prescient.

Thursday (July 10th): Another vivid dream. I almost have to
squint, thinking about it. Can't remember everything, but I remember some. I was climbing the stairs leading from front door up to my
apartment. Up to the landing. But the stairs just kept going, up, up,
up, and every now and then I had to stop and rest. My legs hurt.

Knees and calves and thighs, like having walked a long way in very deep snow. I climbed stairs, sat down, got up, sat down, walked, got up. Looked back behind me, and stairs were a spiral I couldn't see the bottom of. Looked up and same. Felt nauseous, like seasick, and I still do just a little. Went on and on, climbing, trying to get home. Now and then, oddest sense that I wasn't alone, that someone was walking with me. But when I looked, no one was ever there. Once, water ran down the stairs, but stopped after my feet were wet. I don't want to think about this all day.

Note: I did eventually tell Dr. Ogilvy about this dream. It's one of the only things I've told her so far about those months and what happened. But I lied and said I'd only *just* had the dream, a few days before. She said it reminded her of something, but she couldn't recall what. At my next appointment, she read me lines from T. S. Eliot's *The Waste Land*, a passage about a man walking along a snowy white road and the illusion he was being accompanied by a mysterious third companion, though he could never count more than two. She said Eliot was alluding to a peculiar experience Ernest Shackleton described during or after one of his Antarctic expeditions. I had her write it down for me (Shackleton, not Eliot): "I know that during that long and racking march of thirty-six hours over the unnamed mountains and glaciers of South Georgia, it seemed to me often that we were four, not three." She read that to me, and then she asked, "Do you still feel lost, India? Do you still feel as if no one's walking beside you?" I'm not in the mood to write down what I said in response. Maybe some other time I will.

Friday (July 11th): Trying not to wake up Abalyn. She was up later than usual, I think. Does three of these damn dreams a pattern make? Three in three nights, like I've never dreamed before. Flashbulb nightmares. Me and Caroline and Rosemary and Abalyn and some other people I knew in the dream, but don't think I know in real life. Dancing in a circle down on Moonstone Beach, and Eva

Canning was standing in the center of the ring holding a violin (not playing, just holding), singing "The Lobster Quadrille" from Lewis Carroll. There were dead crabs, lobster, fish everywhere, all tangled up and stinking in seaweed. And, Eva, you sang to me, "Sail to me." I was barefoot and dead things under my feet, slippery, slimy, spines slicing the soles of my feet. This is the worst of the three, worse than the stairs.

Saturday (July 12th): Didn't sleep much. Not insomnia, just not wanting to go to sleep, more like knowing the dreams would be there. Reluctance to sleep, not inability. Am I making it worse, recoding [sic] them? Abalyn is already up, and too much sun through window. I'm sweating. But the nightmare, almost same as last night. Dancing in a circle on the beach, like "ring around the roses." There were even beach roses. Dog roses. Caroline and Rosemary weren't with me this time, I was holding Abalyn's right hand, and there was a man on my left. I don't know who he was. We all sang along with Eva, the words to "The Lobster Quadrille." Dancing, I think, counterclockwise, kicking up sand, dead fish underfoot. Stench. Sun high and white, hot, and maybe that was because the bedroom is hot. Then everyone stopped dancing, and Eva pointed the violin bow at me. She said, "I know an old woman who swallowed a fly," but didn't finish with the rhyme. Just that much. I told Abalyn I wanted to go home. I told her I'd left the oven on. She said we'd go home soon, but we didn't.

Note: Ashes in the water, Ashes in the sea, We all jump up, With a one-two-three. (or) She's in the water, she's in the sea. (or) husha husha, we all fall down. See Roud Folk Song Index, #7925 (Roud ID #S263898), and see the website for English Folk Dance and Song Society: 'Twas a dream : Father stay in room : Three beautiful angels : Around bed. (July 10th, 1908; Roud ID #S135469). Hidden meanings: Great Plague of London, 1665 (Ring a-ring o' roses, A pocketful of posies, A-tishoo! a-tishoo! We all fall down; Iona and

Peter Opie, *The Singing Game,* Oxford, 1985, pp. 220–227)—but this interpretation is controversial and hasn't been widely accepted. There are problems. And also, wreck of the *Scandia* and *North Cape* at Moonstone Beach, 1996.

Sunday (July 13th): This one is no better than a fucking cartoon. It's cartoon silly. Abalyn is making breakfast, and she's singing in the kitchen (I like the way she sings. Abalyn, I mean.), and I'm going to write down this silly cartoon dream that didn't and won't bother me because it's no better than slapstick. It won't feel like it's stuck to me somehow, all day, or like it's soaked me and I'll need all day to dry off. Anyway, anyway, this time, I was on the road again, but the road was the river, Blackstone River Gorge rising up on either side, steep granite blacker than the night. The road was wild white water rushing through the gorge, and the car rolled and bobbed and listed this way and that way. I was afraid I would capsize.

Eva Canning was in the car with me, messing with the radio, looking for a channel I don't think even exists. I asked her questions she wouldn't answer. Then the road was just a road, and I'm speeding back towards the city. There are animals watching me from the edges of the highway, and their eyes flash red and iridescent blue-green like Eva's might have flashed (but couldn't have, not really, just me being freaked-out). I saw rabbits, foxes, skunks, weasels, dogs, cats, minks, sheep, coyotes, a bear. Other things I can't remember. When I glanced in the rearview mirror there were big black birds following us. They had Christmas-light eyes. Then it stopped, and I woke up. My chest hurt, like I'd been holding my breath in my sleep. It still aches a little. Dumb fucking dream.

Monday (July 14th): In the bathroom, watching Eva Canning take a shower. The room smells like river water, shampoo, mud, turtles, soap. She is so beautiful. No one is supposed to be as beautiful as that. She shuts off the water and steps out, wincing when her feet meet the tiles. "I'm walking on needles," she said. "I'm walking on sharp knives. The witch, the sea hag, told me that would happen, didn't she? Did I listen?"

I hand her a towel, and notice she leaves bloody footprints on the white tiles. She stands at the mirror above the sink and wipes away condensation from the glass. Eva has no reflection. "What was I to do? He sunk me in the green water below the bridge. They made a violin of my breastbone. They made tuning pegs from my fingers. In the winter, I lay below the ice and the sky was silver and glass." I'm trying to write exactly what she said. It's close, but not exact. This was the worst yet. Call Dr. Ogilvy?

Notes: See *Hans Christian Andersen's Fairy Tales*. Mrs. Henry H. B. Paull, translator. (London: Warne & Co., 1875). See also "The Twa Sisters," *The English and Scottish Popular Ballads*, Francis James Childs (ref #10; 1 10A.7–8), five volumes, 1882–1898.

Tuesday (July 15th): Back to the stairs, only I was walking down. Not up, and the water was continually gushing from above. Several times, it almost knocked me off my feet. Abalyn was calling my name at the bottom of the stairs, but, get this, there wasn't a bottom to the stairs. It was an endless stepwise waterfall. It was a cataract. This has got to stop. I want to tell Abalyn about the dreams, but I absolutely know that I won't. I don't want to tell her; I want them to stop.

There. That's the last of it. The dreams didn't end after that Tuesday. I just didn't write them down anymore. There wasn't any blank space left at the back of *Mansfield Park*, and, besides, I was sick of writing them down. It started to feel like picking though my own vomit to see what I'd eaten. The dreams were making me sick, but I have always been good at hiding my craziness. On Tuesday morning, Abalyn and I fucked like there'd been no nightmare, and I tried to work on my painting. And drew Eva Canning, instead.

Imp typed, "You are a liar. You are a filthy, wicked little liar, and you know it, don't you?"

Yeah, I'm a liar.

I'm a filthy, wicked little liar.

And I know it, sure as shit.

July grew old, as months always and will forever do, and on a day late in July, just before the death of the month and the birth of August, Abalyn and I almost had an argument. Almost, but not quite. In all the time we were together, I don't think we ever had a genuine argument. That sort of thing isn't in either of our natures, and, looking back, I'm grateful for that much, at least. At least we didn't fight and bicker and stab at each other with ugly words we'd spend the rest of our lives regretting, but unable to take back.

So, this is an afternoon, a late afternoon, early evening, almost at the end of July. Which means six weeks or so had passed since Abalyn had come to live with me. The day was exceptionally hot. The sort of day when I really wish my apartment had air-conditioning, even if it costs too much, more than I can afford, and even though I don't need air-conditioning for most of any given summer.

But I did that day. Need air-conditioning, I mean. I had both windows open, in the room where I paint, and I had the box fan running in one of the windows, but it wasn't doing any good. The air was like soup, and the smells of turpentine, linseed, and oils— which I usually found comforting—only added to the oppressiveness of the air. I'd had to take off my smock. I had a bandanna on my head to keep the sweat out of my eyes, but that didn't stop it from dripping off the end of my nose onto my palette. My sweat, mixing with my paint, which struck me as somehow wicked (there's that word again), and somehow dangerous. Painting myself into the canvas, all the minute specks of me trapped in those surface-tension beads of sweat. Locking my *physical* self up within my paintings. I sat there, sweating, sweating, trying to blend a very particular shade of yellow, which I could see plainly in my head, but which kept eluding me. I tried to work, and tried not to think about my sweat in the paint, tried not to think about voodoo and magic and how an artist might become bound to something she's made. How she might lose her soul inside it.

I think it might have been around seven thirty when Abalyn knocked very gently at the door. The sun was getting low, but the room wasn't getting any cooler. She asked if she could come in. If it would bother me if she came in and talked while I was working. I wanted to say no. I probably should have said no, but I didn't. I'd been alone in that room for hours, mixing yellows and sweating into my paint, but not actually putting anything new on the canvas. I couldn't stop working, but I didn't want to be alone in there anymore.

She came in and eased the door shut behind her, careful not to slam it. She sat down on the floor not far from my stool, her back to the wall. For a moment, she stared silently at the window nearest her, at the rooftops and trees and birds.

"Are you getting hungry?" she asked, after a minute or two. "I was thinking I'd make something cold for dinner. Maybe a big salad or something."

"I'm not hungry," I told her, squeezing the tiniest dab of naphthol crimson. I watched as the wrong yellow became an entirely wrong orange. "It's too hot. I can't eat when it's this hot."

"Later, then," she said.

"It isn't going well?" she asked.

"It isn't going at all," I told her. "I can't get this color right. I keep fucking it up, and I'm wasting paint."

"Then maybe you ought to stop for now."

"I don't *want* to stop for now," I replied, and I heard how my voice sounded, almost snapping at her. I apologized and told her the heat was making me irritable.

There was a cigarette tucked behind her left ear, like she was a greaser or a mechanic in some old movie. I thought it was sexy, but I didn't tell her. I just kept stirring at my palette, adding more paint, getting it wronger and wronger.

"Hey, Imp," she said. "You okay?"

"No," I said without looking up. "I'm hot. I'm hot, and I'm wasting paint."

"That's not what I meant. I mean, more like, are you okay, in general?"

I didn't answer right away. I can't remember if I didn't want to answer, or if it was because I was so distracted, so intent on finding the right yellow and all.

"I don't know," I told her eventually. "I guess so. I guess I'm all right as I ever am."

"If you weren't, would you tell me?"

I looked up at her then. Maybe I narrowed my eyes. Maybe I frowned. Her expression changed, as if whatever she saw on my face bothered her or was unexpected.

"I wouldn't lie to you, Abalyn. I wouldn't have any reason to lie to you, right?"

She took a deep breath and let it out in measured exhalations. It made me think of swimming, the way she exhaled. I used to swim a lot, but not anymore, not since Eva. Abalyn breathed in and out and then she glanced at the open window again.

"I know you wouldn't lie, Imp. That's not what I meant. But sometimes there's something wrong, and it's easier not to talk about it."

"That would be a lie by omission," I told her.

"I wasn't accusing you of lying," she said, and I think she held her breath for a moment then. I thought of swimming again. "Maybe I should leave you alone," and Abalyn's beach-glass eyes drifted from the window to the floorboards. Sometimes, my mother used to call beach glass "mermaids' tears."

"No," I said. I probably said it too quickly, with too much urgency. "No, please. Stay. It's okay, really. I'm just irritable from the heat. I don't mean to be."

"Yeah, it's hot as Hades in here. What color of yellow are you after, anyway?" It was obvious she was just pretending to be interested. The words sounded awkward, but she probably believed the silence would be more awkward. It felt like she had to say something to stop the silence from coming back, so that's what she said.

"Don't you mean what *shade* of yellow?" I suggested. I was busy trying to dilute the unfortunate consequences of the naphthol crimson, and it didn't even occur to me this might be a picky, even rude, sort of question until it was already out of my mouth.

"Sure. I guess that's what I meant."

"Well, bright," I replied, chewing my lower lip, stirring at the palette. "Sort of like a canary or goldenrod is yellow. But not too bright, right? Titanium yellow more than Aureolin yellow."

"I don't know what either of those are."

"That's okay. You're not a painter," I said. "You don't need to know. I do. I'm supposed to be able to do this, and if I can't do this, I can't paint."

"I'm worried about you," she said. I want to say "she blurted," but I won't.

I laughed and told her that was ridiculous. "I'll figure it out sooner or later. I almost always do. Sometimes it just takes a while, and the heat isn't helping."

"Imp, I'm not talking about the painting," she said.

I stopped stirring at the glob of oil paint, and stared at the canvas. "Okay. What are you talking about, then?"

"You talk in your sleep," she said. In retrospect, I imagine she'd worked out precisely what she intended to say, and I also imagine this wasn't supposed to be where she started. But it was hot, and maybe none of it was coming out right. I glanced her way, then quickly back to the canvas. So far, it was still mottled red and black, without even a speck of yellow. Abalyn was looking out the window at dusk swallowing Willow Street.

"Abalyn, lots of people talk in their sleep. You probably talk in your sleep sometimes."

"It's what you've been saying in your sleep."

"You lie awake listening to what I say in my sleep?"

"No," she protested. "Usually, it wakes me up."

"Sorry," I said, without a hint of sincerity. I was too annoyed to be sincere. The heat had made me irritable, and now Abalyn was making me angry. "I'm sorry I talk in my sleep and wake you up. I'll try not to do that anymore."

"You talk about her," Abalyn said. "You always talk about her."

"Her who?" I asked, even though I knew exactly what her answer would be.

"That Eva woman," she replied. "You wake me up talking about Eva Canning. Talking *to* Eva Canning. A few times, you were sort of singing. . . ." And she trailed off.

"I most certainly do not sing in my sleep," I laughed. "No one sings in their sleep." I had no idea whether people do or don't sing in their sleep, but when she said that, it gave me a heavy, gelid feeling deep in my belly.

Rosemary Anne, did you sing in your sleep? When they tied you down to your bed in your room at Butler Hospital at 345 Blackstone Boulevard, did you sing in your sleep?

Grandmother Caroline, did you ever dream of songs and sing them to empty rooms where no one could hear?

"Why do you answer the phone when it hasn't rang?" she asked me.

"When it hasn't *rung*," I corrected.

"Why do you do that? I never saw you do it before you brought her home."

"How long had you known me before then, Abalyn? Maybe a week, that's all. I've probably been doing it all my life. You wouldn't know."

"No, I probably wouldn't," she sighed, speaking and sighing in a single reluctant breath. I could tell she wanted to stop, but now that she'd started this, she wasn't going to. Stop, I mean.

Caroline, didn't you ever happen to pick up the telephone when it wasn't ringing?

I thought to myself, *Please don't ask me anything else, Abalyn. I can't mix the right yellow, and I'm sweating like a pig, and please don't keep asking me these questions I can't answer.*

"I found something," she said very softly. I didn't turn to see if she was still gazing out the window. "It was an accident. I wasn't snooping. There was a folder on the kitchen table, and I accidentally knocked it off."

Of course, it was the manila file I'd begun keeping years earlier, the one labeled "Perishable Shippen." What I'd learned about "the Siren of Millville" and *The Drowning Girl.* A day or two before, I'd added Eva Canning's name to the tab. I'd written it in green ink.

"My hand hardly brushed against it."

I kept my eyes on the palette; the paint there had turned a very pale and sickly orange.

"Everything inside spilled out across the floor," she continued. "I was gathering it all back up, to return it to the folder, Imp. I swear, that's all that I was doing."

"You read it?" I asked, biting down on my lip hard enough to taste a faint hint of blood, like iron in water.

She didn't respond.

I set my palette down among the scatter of paint tubes and brushes. "That stuff is private," I said, and my voice wasn't any louder than hers.

"It was an accident," she said again. "I didn't mean to knock the folder off the table. I was cleaning up after lunch yesterday."

"But it wasn't an accident, reading what was in it. No one reads by accident." I didn't sound angry anymore, and I realized that I *wasn't*. The anger had come and gone quick as lightning, and now I just felt sort of tired and weary of the color yellow.

"I'm worried about you, that's all. I wouldn't have brought any of this up, except I'm worried about you. You're obsessed with this woman."

I turned towards Abalyn, and when I moved, the stool wobbled, and I reached out for the easel to steady myself. She wasn't still staring out the window; she was staring at me. She looked concerned. She almost looked frightened. All I wanted to say was that she shouldn't worry, that sometimes I get a thing stuck in my head, but it eventually passes. Just like I always find the colors I need, stuff that gets stuck in my head always gets unstuck, sooner or later. But I didn't say any of that. What I said instead was only meant to make Abalyn stop talking and leave me alone again, not to reassure her.

"I pay a doctor to worry about me," I told her. "Frankly, it seems kind of presumptuous, giving me the third degree when you hardly know me that well. This really isn't any of your business. You're not my keeper. You're only just barely my girlfriend."

She sat there a moment, watching me, before she nodded and stood up. She dusted off the seat of her blue jeans.

"If that came out harsh, it wasn't meant to. But I don't want to discuss this with you."

She nodded and said, "Tell me when you get hungry, and I'll make us something to eat. Or I'll go for takeout. Whichever." She left, easing the door shut, the same way she had eased it open when she came in. I went to the window and stayed there until it was dark.

I'm almost done here. With the pretense of a fourth chapter. Soon, I know, I'm going to quit, and when (or if) I come back to this manuscript, I'll type "5" seventeen lines down a new piece of paper.

No particular reason. The events of that summer are flawless in their continuity, and a more honest woman wouldn't divide it up into episodes. There wouldn't be section breaks, pound signs, and numbers denoting new chapters. If I were telling my ghost story the way I should, there might not even be punctuation. Or spaces between one word and the next. I don't hear punctuation marks in my head. My thoughts all run together, and I slice them apart and nail them into place here. I might as well be a lepidopterist neatly pinning dead butterflies and moths onto foam boards. These words are all corpses now, corpses of moths and butterflies. Sparrows in stoppered jars.

By accident, cleaning up after herself, Abalyn knocked a folder off the kitchen table. I shouldn't have left it there, but I wasn't used to having someone else around. I wasn't accustomed to concealing my fixations. It wasn't her fault. Gravity took over and the pages spilled out, and she read what was on them. What was there, it would have struck her as odd, and we are curious animals, people are, human beings. The folder held an assortment of photocopies from newspapers, magazines, and library books, some of them going back almost a hundred years.

Had she asked, I might have shown them to her.

Or not. She didn't ask, so I can't know.

I never learned which of the pages she read and which she didn't. I never asked, and Abalyn never volunteered the information. She may have read them all, or only a few of them. Those sheets of paper are only butterflies trapped in a killing jar. They're only the feathers of broken, fallen birds. I did wonder, though, which she read. Sitting here in my blue room, I still wonder. But that's only natural, right? It's normal to wonder, even if knowing doesn't matter and wouldn't change anything.

That evening during dinner neither of us said very much. Afterwards, she went to the parlor and the sofa and her laptop, her digital, pixeled worlds. Her time displacement. I went to the bedroom, where I sat reading back over my "clippings" (I think of them that way, even if that's not what they are). I scanned headlines and notes I'd scribbled in the margins. There are two photocopied newspaper articles, in particular, I can remember reading that night. Reading start to finish, I mean.

One bears the headline "Search for Mystery Woman's Body Halted, Hoax Suspected," from *The Evening Call* (Woonsocket, Friday, June 12th, 1914). It describes how two fifteen-year-old boys had been paddling a canoe along the Blackstone River near Millville, Massachusetts, when they'd happened upon the body of a woman floating facedown in the murky water. They prodded her with an oar, to be sure she was dead, but didn't try to pull her from the river. They went at once to a local constable, and that same afternoon, and again the next day, men from Millville probed the river with poles, and used a fishing net to drag the area where the boys claimed to have sighted the corpse. But no corpse was found. Finally, everyone gave up and decided there'd never been a dead woman, that the boys were bored that summer day and fabricated the story to get everyone stirred up.

And the other article I'm fairly certain I read back over that night comes from the *Worcester Telegram & Gazette* ("Bather Claims Attacked and Injured by Unseen Animal," Tuesday, September 4th, 1951). Three girls (their ages aren't given) were swimming above Rolling Dam in Blackstone, near Millville, when one screamed and began thrashing and calling out for help. Her name was Millicent Hartnett (*Mill*icent from *Mill*ville); her friends' names aren't given. When the girls reached the shore, they were horrified to see a deep gash in Millicent's right leg, just above the knee. The wound was serious enough it required twenty stitches. Authorities suspected a snapping turtle (*Chelydra serpentina*) was responsible, or that the girl had caught her leg on a submerged log. Millicent claimed otherwise. She said she'd seen what had bitten her, and that it wasn't a turtle or a log. But she refused to say what it *had* been. "I saw it up close, but no one will believe me," she said. "I don't want people thinking I'm crazy or lying." Millicent's mother told reporters that her daughter was a good student, that she was practical, trustworthy, and not the sort of girl given to tall tales. Swimmers were advised to avoid the dam, and the three girls were said to have been so upset they swore they'd never swim in the river again.

Both boys became soldiers and died in France four years later. Millicent Hartnett grew up, got married, and lives with her oldest son in Uxbridge. It wasn't very hard to find these things out. I've often thought about contacting Millicent, who would be seventy-six or so, and trying to get her to tell me what she saw in the river that day. But I don't think she'd talk to me. She might not even remember, though she must still have a scar on her ankle.

If Abalyn didn't read either of those articles, there are others just as peculiar she might have read, instead. About eleven o'clock, I closed the folder and slipped it under my side of the bed. I switched off the lamp and lay in the dark, listening to the noises rising up from the street and the sounds from the apartments above and below mine. Abalyn slept on the sofa that night, and in the morning we didn't talk about the folder. Mostly, more than anything, I was embarrassed, and was glad I had to be at work early. She was gone when I got home, but had left a note saying she was with friends. The note promised she wouldn't be late, and she wasn't. I didn't tell her how it scared me, coming in and finding she wasn't there, how I'd thought maybe she'd left for good. How I checked to make sure all her stuff was still there. When she got home, Abalyn was a little drunk. She smelled like beer and Old Spice aftershave lotion and cigarette smoke. She told me she loved me, and we fucked, and then I lay awake for a long, long time, watching her sleep.

"The next day," Imp typed, "I apologized."

I'm not sure if I really did. Apologize, I mean. But I like to believe that I did. Regardless, I am sure that was the day I asked her to read a short story I'd written and that had been published a couple of years earlier in *The Massachusetts Review*. If I didn't apologize in so many words, letting her read that story was another and more personal sort of apology. I no longer have a copy of the magazine, but I'm attaching the typescript, because I know it's part of my ghost story. It's a part that I'd already committed to paper well before I met Eva Canning, the first time and the second time, in July and in November. The story's not factual, but it's true. I'm stapling it to this page because I can't find a paper clip.

The Mermaid of the Concrete Ocean

BY INDIA MORGAN PHELPS

The building's elevator is busted, and so I have to drag my ass up twelve flights of stairs. Her apartment is smaller and more tawdry than I expected, but I'm not entirely sure I could say what I thought I'd find at the top of all those stairs. I don't know this part of Manhattan very well, this ugly wedge of buildings one block over from South Street and Roosevelt Drive and the ferry terminal. She keeps reminding me that if I look out the window (there's only one), I can see the Brooklyn Bridge. It seems a great source of pride, that she has a view of the bridge and the East River. The apartment is too hot, filled with soggy heat pouring off the radiators, and there are so many unpleasant odors competing for my attention that I'd be hard-pressed to assign any one of them priority over the rest. Mildew. Dust. Stale cigarette smoke. Better I say the apartment smells shut away, and leave it at that. The place is crammed wall to wall with threadbare, dust-skimmed antiques, the tattered refuse of Victorian and Edwardian bygones. I have trouble imagining how she navigates the clutter in her wheelchair, which is something of an antique itself. I compliment the Tiffany lamps, all of which appear not to be reproductions, and are in considerably better shape than most of the other furnishings. She smiles, revealing dentures stained by nicotine and neglect. At least, I assume they're dentures. She switches on one of the table lamps, its shade a circlet of stained-glass dragonflies, and tells me it was a Christmas gift from a playwright. He's dead now, she says. She tells me his name, but it's no one I've ever heard of, and I admit this to her. Her yellow-brown smile doesn't waver.

"Nobody remembers him. He was *very* avant-garde," she says. "No one understood what he was trying to say. But obscurity was precious to him. It pained him terribly, that so few ever understood that about his work."

I nod, once or twice or three times; I don't know, and it hardly matters. Her thin fingers glide across the lampshade, leaving furrows in the accumulated dust, and now I can see that the dragonflies have wings the color of amber, and their abdomens and thoraces are a deep cobalt blue. They all have eyes like poisonous crimson berries. She asks me to please have a seat, and apologizes for not having offered one sooner. She motions to an armchair near the lamp, and also to a chaise lounge a few feet farther away. Both are upholstered with the same faded floral brocade. I choose the armchair, and am hardly surprised to discover that all the springs are shot. I sink several inches into the chair, and my knees jut upwards, towards the water-stained plaster ceiling.

"Will you mind if I tape our conversation?" I ask, opening my briefcase, and she stares at me for a moment, as though she hasn't quite understood the question. By way of explanation, I remove the tiny Olympus digital recorder and hold it up for her to see. "Well, it doesn't actually use audiotapes," I add.

"I don't mind," she tells me. "It must be much simpler than having to write down everything you hear, everything someone says."

"Much," I say, and switch the recorder on. "We can shut it off anytime you like, of course. Just say the word." I lay the recorder on the table, near the base of the dragonfly lamp.

"That's very considerate," she says. "That's very kind of you."

And it occurs to me how much she, like the apartment, differs from whatever I might have expected to find. This isn't *Sunset Boulevard*, Norma Desmond and her shuffling cadre of "waxwork" acquaintances. There's nothing of the grotesque or Gothic—even that *Hollywood* Gothic—about her. Despite the advance and ravages of ninety-four years, her green eyes are bright and clear. Neither her voice nor hands tremble, and only the old wheelchair stands as any indication of infirmity. She sits up very straight and, whenever she speaks, tends to move her hands about, as though possessed of more energy and excitement than words alone can convey. She's wearing only a little makeup, some pale lipstick and a hint of rouge on her high cheekbones, and her long gray hair is pulled back in a single braid. There's an easy grace about her. Watching by the light of the dragonfly lamp and the light coming in through the single window, it occurs to me that she is showing me *her* face, and not some mask of counterfeit youth. Only the stained teeth (or dentures) betray any hint of the decay I'd anticipated and steeled myself against. Indeed, if not for the rank smell of the apartment, and the oppressive heat, there would be nothing particularly unpleasant about being here with her.

I retrieve a stenographer's pad from my briefcase, then close it and set it on the floor near my feet. I tell her that I haven't written out a lot of questions, that I prefer to allow interviews to unfold more organically, like conversations, and this seems to please her.

"I don't go in for the usual brand of interrogation," I say. "Too forced. Too weighted by the journalist's own agenda."

"So, you think of yourself as a journalist?" she asks, and I tell her yes, usually.

"Well, I haven't done this in such a very long time," she replies, straightening her skirt. "I hope you'll understand if I'm a little rusty. I don't often talk about those days, or the pictures. It was all so very long ago."

"Still," I say, "you must have fond memories."

"Must I, now?" she asks, and before I can think of an answer, she says, "There are only memories, young man, and, yes, most of them are not so bad, and some are even rather agreeable. But there are many things I've tried to forget. Every life must be like that, wouldn't you say?"

"To some extent," I reply.

She sighs, as if I haven't understood at all, and her eyes wander up to a painting on the wall behind me. I hardly noticed it when I sat down, but now I turn my head for a better view.

When I ask, "Is that one of the originals?" she nods, her smile widening by almost imperceptible degrees, and she points at the painting of a mermaid.

"Yes," she says. "The only one I have. Oh, I've got a few lithographs. I have prints or photographs of them all, but this is the only one of the genuine paintings I own."

"It's beautiful," I say, and that isn't idle flattery. The mermaid paintings are the reason that I've come to New York City and tracked her to the tawdry little hovel by the river. This isn't the first time I've seen an original up close, but it is the first time outside a museum gallery. There's one hanging in Newport, at the National Museum of American Illustration. I've seen it, and also the one at the Art Institute of Chicago, and one other, the mermaid in the permanent collection of the Society of Illustrators here in Manhattan. But there are more than thirty documented, and most of them I've only seen reproduced in books and folios. Frankly, I wonder if this painting's existence is very widely known, and how long it's been since anyone but the model, sitting here in her wheelchair, has admired it. I've read all the artist's surviving journals and correspondence (including the letters to his model), and I know that there are at least ten mermaid paintings that remain unaccounted for. I assume this must be one of them.

"Wow," I gasp, unable to look away from the painting. "I mean, it's amazing."

"It's the very last one he did, you know," she says. "He wanted me to have it. If someone offered me a million dollars, I still wouldn't part with it."

I glance at her, then back to the painting. "More likely, they'd offer you ten million," I tell her, and she laughs. It might easily be mistaken for the laugh of a much younger woman.

"Wouldn't make any difference if they did," she says. "He gave it to me, and I'll never part with it. Not ever. He named this one *Regarding the Shore from Whale Reef*, and that was my idea, the title. He often asked me to name them. At least half their titles, I thought up for him." And I already know this; it's in his letters.

The painting occupies a large, narrow canvas, easily four feet tall by two feet wide—somewhat too large for this wall, really—held inside an ornately carved frame. The frame has been stained dark as mahogany, though I'm sure it's something far less costly; here and there, where the varnish has been scratched or chipped, I can see the blond wood showing through. But I don't doubt that the painting is authentic, despite numerous compositional deviations, all of which are immediately apparent to anyone familiar with the mermaid series. For instance, in contravention to the artist's usual approach, the siren has been placed in the foreground, and also somewhat to the right. And, more importantly, she's facing away from the viewer. Buoyed by rough waves, she holds her arms outstretched to either side, as if to say, "Let me infold you," her long hair floating around her like a dense tangle of kelp, and the mermaid gazes towards land and a whitewashed lighthouse perched on a granite promontory. The rocky coastline is familiar, some wild place he'd found in Massachusetts or Maine or Rhode Island. The viewer might be fooled into thinking this is only a painting of a woman swimming in the sea, as so little of her is showing above the water-line. She might be mistaken for a suicide, taking a final glimpse of the rugged strand before slipping below the surface. But, if one looks only a little closer, the patches of red-orange scales flecking her arms are unmistakable, and there are living creatures caught up in the snarls of her black hair: tiny crabs and brittle stars, the twisting shapes of strange oceanic worms and a gasping, wide-eyed fish of some sort, suffocating in the air.

"That was the last one he did," she says again.

It's hard to take my eyes off the painting, and I'm already wondering if she will permit me to get a few shots of it before I leave.

"It's not in any of the catalogs," I say. "It's not mentioned anywhere in his papers or the literature."

"No, it wouldn't be. It was our secret," she replies. "After all those years working together, he wanted to give me something special, and so he did this last one, and never showed it to anyone else. I had it framed when I came back from Europe in 'forty-six, after the war. For years, it was rolled up in a cardboard tube, rolled up and swaddled in muslin, kept on the top shelf of a friend's closet. A mutual friend, actually, who admired him greatly, though I never showed her this painting."

I finally manage to look away from the canvas, turning back towards the woman sitting up straight in her wheelchair. She looks very pleased at my surprise, and I ask her the first question that comes to mind.

"Has *anyone* else ever seen it? I mean, besides the two of you, and besides me?"

"Certainly," she says. "It's been hanging right there for the past twenty years, and I *do* occasionally have visitors, every now and then. I'm not a complete recluse. Not quite yet."

"I'm sorry. I didn't mean to imply that you were."

And she's still staring up at the painting, and the impression I have is that she hasn't paused to *look* at it closely for a long time. It's as though she's suddenly *noticing* it, and probably couldn't recall the last time that she did. Sure, it's a fact of her everyday landscape, another component of the crowded reliquary of her apartment. But, like the Tiffany dragonfly lamp given her by that forgotten playwright, I suspect she rarely ever pauses to consider it.

Watching her as she peers so intently at the painting looming up behind me and the threadbare brocade chair where I sit, I'm struck once more by those green eyes of hers. They're the same green eyes the artist gave to every incarnation of his mermaid, and they seem to me even brighter than they did before, and not the least bit dimmed by age. They are like some subtle marriage of emerald and jade and shallow salt water, brought to life by unknown alchemies. They give me a greater appreciation of the painter, that he so perfectly conveyed her eyes, deftly communicating the complexities of iris and sclera, cornea and retina and pupil. That anyone could have the talent required to transfer these precise and complex hues into mere oils and acrylics.

"How did it begin?" I ask, predictably enough. Of course, the artist wrote repeatedly of the mermaids' genesis. I even found a 1967 dissertation on the subject hidden away in the stacks at Harvard. But I'm pretty sure no one has ever bothered to ask the model. Gradually, and, I think, reluctantly, her green eyes drift away from the canvas and back to me.

"It's not as if that's a secret," she says. "I believe he even told a couple of the magazine reporters about the dreams. One magazine in Paris, and maybe one here in New York, too. He often spoke with me about his dreams. They were always so vivid, and he wrote them down. He painted them, whenever he could. Like he painted the mermaids."

I glance over at the recorder lying on the table, and wish that I'd waited until later on to ask that particular question. It should have been placed somewhere towards the end, not right at the front. I'm definitely off my game today, and it's not only the heat from the radiators making me sweat. I've been disarmed, unbalanced, first by *Regarding the Shore from Whale Reef,* and then by having looked so deeply into her eyes. I clear my throat, and she asks if I'd like a glass of water or maybe a cold cream soda. I thank her, but shake my head no.

"I'm fine," I say, "but thank you."

"It can get awfully stuffy in here," she says, and glances down at the dingy Persian rug that covers almost the entire floor. This is the first time since she let me through the door that I've seen her frown.

"Honestly, it's not so bad," I insist, failing to sound the least bit honest.

"Why, there are days," she says, "it's like being in a sauna. Or a damned tropical jungle, Tahiti or Brazil or someplace like that, and it's a wonder I don't start hearing parrots and monkeys. But it helps with the pain, usually more than the pills do."

And here's the one thing she was adamant that we not discuss, the childhood injury that left her crippled. She's told me how she has always loathed writers and critics who tried to draw a parallel between the mermaids and her paralysis. "Don't even bring it up," she warned on the phone, almost a week ago, and I assured her that I wouldn't. Only, now *she's* brought it up. I sit very still in the broken-down armchair, there beneath the last painting, waiting to see what she'll say next. I try hard to clear my head and focus, and to decide what question on the short list scribbled in my steno pad might steer the interview back on course.

"There *was* more than his dreams," she admits, almost a full minute later. The statement has the slightly abashed quality of a confession. And I have no idea how to respond, so I don't. She blinks, and looks up at me again, the pale ghost of that previous smile returning to her lips. "Would it bother you if I smoke?" she asks.

"No," I reply. "Not at all. Please, whatever makes you comfortable."

"These days, well, it bothers so many people. As though the pope had added smoking to the list of venial sins. I get the most awful glares, sometimes, so I thought I'd best ask first."

"It's your home," I tell her, and she nods and reaches into a pocket of her skirt, retrieving a pack of Marlboro Reds and a disposable lighter.

"To some, that doesn't seem to matter," she says. "There's a woman comes around twice a week to attend to the dusting and trash and whatnot, a Cuban woman, and if I smoke when she's here, she always complains and tries to open the window, even though I've told her time and time again it's been painted shut for ages. It's not like I don't pay her."

Considering the thick and plainly undisturbed strata of dust, and the odors, I wonder if she's making this up, or if perhaps the Cuban woman might have stopped coming around a long time ago.

"I promised him, when he told me, I would never tell anyone else this," she says, and here she pauses to light her cigarette, then return the rest of the pack and her lighter to their place in her skirt pocket. She blows a gray cloud of smoke away from me. "Not another living soul. It was a sort of pact between us, you understand. But, lately, it's been weighing on me. I wake up in the night, sometimes, and it's like a stone around my neck. I don't think it's something I want to take with me to the grave. He told me the day we started work on the second painting."

"That would have been in May 1939, yes?"

And here she laughs again and shakes her head. "Hell if I know. Maybe you have it written down somewhere in that pad of yours, but I don't remember the date. Not anymore. But . . . I *do* know it

was the same year the World's Fair opened here in New York, and I
know it was after Amelia Earhart disappeared. He knew her, Amelia
Earhart. He knew so many interesting people. But I'm rambling,
aren't I?"

"I'm in no hurry," I answer. "Take your time." But she frowns
again and stares at the smoldering tip of her cigarette for a moment.

"I like to think, sir, that I am a practical woman," she says, looking directly at me and raising her chin an inch or so. "I have always
wanted to be able to consider myself a practical woman. And now
I'm very old. Very, *very* old, yes, and a practical woman must acknowledge the fact that women who *are* this old will not live much
longer. I know I'll die soon, and the truth about the mermaids, it
isn't something I want to take with me to my grave. So, I'll tell you,
and betray his confidence. If you'll listen, of course."

"Certainly," I tell her, struggling not to let my excitement show
through, but feeling like a vulture, anyway. "If you'd prefer, I can
shut off the recorder," I offer.

"No, no . . . I want you to put this in your article. I want them
to print it in that magazine you write for, because it seems to me
that people ought to know. If they're still so infatuated with the
mermaids after all this time, it doesn't seem fitting that they *don't*
know. It seems almost indecent."

I don't remind her that I'm a freelance and the article's being
done on spec, so there's no guarantee anyone's going to buy it, or
that it will ever be printed and read. And that feels indecent, too,
but I keep my mouth shut and listen while she talks. I can always
nurse my guilty conscience later on.

"The summer before I met him, before we started working together," she begins, and then pauses to take another drag on her
cigarette. Her eyes return to the painting behind me. "I suppose
that would have been the summer of 1937. The Depression was still
on, but his family, out on Long Island, they'd come through it better

than most. He had money. Sometimes he'd take commissions from magazines, if the pay was decent. *The New Yorker,* that was one he did some work for, and *Harper's Bazaar,* and *Collier's,* but I guess you know this sort of thing, having done so much research on his life."

The ash on her Marlboro is growing perilously long, though she seems not to have noticed. I glance about and spot an empty ashtray, heavy lead glass, perched on the edge of a nearby coffee table. It doesn't look as though it's been emptied in days or weeks, another argument against the reality of the Cuban maid. My arm-chair squeaks and pops angrily when I lean forward to retrieve it. I offer it to her, and she takes her eyes off the painting just long enough to accept it and to thank me.

"Anyway," she continues, "mostly he was able to paint what he wanted. That was a freedom that he never took for granted. He was staying in Atlantic City that summer, because he said he liked watching the people on the boardwalk. Sometimes, he'd sit and sketch them for hours, in charcoal and pastels. He showed quite a lot of the boardwalk sketches to me, and I think he always meant to do paintings from them, but, to my knowledge, he never did.

"That summer, he was staying at the Traymore, which I never saw, but he said was wonderful. Many of his friends and acquaintances would go to Atlantic City in the summer, so he never lacked for company if he wanted it. There were the most wonderful parties, he told me. Sometimes, in the evenings, he'd go down onto the beach alone, onto the sand, I mean, because he said the waves and the gulls and the smell of the sea comforted him. In his studio, the one he kept on the Upper West Side, there was a quart mayonnaise jar filled with seashells and sand dollars and the like. He'd picked them all up at Atlantic City, over the years. Some of them we used as props in the paintings, and he also had a cabinet with shells from Florida and Nassau and the Cape and I don't know where else. He showed me conchs and starfish from the Mediterranean and Japan,

I remember. Seashells from all over the world, easily. He loved them, and driftwood, too."

She taps her cigarette against the rim of the ashtray and stares at the painting of the mermaid and the lighthouse, and I have the distinct feeling that she's drawing some sort of courage from it, the requisite courage needed to break a promise she's kept for seventy years. A promise she made three decades before my own birth. And I know now how to sum up the smell of her apartment. It smells like time.

"It was late July, and the sun was setting," she says, speaking very slowly now, as though every word is being chosen with great and deliberate care. "And he told me that he was in a foul temper that evening, having fared poorly at a poker game the night before. He played cards. He said it was one of his only weaknesses.

"At any rate, he went down onto the sand, and he was barefoot, he said. I remember that, him telling me he wasn't wearing shoes." And it occurs to me then that possibly none of what I'm hearing is the truth, that she's spinning a fanciful yarn so I won't be disappointed, lying for my benefit, or because her days are so filled with monotony and she is determined this unusual guest will be entertained. I push the thoughts away. There's no evidence of deceit in her voice. Art journalism hasn't made me rich or well-known, but I have gotten pretty good at knowing a lie when I hear one.

"He said to me, 'The sand was so cool beneath my feet.' He walked for a while, and then, just before dark, came across a group of young boys, eight or nine years old, and they were crowded around something that had washed up on the beach. The tide was going out, and what the boys had found, it had been stranded by the retreating tide. He recalled thinking it odd that they were all out so late, the boys, that they were not at dinner with their families. The lights were coming on along the boardwalk."

Now she suddenly averts her eyes from the painting on the wall of her apartment, *Regarding the Shore from Whale Reef*, as though she's taken what she needs and it has nothing left to offer. She crushes her cigarette out in the ashtray, and doesn't look at me. She chews at her lower lip, chewing away some of the lipstick. The old woman in the wheelchair does not appear sad, or wistful. I think it's anger, that expression, and I want to ask her *why* she's angry. Instead, I ask what it was the boys found on the beach, what the artist saw that evening. She doesn't answer right away, but closes her eyes and takes a deep breath, exhaling slowly, raggedly.

"I'm sorry," I say. "I didn't mean to press you. If you want to stop—"

"I do *not* want to stop," she says, opening her eyes again. "I have not come this far, and said this much, only to *stop*. It was a woman, a very *young* woman. He said that she couldn't have been much more than nineteen or twenty. One of the boys was poking at her with a stick, and he *took* the stick and shooed them all away."

"She was drowned?" I ask.

"Maybe. Maybe she drowned first. But she was bitten in half. There was nothing much left of her below the rib cage. Just bone and meat and a big hollowed-out place where all her organs had been, her stomach and lungs and everything. Still, there was no blood anywhere. It was like she'd never had a single drop of blood in her. He told me, 'I never saw anything else even half that horrible.' And, you know, that wasn't so long after he'd come back to the States from the war in Spain, fighting against the fascists, the Francoists. He was at the Siege of Madrid, and saw awful, awful things there. He said to me, 'I saw *atrocities*, but this was worse. . . .'"

And then she trails off and glares down at the ashtray in her lap, at a curl of smoke rising lazily from her cigarette butt.

"You don't have to go on," I say, almost whispering. "I'll understand—"

"Oh hell," she says, and shrugs her frail shoulders. "There isn't that much left to tell. He figured that a shark did it, maybe one big shark or several smaller ones. He took her by the arms and he hauled what was left of her up onto the dry sand, up towards the boardwalk, so she wouldn't be swept back out to sea. He sat down beside the body, because at first he didn't know what to do, and he said he didn't want to leave her alone. She was dead, but he didn't want to leave her alone. I don't know how long he sat there, but he said it was dark when he finally went to find a policeman.

"The body was still there when they got back. No one had disturbed it. The boys had not returned. But he said the whole thing was hushed up, because the chamber of commerce was afraid that a shark scare would frighten away the tourists and ruin the rest of the season. It had happened before. He said he went straight back to the Traymore and packed his bags, got a ticket on the next train to Manhattan. And he never visited Atlantic City ever again, but he started painting the mermaids, the very next year, right after he found me. Sometimes," she says, "I think maybe I should have taken it as an insult. But I didn't, and I still don't."

And then she falls silent, the way a storyteller falls silent when a tale is done. She takes another deep breath, rolls her wheelchair back about a foot or so, until it bumps hard against one end of the chaise lounge. She laughs nervously and lights another cigarette. And I ask her other questions, but they have nothing whatsoever to do with Atlantic City or the dead woman. We talk about other painters she's known, and jazz musicians, and writers, and she talks about how much New York's changed, how much the whole world has changed around her. As she speaks, I have the peculiar, disquieting sensation that, somehow, she passed the weight of that seventy-year-old secret on to me, and I think even if the article sells (and now I don't doubt that it will) and a million people read it, a hundred million people, the weight will not be diminished.

This is what it's like to be haunted, I think, and then I try to dismiss the thought as melodramatic, or absurd, or childish. But her jade-

and-surf-green eyes, the mermaids' eyes, are there to assure me otherwise.

It's almost dusk before we're done. She asks me to stay for dinner, but I make excuses about needing to be back in Boston. I promise to mail her a copy of the article when I've finished, and she tells me she'll watch for it. She tells me how she doesn't get much mail anymore, a few bills and ads, but nothing she ever wants to read.

"I am so very pleased that you contacted me," she says, as I slip the recorder and my steno pad back into the briefcase and snap it shut.

"It was gracious of you to talk so candidly with me," I reply, and she smiles.

I only glance at the painting once more, just before I leave. Earlier, I thought I might call someone I know, an ex who owns a gallery in the East Village. I owe him a favor, and the tip would surely square us. But standing there, looking at the pale, scale-dappled form of a woman bobbing in the frothing waves, her wet black hair tangled with wriggling crabs and fish, and nothing at all but a hint of shadow visible beneath the wreath of her floating hair, *seeing* it as I've never before seen any of the mermaids, I know I won't make the call. Maybe I'll mention the painting in the article I write, and maybe I won't.

She follows me to the door, and we each say our good-byes. I kiss her hand when she offers it to me. I don't believe I've ever kissed a woman's hand, not until this moment. She locks the door behind me, two dead bolts and a chain, and then I stand in the hallway. It's much cooler here than it was in her apartment, here in the shadows that have gathered despite the windows at either end of the corridor. There are people arguing loudly somewhere in the building below me, and a dog barking. By the time I descend the stairs and reach the sidewalk, the streetlamps are winking on.

The End

5

I went for a walk while Abalyn was reading "The Mermaid of the Concrete Ocean." Though I probably can't explain exactly why, it just seemed wrong somehow for me to stay in the apartment while she read the story. I feared it might make her uncomfortable. I didn't want her to feel as if I were reading over her shoulder, waiting impatiently for a reaction. Showing her the short story wasn't about whether or not she enjoyed it or thought it was well written. I'm not sure it was even about whether or not she understood it. Possibly, I was rolling over and showing her a soft spot, as an act of atonement for the things I'd said to her the day before in the room where I paint. She'd only been worried about me, but I'd stopped just shy of lashing out at her. We hadn't argued, but there had been a shadow. Possibly, I hoped that by allowing her to read "The Mermaid of the Concrete Ocean," any damage I'd done to the trust between us would be restored. I know what I said earlier, that Abalyn and I didn't fight and bicker and stab at each other with ugly words, that when we parted, we'd not done each other harm that we'd spend our lives regretting.

Often, I say things I only wish were true, as though releasing the words into the world might make them so. Wishful thinking. Magical thinking, part and parcel of my unwell mind. I say things that are not true because I *need* them to be true. This is what liars and foolish people do. As Anne Sexton almost said, "Belief is not quite need."

I know what I mean.

Anyway, I walked from Willow Street to the park, the Dexter Training Grounds where no one trains for anything. I wandered around beneath the trees, picking up acorns and chestnuts and rusty bottle caps and putting them into my pockets. I found myself counting my steps, and tried to remember if I'd skipped my meds. I crossed Dexter Street and went as far east as the intersection with Powhatan before turning back for home. I counted the windows of all the houses I passed. I took care to avoid the eyes of the few people I encountered.

Back home, I found Abalyn in the kitchen, making coffee. She drinks coffee all day long. I've never met anyone who drinks as much coffee as she does. But it doesn't seem to keep her awake or make her nervous. I told her I was home, though, of course, she'd heard me come in. I sat on the sofa, where she'd left the issue of *The Massachusetts Review* with my story in it.

From the kitchen, Abalyn said, "Do you want to talk about it?"

"You mean the story?"

"Yeah. We don't have to, if you'd rather not."

I stared at the cover of the magazine, which was a photograph taken inside an abandoned, decaying schoolroom. There were up-turned desks and chairs, a chalkboard on which was written "Here I am. Here I am." There were holes in the walls and the roof, exposing plaster and lath.

"I don't mind," I told her. And then I asked if she'd liked it, even though I'd promised myself I wouldn't.

Abalyn stepped around the counter that divides the kitchen from the parlor, carrying the huge coffee mug she brought with her when she moved in. She came and sat on the sofa with me, and the copy of *The Massachusetts Review* lay between us.

"I think it's sad and awfully grim," she said. "Not the sort of thing I usually read, left to my own devices. But that's really neither here nor there. Mostly, reading it made me want to know why you don't write more. If I could write that well, Imp, I would."

"You write. You write your reviews."

"You don't seriously think that's the same thing?" she asked, then sipped at her steaming black coffee. When I didn't answer her, she said, "I write *content*. I get paid, when I get paid, to fill space, and that's about it. I tell geeks and nerds what I think of video games, and mostly they ignore me, or worse."

"I haven't even read this one since I finished it. Most times, I'd much rather be painting. Stories occur to me, and every now and then I sit down and make myself write them. Mostly because Rosemary liked my writing. But I only got fifty dollars for that story. It's easier to make money with my paintings. They sell for a lot more. Well, I mean the paint-by-numbers, the ones the summer people buy."

"Those summer-people paintings, they're like my gaming reviews," Abalyn said. "Just content you churn out by rote to make a paycheck. You know there's no art in them, and you don't pretend there is. You told me that much yourself."

"Yeah," I said, "I know," and suddenly I found myself not wanting to talk about "The Mermaid of the Concrete Ocean" and half-wishing I hadn't let Abalyn read it. That I hadn't brought it to her attention. Suddenly, it seemed like my act of atonement was entirely out of proportion to whatever wrong I imagined I'd committed the day before.

I was about to try and change the subject, maybe tell her about my walk, maybe show her my chestnuts and bottle caps, when Abalyn said, "It left me wanting to ask you a question."

"What did?"

"Your story," she sighed, and sort of rolled her blue-green eyes before taking another swallow of coffee.

"Isn't it better with milk and sugar?" I pointed at the mug.

"It is when I want it with milk and sugar," she replied. "When I want black coffee, it's better black." The tone in her voice made me afraid she was going to roll her eyes again. I hate when people roll their eyes at me. But she didn't. Roll her eyes, I mean. She said, "I won't ask it, if you don't want me to. I'm not going to push."

"If you don't, I'll just always wonder. What your question was. When someone tells someone else they have a question, then it sort of has to be asked. It would be indecent, otherwise."

She thought "indecent" was a strange choice of words, but didn't explain herself. I think I know, though; it was an echo from the story. Abalyn asked her question. Then I sat staring blankly at the cover of *The Massachusetts Review* (Volume 47, Issue 4, Winter 2006), and at the floor, and at my shoes. From the kitchen, I could hear the clock ticking loudly, like this was some sort of game show and any moment there would be a buzzer or bell and I'd be told my time was up.

"You really don't have to answer it," she reminded me.

But I did. To the best of my ability, I did. I think I'd rather not write her question down. Or my response. Not now. Maybe later, but not now.

Whichever day was the next day of the week, the next day of the month, I called in sick. I wasn't sick, but I called in sick, anyway. Abalyn and I got up early and took the train to Boston, to Cambridge. We had noodles and miso soup, and then went to a comic-book shop she liked. She knew someone who worked there, a tall, skinny guy named Jip. I don't think Jip was his real name, no, but I never learned any other. Jip and Abalyn had dated briefly, and he always gave her the employee discount. We got ice cream and watched the punks and goths and skater kids. Halfway through the afternoon, I splurged and ponied up eighteen dollars so we could get into the Harvard Museum of Natural History on Oxford Street.

The first time I went to the museum was with Rosemary and Caroline. I think I must have been ten. It really hasn't changed much since then. I don't think it's changed much since it was founded in 1859 by a Swiss zoologist named Louis Agassiz. Lou-ee Aga-see. Especially the enormous Hall of Mammals, with all its tall glass cases and rickety, narrow balconies (or they might be catwalks) and wrought-iron filigree. It smells like dust and time. You can sit on a bench, surrounded by taxidermied giraffes and zebras, a rhino skull, primate specimens arranged to illustrate human evolution, and gigantic whale skeletons suspended from the ceiling high overhead. You can just sit there and marvel and be at peace. I have thought, on more than one occasion, that my great-aunt Caroline, the one who kept dead sparrows in stoppered bottles, might have loved this museum. But I don't think she ever visited. It has a fossil sand dollar collected by Charles Darwin in 1834.

Abalyn wanted to see the dinosaurs first, so we did, but then we walked through narrow hallways filled with hundreds of moth-eaten birds, fish, and reptiles mounted in lifelike positions. Abalyn said she'd never much cared for museums, though she'd been to two or three in New York City and Philadelphia when she was a kid. She told me about the Mütter Museum, which she said has to be one of the weirdest places on earth. I've never been myself, but her description made it sound that way. It's a medical museum filled with slivers of malignant flesh from very famous people, deformed fetuses in jars (she taught me the word *teratology*), and antique wax anatomical models. We sat together beneath the bones of a right whale (*Balaena australis*), and Abalyn told me about seeing the skull of a woman who'd had a horn growing from her forehead.

When no one was looking, we kissed while all those blind glass eyes watched on. I tasted her mouth in that silent reliquary.

I think it was one of the best days we ever spent together. I would press it between wax-paper pages like a rosebud or a four-leaf clover, if I knew how to capture and hold memories that way. But I don't. Know how, I mean. And memories fade. I have no photographs from that day. I have the odd little plastic tag they gave me to wear to show that I'd paid to get in. I have that in a box somewhere. Right after Abalyn left, and after Eva (first and second time), sometimes I would wear that tag.

On the way back to Providence, I dozed. I've always liked sleeping on trains. The steel-wheel-on-rail rhythm of trains lulls me to sleep. I leaned on Abalyn and slept, and she woke me when we were pulling into the station.

I just wanted to write something about that day, because whichever day of the week it was, it was the last day that things were all right that summer. It was the last day, that summer, that I thought Abalyn and I might last. The calm before the storm; sometimes we speak in clichés because there aren't any better words. Anyway. If I manage to tell the story of November wolf Eva, in that version we had many more good days than in this first version of my ghost story.

Abalyn made spaghetti with marinara sauce for dinner, and we watched cartoons.

Sometime past midnight, I was getting sleepy and telling her childhood stories, stories about my mother and grandmother and my asshole father. I promised to show her my "how Daddy should die" list (I never did). She found the idea of the list very funny. I asked her why, as I'd never thought it was funny, and I said so.

"Sorry," she said. "I have my own Nightmare Father tales. At some point, I had to try to stop letting them gnaw at me and try to laugh at how awful and idiotic it all was. Is. You know. I mean, he's still alive."

"Mine might be," I told her. "I have no idea. I don't want to know."

"Good for you," she said, and switched off the television in the middle of an episode of *Ren & Stimpy*. (Abalyn maintained that no good cartoons had been made since the mid-nineties, and wouldn't even talk about SpongeBob. I'd never watched very many cartoons, so I didn't argue.) She set the remote down and folded her legs into a sloppy sort of lotus position. We were sitting on the floor, because she said you should always sit on the floor when you watch cartoons. We were eating Trix cereal, dry out of the box, which she said was another important part of her cartoon-watching ritual.

Abalyn talked about her dad, whom she called the Holy Grail of Douchebags. She told me how he'd punched her in the face when she came out, and she showed me a scar above her left eyebrow. "From his class ring," she said. "Mom, she just said how she wished I was dead, or that I'd never been born. Or, at least, that she wished I was *only* gay. I was sixteen years old, and that was the day I left home."

"Where'd you go?"

"Here and there, couch surfing. Was homeless a couple of times, which wasn't as bad as you might think. It was better than life under the Holy Grail of Douchebags and my mother. There's an old warehouse on Federal Hill where I used to crash with some other kids. We panhandled, Dumpster-dived, turned tricks, shit like that. Whatever it took to get from one day to the next. Things got a lot better later on, when I hooked up with a guy and he asked me to move in with him."

I asked if he was the same guy who'd paid for her reassignment surgery.

"Nah, not him. This was another guy. Phil from Pawtucket."

"You lived in Pawtucket?"

"No, but Phil had, before we met. He always used to introduce himself to people as 'Phil from Pawtucket.' He was sort of a skeeze, but it beat living on the street. And he had a wicked stereo."

"I'm sorry it had to be that way."

"Hey, knew lots of kids had it worse."

"But to have your mother wish you'd never been born?" Which, frankly, shocked me a lot more than getting punched by your father. "How does someone just stop loving her child?"

"No fucking idea. Maybe she never loved me to start with. I always figured that made the most sense. Anyway, that was years and years ago. I don't dwell on it. The past is the past. Let it lie."

I apologized if I'd been the one who'd brought it up, the whole transsexual thing, childhood, parents. I wasn't sure if it had been her or me. She ate a handful of Trix and said not to worry about it, then added, "Like I said, I laugh as much as I can. I laugh to keep the wolves at bay."

I laugh to keep the wolves at bay.

Did you laugh, Mr. Saltonstall? Did you, Mr. Perrault, to keep your wolves at bay? Did you, and then did you each forget how, or did the wolves get too big? Too big, too bad, so they huffed and puffed and, my, what big eyes you have until you fell off that horse and wrecked that motorcycle. Mother, did you have wolves? Caroline, did you?

"Stop it," Imp typed, hitting the keys just a little too hard so that the "O" key punched tiny holes in the paper. "This isn't the *wolf* ghost story. This is the *mermaid* ghost story. Don't mix them up."

Don't mix them up.

That's like trying to keep day and night apart with no twilight or dawn in between. I might as well try that. I'd be just as successful.

Now, I'm well aware that Abalyn's earlier claim to have graduated high school, then attended URI to study bioinformatics, seems to conflict with her story of leaving home at sixteen and living on the street. But it never seemed to matter to me if somehow both were true, or if one was a lie and she was just a lousy liar, mixing up her tales like that. Or if she didn't care what people thought, and maybe she changed her biography as often as she changed her clothes. It was none of my business.

Anyway, "Like I said, I laugh as much as I can. I laugh to keep the wolves at bay."

"I shouldn't have brought it up. We can change the subject if you'd rather not talk about it. I won't mind."

She smiled at me, a very slight sort of smile, and ate another handful of Trix. "It's cool," she said. "It happened. The stuff that happens to you makes you who you are, for better or worse. Besides, you let me read your story. So, it's sort of like reciprocation."

"No, it's not. This is much more personal than my short story."

"I'm a tranny, Imp. Usually, I don't try to pretend any different. If I do, when I have, it just tends to make matters worse. This is me. I live with it."

"Well—and I hope this doesn't sound too freaky—but I think it's kind of neat. I mean, how many people ever experience physical transformation on the level you have? Starting off one thing and becoming another thing. Making that choice. You're brave."

She stared at me a moment, then said, "I've always been a woman, Imp. The hormones and surgery, they didn't change me from one thing to another. That's why I hate the phrase 'sex change.' It's misleading. No one ever changed my sex. They just brought my flesh more in line with my mind. With my gender. Also, not so sure there really was a choice. I don't think I'd be alive if I hadn't done it. If I *couldn't* have done it." She didn't sound angry or put out with me. She spoke patiently, though there was something weary in the back of her voice, and I wondered how many times Abalyn had explained this, and to how many different people. "I don't think it even means I'm brave," she added.

I felt stupid, and started to apologize, but I didn't. Sometimes, apologies don't help at all.

When Rosemary killed herself, the hospital apologized to me. When Caroline killed herself, Rosemary didn't apologize, and it was better that way.

"I still think it's neat," I said. I said lamely. "Even if you had to, even if there wasn't really choice, and if they didn't really change your sex." Truthfully, though, I didn't understand, but I would. In the weeks and months to come, surviving Eva and surviving Eva, I'd learn a lot more—too much—about being one sort of being on the inside and another on the outside. About being held prisoner by flesh, and wanting to be free so badly that death finally becomes an option, the way it became an option for my mother and grandmother. Trapped in a body, trapped in a mind. I don't think the one's so different from the other. No, I am absolutely *not* implying that Abalyn's being transgender was the same as Caroline and Rosemary and me being crazy. There are traps everywhere I look, and I've read the stories about coyotes chewing off their paws to get out of traps. Coyotes and bobcats and raccoons and wolves. And wolves. And wolves. The steel jaws clamp down, merciless, unforgiving, and you hurt until you do what has to be done if you mean to survive. Or leave the world. Which is why, even now, I can't hate Eva Canning. Or any other ghost.

"Maybe," Abalyn said. "I'm not insulted if that's how it strikes you. Someday it's not going to seem so strange to people. At least, I like to hope it won't. I like to believe that someday it will be generally understood it's just how some people are. Gay. Straight. Transgender. Black. White. Blue eyes. Hazel eyes. Fish. Fowl. What the hell ever."

"Crazy or sane," I said.

"Sure, that, too," and she smiled again. It was a less reserved smile than the first time, and I was glad to see it. It made me feel less awkward.

"Have some more Trix," she said, holding the box out to me. "You know, for kids."

"Silly rabbit," I said, then sat picking out a bunch of the lemony yellow ones.

She began talking again, and I just crunched my handful of cereal and listened. She hated her voice, but I miss it so badly some days I don't want to hear anyone else's.

"When I was a child, I used to have this dream. Back before I was even sure what was going on. I must have had it a hundred times before I got the message. I'll tell you, if you really want to hear."

I nodded yes, because I don't like to talk with my mouth full.

"Okay, and this is at least as personal as your short story, and don't try to tell me it isn't."

I swallowed and promised her I wouldn't.

"Okay, when I was a child, before I figured out I wasn't a boy, I used to have this dream. I'm not gonna call it a nightmare. It was scary, but it never struck me as a nightmare." Abalyn reached for her pack of cigarettes and took one out, but she didn't light it. She never smoked in the apartment. "You know the story of Phyllis and Demophoön?"

I did, because I've always loved Greek and Roman myths, but I lied and told her I didn't. I figured it might ruin her story somehow, if she knew that I was familiar with Phyllis and Demophoön.

"Demophoön was an Athenian king, and he married Phyllis, who was a daughter of the king of Thrace. Right after they were married, he had to leave to fight in the Trojan War. She waited and waited for him to come home again. She stood at the seashore and waited, but years passed and he didn't return. She finally hung herself, thinking he'd been slain in battle. But the goddess Athena took pity on her, and brought her back to life as an almond tree. But Demophoön hadn't been killed, and when he came home, he embraced the almond tree and it bloomed."

"That's not how I heard it," I said, and she stopped and glared at me.

"Imp, you just said you didn't know it."

I was annoyed at myself for slipping and blurting out the truth, but I told her I'd forgotten I knew it. "Hearing you tell it, I remembered."

"All right, well, anyway, I think we'd studied the story in school. *Bulfinch's Mythology*, or whatever. Maybe that's how it began."

"You dreamed about them?" I asked, wishing I'd stop butting in, but interrupting anyway.

"No, I didn't. And maybe that wasn't even the right place to start telling about the dreams. It's just the first thing popped into my head. But I did dream that I was a tree. I'd been walking through very narrow city streets, the buildings so close together I could hardly see the sky when I looked up. It was hard to even be sure if it was night or day. I think it was usually day. It was an ugly city, garbage and rats everywhere. The air was so filthy it made my nose sting. The sidewalks were packed with hundreds and hundreds of people, and they were all going one way, and I was trying to go the other. I was terrified that I'd fall and they'd crush me. I knew they wouldn't stop and help me up, or even go around me or step over. They'd just stomp me. I came to an alley that was even narrower than the street, and I managed to get loose from the crowd and hide there."

"But you said you were a tree, right?"

"That part comes later. On the sidewalk and in the alley, I was still just me."

"You were a boy?"

She frowned and said she'd *looked* like a boy.

"I couldn't breathe, not after the press of all those bodies. They'd all kept staring at me, really hatefully, like the sight of me made them furious. When I reached the alley, I saw that it was a dead end. There was just a brick wall at the end and more trash cans, so there I was, thinking I'd live the rest of my life in an alley, because I sure as fuck wasn't going back out into that crowd. But then I saw a fire escape. Someone had left the lowest ladder down, and I went to it and started climbing, just wanting to see the sky again. I climbed for a long time, the building was so tall. And when I passed windows, there were people looking out at me. All the windows had iron bars. Burglar bars, I guess. But it made the people in the apartments seem like they were in jail. Their eyes were white, and I knew they were jealous, even if I didn't know why. Some of them pressed their palms against the glass. I tried hard not to look at them, and I climbed as fast as I dared. I held on tight to the railing and didn't look down through the grating. I never wanted to see that alleyway again. Wherever the fire escape led, I was determined I was never climbing back down again.

"Eventually, I came to the top, but it wasn't the roof of the building. It was a green field. I was so tired from pushing against the crowd, and then having to climb the fire escape, I collapsed in the grass. I wanted to cry, but I didn't let myself. I lay there for the longest time, smelling dandelions, trying to catch my breath. And when I looked up again, there was a woman with white hair, hair so white maybe it was silver, standing above me. She had the astrological symbol for Mars drawn on her forehead in red. Sometimes, it was drawn in ink, and other times in blood. Sometimes it was tattooed on her skin. Her skin was as pale as milk."

"That's also the symbol for male," I said. "The astrological symbol for Mars. The circle with the arrow. The female symbol is associated with Venus. The circle with the cross below it."

"Jesus," she sighed, and glared at me again. "I know that, Imp.

Even then I knew it." She took back the box of Trix. "You want to hear the rest of this or what?"

"I do," I told her. "I really do."

Abalyn set the cereal box down next to the remote control. "So, she stood there over me, this pale, silver-haired woman. And she said, 'Daughter, which will you choose? The Road of Needles or the Road of Pins?' I told her I was sorry, but I didn't know what she meant. I did, but in the dream I didn't remember that I did. She said—"

"It's easier to fasten things together with pins," I whispered, interrupting for the fourth, fifth, or sixth time. But Abalyn didn't look put out with me; she looked surprised. "The Road of Needles is much more difficult, as it's much more difficult to hold things together with needles. Is that what she said to you?"

"Yeah," Abalyn said, not whispering, but speaking softly. The way I recall it, she went a little pale. But that's probably just my memory embellishing. She probably didn't, not really. "That's it, pretty much. You know what it means?"

"It's from one of the old French folk variants of 'Little Red Riding Hood,' back before it was written down. That's the choice the wolf gives the girl when they meet in the forest. In other versions, the roads are called the Road of Pebbles and the Road of Thorns. And the Road of Roots and the Road of the Stones in the Tyrol. I sort of know a lot about 'Little Red Riding Hood.'"

"Clearly," Abalyn said, still not quite whispering.

"I hate that story," I confided, and then I asked, "Which did you choose?"

"I didn't. I refused to choose. And so the silver-haired woman turned me into a tree."

"Like Phyllis."

"Right," she replied, then didn't say anything more for a whole minute or two. That awkward silence felt as if it stretched on forever, but it couldn't have been more than two minutes. I was beginning to think Abalyn wouldn't finish telling me about the dream, when she said, "I was a tree for years. That's how it seemed. I saw the green field turn brown, and then winter came and covered it with snow. And then spring came, and it was green again. Over and over I watched the seasons change. My leaves turned yellow and gold and drifted to the ground. My limbs would bare, and then there would be buds and shoots and there were fresh new leaves. It wasn't unpleasant, especially not after being lost in the city. I almost wanted to stay a tree forever, but I knew the silver-haired woman wouldn't allow it, that, sooner or later, she'd be back to ask the question again."

"What sort of tree?" I asked.

"I don't know. I don't know shit about trees."

"Did she come back?"

"She did. And, like I thought she would, she asked the question again, the Road of Pins or the Road of Needles. I chose the Road of Needles, because I suspected she'd think I was a coward or lazy if I chose the easier of the two. I was grateful, for her letting me be a tree, and I didn't want to disappoint her, or for her to think I was ungrateful."

"Little Red Cap chose the Road of Pins."

"And she got eaten by a wolf."

. . . to keep my wolves at bay.

"I never actually dreamed of walking on the Road of Needles, not literally," she said. "Metaphorically, I did. It was all a metaphor, after all." She looked down at the unlit cigarette between her fingers, and I almost told her to go ahead and smoke. But then she was talking again. "Did I mention that the mark on her forehead wasn't Mars anymore? It was Venus."

"I guessed that part," I told her.

She nodded. "After that, it gets sort of silly. Childish I mean."

"You *were* a child."

"Yeah. Still."

"So, what was so silly? What happened next?"

"She said that I'd learned to be patient. That I'd learned I couldn't get what I wanted all at once, and it was hardly ever easy. I'd learned I might not ever get it. And this is the way of the world, she told me, and I wouldn't receive any special favors. But then, she touched the mark on her forehead, and I became a girl. Just for an instant, before I always woke up. I'd lay there, after, trying so hard to go back to sleep, wanting to find my way back into the dream and never wake up again."

"I don't think that's so childish," I said.

She shrugged and muttered, "Whatever. My shrink was of the opinion I'd never had the dream, that it was only a sort of reassuring story I'd made up to give myself hope or some shit. But I did have that dream, I don't know how many times. I still have it, but not very often. Not like back then."

"It doesn't matter, if it was a dream or a story, does it?" I asked her, and she said she didn't like being called a liar on those occasions when she was not, in fact, lying.

"It helped, though."

That elicited another shrug. "No idea. I can't see how my life would have gone differently without it. My decisions seem almost inevitable in hindsight."

"You never told your parents about the dream." It wasn't a question, because I was already certain enough of the answer.

"Hell no. My mother might have murdered her demon child in its sleep if I'd told her. My dad might have come after me with a hot iron poker." She laughed, and I asked what she meant about a hot poker.

She laughed and put the cigarette back into the pack of Marlboros. "That's what people used to do if they thought the fairies had stolen their child and left a changeling in its place. Fairies can't stand iron, so—"

"But if they were wrong—"

"Exactly," she said.

I remembered then about changelings and hot pokers, or tossing children that might be changelings onto glowing coals, or leaving them outside on a freezing night. (See *Strange and Secret Peoples: Fairies and Victorian Consciousness* by Carole G. Silver [Oxford University Press, 1999], Chapter 2.) But I didn't tell Abalyn I remembered. No, I don't know why. No, I do. It struck me as irrelevant. What I knew and didn't know, it didn't have anything to do with this ghost story, which was Abalyn's and *not* mine. Not mine at all. Except, the bit about changelings, because of what had happened already and what would happen. Seeing an illusion, put there to deceive or protect me, but either way to conceal the truth (or just the facts). Butler Hospital changing its name. Eva and Eva, July and November. *The Drowning Girl* and all those terrible paintings and sculptures Perrault made. In hindsight, as Abalyn said, all these come down to changelings, don't they?

Imp typed, "Eva and Eva, maybe. You're not so sure about all the rest."

No, I'm not. But Eva Canning. What climbed into my car, what I found in a wild place and brought home, what left and bided its time, then came back to me both times.

"Is this the sort of conversation that normal couples have?" I asked Abalyn, and that made her smile.

"You're asking the wrong woman about what's normal," she replied. "Anyhow, is that what we are now, a couple?"

"Isn't it?" Hearing the question, I was suddenly afraid I'd misspoken, or been mistaken, that I'd fucked it all up.

"Sure, Imp. If you want to put a name on it."

"I do, but only if you don't mind. If I'm wrong, if that isn't what we are . . . that would be okay. I mean—"

And then she kissed me. I think she kissed me so I'd shut up. I was glad, because hearing myself, I wanted very badly to shut up. Words start coming out of my mouth like rocks rolling down a hill, and every now and then someone has to stop me. It was a long kiss.

When it was over, I asked if I could play some of Rosemary's records for her, some of the ones that were my favorites. "I'll try to avoid the really schmaltzy stuff. And you don't have to, you know, pretend to like anything you don't," I told her.

"I won't," she assured me, and crossed her heart. "Though, wasn't I gonna give you the musical education, and not the other way round?"

"First, you ought to know what you're up against."

So for the next three hours we lay on the thrift-store cushions in front of Rosemary's turntable and listened to Rosemary's records. I played songs off Elton John's *Madman Across the Water*, *Dreamboat Annie* by Heart (which she decided she liked), Jethro Tull's *Aqualung*, and Blue Öyster Cult's *Agents of Fortune*. She wouldn't let me play anything by the Doobie Brothers or Bruce Springsteen. She got up a couple of times, and strummed air guitar. We listened to the hiss and pop of the scratchy vinyl, and kissed, and didn't talk about bad dreams or childhood or changelings. It was after four before we went to bed and that long, long day ended. Our last good day (in the July ghost story). Our last day before the gallery, and the river, the bathtub, and Abalyn leaving me.

My fingers hurt from typing, and this is as good a place to stop as any. To stop for now, I mean.

I'm not sure how many days transpired between our last good day and the day when, for the first time since I met Abalyn, I visited the RISD Museum. It might have been no more than one or two. Surely, not more than three. I do, however, know it was a Thursday evening, which would have made it the third Thursday of July (admission is free after five, the third Thursday of each month; I try never to pay admission). But I admit this timeline doesn't seem right. There was the afternoon Abalyn and I almost quarreled, and then our last good day, and . . . I don't recall the latter coming so quickly on the heels of the former. So here's something else to cause me to doubt my memories. If it *was* the third Thursday of July 2008 (so, the seventeenth), then Abalyn might not have left until early August, and I was almost certain she went at the end of July. Time is warping. It begins to feel like my *perception* of time is collapsing back on itself, compressing events and recollections.

I'm driving with the window rolled partway down. The city is shrouded in a long summer twilight, no clouds in the violet-blue sky, and I cross the Point Street Bridge. There are two swans floating on the river, and a cormorant is perched on a rotten old piling. The piling juts from the river like a broken bone, and the cormorant spreads its wings, drying its feathers. There's a lot of traffic, and the air stinks of car exhaust and my own sweat. I catch a whiff of scorched crust from a pizza place, just before turning onto South Main. I haven't had dinner, and I skipped lunch; the burned-bread smell reminds me I'm hungry.

I told Abalyn I was going to the library. She didn't ask which one, though if she had, I'd have told her the public library downtown. The central branch of the public library is open until eight thirty on Mondays and Thursdays. She had a deadline, and didn't ask to come along.

"Be careful," she said, without looking up from her laptop.

"I will," I replied, and when she asked if I had my cell phone, I told her I did. I reminded her there was leftover Chinese in the fridge.

The night before, I dreamed of *The Drowning Girl*, and the next day—this day—I couldn't stop thinking of the painting. I was distracted at work, and kept making stupid mistakes when I rang people up or tried to show them to the aisle they were looking for. Then, on the way home from work, I turned on the wrong street and got lost. I hardly said a word to Abalyn until I told her I was going out. I had it in my head that if I saw the painting, if I confronted it, maybe I could stop obsessing over it.

There are trees on South Main, and the wind through the Honda's open window smells less of automobiles. I park opposite the museum gift shop, and linger by the car a moment, thinking it might be a mistake, coming here. Wishing I'd have asked Abalyn to come with me. I could climb back into the Honda and drive straight home again. Then I tell myself that I'm behaving like a coward, stuff the keys in my pocket, cross the street, and go inside, where it's cool and the air smells clean.

There's a special exhibit up devoted to artists' models as depicted *by* artists, and I use it as a convenient excuse to avoid confronting *The Drowning Girl* for another twenty minutes or so. There are pieces on display by Picasso, Klimt, Matisse, Angelica Kauffmann, paintings and charcoal studies and photographs, a cartoon from *The New Yorker*. I stop and examine each one closely, but I can't really focus on any of them. It's impossible to concentrate on these images, no matter how exquisitely executed or revealing or intimate they might be. This isn't why I've come.

Get it over with, I think. But not in my *own* thought voice. This is the voice I dreamed of the night before, the voice I've dreamed repeatedly, the voice I first heard that night by the Blackstone River. I take out my phone and almost call Abalyn. I notice one of the docents watching me, and I return the phone to the bag I'm carrying and walk away. I move through one gallery after the other until I come to that small octagonal room with its loden-green walls and ornate gilt frames. There are eleven oil paintings by New England artists, but the first one you see, entering from the south, is Saltonstall's. I quickly avert my eyes and turn my back on it. I slowly move around the room clockwise, pausing before each canvas before moving along to the next. Each painting brings me a few steps nearer *The Drowning Girl*, and I keep reminding myself it's not too late; I can still leave the museum without having caught more than the briefest glimpse of the thing.

(*Thing.* I type the word, and it seems hideous to me. It seems filled with an indefinable threat. It has too many possible meanings, and none of them are specific enough to simply dismiss out of hand. But by that evening I had made a thing of *The Drowning Girl.* Probably, I'd been busy making a thing of it since Rosemary brought me to the museum on the occasion of my eleventh birthday, almost eleven years before.)

There's a docent in this room, too, and he's watching me. Do I seem suspicious? Does the anxiety show on my face? Is he just bored, and I'm something new to occupy his attention? I ignore him and try hard to pretend to be interested in those other compositions—two landscapes by Thomas Cole (1828 and 1847), Martin Johnson Heade's *Brazilian Forest* (1864) and *Salt Marshes of Newburyport, Massachusetts* (1875–1878), and the last before Saltonstall, William Bradford's *Arctic Sunset* (1874). That makes five. Were I the Catholic that my mother cautioned me against becoming, it would make somewhat more sense that it suddenly occurs to me how this was like the grim, grotesque procession of the Stations of the Cross, stopping before each painting. But I'm not Catholic, and it seems very odd. This, the fifth, *Arctic Sunset*, would be the scene where Simon of Cyrene carries the cross for Christ, and the next, the next will be Veronica wiping the brow of Jesus. The comparison is alien, another *thing* rising up to haunt me, and I push it away.

I push it away and, my mouth gone dry as dust and ashes, turn to confront the *thing* that has brought me here. And I do, but that thing, it's not Phillip George Saltonstall's painting of a woman standing in a river. I turn, and Eva Canning is standing in front of me. Just like that, as ridiculous as a scene in a horror movie, a scene that's meant to be unexpected, to startle you and make you jump in your seat. When it's over, you laugh nervously and feel silly. I don't jump. I don't laugh. I don't even breathe. I just stand there, staring at her. She's wearing the same red dress she might have been wearing the day I thought I saw her at Wayland Square. The same sunglasses, round lenses in wire frames that make me think of John Lennon. She smiles, and her limp blonde hair glimmers faintly beneath the lights. She isn't barefoot this time. She's wearing very simple leather sandals.

"India. What a pleasant surprise," she says. "You're the very last person I expected to see tonight." Her tone is warm and entirely cordial, as if we're nothing more remarkable than two old friends, meeting by chance. It's just a happy coincidence, that's all.

And I say the very first thing that occurs to me. I say, "You were in my head. A few minutes ago. You said, 'Get it over with.' " There's a tremble in my voice. My voice is a counterpoint to Eva's, as is what I've said, implying that this coincidence *isn't* happy. It may not even be a coincidence.

Her smile doesn't waver. "Was it, now?" she asks me, and I nod. "Well, you were dawdling. You were getting cold feet, weren't you?"

I don't say yes or no. I don't have to. She already knows the answer. Standing here before me, in such mundane surroundings, she strikes me as a *thing* taken out of context. The sight of Eva naked at the side of the road made more sense to me than the sight of her in the gallery, and in some ways she seems more naked here than she did when I first saw her. There's a wooden bench directly in front of *The Drowning Girl*, and she sits and motions for me to do the same. I glance at the docent, and he's still watching me. No, now he's watching us. I sit beside her.

"You came to see my painting," she says. (I'm very sure that's what she said. *My* painting. Not *the* painting.) "Where's Abalyn?" she asks.

"Home," I reply, the tremble fading from my voice. "She doesn't much like museums."

"I've been meaning to call and thank you. No telling what would have become of me if you hadn't come along. It was rude of me not to call. Oh, and I still have the clothes you lent me. I need to get those back to you."

"It wasn't an accident, was it? That night, I mean."

"No," she says. "No, Imp, it wasn't. But you didn't have to stop for me. That much was left up to you."

She isn't lying to me. There's no hint of deception here. She isn't denying anything, though I wish she were. I wish she would at least try to make it all less real. Do her best to render these events perfectly ordinary. I sit and stare at *The Drowning Girl*, and catch the familiar, comforting scent of the sea coming off Eva. It doesn't strike me as odd, her smelling like the sea. If anything, it only seems appropriate, consistent, inevitable.

"He was a sad sort of man," she says, and points at the painting. "He was a melancholy man. It was a shame, him dying so young, but hardly unexpected."

"So you don't believe his fall from the horse was an accident?"

"That's twice now you've used that word," she says. "You seem preoccupied with causality and circumstance. But no, I seriously doubt it was an accident. He was a very accomplished horseman, you know."

"I didn't know that," I tell her, and I don't take my eyes off the painting. Ironically, it strikes me as the safest place in the entire gallery to let my eyes linger, even though the dark woods behind Saltonstall's bather appear more threatful than they ever have before.

"I didn't have to stop," I say. "You mean that. I truly had a choice?"

"You did, Imp. You could have kept on driving and never looked back. No one's ever had to stop for me. Or even hear me. Anyway, you did, and now I'm afraid the time for choice is behind us both."

These words could have so many different meanings, and I don't want to know precisely which meaning she intends for them to have. So, I don't ask her to explain. I think, *I'll find out soon enough.*

"Was it because I'm crazy?" I ask, instead. "Is that why I heard you?"

"You're too hard on yourself," she says, and I don't really know what that means, either.

"Can I ask what happens next?"

She smiles again, but not the same way she smiled before. This smile makes her look frayed, and there's a sadness about it that makes me think of what she said about Phillip George Saltonstall.

"There's no script," she says, and straightens her spectacles. "No foregone conclusions. So, we'll both just have to wait and see what happens next. Me, as much as you."

"I don't want Abalyn to get hurt."

"You're not the sort of person who wishes harm to come to much of anyone, are you, Imp? Well, except your father, but I can't blame you for that."

I don't ask her how she knows about my father. I'd figured out enough to understand it's not important. Sitting there with her, I'm overwhelmed by an instant of déjà vu, stronger than any I've ever felt in my life. It makes me dizzy. It almost makes me ill.

"I should be getting home," I say, and shut my eyes.

"Yes, you should. She's waiting for you. She worries when you're out alone." And then Eva leans near and whispers into my right ear. Her breath is warm, but the smell of the sea grows cloying with her face so near mine. She exhales, and I think of mudflats at low tide. I think of mud and reeds and crabs. Quahogs waiting to be dug from their snug burrows. Stranded fish at the mercy of the sun and the gulls. Her words are drops of brackish, estuarine water, dripping into me, and I bite my lip and keep my eyes squeezed closed as tightly as I can.

" 'Turn not pale, beloved snail,' " she whispers. " 'But come and join the dance. Will you, won't you, won't you, will you join the dance? I'm waiting to hold you.' "

Her lips brush my earlobe, and I flinch. And I want to kiss her. I imagine those lips prowling over every inch of my body. The words drip, and I wonder how much water will fit inside my ear, inside my skull. How much before it spills out into my mouth and down my throat and I drown in the gentle flow of Eva Canning's words.

She whispers, " 'What matters it how far we go?' his scaly friend replied. 'There is another shore, you know, upon the other side.' "

Then she isn't speaking anymore, and I can no longer smell the tidal flats. I can only smell the clean museum air. I know she's gone, but I keep my eyes shut until the docent walks over and asks me if anything's wrong, if I'm okay. I open my eyes, and see that Eva's no longer sitting there beside me.

"Where did she go?" I ask. "Did you see her leave?"

"Who do you mean, ma'am?" the man wants to know, and he looks confused. He has that quizzical expression people get when they begin to realize there's something wrong with me.

I don't bother asking him a second time.

I've been thinking about what I wrote earlier regarding the word *thing*, and how a *thing* imperfectly defined, only half-glimpsed, has the potential to be so much more fearful than dangers seen with perfect clarity.

I spent a day and a half composing that sentence. I must have written twenty-five or thirty versions of it on various scraps of paper before letting myself type it here. I'm not a careful writer, not usually, and I've been especially lackadaisical writing this all out (another word Abalyn kidded me for using: "Imp, no one actually says 'lackadaisical'"). I've made little or no effort to rein in my disordered mind. As long as I set down the events, to the best of my ability, it hardly matters whether or not this manuscript is orderly.

But—the word *thing*. The vague concept of a *thing*, versus the concrete image of any given *thing*. I started thinking about the movie *Jaws*. I've already mentioned that I'm not particularly interested in movies, and I haven't seen all that many of them. Not compared to most people, I would think. Not compared to Abalyn, who often spoke in dialogue borrowed from movies, who peppered our conversations with allusions to films I'd never seen, but which she seemed to know by heart. Anyway, I have seen *Jaws*. I saw it before Abalyn and before Eva Canning. I'm still not sure whether or not I liked it, and that doesn't really matter. I'm sure it was one of the many things that inspired me to write "The Mermaid of the Concrete Ocean."

The film begins with the death of a young woman. Unlike the later victims, she isn't killed by a shark. No, she's killed and devoured by a *thing* we never see. She leaves her friends and the warmth of a campfire, leaves her friends and the safety of the shore, and she enters the cold sea. The sun is rising as she strips off her clothes and enters the sea. The water is black, and anything below it is hidden from our view. Some*thing* under the water seizes her, and she's hurled violently from side to side. She screams and desperately clutches at a bell buoy, as though it might save her. We hear her cry out, "It hurts." *It*, a word as terrible and empty of specificity as *thing*. The attack doesn't last very long. Less than a minute. And then she vanishes, pulled down into that black abyss off Amity Island, and we can only guess at *what* pulls her down. The sea is an accomplice to her attacker, concealing it, though this unseen force must lie only inches below the surface.

Later, when I encountered the story of Millicent Hartnett's having been bitten by some*thing* in the Blackstone River at Rolling

Dam, a some*thing* her friends never saw, I thought at once of this scene. I thought about how lucky Millicent Hartnett was that day in the summer of 1951. She might have been that girl who was pulled under in *Jaws*.

I didn't find the rest of the movie scary. It's only about a very large shark, which we are shown again and again and again. We are shown the shark, and then nothing is left to the imagination. A shark can only kill a woman. And a shark can be understood and reckoned with. A shark is only a fish that can be tracked down and destroyed by three men in a leaky little boat. It's no*thing* even as remotely unsettling as the opening scene's ~~villain~~.

I shouldn't have written *villain*, so I've struck it out. After all, whatever mauled and pulled the unlucky girl down to her death, it was only being whatever it was. She was the interloper. She came to *it*, invaded its world, not the other way round.

In Phillip George Saltonstall's painting, the threat is completely shrouded. It is a *thing* only implied. The nude woman stands in murky river water, the same murky river where, fifty-three years after the painting was finished, Millicent Hartnett would be bitten by some*thing* no one ever saw. The same murky water said to be haunted by "the Siren of Millville." The woman in the painting is glancing back over her shoulder towards the shore and a shadowy forest that imply threat. She has turned away from the placid water in the foreground, which may be as charged with menace as the trees. The trees might only be misdirection, an act of prestidigitation fashioned to distract the woman from a hazard that doesn't lurk behind the trees, but beneath the deceptively calm water.

She stands poised between Scylla and Charybdis, having waded naively into a makeshift New England equivalent of the Strait of Messina.

It isn't what we see. It's what we are left to envision. This is the genius of *The Drowning Girl*, and the genius of so many of Albert

Perrault's loathsome paintings. We are told that the hulking forms surrounding the kneeling girl in *Fecunda ratis* are wolves, but they don't exactly look like wolves. They might be any*thing* else. This is *Jaws*' and Saltonstall's trick reversed, but to the same effect. The summoning of the unknown.

It isn't the known we fear most. The known, no matter how horrible or perilous to life and limb, is something we can wrap our brains around. We can always respond to the known. We can draw plans against it. We can learn its weaknesses and defeat it. We can recover from its assaults. So simple a thing as a bullet might suffice. But the unknown, it slips through our fingers, as insubstantial as fog.

H. P. Lovecraft (1890–1937), a reclusive writer who lived here in Providence (and to whom I am distantly related), wrote, "The oldest and strongest emotion of mankind is fear, and the oldest and strongest kind of fear is fear of the unknown." I've never much cared for Lovecraft. His prose is too florid, and I find his stories silly. But Abalyn was a fan of his writing. Anyway, he's not wrong about our fear of the unknown. He hits the nail on the head.

"What are you getting at?" Imp typed. "You're losing me. You were sitting on a ~~beach~~ bench in a museum with Eva Canning, and first she was there and then she wasn't anymore. First, the docent saw her, and then he hadn't. And she wasn't hidden. You saw her plain as day. A pale, blonde woman in a red dress and leather sandals. A pale woman with cornflower blue eyes, who sat next to you, who leaned in and touched you. She hid nothing."

No. No.

That's a lie. What she let me see was some*thing* like the tangible, ordinary, vulnerable flesh of the shark we finally see in *Jaws*. She showed me that to conceal the scene at the beginning of the movie, to mask the unknown swimming below the surface of her. That evening was the third time she came to me clothed in the skin of a woman, because, I think, she knew I wasn't yet ready to see the truth of her. The truth of her was then and always will be, ultimately, unknown. Very soon, she would show me things I could only halfway comprehend, but no mystery I'd ever actually penetrate. The unknown is immune to the faculties of human reason. Eva Canning taught me that much, if she taught me nothing else.

> *"Will you walk a little faster?" said a whiting*
> *to a snail.*
> *"There's a porpoise close behind us, and he's*
> *treading on my tail."*

Imp types, "That evening in the museum, even if she hid her true face, she didn't lie to you. She answered all your questions. She warned you what was coming, even if the warning was veiled. This is, at best, a paradox."

Imp types. I type. "I see that, too."

> *"Will you, won't you, will you, won't you,*
> *will you join the dance?"*

Perhaps I should rip up these last few pages. Maybe I have no idea what I'm trying to say. Or I should have spent many more days working out each and every sentence on countless scraps of paper, not daring to fit them together until every word had been unerringly selected.

I am not even sure I can hear my own voice anymore. Very soon now, as I tell my ghost story, that's what I'll say to Abalyn, that I'm not even sure I can hear my own voice anymore.

Did *you* join the dance, Rosemary Anne? That last night in the hospital, did a siren come to you and tell *you* how delightful it would be when they take us up and throw us with the lobsters out to sea? Did you listen?

"So, Saltonstall went to the Blackstone River, and he saw something there, something happened there, and it haunted him." I wrote that sentence many pages ago, back when I was pretty sure I'd never get this far with the story of my ghost story. I need to return to what Saltonstall saw before moving along to the worst of it. I mean, the worst of *this* first incarnation of my haunting.

The detached sliver of my mind that is acting as The Reader is eager to know what happens next, even though she ought to comprehend that I'll only divulge the narrative in my own time, as I find the courage to do so. I didn't set out to appease the Tyranny of Plot. Lives do not unfold in tidy plots, and it's the worst sort of artifice to insist that the tales we tell—to ourselves and to one another—must be forced to conform to the plot, A-to-Z linear narratives, three acts, the dictates of Aristotle, rising action and climax and falling action and most especially the artifice of resolution. I don't see much resolution in the world; we are born and we live and we die, and at the end of it there's only an ugly mess of unfinished business.

There was no resolution for me and Abalyn, and as for Eva Canning, I'm still chasing closure. That's such an idiotic word, such an idiotic concept, closure.

Saltonstall died still searching for closure. Albert Perrault died before he ever got that far.

It's just an accident that I found out exactly what Saltonstall claimed he saw at Rolling Dam that inspired *The Drowning Girl*. It's something else buried in his correspondence with Mary Farnum, letters that'll likely never be indexed or published, and that are scattered between three different institutions. That afternoon in August 2002, the day I found a brief mention of Saltonstall and the phantom said to haunt the Blackstone River in Smithfield's *A Concise History of New England Painters and Illustrators*, a librarian at the

Athenaeum who knew I was trying to dig up whatever I could on
Saltonstall mentioned that some of his letters had ended up in the
John Hay Library at Brown University. She had an acquaintance
there and volunteered to give him a call and schedule a time I could
examine them. I went to the Hay a week later, and this is what I
found (in a letter to Mary, dated March 7th, 1897):

My Dearest, Darling Mary,

*I hope that you and your mother are well, and that your
father is doing better than when last I visited. In three short
days, I'll be leaving for Baltimore, and I felt I should write
once more before my trip south. If I am very fortunate,
the journey will prove a success and I'll return with some
measure of financial security guaranteed for the year to
come! I wish you were coming with me, as I feel certain
you would love that city and all its delights.*

*In your last letter you asked about my fright last summer
at the dam, and I admit I'd not intended to elaborate on
that strange day. Indeed, I do now regret ever having
mentioned it to you. I'd prefer you not spend your evening
dwelling on such morbid, uncanny affairs, which would be
more at home in a story by Poe or Le Fanu than in our
exchange of letters. But you were so insistent, and you
know that I have yet to discover the resolve to deny you
that which is within my power to grant. And so, I will
relent, but have you know I've done so reluctantly.*

*That particular afternoon I'd decided to move farther
away from the dam (on the Millville side). A man in town
had been kind enough to inform me of a level, stony patch
of bank much favored by local fishermen and by the boys
who come down to swim. I found it a most agreeable
vantage point, affording me a clear and unobstructed view*

of the last bend in the river, just past the boggy slough. I would say there is an eeriness about the spot, but my opinion has undoubtedly been colored by the occurrence I'm about to relate. Still, being in that place made me uneasy, despite the amenable field of vision, and I wondered that the spot was said to be so popular.

It was quite late, and I was catching the last good light, finishing up one last sketch before packing away my charcoal and easel. My attention was occupied by the forest directly opposite where I stood. The river is, at this spot, fifty feet across, hardly more than the breadth of the dam. So what I saw, I saw clearly. There was a rustling in the underbrush on the farther shore, which I at first took to be a deer coming down to drink. But instead a young woman emerged from the thick growth of maples (uncommonly dense there, I'd add). She was attired very plainly, and I imagined her a woman from Millville or Blackstone. She looked my way, or seemed to, and I waved, but she showed no sign of having seen me. I called out to her, but still failed to get her attention, unless, of course, she was purposely ignoring me. Supposing her business to be none of mine own, I quickly added her to my sketch. I took my eyes away from her no more than the space of half a minute, but when I looked again, she'd undressed and stepped into the water far enough that it reached her knees. I do not wish you to think me a man of dissolute morals (though I know all artists are generally supposed to be just that), but I didn't immediately look away. She glanced back at the trees several times, and it occurred to me how very deep the shadows were beneath the maples. The shadows there seemed almost possessed of a solidity, a quality more than the mere absence of light caused by their boughs blocking the daylight. Returning to my earlier mention of a deer, it struck me that she had about her the same wariness as a doe, having heard the approach of footsteps in the moment that she raises her head before dashing away to safety.

Now, Mary, this next part I shall not be offended if you discredit completely, writing it off to the heat of the day, to my having taken too much sun, and to my general exhaustion. In fact, I'd prefer you did just that. All at once, there was a commotion in the water only a yard or so from the woman, as if a large fish were thrashing about just below the surface. You are no doubt familiar with that sight, a very large carp or salmon breaking the surface in pursuit of an unlucky dragonfly. But this disturbance persisted beyond the duration one would expect to be produced by a hungry fish. The initial splash grew into a froth. I can think of no more apt word for what it was than that. And a few seconds later, the unclothed woman turned to face the churning river. I stood up, alarmed, believing that surely she'd back away, returning to the shore lest the commotion prove a threat. But she did not. Rather, she appeared to stare at it most intently.

It was then that a pitchy shape leapt up from the river. I know that is a vague description, but I can do no better. It was visible only for an instant, and it never coalesced into anything more distinct. Still, it left me with the disquieting impression that I'd beheld not any manner of fish, but possibly a great serpent, thick around as a telegraph pole and greater in size than any serpent I'd imagined lived anywhere outside the African or Amazonian tropics. Not a genuine serpent, but that's the nearest comparison I can

*draw, if I attempt to fashion of it anything more substantial
than the shadows beneath the maples. I made to shout to
the woman to move away, but by then the shape had
vanished, as had the woman, and the water was so calm I
could scarce believe I'd actually seen anything at all. At
once, I began packing my things, genuinely disturbed and
desiring nothing more than to be clear of the river with all
possible haste.*

*There. Now you have it, Mary. The entirety of my
macabre episode by the river, and I should think your
curiosity duly satisfied and ask you to put the affair out of
your mind. It is wholly absurd, and I do not credit my
senses with having been faithful to me on that day. On my
way back through Millville, I did happen to mention what I
thought I'd seen to a man at the mercantile, and clearly he
suspected me unhinged and he politely refused to speak on
the matter. I'd not have people regarding you with the same
dubiety!*

*I will close, but be assured I shall send, at the least, a
picture souvenir card while in Balt. Be well.*

Fondly,
PG

Had Saltonstall heard the tales of the ghost of Perishable Shippen? I've found nothing in any of his letters to indicate he had. If he
had, wouldn't you think he'd have mentioned the tradition here?

My eyes are smarting, and my fingertips are sore. These keys are
sticky and need oiling. Anyway, I don't have the heart, or the stomach, or whatever, to write about the things that happened after Eva
came to me at the museum. Not just yet. Tomorrow, maybe. Maybe
tomorrow.

"Imp, it won't be any easier tomorrow than it would be today. Don't fool yourself into thinking it will."

I didn't say it would be easier. I said I'm just not up to it right now. I want to get this over with. I want to spit it out so I don't have to dread spitting it out. It's a goddamn lump in my throat. It hurts, and I want to cough it up, please.

6

(A PLAY IN FIVE ACTS)

RISING ACTION (1)

Act One: Hairshirt

Abalyn and I didn't go to the Blackstone River the day after Eva Canning came to me in the museum. Usually, it seems that way, but then I stop and think, and realize there were days in between. There was a visit to Dr. Ogilvy in between. I didn't hear the receptionist when she said I could go in. I was too busy scribbling in the margins of pages in a year-old issue of *Redbook*. Eventually, Dr. Ogilvy came out to see if there was something wrong, and she found me writing in the magazine. I'd written lines from "The Lobster Quadrille" over and over again, over and over, out of order. She asked if I was okay, "Imp, is something wrong?" and when I didn't answer (I was trying to, but my head was too full of Lewis Carroll) she asked if she could look at what I'd written. I blinked a few times and relinquished the copy of *Redbook*.

She stared at my messy handwriting, and then wanted to know what it meant. Not what it *was*, but what it *meant*.

"I don't know," I said, tapping my pen against my leg and reaching for another magazine (*Cosmopolitan*, I think). "But I can't get it out of my head."

She said it would be better to talk in her office, and she said if I needed to take the magazine in with me, that was perfectly okay. By then, I was fifteen minutes into my hour. Dr. Ogilvy's office is small, and decorated with butterflies and beetles and other colorful insects pinned inside glass frames. She once told me she almost studied entomology in college.

"India, when you say you can't get this out of your head, I assume you mean the thoughts are involuntary and unwelcome."

"I wouldn't want them to go away if they were welcome, would I?" And I wrote

> *They are waiting on the shingle—will you*
> *come and join the dance?*

in the margin of an article about spicing up your sex life by learning the secret sexual fantasies of men.

"How long has this been going on?"

"I'm not sure," I lied. It started when Eva whispered in my ear, of course. But I knew better than to start talking to Dr. Ogilvy about Eva Canning.

"More than a day?"

"Yeah."

"More than two days?"

"Maybe."

"Have you told anyone?" she asked, and I told her that my girlfriend had caught me writing the poem on the back of a napkin the day before. We'd gone out for hamburgers.

"What did you tell her?"

"I said it was nothing, and I threw away the napkin."

I scribbled

Beneath the waters of the sea
Are lobsters thick as thick can be—
They love to dance with you and me.
My own and gentle Salmon!

in the copy of *Cosmopolitan*.

"It's been a long time since it was this bad," I said. "I couldn't go into work yesterday. My manager's not happy. I'm afraid he's going to fire me, and I can't afford to lose my job."

"You've been missing a lot of days."

"Some," I said. "I keep telling him I'm sick when I call in, but he doesn't believe me anymore. I've always been a good employee. You think he'd cut me some slack."

"India, would you like me to call him and explain?"

"No," I replied. I said no seven times, and didn't look up because I didn't want to see Dr. Ogilvy's expression. I knew what it was without having to look. I wrote

Salmon, come up! Salmon, go down!
Salmon, come twist your tail around!
Of all the fishes in the sea
There's none so good as Salmon!

and she asked if I'd stopped taking my meds. I told her no, that I hadn't missed a single dose. That was the truth. Then she asked if I would give her the magazine. I clutched it tightly, so tightly I tore the page I'd been writing on, but then I gave it to her. I apologized for ruining it, and offered to replace it and the copy of *Redbook*.

"Don't worry about that. They're not important." She stared at the page a moment, then asked, "You do know what this is, I assume?"

"The Mock Turtle's song. From the tenth chapter of *Alice's Adventures in Wonderland*, first published in London in 1865 by Macmillan and Company."

I was tapping the pen very hard against my knee, tapping seven times, then seven times, then seven times.

"We're going to adjust the levels of your medications," she said, and passed the magazine back to me. "Are you okay with that?"

She scrawled illegibly on a prescription pad, and I scrawled almost as illegibly in *Cosmopolitan*:

> *Will you, won't you, will you, won't you,*
> *will you join the dance?*

"When did you memorize that poem?" Dr. Ogilvy asked me, and before I thought better of it, because I was too busy writing, I said, "Never. I never memorized this poem or any other poem."

She tore two pages from the pad, but didn't immediately hand them to me. "If I send you home today, will you be safe? Can you drive?" I told her I'd taken the bus from Willow Street, and she said that was for the best.

"You'll be safe?" she asked again.

"Safe as houses," I answered. When I glanced up, she was staring at me skeptically.

"Your girlfriend knows about your condition?"

"Yeah. I told her right after we met," and I wrote:

> *When the sands are all dry, he is gay as a lark.*
> *And will talk in contemptuous tones of the*
> *Shark:*
> *But when the tide rises and sharks are around,*
> *His voice has a timid and tremulous sound.*

She handed me the prescriptions, and asked me to please be careful, and to try to go to work, and to call her if it got any worse, or if I wasn't better in a couple of days. I could tell she didn't want to let me leave, that she was thinking about the hospital. She knows, and she knew back then, that she'd have to force me to spend even a single night in a hospital. She knew almost everything there was to know about Rosemary Anne. She knew it would have to get a lot worse than obsessively copying Lewis Carroll onto napkins and old magazines before I'd go, and that even then I'd go kicking and screaming.

I said, "St. Ignatius of Loyola had obsessions. Intrusive thoughts, I mean. He was terrified of stepping on pieces of straw forming a cross, because he was afraid it showed disrespect to Christ. I don't know where I read that. I must have read it somewhere. I think a lot of people that got to be saints were really only crazy." I pressed too hard and tore the page.

Dr. Ogilvy was silent for a while.

"You know I'm not religious," I said. "You know I've never believed in God and all that."

"Will you sit in the waiting room for a couple of hours?" she wanted to know. "You can leave anytime, but I think it would be a good idea if you stuck around for a bit, just in case."

"No," I replied, and shut the magazine. I rolled it into a tube and squeezed it. "I need to get home. I'll be fine, I swear. I'll call you if it gets worse."

"And you're sure you don't know what triggered this episode?"

"I'm sure," so there was my second lie.

"Will you call when you get home?"

I told her I would. It was a small enough price to pay to escape her office and get out of the clinic and away from her scrutiny and questions. She followed me back out to the receptionist, and I wrote a check for the cost of the session. We said good-bye. I had to pee, and I ducked into the restroom before I left the building. I sat on the plastic toilet lid and wrote

Then turn not pale, beloved snail, but come
and join the dance.

and I even drew a snail beneath the verse. I almost missed my bus. But only almost. I was home by four o'clock, but Abalyn had taken the Honda and gone to the market. She'd left a list explaining that she'd gone to get milk, coffee, cereal, peanut butter, "feminine hygiene products," AAA batteries, Red Bull, and carrots. I called Dr. Ogilvy, but she was with another patient, so I had to leave a message with her voice mail. I sat on the sofa and waited for Abalyn to come home. I tossed the magazine at a wastepaper basket and missed. I'd left one of my drawing pads on the sofa the night before, and so I wrote lines from "The Lobster Quadrille" in it, instead. When my pen ran out of ink, I stopped long enough to find another.

RISING ACTION (2)

Act Two: Find the River

Abalyn and I are sitting together at one of the long oak tables in the downstairs reading room of the Athenaeum. The library, as usual, is noisier than most libraries, but I've never minded. The voices of the librarians have always comforted me, just like the building comforts me, the stones and mortar set in place one hundred and seventy years ago, fifty-eight years before Saltonstall saw what he saw in the Blackstone Gorge. Do the math. Draw the parallel lines and abrupt angles, then mark the intersecting points. The library comforts me. I am wrapped in the aroma of antique books, dust, everything that has aged and is still aging. The Athenaeum is a shroud I hide within. I'm sitting across from Abalyn. I have a college-ruled notebook open in front of me. I bought it at the Walgreens on Atwells Avenue the day before, and the first seventy-four pages are filled, front and back, with lines from "The Lobster Quadrille," written down in no particular order. The number seven appears at the four corners of every page. I write in my notebook, and Abalyn talks, not quiet whispering.

"It's a bad idea," she says, staring at my notebook. She's afraid. I would say that I can smell her fear, but I can't. Maybe I feel her fear, or only see it in her green eyes, the color of mermaids' tears. She keeps trying to take the notebook away from me, even though that's exactly the wrong thing to do. Last night, she called Dr. Ogilvy's emergency number, but Dr. Ogilvy apologized and refused to speak with her about me. I haven't signed a release form permitting my psychiatrist to discuss my case with anyone.

"It might work," I say, not looking up from the notebook. I come to the last line; then I carefully place the four necessary sevens before turning to the next page. Seven, seven, seven, seven, twenty-eight.

"You don't know that, Imp. You might only make this worse. That could happen, couldn't it?"

"Almost anything could happen," I say. "Almost anything at all. You don't have to go with me. I keep telling you I can go alone."

"The hell you will," she says. "I'm afraid to let you out of my sight."

I glance up at her then, and it hurts to see her so frightened. "Don't say things like that. Please don't. Don't make me feel trapped."

"You know that's not what I'm trying to do."

I go back to scribbling, because I have to, and so I don't have to look at the expression on her face. "I know. But that's what you're doing."

We leave Providence about one o'clock. It's hot that day, up in the nineties. The wind through the open windows does nothing much to keep us cool, and the smell of sweat puts me in mind of the sea, which puts me in mind of Eva Canning. I write in my notebook, and ~~Eva~~ Abalyn drives and stares straight ahead. She never takes her eyes off the road.

The night before, Abalyn googled Eva Canning. It's weird all the words I never knew existed before Abalyn came to live with me, words like "googled." I told her it was amazing how much she'd found, and she said, "Yeah, well. I was going to open a private-detective agency, but the name Google was already trademarked." She got 473 hits, almost all of which were clearly other people and not *my* Eva Canning. But there was one thing. I have Abalyn's printouts here beside me. One article from the *Monterey County Herald* and another from the *San Francisco Chronicle*, a few others, all from April 1991. They connect a woman named Eva Canning to a woman named Jacova Angevine. In one of the articles there's a photograph of Eva standing beside Jacova Angevine, who was the leader of a cult, a cult that ended in a mass drowning, a mass suicide in the spring of 1991. Angevine led them into the sea at a place called Moss Landing in California, not far from Monterey. I'll quote a short passage from the *Herald* and then one from the *Chronicle* article here:

"The bodies of 53 men and women, all of whom may have been part of a religious group known as the Open Door of Night, have been recovered following Wednesday's drownings near Moss Landing, CA. Deputies have described the deaths as a mass suicide. The victims were all reported to be between 22 and 36 years old. Authorities fear that at least two dozen more may have died in the bizarre episode and recovery efforts continue along the coast of Monterey County" (*Monterey County Herald*).

And:

"The protestors are demanding that the Monterey Bay Aquarium Research Institute (MBARI) end its ongoing exploration of the submarine canyon immediately. The 25-mile-long canyon, they claim, is a sacred site that is being desecrated by scientists. Jacova Angevine, former Berkeley professor and leader of the controversial Open Door of Night cult, compares the launching of the new submersible *Tiburón II* to the ransacking of the Egyptian pyramids by grave robbers" (*San Francisco Chronicle*; note that *tiburón* is Spanish for shark).

Obviously, the second article was written before the first. In an article from a website devoted to suicide cults, the names of most of the people who drowned themselves are listed. One of them is a thirty-year-old woman named Eva Canning from Newport, Rhode Island. The website speculates that she was Jacova Angevine's lover, and listed her as a priestess in the Open Door of Night (which some journalists called the "Lemming Cult"). The name Eva Canning appears in the acknowledgments of a book, *Waking Leviathan*, that Jacova Angevine published several years before, and something somewhere said the book was written before the cult was actually formed.

I sat and listened and wrote in my notebook while Abalyn read the articles to me. When she was done, there was a long silence, and then she asked, "Well?"

"I don't know what any of that means," I replied. "It can't be the same Eva Canning."

"I showed you the photograph, Imp."

"The photograph isn't very clear." (That's true. It wasn't.) "It can't be the same Eva Canning, and you know it. I know you know that."

Abalyn pointed out that one of the articles mentioned many of the bodies being in "an advanced state of decay" by the time they were recovered by the Coast Guard. Some appeared to have been fed upon by sharks (id est, *tiburón*).

"Maybe she didn't drown there, Imp. Maybe they made a mistake when the bodies were identified, and she came back East. That's practically murder, leading those people to their deaths like that. She'd be hiding."

"And not using her real name," I pointed out.

Abalyn stared at me, and I stared at the parlor window, the moon, and the headlights of passing cars down on Willow Street. There was a question I didn't want to ask, but finally I asked it anyway.

"Did you ever hear of this cult? Before today, I mean. I never did, and wouldn't this have been a pretty big deal? Wouldn't we have heard about it before now?"

Abalyn opened her mouth, but then she shut it again without actually saying anything.

"I don't know what any of this means," I said again. "But it can't be the same Eva Canning. It doesn't make any sense. It doesn't make any sense neither of us ever heard of this before."

"We were just kids," she said.

"We weren't even born when Jim Jones made all those people poison themselves, or when Charles Manson went to prison. But we know all about them. This sounds at least as awful as both of those, but we've never heard of it. I think it's a hoax."

"It's not a hoax," she said, but then dropped the subject. She threw the printouts away, but later, when she wasn't watching, I fished them out of the kitchen trash and wiped the coffee grounds off them. I added them to my file devoted to the Siren of Millville, the file I'd also labeled "Eva Canning."

The sun is a white devil, the broiling eye of a god I don't believe in, gazing down at all the world. The Honda's tires hum against the blacktop. We drive north and west, following the heat haze dancing above 122, through Berkeley, Ashton, Cumberland Hill, Woonsocket. We cross the state line into Massachusetts, and we cross the Blackstone River, and we drive slowly through Millville. I see a black dog at the side of the road. It's busy chewing at what I think might be a woodchuck that'd been hit by a car as it was trying to cross the road.

"You'll have to show me where," Abalyn says. She sounds hot and scared and tired. I know she's all those things. I'm only hot and tired. My head is too filled with Lewis Carroll to be scared. "The Lobster Quadrille" rattles and bangs through my head, like church bells and thunder.

I showed her the place where I'd found Eva, and the spot where I'd pulled over that night. She turned around in someone's drive, so we wouldn't have to cross the highway, and she parked my car almost exactly where Eva was standing, naked and dripping wet, when I first spoke to her. It's so hot I can hardly breathe. I think I'll smother, it's so hot. It's a little after two o'clock, but sometimes the clock set into the dash runs slow, and other times it's fast. You can't ever trust that clock. It's fickle.

"This is such a bad idea," she says again, before we get out of the car. I don't reply. I take my notebook with me. We leave the windows rolled down.

It's easy to find the trail leading down to the river, though it's half-hidden between the brush. I go ahead of Abalyn, and we're careful to watch for poison ivy. I cut my ankle on creepers and blackberry briars. The trail is steep, and no more than two feet wide. Here and there, it's deeply gullied from rain. The farther we walk from the road, the more the air smells like the Blackstone River and the plants growing all around us, and the less it smells like the road and melting asphalt. There are monarch butterflies and clumsy, bumbling bumblebees.

At the bottom of the winding trail, there are a couple of trees, but it's not much cooler in the shade than in the sun. I've counted my steps from the car, and I took fifty steps. We've come to a wide rocky clearing. There are patches of mud between the granite boulders. The river's the color of pea soup, and the water's so still it hardly seems to be flowing at all. I spot three turtles sunning themselves on a log, and I point them out to Abalyn. Iridescent dragonflies skim low over the pea-green river, and the air throbs with the songs of cicadas and other insects. Every now and then, a fish causes ripples on the surface. I will wonder, hours later, if this is the same spot where Saltonstall was sketching the day he saw the woman come down from the woods on the other side.

Abalyn sits down on one of the boulders and uses the front of her T-shirt to wipe the sweat from her face. She takes out her cigarettes and lights one, so that now the air also smells of burning tobacco.

"So, just what are we looking for, Imp?"

"Maybe we're not looking *for* anything," I reply. "Maybe we're just looking," and she shakes her head and stares out across the river.

"This is bullshit," she says. She almost hisses the last word. She sounds like an impatient snake would sound, if impatient snakes could talk. Sibilant, as though a forked tongue is flicking out between fangs. She sits on her rock, and I stand near her. I'm not sure how long, but no more than twenty minutes, I think. Yeah, twenty minutes, at the most.

"Imp, there's nothing to see," Abalyn says, in an imploring sort of tone that also says, *Can we please get the fuck out of here?* Out loud, she adds, "I think I'm about to have fucking heatstroke."

And then I see the footprints in the mud. They must have been there the whole time, but I was too busy searching the river and the trees on the other side of the river to notice them. They're small, slender, long-toed. They might have been left by a kid who came down to swim. Anyway, that's what Abalyn says when I point them out to her. They lead out of the water, then back in again, making a half circle on the shore. They don't seem to lead back up the trail towards the highway. But, I tell myself, maybe the dirt trail is too hard and dry for bare feet to leave footprints.

"Come on, Imp. We're going home. You need to get out of this heat," she says, and flicks the butt of her cigarette into the river. She stands and very gently touches my left elbow.

I clutch my notebook to my chest and stare at the footprints for a couple more minutes, "The Lobster Quadrille" louder than the cicadas screaming in the trees. I think of seeing Eva (or only thinking I was seeing Eva) that day at Wayland Square, and how she hadn't been wearing any shoes.

"I'm sorry," Abalyn says. "If this didn't help you, I'm sorry."

"I'm sorry I dragged you all the way out here," I reply, and my voice has the odd rhythm that comes from taking great care to insert each word between the syllables of "The Lobster Quadrille."

"When we get home, promise me you'll call your doctor again, okay?"

I didn't. Promise, I mean. But I let her lead me back to the car.

CLIMAX

Act Three: 7 Chinese Brothers

I t didn't get any better after the drive to the river. The earwig, I mean. That's what Caroline used to call getting something stuck in your head—a song, a jingle from a television commercial. I'm sure she would have called getting "The Lobster Quadrille" stuck in my head an earwig, too. Also, I remember an episode of a TV show called *Night Gallery*, one I saw when I was living with Aunt Elaine in Cranston. In the episode, a man pays another man to place an earwig in the ear of a third man, a romantic rival. But there's a mix-up. The earwig is mistakenly inserted in the ear of the man who paid the man, and it lays eggs in his brain. Earwigs don't really do that, tunnel into people's brains and lay eggs in their heads. But it scared me all the same, and for a while I slept with cotton stuffed in my ears. In the *Night Gallery* episode, the man with the earwig in his head was in unspeakable agony as the insect ate its way through his brain. I don't think it was all that different from what Eva Canning did to me, when she leaned close that day in the RISD Museum and whispered in my ear.

This earwig of mine, these intrusive, echoing thoughts, she set them in motion. She said the words that turned the Aokigahara into the Suicide Forest. She laid her eggs between the convolutions of my cerebellum. She honeycombed the living gray matter, reshaping it to her own ends. I knew that, though I didn't dare tell Dr. Ogilvy or Abalyn or anyone else. I was crazy enough without telling tales of a siren who'd bewitched me because I'd not had the good sense to follow the example set by Odysseus' crew and fill my ears with wax. Or even cotton balls. I brought her home, and she rewarded me with a cacophony of Victorian nonsense.

I didn't call Dr. Ogilvy when we got home. Abalyn kept asking me to, but I didn't. I told her it would pass, because it always passed. But it wouldn't, not this time, so I knew that I was lying.

And then there was another day, and I filled up my notebook and then bought another. I used up two ballpoint pens and started on a third. It had never, ever been even half this bad, the unwelcome, deafening thoughts clanging about my mind, not even before my meds. I don't suffer from migraines, but maybe migraines are like having the same string of words running on an endless loop through your skull day and night and even when you dream. The compulsion to set the words to paper, and the inability to stop. I doubled my Valium dose, then tripled it. Abalyn watched, except when she was trying not to watch. She tried to get me to eat, but the Valium was making me sick to my stomach, and, besides, it was hard to eat while writing in my notebooks.

Finally, on the day *after* the day after the day at the Blackstone River, she grew so scared and angry, she threatened to call an ambulance. But she didn't. Instead, she started crying and went for a walk. I'll say that this was the third of August, even if it wasn't. The sun was down, and the apartment was stifling, though all the windows were open and the fans were running on high.

Abalyn slammed the door, and the very next second the telephone rang. Not my cell phone, but the old avocado-colored phone mounted on the kitchen wall. The one I hardly ever use. It's so old it has a dial. Hardly anyone ever calls me on that phone, and I've often wondered why I keep paying not to have the service shut off. The door slammed; the phone rang. I was sitting on the sofa, and I stopped writing halfway through the line about how delightful it will be when they take us up and throw us with the lobsters out to sea. The phone rang at least a dozen times before I got up and crossed the parlor to the kitchen and answered it. Maybe it was my boss, calling to tell me I was fired. Maybe it was Aunt Elaine, or even Dr. Ogilvy, though they both always called my cell number.

I lifted the receiver, but I don't think I heard anything for a whole minute. Sometimes I believe I *did* hear something, the same sound you hear when you put a conch shell to your ear. So, either there was silence or there was a sound that imitated the sea and wind. When Eva Canning spoke, I wasn't even a little bit surprised. I don't know what she said. I'm pretty sure I forgot it as soon as she stopped talking and I hung up. But it seems as though she talked for a very long while. It seems she told me great and wonderful secrets, and also secrets that were ugly and malicious. When it was over, "The Lobster Quadrille" was still reverberating in that constructed space between my eyes and pounding at my temples and slithering in through my ears. But I no longer needed to write it down, and that may have been the greatest relief I've ever known (at least in the July version of my haunting).

I walked back to the parlor and went to the window and stood contemplating Willow Street. There were chimney swifts swooping low above the roofs, chasing mosquitoes. Several Hispanic teenagers had set up a table across the street and were playing dominoes by streetlight and listening to loud Mexican pop music. There was no breeze whatsoever. Far off to the north I heard a train whistle. It might almost have been any summer night in the Armory. Maybe I was waiting for Abalyn to come home. Maybe I was standing there watching for her.

> *Beneath the waters of the sea*
> *Are lobsters thick as thick can be—*

When Abalyn didn't come back, I shut the window and locked it. I didn't go to any of the other windows to shut and lock them. It was only important that I shut and locked *that* one. There was something symbolic in the gesture. Closing a window was shutting a door. The Open Door of Night? It was Caroline turning on the gas, and Rosemary Anne growing tired of fighting her restraints and finding the resolution to swallow her own tongue.

> *They love to dance with you and me,*
> *My own, my gentle Salmon!*

I recall all those little details about what I saw outside the window, but I can't remember walking to the bathroom. I don't remember anything between the window and being in the bathroom, flipping the light switch (on and off seven times) and turning the cold water (on and off seven times). I remember the bathroom smelled like Abalyn's peppermint soap, and that I could still hear the music coming from the street, even over the singsong drone of "The Lobster Quadrille." I sat on the rim of the tub and watched as the cast-iron tub filled. The heat was so unbearable, and I knew the water would be heaven. I couldn't imagine why I hadn't thought of taking a cold bath earlier that day. I blamed the notebook and the pen and Abalyn being so upset.

I held my hand beneath the tap, and it was like dipping my fingers into liquid ice, almost *too* cold. I undressed, and let my clothes lie where they fell on the blue and white tiles. When the tub was full enough it might slosh over, I shut off the faucet and stepped into the water. It burned, that's how cold the water was. But I knew it would only burn at first, and then I would be numb, and I wouldn't have to be hot anymore or ever again. I stood in the burning water, thinking how this water had come all the way from the Scituate Reservoir, seven or eight miles to the west. In the winter, the reservoir sometimes freezes over and there are skaters. In the summer, it is the darkest dark blue. I thought about the many streams that flow into the reservoir, and the water that comes from underground, and about the rain, and how, in the end, it all comes from the sea. And how, in the end, it all goes back to the sea, one way or another.

> *"You really have no notion how delightful*
> *it will be*
> *When they take us up and throw us, with the*
> *lobsters, out to sea!"*

I lay down in the tub, and gasped and tightly clutched the edges until the initial shock passed.

> *"See how eagerly the lobsters and the turtles*
> *all advance!"*

My hair flowed out around my shoulders, across my breasts and belly like seaweed floating in a tide pool. As I sank deeper and deeper, the tub began to overflow and splash the floor.

"What matter it how far we go?"

I didn't shut my eyes. I didn't want to shut my eyes, and I knew Eva wouldn't want me to. I sank in the shallows of the tub. I pulled my head under, and marveled at the silvery mirror above me. It might as well have been mercury spilled across the sky, the way it shimmered.

"There is another shore, you know, upon the other
side. . . ."

The first breath was easy. I just opened my mouth and inhaled. But then I was choking, my entire body fighting the flood pouring down my throat and into my lungs and belly. I fought back, but I almost wasn't able to manage the second breath.

Then turn not pale, beloved snail, but come
and join the dance.

I was taking the sea inside me, even if I couldn't taste salt. I was taking the sea inside, and as my lungs caught fire and my body struggled against me, the earwig died. It died, or it merely faded away, and there was no noise remaining in my head except the sloshing of water and the stubborn, insistent beating of my heart. The mercury sky swishing to and fro above was going black, and I shut my eyes and gritted my teeth.

FALLING ACTION

Act Four: Try Not To Breathe

And then Abalyn's strong hands were digging into my shoulders, hauling me up and out of the ice, lifting me from the tub. Maybe I don't *truly* remember this part. Maybe I was unconscious for this part, but if these aren't genuine memories, they've fooled me for two and a half years. Abalyn set me down on the bathroom floor, and held me while I coughed and vomited water and whatever I'd had for lunch until my throat was raw and my chest ached. She was cursing herself and cursing me and sobbing like I'd never heard anyone cry before or since. I've never cried the way she was crying, never been so wracked with sorrow and anger and confusion that I *had* to cry that way. Sorrow and anger and confusion. It's presumptuous of me, acting like I know what she was feeling while I puked and sputtered in her arms.

When there was nothing left inside me, Abalyn picked me up again and carried me to bed. I'd never realized she was so strong, strong enough to carry me like that. But she did. She bundled the sheets and comforter about me, and kept asking what the hell I thought I was doing. I couldn't possibly have answered, but she kept asking me anyway. *Imp, what the hell were you trying to do?*

She wanted to call an ambulance (again), but I was able to shake my head, and that stopped her. I'm surprised that stopped her, but it did.

Two days later, Abalyn left me, and she never came back again.

"Stop this," Imp typed.

I also typed.

"You don't have to do this anymore. You need to stop. It doesn't matter what she said. So stop. Stop and put these pages away and be done with this bullshit. Have mercy for yourself."

"No," I type. "You can only set it aside for now. But you *can* do that. You've said what matters. You didn't drown, and the earwig died, and Abalyn left, and you can get to the rest of it tomorrow or the next day."

It's such a wicked, selfish fucking thought, but I wish she'd let me go that day. I wish that as hard as I wish the telephone would ring, and this time it would be Abalyn.

Stop. Enough. Enough for now.

Enough forever.

DENOUEMENT

Act Five: The Wake-Up Bomb

There weren't supposed to be five acts. But I was wrong, and there are.

Four days ago, I said "enough forever," and for four days I haven't sat down in this chair in the blue-white room with too many books. But here I am again. Here I am, because, because, because . . . even as I have tried to tell my ghost story, my mermaid and my werewolf story, as a thing that *happened* to me in the past, stuff keeps happening. New events stubbornly occur that I know are part of the story, which continues to unfold around me, rudely making a worse tangle of my hopelessly tangled mess. All along, I've desperately wanted to say these days *were*, and now it's over, right? So, I'm only recording history. I've been pushing away, trying to put behind.

And yeah, history has consequences, but at least it's *over*. You remember it, but you don't live it. This is what I think most people believe, and what I wanted to believe, because maybe believing that I could stop living the ghost story. I would type THE END, and walk away, and there would be no more sorrow and no more fear. No more thoughts of Abalyn and Eva and wolves and sirens and snowy roads and muddy rivers. No more Saltonstall. No more Perrault.

But. In *Long Day's Journey Into Night*, Mary says, "The past is the present, isn't it? It's the future too. We all try to lie out of that but life won't let us." (Rosemary was very fond of Eugene O'Neill.) I searched through a book of plays after work last night, because I wasn't sure I was remembering that line exactly right, but I was. Past is present. The future is present, too. And hey, look at me trying to sound like I know something, when the whole point here is that what I thought I knew I'm no longer sure I ever knew at all. Because it's still happening, and the past is present, like Mary Cavan Tyrone said. She took morphine, and she was crazy, too, plus she's only alive when actresses bring her to life, but she saw. She saw, and all I can do is borrow her vision.

This happened (happens) to me yesterday (now):

I was at work, and on my break, I felt like walking. This isn't unusual. I left the art supply store and walked around the corner to Elm Street, and then I turned again onto Hospital Street. I was walking past the parking lot for the Providence Children's Museum when I saw Abalyn and another woman, whom I'd never seen before, and a little girl, getting out of a red car parked close to the sidewalk. I could have turned around and headed back to work. If I had, everything would be different, and I wouldn't be writing this. But "if I had" doesn't matter, because I didn't turn around. I just stopped, and stood there, hoping Abalyn wouldn't see me, but also so happy to see her again after so long that I felt dizzy, but also so dizzy from the pain of having lost her twice welling up like it had all just happened. Like the pain was fresh. The way it felt, we might only have split up a week ago.

She did see me, and she glanced at the other woman, as if waiting for some sort of cue or for permission, or as though she were going to beg my pardon for something she hadn't yet done. And then she spoke words I couldn't hear, so she couldn't have said them very loudly, and walked over to where I was standing.

"Hey, Imp," she said. Her hair isn't black anymore. She's letting it grow out, and mostly it's blonde, but the color of her eyes hasn't changed.

"Hi," I said, and had no idea what to say next.

"It's been a long time," Abalyn said, like somehow I wasn't aware of that. "You doing okay?"

"Yeah," I replied. "I'm doing okay. Who are your friends?"

She looked over her shoulder, back to the other woman and the little girl waiting in the parking lot by the red car. She turned back to me. When she spoke again, she sounded as anxious and dizzy as I felt.

"Oh, yeah. That's Margot and her niece, Chloe. We're taking Chloe to the museum. She's never been before."

"You don't like museums," I said.

"Well, it's for Chloe, not me."

"Margot's your new girlfriend?" I asked, hearing the words and knowing that I was saying everything I shouldn't be saying, but saying them anyway.

"Yes, Imp," Abalyn answered, and the smallest bit of a smile creased the corners of her mouth. "Margot's my girlfriend."

There were a few seconds of awkward silence that likely seemed longer than they actually were, and then I said—no, then I *blurted*, "I've been writing it all down."

She stared at me, still almost frowning, and she asked, "Writing all what down?"

Wishing I could take back what I'd blurted out, wishing I were sitting in the break room at work, or out in the courtyard, instead of standing on the sidewalk with Abalyn staring at me, I said, "You know, what happened. What happened before you left. The river, and the two Evas. I've only gotten as far as trying to drown myself in the bathtub, but I don't think I'm going to write any more. I've told the July story, and I don't think I really have to tell the November story."

Words tumbling out of me, like I was someone with Tourette's and couldn't help myself. She looked over her shoulder at Margot and Chloe, and then turned back to me.

"The *two* Evas?"

"Yeah," I replied. "Both of them. July and November."

There was an even longer awkward silence than the first one, and she tried to smile, but didn't do a very good job of it. "I'm not sure what you mean, Imp. There was only ever one Eva Canning. You've lost me." She stopped, glanced up at the sun, and squinted. And I thought she was about to ask me if I'd been skipping my meds, missing doses. That was the sort of expression she had. All at once, it felt like my belly was full of rocks.

"There was July, and then there was November," I told her, the words still tumbling, sounding insistent when I'd only meant to sound certain of myself and a little perplexed. "There was the first time you left, right? And then there was—"

"I'm sorry, Imp," she interrupted. "It's really good to see you again. Really, but I need to go."

"Why are you acting like you don't know what I mean?"

"Because I don't. But that's all right. It doesn't matter. Anyway, I have to go now."

"I miss you," I said. I shouldn't have, but I did.

"We'll talk sometime," she promised, but I knew she didn't mean it. "Take care of yourself, okay?"

Then she was gone. I stood on the sidewalk, and I watched her and the woman named Margot and the little girl named Chloe go into the children's museum.

There was only ever one Eva Canning.

Only one.

All the way back to the store, and the rest of the day, and most of last night, I tried to only be angry and only pretend it had pissed her off, embarrassed her, running into me like that. Or it was a cruel joke. Perhaps she hadn't meant it as a cruel joke, but that's what it was. Phillip George Saltonstall hadn't meant to perpetuate a haunting when he painted that picture, and neither had Seichō Matsumoto when he published *Kuroi Jukai* and changed a forest into a place where people went to die. I might have called Abalyn last night, if I had her phone number. I might have called and demanded that she apologize and explain herself, tell her how it felt like she'd been making fun of me. I stood by the telephone in the kitchen, and sat on the sofa holding my cell phone. I probably would have been able to find her number if I'd tried, but I didn't. I considered emailing her, because I'm pretty sure her email hasn't changed, but I didn't do that, either.

Abalyn never played tricks on me. Why would she do it now, even if she was embarrassed at having to talk to me while her new girlfriend was standing there, close enough to hear everything we said? No matter how much easier it would be if she had, I don't think she was lying to me. Which means she might just have been confused and not remembering it right, but that's ridiculous. That would mean she's forgotten months and months and so many awful things. If she thinks there was just one Eva, whether it was the first or the second, she would have to have forgotten things so terrible they're impossible to forget.

Last night I didn't sleep. I lay awake until the sun came up, forcing myself to ask the worst question, first to myself and then aloud. Forcing myself to let it become solid as concrete, so I can't deny it. Because Eva taught me the unknown is immune to the faculties of human reason, that something hungry below the water that you can't see is scarier than a hungry twenty-foot-long shark. Because the unknown is even scarier than a truth so appalling that it breaks your whole wide world apart.

Almost three hundred pages ago, I typed, "I said there's no reason doing this thing if all I can manage is a lie." If I wasn't sincere, then none of this has meant anything, and I might just as well have been typing the same sentence over and over again. Or not even a real sentence, just the same letter hundreds of thousands of times. I didn't mean what I said, that's all I've done.

Was there only one Eva Canning, and, if so, which one is the real one?

Writing makes it even harder than concrete. Writing makes it hard as diamond.

But questions don't come with answers conveniently attached, and I always knew there was a paradox. A particle and a wave. Spooky action at a distance. July and November. Asking my appalling question out loud doesn't bring any sort of resolution. I know less than I ever thought I knew. That's all being able to ask the question means.

Except it also means that I can't stop here.

7/7/7/7
7/7
7
SEVEN
7
7/7
7/7/7/7

All our thoughts are mustard seeds. Oh, many days now. Many days. Many days of mustard seeds, India Phelps, daughter of mad-women, granddaughter, who doesn't want to say a word and ergo can't stop talking. Here is a sad, sad tale, woebegone story of the girl who stopped for the two strangers who would not could not could not would not stop for me. She, she who is me, and I creep around the edges of my own life afraid to screw off the mayonnaise lid and spill the mustard seeds. White mustard, black mustard, brown In-dian mustard. She spills them on a kitchen floor and so has to count them seven times seven times before returning them to the spice jaw jar jaw jar. Screwed the lid on tight, because once was plenty enough of that, thank you. She exaggerates, but counting them more than once, there's no getting past that, right? A careless elbow, and India Phelps loses one whole fucking hour and a half counting the seeds scattered all over the inconsistent floor, caught in cracks between boards, rolled away under the fridge and the stove and so having to be retrieved and no matter how long it takes. My time is mine. Black hands, hour hand, swift second hand, right and left hand dominant hand, minute hand, life line, soul line, all counterclockwise widdershins pockets full of posies. India Morgan Phelps, imp, demon, everyone calls her demon her whole life long thinking it was cute, her heart as rotten as old apples on the ground. These black enameled keys are good as mustard seeds, if I stop to consider the sound they make.

There she was with a girl named Chloe and a woman she named Margot, but how would I know she wasn't lying? To herself, to me, drawing names out of a hat. She didn't ask if I was off my meds, but I saw it in her eyes, eyes green as wave-tumbled Coca-Cola tins. Saying there was only one story happened, when I've got two in my head, and how, how. How. Haven't picked up the phone. No, picked up the phone, but haven't called you Abalyn or Ogilvy or anyone at all. Thinking she might be right is worse than knowing, but still easier than picking up the phone or an email to steer my demonic self towards confirmation. The unknown is terrifying, but certainty damns me. Strike, strike, strike, strike a typewriter key, strike a match, strike a deal, strike a cord or is it chord? strike a bargain, strike me dead. The thought has crossed my mind many times the last several days counting my spilled mustard seeds. It would be easy, though bodies never want to give up the ghost easily, but with a little luck this would be ended and no more playing games of this is true or that is true but only the madwoman on Willow Street would dare be such a fool as to think both are true.

Which brings me to Wolf Den Road, so called, so-called sobriquet Wolf Den Road traced in dirt between banks of snow forest in north and eastern Connecticut. I didn't know the etymology that November night but I know it now. I know Israel Putnam's crime of the winter of 1742, 1743, as winters span or straddle one year and the next. The justifications are almost as wild and unlikely as the legends of Gévaudan, La Bête du Pomfret we are told by history slaying sheep all that long winter, the tally varying from one source to the next. I don't think any are reliable. I think the wolf was framed, and that sets me wondering about the wolf and the girl in red and who was it stalked who? Seventy sheep and goats on a single night. I don't buy that, but I don't buy many things others swallow whole, for the woodsman to cut free, half-digested, from distended lupine bellies. Lambs and kids mutilated, the survivors maimed badly enough to be put down like mad dogs, madwoman demonic disbelieving Imp. Devastated sheepfolds. Devastated shepherds of Connecticut. So there was a posse of Israel Shepherds and Oddfellow friends of sheep and goats and she'd left her fresh, incriminating paw prints in the new fallen snow so they'd have no trouble at all stalking her right back again. Makes me wonder if she wanted to die, too, and meant to be found, even if she didn't make it entirely easy for those vengeful men of God. The dogs went down that stone throat and came out whimpering, tails between skinny legs, I think that's shameful, sending dogs to do the bloody work of men, setting dogs against their forebears.

Eva Canning, you of November evenings, lost and hopeless and hungry, crouched in the dark, sending the hounds scrambling back to their vexed masters. They'd already slaughtered so many of your children. And here the men sit all a long winter's night, at the mouth of your den in the rocks, vexing themselves. Rocks slippery with snow and ice and the blood not yet spilled to avenge livestock. Putnam made a torch of birch bark and with a rope he bade them lower him into the crevice because if you want something done they say do it yourself if you want it done right. Don't leave it to the dogs who once were wolves themselves, so let's consider a conspiracy of canine coconspirators. Let's suppose, as we suppose uncounted mustard seeds spell certain and not unknown doom. Good and righteous Squire Putnam, Patron Saint of sheep and goats, kids and lambs, mutton chops, lowered head down into the stinking maw of surely unknown blackness to exorcise the imp of Pomfret which was known lately to stalk frosty fields. Here he is, choosing the Road of Needles, for the sake of good Christian farmers of New England. Wolves who do evil out of ravenous hunger in the dead of winter. My headlights illuminating along back roads, not going anywhere on purpose, and ignorant of the mock-turtle heroics of Israel Putnam and the ghost he let loose that night so long ago when all my research has revealed the Holy Bible makes thirteen references to wolves. I've got a list right here. Try Acts 10:29. Skip this version. Remind me later.

Canto 1, *Inferno*, Dante Alighieri, who wrote, but emphatically not of Israel Putnam the wolfslayer of Pomfret, lost in primeval glades and confronted by three wild beasts. One was a she-wolf. Good Friday, 1300 AD: *Ed una lupa, che di tutte brame,* And a she-wolf, that with all hungerings; *sembiava carca ne la sua magrezza,* seemed to be laden in her meagreness; *e molte genti fé già viver grame,* she brought upon me so much heaviness. The depredations of all these misbegotten bitches, woebegotten, so you'd think it was a bitch wolf in Eden and not a snake at all.

(where you shall hear the howls of desperation)

She didn't see me at first. I'm not sure when she noticed me, but not until I stopped for her, Mr. Putnam. It's not as if she were stalking me that night to do me mischief in that wood of barren limbs and snow crust to decently hide a billion shed leaves from my sight. It's not like she was out hunting that night. I came upon her, Abalyn. I was out hunting, and it wasn't her.

I'm going to call this part "The Wolf Who Cried Girl."

But hunched here in my seat by the window on Willow Street I'll not let Israel Putnam off the hook by straying back towards the road to Eva Canning (that's the Second Coming, and not the first, this rough slouching beast).

(which, even as she stalked me, step by dogged step)

What I read says it was fifteen feet deep, the pit down to the haunt of the she-wolf of Pomfret. Then another horizontal ten feet hardly a yard from side to side and the ceiling so low Saint Wolf-slayer had to crawl on his belly. This story grows ever more un-likely, just like Margot not being a not-quite-clever-enough nom de guerre, and what child's name was India Imp, your guess is as good as mine. Fuck. Fuck. The mustard seeds keep coming back, and even without them I'd probably keep losing my way, straying from the path, but the mustard seeds aren't helping one little biddy bit. Mr. Putnam said the wolf had fiery eyes. He *would* say that. He would embroider as hunters and fishermen are wont to do. All my Eva's eyes flashed red. No, I mean that. So, Israel Putnam loaded his black-powder musket with nine deadly buckshot and killed the snarling, fire-eyed she-wolf bitch and dragged her out to the cheer-ing crowd assembled above. She, dead, was dragged a corpse a mile from her sanctuary and nailed with an iron spike to a barn door or something of that sort. She was proof of the primacy of man, and of Putnam's guilt but I see no proof hear no evidence (these lines I hear) beyond the merely circumstantial that she committed any crime. Remind me later.

So it was named Wolf Den Road, but technically I was on Val-entine Road when I found Eva the wolf and I'm embellishing. She would have wandered Wolf Den Road, though. I think she must have.

He murdered the wolf at ten o'clock, and they say that was the last wolf in Connecticut. General Israel Putnam, to be a hero in wars to come—American Revolution and French and Indian. But I still will call him a murderer, and I will call him the murderer who set loose the ghost I found that freezing night, naked and lost and frightened on the icy dirt road. She must have come to him, like the Exeter vampire specter of Mercy Brown visiting her sisters and broth-ers. She must have haunted him, and in his guilt he fought in those latter wars hoping against hope to assuage his guilt in the affairs of the winter of 1742 and 1743.

That's a terrible burden to carry, and I don't care even if you're a pious Saint armed with lead buckshot, that's a terrible burden, finding himself the hand of extinction of the race of wolves in all Connecticut. He might have worn it like a badge of honor, oh I'm sure but I'm supposing it was a put-on so others wouldn't see his guilt.

Eva spake, "You found me." But it came out more like a growl than English. She didn't, of course, right? She didn't say anything that night, or lots of nights after I brought her home to my Willow Street den and Abalyn who was duly horrified and wanted to send her away but I didn't. Abalyn called her something I'll not here repeat broken lovelorn on your rocks.

Eva Canning was the ghost of the last dead wolf, just as sure as she was surely also the ghost of Elizabeth Short, Black Dahlia, werewolf murder, all the way faraway where I have never been to Lost Angels and that was in the winter of 1947. That was in that other winter at the edge—the opposite edge—of a continent. I think she, she being Elizabeth Short, she being the inverted reincarnation of Eva Canning, she being the reincarnated ghost of the final wolf of the Great State of Connecticut . . . I think SHE in capitals SHE must have taken the Road of Pins. She must have worn a red cape, to have been sliced in half like that, drained her blood, face carved like a jack-o'-lantern, carved ear to ear with the Glasgow Smile, the werewolf smile I think some journalist started that, which is how it was the werewolf murder because wolves have such wide smiles, such big teeth. Sometimes, I think the journalists meant she was the murdered werewolf and other times they without any doubt meant, no, she was murdered by the wolf. They made her eat shit, feces, said the coroner. All her teeth were rotten like apples lying on the ground late in the summer. They, the police, thought it was a blow to the head that killed her, not the being cut in half, which I guess is merci-ful. Like stopping by the woods on a snowy evening because she would not could not would not stop for me.

Once. Not twice. There was only one Eva.

Imp, you see? You see what this is, paper in the carriage? Pump-kin. Twelve enchanted mice. You have eyes and see, right, what and how you need to please stop this nonsense before it gets any worse rotten cider and you have to start in again on the goddamn mustard seeds? The words you won't be able to pick up like mustard seeds and put back from all the places they've come from. You see that, right? Oh, god. Oh my god.

I am a dead woman. Dead and insane.

7/7/7

7/7

7

Isn't the number seven a holy number? It is, isn't it? God's num-ber. So, I'm laying down these sevens against the ghosts crowding my head, and against the imp who I am, against demons, were-wolves, sirens, hunters with muskets, lovers lost, women who can't really be named Margot and little girls not named Chloe, against the blowback, the consequences, the backdraft, the mustard seeds. Against the ire and absence of Messieurs Risperdal, Depakene, and Valium, all of whom I have neglected in the worst sort of fashion, leaving my gentlemen to languish, jilted, uselessly ~~in Baltic amber specked with carbonized ants and gnats~~. I put them away in the bathroom medicine cabinet. I put them away. They obscure the true things. Dr. Ogilvy knows that, that need is not quiet relief, that rats live on no evil star. She's told me as much, if I don't want to wind up like Rosemary Anne. I don't, but my sevens are just as fierce as my psychoactive paramours. I want to hear the real me, not the false, inconstant me whose truer thoughts are all boxed up and hidden in a suitcase beneath my bed where no one might get hurt by sentences honed sharp as razors. I'm only cutting *myself* off at the knees.

I kindly stopped, though. The woman stood naked in the snow at the side of ~~Wolf Den Road~~ Valentine Road, Road of Needles, Bray Road of road of yellowcake and the Trail of the Coeur d'Alenes. I stopped, and oh what big eyes she had, eyes of deepest golden-brown honey butterscotch agate and what big teeth of ivory so she rends me apart and gaily strews the pieces to the winds, so now my foolish heart. What long-leggedy beast, she, sidhe, Eva the Second Coming after my failed Ophelia. What sharp claws. She creeps along country roads and railroad tracks, and I'm no more than meat. She no more than a wisp of smoke, if you do not look directly at the creeping taxidermy of her. But she rends me and scatters the fruits of her efforts—pomegranate seeds, peach pits, bitter almonds the taste of cyanide monsoons boat is leaning. Opening the door of my Honda, the night spills in because she owns the night, and it does her bidding. Israel Putnam pulled the trigger and set her free. Ghosts must be liberated from the prisons of flesh and bone, autocracy of sinew and gray matter. She crept between the trees to me and I asked her if I could help and to smother in those golden sunset eyes, pupils eating up the sky. Pay attention, Imp. Pay attention, or it will come to collect the debt. Eva collected me in sickle talons, and rolled the bones on a snowy evening.

Yeah, this is the conclusion I am arriving at without the fog of my Messieurs. I died, and what came home was as much a phantom as the last wolf in Connecticut. Eva buried my festering, grateful corpse below ~~frost~~, leafy detritus frozen hard until spring thaw but her claws made short work of the crust, and neatly carved the soil for my grave. She prayed a wolfish, blasphemous mass over my funerary sleep, and there would have been twine bundles of bergamot, black-eyed Susans, columbine and marsh marigolds, had it been that night another season (I would give you some violets, but they wither'd all when I planned my runaway father's demise). Instead, just rotting leaves and shivering worms. The interment rudely woke sleeping earthworms and clicking black beetles. But they forgave me, and I was schooled in the tongues of annelids and insects. Beetles have a peculiar dialect. Grubs are fiends of glottal stops. I told them I was a painter who wrote stories about paintings of mermaids and dead motorcycle slain multimedia men obsessed with murdered women and fairy tales. Whether or not they believed me, I was duly humored. I think this is most certainly what happened on WolfsValentineDenRoad. Be mine. And I can still smell Eva crouched on the raw dirt above me, pissing, shitting wolf lady, and she raises her head, throws back her head, wishing there were a full moon that night, howling anyway. I think, howling because there *wasn't* the moon, her faithful brutal sweet rapist. Her rapacious satellite. Her tidal puller. Pray you, love, remember, how could you use a poor maiden so? Where were you? Underground, on my bed of sticks, bed of Styx, I prayed for her full sail. Here in November is a good month for giving up the ghost, she whispered, and I wouldn't have argued, even if she'd not stilled my lips.

It's all well and good, India, but you can't tell stories for shit, can you? You make a muddle, and it's gonna be no worth to anyone.

You can't draw a straight line.

But I can walk a crooked mile.

When the subterranean insect catechism had ended, with hours yet before dawn, she exhumed whatever was left. She licked clean my skull and breast, until the bones were bright alabaster as her wayward rakish moon. This was to make plain and without a doubt her gratitude that I'd died for her sins. I mean, of course, the sins of Putnam, which she accepted as her own while he scuttled away to fight the redcoats and Iroquois and Mississauga during *la Guerre de la Conquête*, so had no time to bear his cross. Dead wolves are sin-eaters. She was nailed with iron spikes to a smokehouse wall and gawkers game from all around to bear witness to laid low Christ Wolf in her mock Calvary tribulations. There was no Mary Magdalene or Queen of Heaven to cry for a wolf, only owls and the crows who came to peck at her flesh, making her alive again. Eva Canning was resurrected in the bodies of crows, black birds are a sure sign of a lie, all black birds, even corvids not black burnt, and all black birds took her into themselves so she soared high, victorious above fallow fields. Transubstantiation.

She pawed open the ground again (prematurely) that I might gaze in wide-eyed wonder upon the splinters of the one true barn door cradled in her gory, reliquary palms.

She whispered in my ear and I smelled her sickly sweet carrion breath. She whispered there would be lies farther down the road. Abalyn, she would betray me three times, and instill a doubt so profound it would leave me clutching at Judas straws and shutting my pills behind a mirrored door. I cried when Eva told me this, and she wiped my tears away with flickering hands unable to decide if it was best to be paws or hands. She was all of a splendid metamorphosis, like the grubs who'd spoken while I slept. She was first this one thing and then that other, right before my eyes. She was a kaleidoscope chrysalis of shifting skeletons and muscle and marrow, bile and the four richly appointed chambers of a mammalian heart. The heart, the chest's pumping aqua vitae tetragrammaton, for the life of the flesh is in the blood, blood is the life. She was never for an instant only a single beast, as I will not accept the deceit that there was only ever one of her, that I must choose between July and November. Why can't she, Abalyn, see this, when she, herself, like Tiresias, has turned her gender lycanthropy trick on her own? Isn't that an hypocrisy? She is a paradox, and wants to take mine away, and wants me to believe it impossible? She slipped out of a skin she hated and into one she wished, and so a particle and a wave and so Eva and Eva, right?

~~Abalyn would scowl her priestly scowl and say no.~~

If I'd not divorced my Messieurs I would have remained dumb and deaf to all this, and might have lain down and died. Choose the bathtub again, or open my wrists? It wouldn't matter, either way I'd be silenced. The inconvenience would be done away with. Neatly, neatly. Safe as houses. You love someone, you don't leave her to drown, and you don't tell her she's crazier than she already knows that she is.

There's a crow on the windowsill. He thinks I'm not watching him watching me. He probably hasn't been told that I saw four people strolling along together in the park. Back from the streetlamps and under the trees, where it was the darkest. Not nuns, in their heavy flowing cloaks, but either human crows or actually (and this I concede most probable) plague doctors, beak doctors, slipped from their right century with salves of balm-mint leaves, amber camphor, rose, laudanum, myrrh, storax, waxed leather hoods, their bills with antidotes all lined, that foulsome air may do no harm. Medico Della Peste, glass-eyed, not like the black-eyed crow on my windowsill. Like wicked Hieronymus Bosch's earthly delights. Maybe Abalyn kept secrets and can become a crow, and there now she sits spying as I type. But I have my seven charm, and when I set down

7/7/7/7

7/7

7

seven

7

7/7

7/7/7/7

VII

7

she spreads her ebony wings and flies away home to the hell with
not-Margot and not-Chloe paper dolls she's wrought for herself. But
I digress. The distraction of a blackbird attempting to bury me in a
new tumult of self-doubt, recalling Caroline's warning, black birds
come to liars. So, where was I?

Chasing Eva Canning beneath a moonless winter sky.

Or late autumn sky, but cold as fucking winter. Hurry along
now, child. This clarity may not last forever. They have ways of
stealing it back.

I didn't need my Honda any longer, not with Eva the Wolf of
Israel Putnam calling out for me to run ~~along~~ on my dead legs and
keep up, keep up. Wild, wild night. She planted a corpse and sprouted
a swift-footed dead woman zombie racer who, try as she might,
would not ever keep up. This doesn't matter, as that night it didn't
matter. Only the effort was of importance. She knew I was running
as fast as I could, on those rattling bony legs of mine. She understood I couldn't go down on all fours with her, though I longed for
that earthly delight so badly it ached. She was the ghost of a wolf,
and I wished to join her. The ghost of a wolf is freer than a madwoman with a belly full of drugs. It was the pills that made me too
immutable to run on all fours, not morphology of sacrum, pelvis,
femur. They were the poison even she was helpless against.

On two feet, upright, I ran until the souls of my feet bled. The
soles. She removed all my ragged clothes, torn by her hunger, before
laying me to rest, so upon my restoration I was naked as was she. I
was her crippled sister, alike in intent if not her fearful symmetry
burning bright down Valentine Road of Needles while unsuspecting
farmers and the wives of farms slept snug in their beds. The horses
heard us, though, and the cows. Goats, they heard us, too. I had
strayed from the path of my life and illusions of medicated surrogate
sanity. I strayed, and Eva let me dance beneath the starry sky with
the long-leggedy beast the naked woman at the side of the road had

become. You really have no notion how delightful it will be, was, at the inevitable convergence of those two roads full sail. That's what Abalyn would steal from me, the knowledge of the glory of that tarantella danse macabre dervish. I fell down among quiescent fields, pale as sugar-powdered confections, divided by fieldstone walls since the days of Israel Putnam. I lay down, and she climbed on top of me. She glared down at me, all iridescent crepe-paper crimson eyeshine appetite, insatiable and wanton, and I spread my legs for the wolf she'd always really been. Her wet black nose snuffled my welcoming sex, her lolling mottled ice-cream licking me apart before she roughly rolled me over onto my stomach and wounded breasts and mounted me in the fashion of a wolf.

"You are in the House of the Wolf, *casa del lobo*, young lady, and so you'll fly right and do as is our custom. You will fuck as wolves fuck."

A woman in a field—something grabbed her.

Fecunda ratis.

She plowed me, as the fields would be plowed come spring. She planted me, a second time, sowing later jealousy, as I am certain Abalyn would have smelled her musk on me when I came home that night. It's a fairy tale, isn't it? Yes, it's all a fairy tale, even if there are no fairies, per se. Pixie-led, pixilated, the foolish disobedient child wanders into the heart of a haunted wood and meets a ravenous lupine devil who, in short order, promises I will race you to Caroline's house, and what's more, I'll love you true, let me enfold you and I don't care that you're insane. I will love you forever and forever. Pull back the covers to find her waiting in the fallow fields, to plow.

(Abalyn is at the window again, but this time I'm ignoring her.)

The carmine girl who was me, is me, came up from the hollow hills, hand in hand with La Bête, thinking how lucky I was. Hoping I might bear her pups, and not be empty anymore. Empty cockleshell girl behind the register, and people whisper about her behind her back, and they don't know she knows or they just don't fucking care. I wager the latter. Empty oyster girl at last not empty anymore. I came back to my car, and the headlights were still blazing white shafts in the gloom, making the snow sparkle. Eva was with me, on my left, and she let me fasten the seat belt around her. The roads were slick and treacherous, and sometimes I drive over the speed limit. Pixie-led girls who stray from the path aren't the sort to worry too much about breaking traffic laws. They have their own limits painted indelibly on their palimpsest skin for wolves to read.

This is my ghost story of the wolf who cried girl. The murdered wolf ghost who roamed centuries after a musket blast, without other wolves, except other wolf ghosts, for company. And somehow she forgot she ever was a wolf, deprived of others of her kind to provide perspective. She forgot. But she saw so many human beings, men and women and children, and having forgotten herself she mistook herself for nothing more than a naked woman at the side of Valentine Road. Or it wasn't entirely a matter of forgetting. What if she learned her lesson, that wolves are not safe from men, but women are just a little safer from men, so she sewed herself a woman's skin and crawled inside? The fit was snug, and she had to take great care her claws didn't rip the skin gloves, and that no one saw her fangs.

The ghost of a wolf in disguise.

Madwomen can see such apparitions, and our touch can render them corporeal. Which is how Abalyn saw her when we got back to Willow Street. If Abalyn had met what I came upon, it would have been invisible and she'd have kept right on driving drive, drive, drive, drive ignorant of what a miracle. Since 1742 or 1743 or 1947, that's what everyone before mad India Morgan Phelps the Imp of Willow Street pulled over and asked if she was okay or if she needed help. I saw she had no voice, had not learned yet to use her pilfered woman's tongue. She would, eventually, and that means she lost herself that much more in the cacophony clash of nouns, vowels, participles, adjectives, verbs, and all. ~~I blame myself for that a little. I was an enabler to her psychotic amnesiac masquerade.~~

While I wasn't looking the Abalyn Crow flew away again. I think it won't be back. Not tonight, at least. A black bird means a lie, unless a black bird *is* a lie. When moving through fairy tales, one must obey the laws of fairy. When moving through a ghost story, Gothic and Victorian law applies. Here I creep my footpath through both at once and the dictates are unclear, winding together in greenbrier snarls I'll have to prick my fingers on spinning wheel spindleshanks to comprehend. It must have been worse on Eva. I was on the outside looking in and she was locked in the lie she'd told herself not to go mad as India Morgan Phelps or her mother.

All my telephones keep ringing, but I know better than to answer. I know what seeps through telephones. I know the Messieurs would have me answer, and I know they're lying sons of bitches. Liars very much count on our not recognizing a lie when we hear one. Even when, like a lost wolf, we are lying to ourselves.

I ran poor, poor Eva Wolf a bath with iodine water the color of Coca-Cola tins straight from Scituate and so come indirect from the sea. Abalyn went for a walk and a smoke, hating what I'd done, afraid and we hate what scares us, what we don't understand, and she couldn't fathom Eva any more than she could fathom me. I was careful the water was warm, to chase away the chill shot through her crystalline veins, through otherwise unblemished lacteous calcite veins. I helped her into the tub, and she folded up easy as a Japanese fan, all knees and elbows and those xylophone ribs showing from beneath her filthy bleached hide. It pained me to see anything that starved. I'd have to learn what ghost wolves eat. I used Abalyn's peppermint soap to scrub her clean. I found cuts, scrapes, scratches, welts, offal and twigs matted in her chestnut hair, and I took all that away and left her purified as if I'd used salt and holy water. I made her baptism in chlorination and shampoo. But, deceive the deceivers thus neither the angels in heaven above nor the demons down under the sea can ever dissever my soul from the soul of what I know to be the truth. Not even Abalyn, however much she knows I still love her.

That's it. Or that's all I'm allowing for now. The story of the wolf who cried girl when there was no one but me to finally show up and hear her. Once upon a time, she got hunted down and nailed to a wall, and I wrenched the cold iron spikes from her pelt and a thorn from the callused pad of a bloodied paw. There is more, yes. That's no decent conclusion. But I have been typing now for so many hours I can't count, but a long time because the sun was going down and now it's rising. I'm sleepy. I can't recall ever before having been half this sleepy. But here it is, here I am, here I am, and I can see it, and this undoes all Abalyn's lies that there was only ever one Eva Canning.

Go away, crow tapping at my window. One brings only sorrow; it takes ~~too~~ two for mirth.

Don't think I don't know that. Don't think I can't see you there. Before I go to bed, I'll seal the window with seven mustard seeds and seven bottle caps and seven bay leaves, and I won't even have to dream of you, Abalyn.

7/7/7/7

7/7

7

seven

7

7/7

7/7/7/7

8

(Little Conversations)

⌀

Selected telephone messages, last week of October 2010 (offers of aid, concerned voices neglected):

"Imp, look [pause] I know this is weird, calling and all. Especially after that scene in the parking lot last week. It was awkward, and I'm sorry about that. Maybe I shouldn't have said what I said. Anyway, hey [pause] I'm worried about you, Imp. Let's talk, okay. I think it would be good if we could talk."—Abalyn Armitage

"India, this is the receptionist from Dr. Ogilvy's office, calling to remind you of your appointment at five p.m., day after tomorrow. Please let us know if you can't make it and need to reschedule. Thanks."

"Hi, Imp. You can't keep missing work like this. I can't continue to ignore it. You're not even bothering to call in sick, and I can't keep letting you slide. You know that. You need to call me, as soon as you hear this message. We have to talk."—Bill, my ex-manager from work

"India, it's Dr. Ogilvy. You missed your five o'clock yesterday. We're going to have to charge you for the session, since you didn't cancel. You've never missed and not let us know ahead of time, so I'm just a little concerned especially after our last session. Give me a call when it's convenient."—Dr. Magdalene Ogilvy

"It's Bill again. I've left messages on your cell and your landline, and you haven't called back. I don't know what's going on. I hope you're okay, but I don't have any choice but to let you go. I'm really sorry. You gotta know I didn't want it to come to this. You've always been a great employee. But you've left me no choice. Anyway, come by when you can and pick up your last check. Thanks."—Bill (fourth call in four days)

"Imp, it's Abalyn again. Please call me." (second call)

"India, it's your aunt Elaine. I got a call this morning from your psychiatrist. She says you missed your last appointment, and didn't even bother to call. That's not like you, and she agreed. She's worried, and so am I. Call me, baby. Let me know you're okay."

"India, it's Dr. Ogilvy again. I spoke with your aunt yesterday, and she says she hasn't talked to you in a couple of weeks. I know you need refills on two of your prescriptions. And, well, you've always been so good about getting in touch when you need to reschedule. Please call." (second call)

"Abalyn again. I guess I've pissed you off. I'm not going to call again. I feel stupid, leaving all these messages. I truly did not mean to upset you that day. If you're pissed, I probably have it coming. [long pause] So, yeah, I'm not going to call again. I can't stand being a pest. But I still wanna talk. Call me, or don't. Either way, I hope you're okay. I'm not just saying that." (sixth message)

"India, just a reminder that the rent check was due last week. Just a reminder. We'd hate to have to charge you the late fee."—Felicia, my landlord

"Baby, I still haven't heard from you, and it's been days since I called. If something's wrong, you need to let us know. I talked to Dr. Ogilvy again this afternoon. She said she's still not heard from you, and we're both worried. I'm thinking about dropping by. Call me."—Aunt Elaine (second call)

"India, please pick up if you're in. I spoke with your aunt again about an hour ago. If you're off your medication, we need to know."—Dr. Ogilvy (third call)

"Hey, I know I said I wasn't going to call again, but I had a really fucked-up dream about you last night."—Abalyn (seventh and final message)

"India, about the rent . . ."

Part of me always thought no one would much care if I ever dropped off the face of the earth. Obviously, I was mistaken. People kept calling until the answering machine and voice mail were full. I was only half-aware the phone kept ringing. That was two and a half weeks ago. Halloween came and went; I'm not sure I even noticed. Now it's the middle of November, and the trees along Willow Street are almost bare. Willow Street has no willows by the way. Oak Street has no oaks. Maybe they did once upon a time. Like I said, lots of things in Providence have names that no longer fit.

On the twenty-sixth of October, the day after I ran into Abalyn outside the children's museum, I stopped taking my meds. At first, I just forgot. I'm not bad about forgetting, 'cause it's been so many years, me and the meds. But after a day or two I was aware I wasn't taking them because I didn't *want* to take them. I was getting paranoid. That can happen pretty quickly, and I thought . . . well, it's there in the stuff I wrote during the relapse. I got it in my head the pills were messing with my memory. After Abalyn said what she said, I panicked. Someone tells me I can't remember what I definitely *do* remember, and sometimes I panic. I'm not as used to it as I often pretend. As I pretend to be used to it, I mean to say. The false memories. That hasn't happened in a long time, a full-on bahooties return to the worst it can get. I'm trying not to dwell on what might have happened, because it didn't, and nothing good's gonna come of fretting over spilled milk, right?

Anyway, here I am on the other side, and I put people through shit, and I lost my job, and I feel like an idiot. Maybe it was something I had to do. I read back over what I wrote, and I can't help but think maybe it was necessary, a trigger for a *thing* I might never have managed otherwise. But I still feel like a heel for having done it. I don't like to frighten people who care about me, and now I'm out of work and owe $125 for a missed session, and I can't afford that even more than usual because Bill fired me. I don't blame him, but I have no idea what I'm going to do until I can find another job. Money's gonna get tight fast, trust fund or no trust fund.

Dr. Ogilvy apologized, but said she can't make an exception. The hospital sets the rules, not her.

Finally, Abalyn stopped calling and came to see what was wrong. Someone let her in the house, though they're not supposed to do that. Let in people who don't live here anymore. Maybe whoever did it, the college students upstairs or the mathematician from Brown who lives downstairs, maybe they weren't aware Abalyn had moved out. She says she stood outside my door knocking for almost half an hour, then she used her key. I never asked for it back, and she never volunteered. Neither of us thought about it, I suppose. My car was in the driveway, and though she's aware I often walk and take the bus, she knocked and knocked and waited, then gave up and used her key. I'm not going to be cross with her about it. I know how shitty it would be if I were. To be cross with her over using the key. Oh, she'd lost her key to the building, but not the one to my apartment.

Abalyn let herself in, and she found me holed up in my bedroom. I'd locked the door, so that was another barricade she had to get past. I'm not sure how long I'd been shut away in there, hours or days. I don't remember, and I don't have any way of finding out. It doesn't matter now. She said I was crying, that she could hear me crying and talking to myself. She went to the kitchen and got a butter knife, and she was able to use it to jimmy the lock. She found me in nothing but my panties, hiding in a corner by the window. She didn't say I was hiding, but I believe I must have been. Corners have always felt like safe places. Nothing can sneak up behind you in a corner, even a corner near a window. She found me with my back to two walls, squeezed into a corner, but I'm not going into detail. It's too embarrassing, how she found me, what I was doing, the state I was in. But I was dehydrated. I hadn't eaten in, I don't know, days. I hadn't been flushing the toilet. At first, she was angry, but then she held me and cried. Don't know for how long, but I remember telling her to stop a bunch of times. I struck her, too. I have to admit that part. I hit her several times while she was trying to calm me down and find out what was going on, and I blacked her right eye. I wish she'd hit me back, but she didn't. She just held filthy, hysterical me there in my corner until I stopped freaking out. Later, she stood near the fridge, silent, calm, holding a bag of frozen peas against her face. Every time I remember that, her standing there, I wish all over that she'd hit me back.

Anyway, then the chain of events went something like this: Abalyn called Dr. Ogilvy's emergency number, and someone, whomever she talked to, told her to try to get some Valium in me and call my aunt. But I didn't want Aunt Elaine around, and apparently I told Abalyn that. She did call Aunt Elaine, but convinced her not to come to my apartment, got her to agree that she wouldn't so long as Abalyn kept her in the loop. The clinic said if someone would stay with me, and if I didn't seem like a danger to myself or anyone else, it wouldn't be necessary to call an ambulance (again, again). Dr. Ogilvy phoned. I said something to her, but I don't for the life of me know *what* I said. Abalyn agreed to stay with me, and Dr. Ogilvy told her to wait twenty-four hours, then get me back on my drug regime. She also told Abalyn to try to figure out how long it had been since I'd stopped taking my meds. Either I couldn't remember, or I just wasn't willing to tell anyone (back to the paranoia, I didn't want Abalyn or anyone else near me). The best she, Abalyn, was able to do was find my pillbox, which holds a week's worth of pills, Sunday through Saturday, contained in their own discrete plastic compartments—S, M, T, W, T, F, S. There was six days' worth in the box, which only told her it had been a minimum of six days. She knew it might have been quite a bit longer.

Abalyn called Margot, the new girlfriend, and they had a big fight. Margot said none of this—meaning me—was Abalyn's responsibility, and I was being manipulative. They fought some more, and eventually Abalyn told her to fuck off, and now they're not together any longer. So, I scared Abalyn half to death, punched her in the eye, and made her lose her girlfriend. Way to go, Imp. You're a peach, you are.

She's staying here, because she didn't have anywhere else to go, and it was the very least I could do after what she did for me and what it cost her. She's only *staying* with me; she isn't *living* with me. I can see it's hard on her. We try to keep out of each other's way. You can care about someone deeply, but not be able to live with them, not easily. I look at Abalyn and I see how true this is; before the relapse, I probably didn't understand how true that is. I made a joke about her being my knight in shining armor, but it wasn't funny, and neither of us laughed.

There hasn't been much of that, laughter, around here since she found me cowering in that bedroom corner. I live in a house where people upstairs laugh, and people downstairs laugh. I hear them through the floorboards, laughter going down, laughter coming up.

A couple of days after Abalyn found me, we were eating Trix cereal and watching cartoons, just like the old days. Except *Ren & Stimpy* and *The Angry Beavers* weren't hilarious like they used to be, and the cereal tasted like tiny fruit-flavored balls of paper. Halfway through a cartoon, I said I didn't want to see any more, so Abalyn picked up the remote and her TV went black (she had to move all her stuff back here, of course). She's been so accommodating, which helps, but which also makes me feel even more ashamed. We both just sat there a few minutes, silent, picking at dry Trix, and the street noise seemed louder than usual. The Mexican boys, passing cars, autumn birds. Abalyn spoke first, and it was a relief, dispelling that not-really-quiet hanging between us. I'd still say it was a relief, even considering the stuff we both said immediately afterwards.

"I read it," she said, and I nodded. I'd given Abalyn the pages I typed during the crazy spell and asked her to read them. She hadn't wanted to, but I told her it was important.

"Thank you," I said.

She asked, "Did it help?" and I shrugged.

"Probably too soon to say, but I don't especially think so. I think it was a start, and I had to start somewhere, but I'm still scared." I almost said something Dr. Ogilvy would have said, like "there's still a high degree of cognitive dissonance," but, fortunately, I thought better of it and said what I said, instead.

"But it was a start," she said, and I noticed she was picking all the lemon-yellow Trix out of her bowl and lining them up single file on the floor in front of her. It reminded me of something I'd do. "I can't stop feeling like none of this would have happened if only I'd been a little more tactful that day."

"You shouldn't have to walk on eggshells around me," I told her. It was something I'd said to her before. "I don't expect you to coddle me."

"Still . . . ," she said, and trailed off.

"You didn't even know I had those two versions of Eva in my head, Abalyn. There was no way you could have known, not if only one of them actually happened."

She plucked another yellow Trix from her bowl and lined it up with the others.

"You believe that now?"

She wanted me to say yes, I did. But she'd been too good to me, and she deserved more than a lie. So I said, "No, but I'm working on it. I mean, I see Dr. Ogilvy in a few days . . . and I'm working on it. I know something's wrong now, and that's a start. I know something's gone wrong in my head."

"You're a brave lady, Imp. I swear I couldn't live with shit like that. You're stronger than me."

"No, I'm not. I'm just used to it. I haven't ever been any other way. Not really. Besides, you've been through at least as much. I can't imagine having the courage to do what you've done." I was talking about coming out and her reassignment surgery, but she knew that without me having to spell it all out. "People do what they have to do. That's all."

"Listen to us," she said, and she almost smiled, and she almost laughed. "Imp and Abalyn's Self-Congratulatory Society of Mutual Admiration."

I smiled, but didn't try to laugh.

Then Abalyn said, "Maybe if you wrote. Not the way you wrote it when you were sick. I mean, if you wrote it as one of your short stories."

"I'm not a writer. I'm a painter."

"I know that. I'm just saying, it might help."

"I haven't written a story in a long time."

"I figure it's like riding a bicycle," she said, then picked up one of the lemon-yellow Trix and ate it.

"It's strange enough, that you've read what you've already read."

"That was your idea," she reminded me.

"I know, but that doesn't make it any less strange."

"You know what part surprised me most? The lines about the Black Dahlia. That's the part that really put its hook in me. And I feel responsible for that, too. Seeing the Perrault exhibit was my idea."

"So, that really did happen?"

"Unless we're both crazy. Fuck knows, my mother and father would tell you I'm crazy as a shithouse rat."

"Your mother and father don't know you," I told her, trying hard not to think about having to be despised by one's parents. I silently wished Abalyn could have had a mother like Rosemary Anne, a grandmother like Caroline. If I'd ever told Rosemary I was a boy, not a girl, I'm sure she'd have been mostly fascinated. Maybe concerned, too, because of the way the world treats transgender people, but mostly fascinated. She probably would have gone so far as to insist it was marvelous.

"Anyway, yes. We went to the Perrault exhibit, and there was that Black Dahlia sculpture. I'm never gonna forget how much it upset you."

"It shouldn't have. I overreacted."

"It was damned creepy. It's even worse if you stop to consider he had to look at it every day for who knows how long it took to finish. Months maybe. Months coming back to the same grotesque subject day after day, and all the research he would have needed to do. I read there was a feminist victims' rights sort of group out in California tried to get the exhibit banned because of that sculpture. Hell, I almost halfway don't blame them."

"I'm not for censorship," I said, "no matter how awful art gets."

Abalyn frowned and stared at a lemon-yellow Trix held between thumb and index finger, only halfway to her mouth. "You know I'm not in favor of censoring art, Imp. I was only saying I can see how that sculpture could elicit so strong a response."

We were talking about *Phases 1–5*, of course, the grotesque pinwheel Perrault made using life casts and taxidermy to depict Elizabeth Short transforming into a werewolf. The last piece we'd seen before I couldn't stand seeing any more and we'd left the gallery.

"If writing a story would help you sort through that second Eva you remember, it might help," she said. "I'm here to help, you know. If you want me to help. I didn't mean to be presumptuous."

"I know."

"And I'm sure Dr. Ogilvy would help."

I told Abalyn that I'd never talked to Dr. Ogilvy about Eva Canning, and she looked kind of dumbfounded.

"Imp, whatever really happened with her, don't you think that's sort of a big thing not to tell your psychiatrist? Isn't that what you pay her for?"

"I don't think she believes in ghosts. And certainly not were-wolves, or mermaids."

"Does it matter what she believes in? You gotta figure she's heard weirder shit than this."

I told Abalyn I seriously doubted she had.

"Okay, but what's the worst she can do? Have you committed? From what I saw, and what you've told me, I think if she was going to try to do that, she'd have already done it."

I wanted to say, let's please stop talking about this. Possibly, I was getting angry, and, possibly, I wanted to tell Abalyn she simply didn't *get it*, that there's crazy and then there are crazy people who believe in mermaids and werewolves and unicorns and fairies and shit. But I didn't. Surely, she'd earned the right to speak her mind. I'd be in the hospital, or worse, if she hadn't found me when she did. If she hadn't cared enough to come looking, and then cared enough to stick around. And, anyway, down inside, I knew she probably wasn't wrong about Dr. Ogilvy.

"Okay," I said.

"Okay what?"

"Okay, I'll talk to her. I'll try to consider writing a story."

"And I'm here, if you need me."

"Because you don't have anywhere else to go."

"Jesus, Imp. No, not because I don't have anywhere else to fuck-ing go."

"Well, you don't, do you?"

She didn't answer me. Conversation ends here. She shook her head and sighed, then took her cereal bowl and the box of Trix, stood up, and went to the kitchen. I sat on the floor in front of the blank television, trying to imagine what I was going to say to my psychiatrist, if that's what I was going to do. *How* I would say what

Abalyn thought I ought to say, because I realized it wasn't so much the *what* of Eva as it was finding the necessary words.

We didn't talk much the rest of that day. Aunt Elaine called sometime after dark, and I worked on a painting until I was tired enough to try to sleep.

I'm piling contradictions upon contractions, building myself a house of cards or a deadfall jumble of pick-up sticks. I told Abalyn that I've never spoken with my psychiatrist about Eva Canning, but that's not true. Just look back at pages 115 and 166, where I wrote: "I've not mentioned that I'm writing all these things down, though we [Ogilvy and I] have spoken several times now of Eva Canning, both the July Eva and the November Eva, just as we've talked about Phillip George Saltonstall and *The Drowning Girl* (painting and folklore) and 'The Little Mermaid.' Just as we've talked about Albert Perrault and The Voyeur of Utter Destruction (in Hindsight) and 'Little Red Riding Hood.' "

When I told Abalyn I'd kept it from Dr. Ogilvy, was I mistaken, or was I simply lying? Why would I have lied? Was it misremembering? Also, I wrote that Abalyn told me she and I went to the exhibit together, but we didn't. My friend Ellen from the used bookstore, she asked me to go, not Abalyn, and that was in late September, after Abalyn says she'd already left.

I'm not trying to lie.

I'm lying.

I tell you this, India Morgan Phelps, daughter of Rosemary Anne and granddaughter of Caroline, you don't even guess your own motives. You obfuscate and deny and spin falsehood (consciously or unconsciously), and you can't say why. It's deranged, and it's *all* deranged. No, it's worse than that. I'm beginning to lose the threads of my ghost story. I'm no longer even certain that it *is* a ghost story, and if it's not, I don't know what else it could be. Or how to proceed.

I'm setting aside the questions I posed last time I sat down at my grandmother's typewriter. Not because they're invalid questions, but because . . . because. Maybe, they've been answered, and that's the because. I choose to posit that's the truth of it.

Yesterday, I saw Dr. Ogilvy for the first time since the episode, and I want to write about that this evening, about seeing her, what I said and what she said. What was said. But I woke up this morning with a headache, and it's only gotten worse. My usual cocktail of Excedrin and aspirin hasn't helped. There's a railroad spike in my left eye, and there are gremlins running around in my skull banging on pots and pans. Skull goblins. Abalyn has a bottle of codeine that a friend gave her, and she offered me one. But I don't like to take other people's prescriptions (evidently, Abalyn has no such qualms), so I said thank you, but no thank you. It might have helped, but I didn't know if it would interact with my meds, and I didn't feel like calling the pharmacy to find out. Abalyn offered to look online for any information regarding the possibility of negative interactions, but I don't trust stuff about drugs posted on the internet; how do you know if whoever wrote it knows what he or she is talking about?

Dr. Ogilvy is in her fifties, probably close to sixty. I haven't ever asked her age, but I've always been pretty good at guessing how old people are. Her hair is long, and she wears it pulled back in a pony-tail. Where it comes free of the ponytail, it sticks out, sort of crinkly or kinky. It's almost all gray, except for a few stubborn streaks of auburn. Those streaks aren't crinkly. Her eyes are kind and alert. They're hazel, closer to hazel green than hazel brown. There are fine wrinkles all around her kind, alert, hazel-green eyes. She smiles a lot, but it's a soft smile that doesn't show her teeth. She doesn't grin, and that's good, because it unnerves me when people grin. Her nails are usually polished.

I've mentioned all the insects in her office, right? And how she almost studied to be an entomologist in college? Well, her office, where the walls are painted a dark red that's more comforting than most people might expect it to be. Dark red, but not maroon. There's something of purple in maroon, and there's nothing of purple in the red of her office walls. The first or second time I saw her, I asked about all the insects in their frames, and she told me about a lot of them. Many, many beetles, and she said that beetles really were her favorites. She called her passion for beetles "avocational coleopterology." Coleopterology (kō-lē-op-ter-ology) being the branch of entomology that studies beetles. She said that twenty-five percent of all species on earth are beetles. "God," she said, "if He exists, has an inordinate fondness for beetles." She told me she was paraphrasing a British biologist named Haldane.

She was especially proud of a gigantic four-and-a-half-inch black-and-white beetle called the Goliath beetle (*Goliathus goliatus*), which she collected herself on a trip to Cameroon, which is in western Africa.

"It wasn't a safe place to go," she told me. "It's even less safe now. You'd probably be better off not ever visiting Cameroon. It's a beautiful country with beautiful people—and beautiful beetles—but too much political unrest. Don't go to Cameroon, Imp."

I replied it was unlikely I ever would, that I'd ever be able to afford to even if I wanted to go. Then she showed me dozens of butterflies and a praying mantis that looked like a leaf. "I didn't collect most of these," she said. "There's a shop in New York—Maxilla and Mandible, on Columbus, just around the corner from the American Museum of Natural History—and I buy many of them there." I asked why she had no spiders on her walls, and Dr. Ogilvy reminded me spiders aren't insects, that they're arachnids, like scorpions and ticks. "I don't collect arachnids," she said.

"Well, you've got a lot of bugs."

"This is nothing. You ought to see my house."

I'm not supposed to be writing about Dr. Ogilvy's insects, so I must be stalling.

"It's what you do," Imp typed. "You procrastinate, like it'll ever get easier. Like, if you wait long enough, it'll be a breeze."

It won't be. Not ever. It'll be a hurricane.

Here's what I "know," after yesterday's session. I have been talking with Magdalene Ogilvy about Eva Canning, on and off, since December 2008—so for the past twenty-two months. That's what her records indicate, which would be long after July Eva, and during November Eva (whom, increasingly, I've begun to dismiss as . . . well, I'll get back to that). Dr. Ogilvy was aware I've wrestled with the paradox of the two Evas and Abalyn having left me twice. She showed me the notes to prove it. It's a very thick sheaf of notes. Does she believe in ghosts, werewolves, and/or mermaids? She said that wasn't relevant, and I suppose I see her point.

However, she didn't know I've been writing this manuscript. She was surprised to learn of it, I could tell, though I think she made a concerted effort not to *appear* surprised. The first thing I did yesterday was show her what I think of as the "7 pages," what I wrote during the episode. She asked if I minded her reading them aloud, and I said I didn't (which definitely wasn't true). When she was done, I was almost shaking, and I wanted to leave.

"It's very powerful," she said. "It reads almost like an incantation."

"An incantation against what?"

"Depends," she said. "These ghosts of yours, and perhaps your illness. The anomaly you've been struggling with so long now. The contradictions. But it also reads like a declaration. It's a bold thing you've set down on paper. Obviously, you shouldn't have stopped your medication, but . . ." And she trailed off. I was pretty sure I knew how she would have finished the sentence.

"Do you believe these events happened?" she asked, and tapped at the pages. "As you've written them?"

I hesitated a moment, then said, "I don't. I freaked, and I was hammering at what Abalyn claimed, the existence of only one Eva. I was clutching at . . . I don't know. I can't see how, if I somehow invented the second Eva, it could have been any sort of consolation."

"So maybe that's the question we need to find the answer to." Then she corrected herself. "No, the question *you* need to answer for yourself, Imp." And she brought up that Joseph Campbell quote I wrote down earlier (or did I?), about being permitted to "go crazy" and find your own way out again. "This is your journey, and if it's ever going to let you rest, I believe it's a problem you should try to solve for yourself. I'm here, of course, if you need me. I can be a guide, maybe, but it feels like you're beginning to put the pieces together. I think Abalyn's helping."

"She wants me to write a story. About the second part, Albert Perrault and the exhibit and all."

"Do you think you can?"

We'd already discussed the Perrault exhibition, and how it did, or didn't, fit in with my garbled chronology of the events between late June and the winter of 2008–2009. July and November and what have you. I told her that Abalyn said she hadn't gone to the exhibit with me, but that I was sure I hadn't gone alone. I wouldn't have dared to go alone.

"That's where I want to begin," Dr. Ogilvy said. "Where I want *you* to begin." And she stared down at my thick file lying open in her lap. "There's a reason you fabricated the second story, assuming you fabricated the second story, and, more than anything, you need to know why that was."

"I don't know why."

"I know, but I think you can learn why. Or relearn why. It's there in your mind, somewhere. You haven't lost it, even if you have repressed it. You've just hidden it from yourself. Maybe you're trying to protect yourself from something."

"Worse than two Evas, and worse than mermaids and were-wolves?" I asked, not making much of an effort to hide my skepticism.

"That's your question," she said. "Not mine. But I have an exercise I'd like you to try. I'd like you to make a list for me. I'd like you to list those things you are starting to believe are false, that you previously thought were part of the truth." (She meant *factual*, not *true*, but I didn't correct her.)

"About Eva Canning," I said.

"Yes. About her, and these events which seem associated with her. Are you up to that?"

"Yeah," I said, even though I wasn't certain if I was.

She handed me a yellow legal pad and a number two pencil (#2, hexagonal in cross section, Palomino Blackwing, high-quality graphite), and said she'd leave me alone while I wrote my list. "I'll be right outside in the hallway. Just let me know when you're done." And here's what I wrote (she made a photocopy for herself, then let me take the original home):

1. Eva Canning only came to me once.
2. It was July when I found her, not November.
3. Abalyn left me early in August.
4. It may be impossible for me to set forth a strictly accurate chronology/narrative of these events.
5. There was a siren. There was no wolf.
6. Abalyn didn't go with me to the Perrault exhibit. Ellen did. And that was after Abalyn left me.
7. I created the wolf/2nd Eva/Perrault exhibit as a defense mechanism against the events of the July Eva.
8. There was only one Eva Canning.

And then I stood up and opened the door to find Dr. Ogilvy just outside, talking with a nurse. She came back in and I sat again. She sat and read my list two or three times. "This last one," she said. "I want to focus on this last one before you leave," and she looked at the clock. I had five minutes before my time was up.

"Okay," I said, and reached for my shapeless cloth bag, one of Rosemary's old purses, and held it in my lap. Holding the bag made me feel safe, and, besides, I didn't want to forget it.

"This is admitting to a lot," Dr. Ogilvy said. "And it shows a considerable amount of understanding of what may have happened to you." She seemed to expect me to say something then, but I didn't.

"Why, Imp, do you suspect you'd have needed a defense mechanism or coping strategy against the July Eva?"

"Isn't it obvious?"

"Maybe, but I'd like to hear you say it."

I stared at her for a minute. I probably mean that literally. I stared at her for a full minute. Probably, she saw reluctance and unease in my eyes.

"Sirens," I told her, "sing you to drowning or sing you to shipwreck. They sing, and, if you're listening, their song compels you to do things you wouldn't do otherwise. They manipulate you to their own ends. I despise the idea that I was manipulated. But the wolf, the wolf was helpless and only a ghost that needed me to remember it was a wolf, so that it could also remember it was a wolf."

She smiled a little wider than usual, and I glanced down at my bag.

"What do you think July Eva made you do, Imp?"

"I can't say that. Later, maybe, but not now. Don't ask me that again, please."

"I'm sorry. I didn't mean to push."

And then I pointed out that my time was up, and she tapped at her computer and made my next appointment, and wrote prescriptions for my refills, writing in that secret language only doctors and pharmacists can decipher.

"Think about number seven," she said, just before I left. "Just think about it." (7/7/7)

"I think about it a lot," I replied. It was raining when I left, and the rain falling on the mounds of dirty snow was ugly, so I watched the sky, instead.

On the bus home, there was an elderly Portuguese woman with ill-fitting dentures and a very large mole between her eyes. There were three thick white hairs growing from the mole. Despite the cold, she was wearing lime-green flip-flops and a T-shirt. She was like me, not sane, except I don't think she was on any sort of medication. She was sitting across from me, talking to herself, and it was annoying other passengers, who kept glaring at the woman.

"Are you cold?" I asked her. She seemed startled that anyone would choose to speak to her.

"Isn't everyone, this time of year?"

"You ought to wear a coat. And better shoes."

"I should," she agreed. "But, you know, shoes and coats hide too much skin."

"You need to see your skin?"

"Don't you?"

"I've never thought about it." I asked her name, and she squinted at me, as if trying to puzzle out some devious ulterior motive for my having asked.

"Teodora," she said. "When I had a name, it was Teodora. But it went away one day when I forgot to watch my skin. Now, I don't know. But once it was Teodora."

"My name is India," I told her, and she laughed, which made those loose dentures slip around a bit.

"That's a strange name, little lady."

"My mother got it from *Gone with the Wind*. It's a book, and there's a woman in it named India Wilkes."

"It's a book," she repeated. Then added, "It's your name. You're a book," and stared out the window for a while at the storefronts along Westminster.

"I'm sorry if I bothered you," I said.

She sighed and didn't take her eyes off the window. "You haven't bothered me, India Wilkes. But watch your skin. Don't you wear so many clothes. Nobody knows to watch after their skin anymore. Look at 'em. Nobody on this bus watches their skin, so it waltzes in the night. You watch skin, or it moves around."

I gave her five dollars, though she didn't ask me for it. She held the bill wadded up in her left hand, which wasn't clean. She didn't appear to have bathed recently.

"I'll watch my skin more closely," I assured her. "You stay warm, and get something to eat."

She didn't reply, and I got off at the next stop. The bus driver wanted to know if Teodora had been bothering me, or panhandling. "No," I told him. "We were just talking." Then he looked at me funny. "You say so," he said.

Back home on Willow Street, Abalyn was sitting cross-legged on the floor in front of her television playing a game called *Fallout: New Vegas*. I only knew the name because she'd told me the night before. She was playing a character named Courier who was wandering about a post-apocalyptic Mojave Desert trying to find a lost package containing a platinum poker chip. None of it made much sense to me. I told her I was going to write the story, and that I'd be in the blue room with too many bookshelves.

"Do you want me to remind you about dinner?" she asked. I said if I got hungry—and I knew I probably wouldn't—I'd come out and find something to eat. But I thanked her for offering, anyway.

And so I wrote my story about the November Eva I didn't find on Valentine Road, only it came out more of a story about Albert

Perrault and Elizabeth Short. It came out as it needed to come. Because I couldn't manage a recitation of false facts, I managed a recitation of truth. I was worried Dr. Ogilvy might question the utility of having written a story about the wolf that was only indirectly my story of the wolf. But she didn't, even when I suggested I'd only set one box within another, that all I'd accomplished was the creation of a fiction to contain another fiction.

"If the fiction has been contained," she replied, "then you've gained control over it." And I didn't argue with her. It took me five days (and nights) to write "Werewolf Smile," and I'm never going to try to sell it to a magazine. It belongs to no one except me.

Werewolf Smile

BY INDIA MORGAN PHELPS

I don't know whether it's true that Eva slept with Perrault. Probably it is. I know she slept with plenty enough men—men and other women—those nights when she'd slip away from me, wrapped in a caul of cigarette smoke, perfume, and halfhearted deceit. She'd laugh whenever anyone dared to call her polyamorous. Unless, of course, she was in one of her black moods, and then she might do something worse than laugh. I never called her polyamorous, because I knew that she never *loved* any of them, any more than she loved me. There was no amour in those trysts. "I fuck around," she would say, or something like that. "It doesn't need a fancy fucking Greek word for it, or a fucking flag in a pride parade. I'm a wanton. I sleep around." Then, she might ask, "What's got me wondering, Winter, is why you *don't*." She almost never used my actual name, and I never asked why she'd started calling me Winter. We met in July, after all. On a very hot day in July. But, sure, she might have slept with Albert Perrault. She liked to call herself his disciple. I heard her call herself that on more than one occasion. She fancied herself somehow favored by him. Favored beyond the bedclothes, I mean to say. It pleased her, imagining herself as more to him than a mere student, as though he were some unholy prophet, Eva's very own *bête noire* come to lead her down to places she'd spent her life only half imagining and never daring to dream she might one day glimpse. She assumed—from his paintings, from *what* he painted—*he* had glimpsed them, from his paintings, from *what* he painted. She assumed he had something to show anyone *besides* the paintings. Eva assumed a lot of things. But don't ask me what he truly thought of her. I hardly ever spoke with him, and then only briefly, and it was never anything but the most superficial sorts of conversation. Our exchanges were cursory, perfunctory, slipshod, though never exactly awkward. I don't know what he thought of her as an artist, or as a lover, or if he derived some satisfaction from my suspicion about the two of them. Sometimes, I wanted to warn him (I'd often wanted to warn others about Eva), but I never had the nerve, or I never had the heart, and, besides, that probably would have been like warning Herod about Salome. And, likely, I'd have only succeeded in appearing jealous, the disgruntled green-eyed third in a disconnected *ménage à trois* trying to gum up the works. I can see how my feelings for Eva might be misinterpreted. But I do *not* hate her. I love her, as I have loved her since the hot July day we met, almost five years ago, and I know that's why I'm damned. Because I cannot push away. I am unable to push away. Even after all her lovers, after Perrault, and the Dahlia, and all the things she's done and said, the hideous things I've seen because of her, all that shit that's going to be in my head forever and ever, I still love her. I seem to have no choice whatsoever in the matter, because I have certainly *tried* to hate Eva. But I have found that trying not to love her is like someone trying to wish herself well; thinking, for example, I could simply will a gangrenous wound back to healthy pink flesh again. You cut away necrosis, or you die, and I plainly lack whatever cardinal resolve is necessary to cut Eva out of *me*. And I wonder, now, if

she ever had these same thoughts, about me, or about Albert Perrault? I cast her as I have, and as she claims herself to be, a willing
plague vector, but perhaps Eva was also merely one of the infected.
She may well not have been a Typhoid Mary of the mind and soul.
I can't know for sure, one way or the other, and I'm weary of speculation. So, better I restrict these meanderings to what I at least *believe*
I know than to speculate, yes? And when I sat down to write about
her and about Perrault, I had in mind the Dahlia, in particular, not
all these useless (and generally abstract) questions of love and fidel-
ity and intent. How can I pretend to have known Eva's intentions?
She called herself a liar as frequently as she called herself a wanton
and a slut. She was the physical embodiment of the pseudomenon,
a conscious, animate incarnation of the Liar's Paradox.

"Oh, Winter, everything I've ever told you or ever will tell you
is a lie, but *this*, this *one* thing is true."

Now, work with that. And I'm not speaking in metaphors, or
paraphrasing. And I do not, here, have to rely upon an inevitably
unreliable memory, because when she said those very words, I was
so taken aback, so galled at the audacity, that, less than an hour
later, I scribbled it down in the black Moleskine notebook Eva presented me on the occasion of my thirty-fifth birthday. That *is* what
she said. And I sat very still, and I listened, because how could I
refuse to hear the one truth uttered by a woman who will never be
permitted to speak one truth? I sat on the floor of my apartment (I
never thought of it as *our* apartment), and I listened. "It scared the
living shit out of me," she said, "and I have never seen anything so
beautiful." This, I suppose, was her one true thing, which, perforce,
must also be false. But she continued for quite some time thereafter,
and I sat beneath the window, not *not* listening. There was a Smiths
CD in the stereo, set on repeat, and I think the disc played twice
through before she was done describing to me plans for Perrault's
new installation. "The parallel is obvious, of course, and he ac-

knowledges that up front. *Le Petit Chaperon Rouge*, Little Red Riding Hood, *Rotkäppchen*, and so forth. The genius is not in having made the association, but in the execution. The cumulative effect of the assembled elements, both his paintings and the reproductions of various artifacts relating to the murder of Elizabeth Short." Eva laughed at me when I told her it all sounded pretentious and unspeakably morbid. She laughed loudly, and reminded me of games that we had played, of scenes beyond counting. "I know, Winter, you like to pretend your heart's not as rotten as mine, but do try not to be such a goddamn hypocrite about it." And there's our lovely paradox once more, because she was absolutely right, of course. I don't recall interrupting her again that night. I can't even recall *which* Smiths CD was playing. Not so much as one single song. "You know," she said, "before the 'Black Dahlia' moniker stuck, the newspapers in Los Angeles were calling it the 'werewolf murder.'" She was silent a moment then, just staring at me, and I realized I'd missed a cue, that I'd almost forgotten my line. "Why?" I asked belatedly. "Why did they call it that?" She lit a cigarette and blew smoke towards the high white ceiling. She shrugged. "Albert tried to find out, but no one seems to know. Back then, LA journalists were always coming up with these lurid names for murders. Lots of times, they had to do with flowers. The White Gardenia Murder, the Red Hibiscus Murder, and so on. He thinks the werewolf thing maybe had something to do with the smile the killer carved into her face, pretty much ear to ear. That it sort of made Short *look* like a wolf. But that still doesn't make much sense to me. I assumed that the newspapermen were referring to the murderer as the werewolf, not to the victim." That's the only time I ever heard Eva disagree with Perrault. She shrugged again and took another drag off her cigarette. "Either way, it's a great angle, and he means to make the most of it. He hasn't told me exactly how, not exactly, not yet. But I know he's been talking to a taxidermist. Some guy he worked with once before." And she went on like this, and I sat and listened. "It's very exciting," Eva continued, "seeing him branch out, explore other media. He did that thing with the stones last year in New York, the stones inside their cages. That's what really set him moving in this direction. That's what he says. Oh, and I haven't told you. He got a call from someone in Hollywood last week. He won't say who, but it's someone big." I promise, for what that might be worth, I am not trying to make Eva sound any more or less insipid or sycophantic than she actually did that night. She knew I didn't care for Perrault's work, that it gave me the willies, which is probably why she spent so much time talking about it. Come to think, that's probably why she started fucking him to begin with (assuming that I am not mistaken on that count, assuming she actually *did* fuck him).

But wait.

I've said too much about that night. I didn't intend to drone on about that night, but merely present it as prologue to what came afterwards. It was winter, late winter in Boston, and an especially snowy winter at that. I'd just started the bookshop job, and sometimes I picked up a spare shift at a coffeehouse on Newbury Street. I don't think Eva was working at the time, except she'd taken to calling herself Perrault's personal assistant, and he'd taken to letting her get away with it. But I'm not sure any genuine work was involved; I'm certain no money was. Eva was only a slut. She never had the requisite motivation to be anything so useful or lucrative as a whore. But, playing his PA, she was involved in all the nasty shit he was getting up to that winter, planning the show in LA, the Dahlia. Perrault decided early on to call the installation The Voyeur of Utter Destruction, after some David Bowie song or another. I heard through Eva, Perrault had landed a book deal from a Manhattan publisher, a glossy, full-color folio affair, though it wasn't paying much. I heard from Eva he didn't care about the small advance, because he'd gotten color. Frankly, I heard most of what I heard about Albert Perrault through Eva, not via my own aforementioned perfunctory conversations with the man. Anyhow, the same day Eva told me about the book, she also told me that she was going to be his model for several of the sculptural pieces in the installation. Life casts had to be made, which meant she had to fly out to LA, because he had a makeup-artist friend at some special-effects studio or another who'd agreed to do that part free of charge. I understand Perrault was quite good at getting people to do things for him for free. Eva, for example. So, she was gone most of a week in February, during the worst of the snow, and I had the apartment and the bed all to myself. When I wasn't working or slogging *to* or home *from* work through the black-gray slush drowning the streets, or riding the T, I slept and watched old movies and halfheartedly read from a collection by Nabokov, *A Russian Beauty and Other Stories*. The book was a first edition, signed by the author, and actually belonged to Perrault. He'd loaned it to Eva, advising her to read it, cover to cover, but Eva rarely read anything except astrology and self-help crap. Oh, she had subscriptions to *The New Yorker* and *Wired* and *Interview*, because she thought they looked good lying on the coffee table. Or rather, because she thought they made *her* look good. But she never read the magazines, and she'd not read a page of the Nabokov collection, either. I read most of it while she was gone to California, but can only recall one story, about a midget named Fred Dobson. Fred Dobson got someone pregnant and died at the end, and that's about all I remember. Eva came home on a Friday night, and she was uncharacteristically taciturn. Mostly, she sat alone in the kitchenette, smoking and drinking steaming cups of herbal tea. On Saturday night, we fucked, the first time since she'd started seeing Perrault. She had me use the double-ended silicone dildo, which was fine by me. I came twice. I'm not sure how many times Eva came, because she was always so quiet during sex, always so quiet and still. Afterwards, we lay together, and it was almost like the beginning, right after we met, before I understood about necrosis. We watched the big bay window above the bed, flakes of snow spiraling lazily down from a Dreamsicle sky. She said, "In Japan, they call them *harigata*," and it took me a moment to realize she was talking about the double-ended dildo. "At least that's what Albert says," she added, and the illusion that we might be back at the start, that I did not yet know the truth of her, immediately dissolved. I lay still, Eva in my arms, watching the snow sticking to the windowpane. Some of it melted, and some of it didn't. I asked her if she was okay, if maybe something had happened while she was away in Los Angeles. She told me no, nothing had happened, but it was intense, all the same, working that closely with Perrault. "It's like being in his head sometimes, like I'm just another canvas or a few handfuls of clay." She fell asleep not long afterwards, and I got up and pissed, checked my email, and then watched TV almost until dawn, even though I had to work the next day. I didn't want to be in the same bed with whatever she was dreaming that night.

I didn't see her again for two or three days. She took the train down to Providence, some errand for Perrault. She didn't go into the details, and I didn't bother to ask. When she came home, though, Eva was mostly her old self again. We ordered Chinese takeout, moo goo whatever, kung pao pigeon, and she talked about the life castings she'd done. Her body nude and slicked with Vaseline, and then they'd covered her with a thick coating of blue alginate, and when that had set, they'd covered the alginate with plaster bandages, making the molds for Perrault's sculptures from her living corpse. I asked if they put straws up her nose so she could breathe, and she laughed and frowned. "They don't do that," she replied. "They're just careful not to cover your nostrils. It was claustrophobic, but in a good way." She told me that each mold would be used only once and then destroyed, and that they did five separate life castings of her over five consecutive days. "When it hardens, you can't move?" I asked, and she frowned again and said, "Of course you can't move. That would ruin everything, if you were to move." I didn't ask exactly what Perrault intended to do with the casts, and Eva didn't say. It was the next evening, though, that she produced a photograph of one of Albert Perrault's paintings and asked me to look at it, please. Eva never, ever fucking said please, so that was sort of a red flag, when she did. She was sweating, though it was chilly in the apartment, because the radiator was acting up again. She was sweating, and she looked sick. I asked if she had a fever, and Eva shook her head. I asked if she was sure, because maybe she'd picked up something on the plane, or while she was in LA, and she made a snarling sound and shoved the photograph into my hands. It was in color, an eight-by-ten printed on matte paper. There was a sticker on the back with the painting's title typed neatly, black Courier font on white. It read *Fecunda ratis*, and there was a date (which I can't recollect). Written directly on the back of the photo, with what I took to have been a ballpoint pen, were the words "De puella a lupellis seruata," about a girl saved from wolf cubs, circa 1022–1024; Egbert of Liège. "So who is this Egbert of Liège?" I asked. She glared at me, and for a second or three I thought she was going to hit me. It wouldn't have been the first time. "How the hell am I supposed to know?" she snapped, trading in my question for a question of her own. "Will you fucking look at the *front*? Winter, look at the front of the picture, not the goddamn back of it, for Christ's sake." I nodded and turned the photograph over. I recognized it immediately as one of Perrault's, even though I'd never seen that particular painting before. There's something about the easy violence, the deliberate carelessness of his brushstrokes. Almost like Edvard Munch trying to forge a Van Gogh, almost. At first, any simple representational image, any indication of the painting's composition, refused to emerge from the sooty blur of oils, the innumerable shades of gray broken only by the faintest rumors of green and alabaster. There was a single crimson smudge floating near the center of the photo-graph, a chromatic counterpoint to all the murk. I thought it looked like a wound. I didn't say that to Eva, but that's the impression I got. As if maybe someone, Perrault or someone else, had taken a knife or a pair of scissors to the canvas. Heaven knows, I've wanted to do it myself, on more than one occasion. I would even argue that, at times, his art seems intended to provoke precisely that reaction. Art designed, premeditated, to elicit the primal fight-or-flight response, to reach in and give the hindbrain a good squeeze, dividing the predators from the prey. "What do you see?" Eva asked me. And I said, "Another one of Perrault's shitty paintings." "Don't be an ass," she replied. "Tell me what you *see*." I told her I'd thought she wanted my honest opinion, and she gave me the finger; I had it coming, I suppose. I looked at her, and she was still sweating, and was also chewing at her lower lip. Peering into her eyes was almost as bad as trying to make sense of *Fecunda ratis*, so I turned back to the somber chaos of the photograph. "Is this one going to be in the show?" I asked. "No," she said, and then, "I don't know. Maybe, but I don't think so. It's old, but he says it's relevant. Albert doesn't have it any-more, sold it to a collector after a show in Atlanta. I don't know if he still has access to it." I listened, but didn't reply. Her voice was shak-ing, like the words were not quite connecting one against the other, and I tried harder to concentrate on making sense of *Fecunda ratis*. I wished I had a drink, and I almost asked Eva for one of the Ameri-can Spirit cigarettes she'd begun smoking after meeting Perrault, though I'd stopped smoking years before. My mouth was so dry. I felt as though my cheeks had been stuffed with cotton balls, my mouth had gone so dry. "What do you see?" she asked again, sound-ing desperate, almost whispering, but I ignored her. Because, sud-denly, the blur was beginning to resolve into definite shapes, shadows and the solid objects that cast shadows. Figures and land-scape and sky. The crimson smudge was the key. "Little Red Riding

Hood," I said, and Eva laughed, but very softly, as if she were only laughing to herself. "Little Red Riding Hood," she echoed, and I nodded my head again. The red smudge formed a still point, a nexus or fulcrum, in the swirl, and I saw it was meant to be a cap or a hat, a crimson wool cap perched on the head of a nude girl who was down on her hands and knees. Her head was bowed, so that her face was hidden from view. There was only a wild snarl of hair, and that cruel, incongruent red cap. Yes, that *cruel* red cap, for I could not then and cannot now interpret any element of that painting as anything but malevolent. Even the kneeling girl, made a blood sacrifice, struck me as a conspirator. She was surrounded by pitchy, hulking forms, and I briefly believed them to be tall standing stones, dolmens, some crude megalithic ring with the girl at its center. But then I realized, no, they were *meant* to be beasts of some sort. Huge shaggy things squatting on their haunches, watching the girl. The painting had captured the final, lingering moment before a kill. But I didn't think *kill*. I thought *murder*, though the forms surrounding the girl appeared to be animals, as I've already said. Animals do not do murder, men do. Men and women, and even children, but *not* animals. "I dream it almost every night," Eva said, near to tears, and I wanted to tear the photograph apart, rip it into tiny, senseless shreds. I'm not lying when I say that I loved and still love Eva, and *Fecunda ratis* struck me as some sick game Perrault was playing with her mind, giving her this awful picture and telling her it was *relevant* to the installation. Expecting her to study it. To fixate and obsess over it. I've always felt a certain variety of manipulation is required of artists (painters, sculptors, writers, filmmakers, etc.), but only a few become (or start off as) sadists. I have no doubt whatsoever that Perrault is a sadist, whether or not there was a sexual component present. You can see it in almost everything he's ever done, and, that night, I could see it in her eyes. "Eva, it's only Little Red Riding Hood," I told her, laying the photograph facedown on the coffee table. "It's only a painting, and you really shouldn't let him get inside your head like this." She told me that I didn't understand, that full immersion was necessary if she was going to be any help to him whatsoever, and then she took the photograph back and sat staring at it. I didn't say anything more, because I knew nothing more to say to her. There was no way I would come between her and her *bête noire*, nor even between her and the black beasts he'd created for *Fecunda ratis*. I stood up and went to the kitchenette to make dinner, even though I wasn't hungry and, by then, Eva was hardly eating anything. I found a can of Campbell's chicken and stars soup in the cupboard and asked if she'd eat a bowl if I warmed it up. She didn't reply. She didn't say a word, just sat there on the sofa, her blue eyes trained on the photograph, not sparing a glance for anyone or anything else. And that was maybe three weeks before she flew out to Los Angeles for the last time. She never came back to Boston. She never came back to me. I never saw her again. But I suppose I'm getting ahead of myself, even if only slightly so. There would be the one distraught phone call near the end of April, while Perrault would still have been busy working on the pieces for his installation, which was scheduled to open on June 1 at a gallery called Subliminal Thinkspace Collective. It's easy enough, in retrospect, to say that I should have taken that phone call more seriously. But I was working two jobs and recovering from the flu. I was barely managing to keep the rent paid. It's not like I could have dropped everything and gone after her. I make a lousy Prince Charming, no fit sort of knight-errant. Anyway, I'm still not sure she wanted me to try. To save her, I mean. It's even more absurd to imagine Eva as a damsel in distress than to imagine myself as her rescuer. Which only goes to show the fatal traps we may build for ourselves when we fashion personae. Expectation becomes self-fulfilling. Then, later on, we cry and bitch, and pity ourselves, and marvel stupidly at our inability to take action. The therapist I saw for a while said this was "survivor's guilt." I asked him, that day, if the trick to a lucrative career in psychology was to tell people whatever might make them feel better, by absolving them of responsibility. I look around me, and I see so many people intent upon absolving themselves of responsibility. On passing the buck, shifting the blame. But I'm the one who did not act, just as Perrault is the one who messed with her head, just as Eva is the one who needed that invasion so badly she was willing to pay for the privilege with her life. All I was paying the therapist was money, and that's not even quite the truth, as I was piling it all on a MasterCard I never expected to be in a position to pay off. Regardless, during our very next session, Dr. Not To Be Named Herein suggested that some of us are less amenable to therapy than are others, that possibly I did not *wish* to "get better," and I stopped seeing him. I can be a guilty survivor on my own, without incurring any additional debt.

Eva called near the end of April. She was crying.

I had never heard Eva cry, and it was as disconcerting a sound as it was unexpected.

We talked for maybe ten or fifteen minutes, at the most. It might have been a much longer conversation, if my cell phone had been getting better reception that afternoon, and if I'd been able to call back when we were finally disconnected (I tried, but the number was blocked). Eva was not explicit about what had upset her so badly. She said that she missed me. She said it several times, in fact, and I said that I missed her, too. She repeatedly mentioned insomnia and bad dreams, and how very much she hated Los Angeles and wanted to be back in Boston. I said that maybe she ought to come home, if this were the case, but she balked at the idea. "He needs me *here*," she said. "This would be the *worst* time for me to leave. The absolute worst time. I couldn't do that, Winter. Not after everything Albert's done for me." She said that, or something approximating those words. Her voice was so terribly thin, so faint and brittle in the static, stretched out across however many thousands of miles it had traveled before reaching me. I felt as though I were speaking to a ghost of Eva. That's not the clarity of hindsight. I actually *did* feel that way, *while* we were speaking, which is one reason I wouldn't permit my therapist (my ex-therapist, now that we're estranged) to convince me to lay the blame elsewhere. I clearly heard it that day, the panic in her voice. Hers was such a slow suicide, a woman dying by degrees, and it would be reprehensible of me to pretend that I'm not cognizant of this fact, or that I did not yet have my suspicions that day in April. She said, "After dark, we drive up and down the Coast Highway, back and fucking forth, from Redondo Beach all the way to Santa Barbara or Isla Vista. He drives and talks about Gévaudan. Winter, I'm so sick of that goddamn stretch of road." I didn't ask her about Gévaudan, though I googled it when I got home. When we were cut off, Eva was still sobbing, and talking about her nightmares. Had it been a scene in a Hollywood melodrama, I would surely have dropped everything and gone after her. But my life is about as far from Hollywood as it gets. And *she* was there already.

A few days later, the mail brought an invitation to the opening of The Voyeur of Utter Destruction. One side was a facsimile of a postcard that the man purporting to have murdered Elizabeth Short, the Black Dahlia, sent to journalists and the police in 1947. The original message had been assembled with pasted letters snipped from newspapers, and read "Here is the photo of the werewolf killer's/I saw him kill her/a friend." There was an indistinct photo in the lower left-hand corner of the card, which I later learned was of a boy named Armand Robles. He was seventeen years old in 1947, and was never considered a suspect in the Dahlia killing. More mind games. The other side of the postcard had the date and time of the opening, please RSVP, an address for Subliminal Thinkspace Collective, etcetera. And it also had two words printed in red ink,

handwritten in Eva's unmistakable, sloppy cursive: "Please come."
She knew I couldn't. More than that, she knew I *wouldn't*, even if I
could have afforded the trip.

Like I said, I googled "Gévaudan." It's the name of a former
province in the Margeride Mountains of central France. I read its
history, going back to Gallic tribes and even Neolithic people, a
Roman conquest, its role in medieval politics, and the arrival of the
Protestants in the mid-sixteenth century. Dull stuff. But I'm a quick
study, and it didn't take me long to realize that none of these would
have been the subject of Perrault's obsession with the region. No,
nothing so mundane as rebellions against the Bishop of Mende or
the effects of WWII on the area. However, between the years 1764
and 1767, a "beast" attacked as many as 210 people. Over a hundred
of them died. It might have been nothing more than an exceptionally large wolf, but has never been conclusively identified. Many
victims were partially eaten. And I will note, the first attack occurred on June 1, 1764. From the start, I saw the significance of this
date. After Eva's call, I could hardly dismiss it as a coincidence. Perrault had knowingly chosen the anniversary of the beginning of the
depredations of the infamous *Bête du Gévaudan* as the opening night
of his installation. I spent a couple of hours reading websites and
internet forums devoted to the attacks. There's a lot of talk of witchcraft and shape-shifting, both in documents written during and
shortly after the incident and in contemporary books, as well. Turns
out, Gévaudan is one of those obscure subjects the crackpots at the
fringe keep alive with their lavish conspiracy theories and pseudo-
scientific, wishful blather. Much the same way, I might add, that the
true-crime buffs have kept the unsolved Dahlia case in the public
eye for more than half a century. And here, Albert Perrault seemed
intent upon forging a marriage of the two, along with his unrelent-
ing fairy-tale preoccupations. I thought about the life casts, and
wondered if he'd chosen Eva as his midwife.

I stuck the postcard on the fridge with a magnet, and for a few days I thought too much about Gévaudan, and was surprised by how much I worried about Eva, and how frequently I found myself wishing that she would call again. I sent a couple of emails, but they went unanswered. I even tried to find a contact for Perrault, to no avail. I spoke with a woman at Subliminal Thinkspace Collective, a brusque voice slathered with a heavy Russian accent, and I gave her a message for Eva, to please have her get in touch with me as soon as possible. And then, as April became May, the humdrum, day-to-day gravity of my life reasserted itself. I fretted less about Eva with every passing day, and began to believe that this time she was gone for good. Accepting that a relationship has exceeded its expiration date is much easier when you always knew the expiration date was there, waiting somewhere down the road, always just barely out of sight. I missed her. I won't pretend that I didn't. But it wasn't the blow I'd spent so much of our four years together dreading. It was a sure thing that had finally come to fruition. Mostly, I wondered what I should do with all the junk she'd left behind. Clothing and books, CDs, and a vase from Italy. All the material ephemera she'd left me to watch over in her absence, the curator of the Museum of Her. I decided that I would wait until summer, and if I'd not heard from Eva by then, I would box it all up. I never thought far enough ahead to figure out what I'd do with the boxes afterwards, once they were packed and taped shut. Maybe that was a species of denial. I don't know. I don't care.

The first of June came and went without incident, and I heard nothing more from her. I don't think of myself as a summer person, but, for once, I was glad to have the winter behind me. I welcomed the greening of Boston Common, the flowers and the ducks and the picnicking couples. I even welcomed the heat, though my apartment has no AC. I welcomed the long days and the short nights. I'd begun to settle into a new routine, and it seemed I might be discovering an equilibrium, even peace, when I got the letter from Eva's sister in Connecticut. I sat on the bed, and I read the single page several times over, waiting for the words to seem like more than ink on paper. She apologized for not having written sooner, but my address had only turned up the week after Eva's funeral. She'd OD'd on a nortriptyline prescription, though it was unclear whether or not the overdose had been intentional. The coroner, who I suspect was either kindly or mistaken, had ruled the death accidental. I would have argued otherwise, only there was no one for me to have the argument with. "I know you were close," her sister wrote. "I know that the two of you were very good friends." I put the letter in a drawer somewhere, and I took the postcard off the refrigerator and threw it away. Before I sat down to write this out, I promised myself I'd not dwell on this part of the story. On her death, or on my reaction to it. That's a promise I mean to keep. I will only say that my mourning in no way diminished the anger and bitterness that Eva's inconstancies had planted and then nourished. I didn't write back to her sister. It seemed neither necessary nor appropriate.

And now it is a cold day in late January, and soon it will have been a year since the last time I made love to Eva. The snow's returned, and the radiator is in no better shape than it was this time last year. All things considered, I think I was doing a pretty good job of moving on, until a shipment of Perrault's book arrived at the shop where I (still) work. It came in on one of my days off, and was already shelved and fronted, right up front, the first time I set eyes on it. The dust jacket was a garish shade of red. Later, I would realize it was almost the same shade of crimson as the girl's cap in *Fecunda ratis*. I didn't open it in the store, but bought a copy with my employee discount (which made the purchase only slightly less extravagant). I didn't open it until I was home and had checked twice to be sure the door was locked. And then I poured myself a glass of scotch, and sat down on the floor between the coffee table and the sofa, and scrounged up the courage to look inside. The book is titled simply *Werewolf Smile,* and opens with an epigraph and several pages of introduction by a Berkeley professor of modern art (there is also an afterword by a professor of Jungian and Imaginal Psychology at Pacifica Graduate Institute). I saw almost immediately that Perrault had dedicated the book to "Eva, my lost little red cap." Reading that, I felt a cold, hard knot forming deep in my belly, the knot that would soon become nausea as I turned the pages, one after one, staring at those slick full-color photographs, this permanent record of the depravity that Albert Perrault was peddling as inspiration and genius. I will not shy away from calling it pornography, but a pornography not necessarily, or exclusively, of sex, but one effusively devoted to the violation of anatomy, both human and animal. And the freeze-frame violence depicted there was not content with the canvas offered by only three dimensions, no, but also warped time, bending the ambiguities of history to Perrault's purposes. History and legend, myth and the Grand Guignol of *les contes de fées.*

I should—though I can't say why—include that epigraph, which sets the book in motion. It was written by a Boston poet I'd never heard of, but since there are many Boston poets I've never heard of, that means next to nothing, doesn't it? I live here, and work in a bookstore, but that hardly seems to matter. It's no protection against ignorance. The text of the epigraph appears first in Latin, and is then translated into English. It is titled "The Magdalene of Gévaudan":

Mater luporum, mater moeniorum, stella montana, ora pro nobis. Virgo arborum, virgo vastitatis, umbra corniculans, ora pro nobis. Regina mutatum, regina siderum, ficus aeterna, ora pro nobis. Domina omnium nocte dieque errantium, nunc et in hora mortis nostrae, ora pro nobis.

Mother of wolves, mother of walls, star of the mountains, pray for us.
Virgin of trees, virgin of desert, horned moon's shadow, pray for us.
Queen of changes, queen of constellations, eternal fig-tree, pray for us.
Mistress of all who by night and day wander, now and at the hour of
our death, pray for us.

It doesn't actually feel like a poem. It feels like an invocation. Like something from Aleister Crowley.

I am becoming lost in these sentences, in my attempt to convey in mere words what Perrault wrought in paint and plaster, with wire and fur and bone. The weight and impotence of my own narrative becomes painfully acute. Somehow, I've already said too much, and yet know that I will never be able to accurately, or even adequately, convey my reaction to the images enshrined and celebrated in Perrault's filthy book.

I am a fool to even try.

I am a fool.

I am.

He festooned the gallery's walls with black-and-white photos of Elizabeth Short's corpse, those taken where she was found in the weedy, vacant lot at Thirty-ninth and Norton in Leimert Park and a few more from the morgue. These photographs were so enlarged that a great deal of their resolution was lost. Many details of the corpse's mutilation vanished in the grain. There was also a movie poster from George Marshall's 1946 film noir, *The Blue Dahlia*, written by Raymond Chandler, which may (or may not) have served as the inspiration for Short's sobriquet. Hung at irregular intervals throughout the gallery, from invisible wires affixed to the ceiling, were blowups that Perrault had made of newspaper accounts of the murder, and there were the various postcards and letters taunting the LAPD, like the one that had been used for my invitation to the installation's opening.

I have decided not to surrender Too much fun fooling the police
Had my fun at police
Don't Try to find me.
—catch us if you can

Scattered among these gruesome artifacts of the Black Dahlia murder were an assortment of illustrations that have accompanied variants of the "Little Red Riding Hood" tale over the centuries. Some were in color, others rendered only in shades of gray. Gustave Doré, Fleury François Richard, Walter Crane, and others, many others, but I don't recall the names and don't feel like searching through the book for them. They would have only seemed incongruous to someone who was blessedly unaware of Perrault's agenda. And displayed among the postcard facsimiles and the red-capped girl children were eighteenth-century images of the creature believed to have been responsible for all those attacks in the Margeride Mountains. From my description, it may seem that the installation was busy. Yet somehow, even with so many objects competing for attention, through some acumen on the part of the artist, just the opposite was true. The overall effect was one of emptiness, a bleak space sparsely dotted with the detritus of slaughter and lies and childhood fancy.

But this odd assemblage, all these sundry relics—*every bit of it*—was only a frame built to mark off Perrault's own handiwork, the five sculptures he'd fabricated from Eva's life casts and, presumably, with the aid of the taxidermist acquaintance she'd mentioned to me. The centerpiece of The Voyeur of Utter Destruction and, later on, *Werewolf Smile*. The desecration made of the body of Elizabeth Short, as it had been discovered in that desolate lot in Leimert Park at about ten thirty a.m. on the morning of January 15, 1947. Here it was, not once, but repeated five times over, arranged in a sort of pentagram or pinwheel formation. The "corpses" were each aligned with their feet towards the wheel's center. Their toes almost, but not quite, touching. There are twenty or so photographs of this piece in the book, taken from various angles, the sculpture that Perrault labeled simply *Phases 1–5*. I will not describe it in any exacting detail. I don't think that I could bear to do that, if only because it would mean opening up Perrault's book again to be certain I was getting each stage in the transformation exactly right. "It's not the little things," Eva once said to me. "It's what they add up to." That would have served well as an epigraph to *Werewolf Smile*. It could have been tucked directly beneath the author's dedication (as it happens, the actual epigraph is by Man Ray: "I paint what cannot be photographed, that which comes from the imagination or from dreams, or from an unconscious drive"). What I will say is that *Phase 1* is an attempt at a straightforward reproduction of the state in which Elizabeth Short's naked body was discovered. There's no arguing with the technical brilliance of the work, just as there's no denying the profanity of the mind who made it. But this is not Elizabeth Short's body. It is, of course, a mold of Eva's, subjected to all the ravages visited upon the Black Dahlia's. The torso has been bisected at the waist with surgical precision, and great care has been taken to depict exposed organs and bone. The severed arms are raised above the head, arranged in a manner that seems anything but haphazard. The legs are splayed to reveal the injuries done to the genitalia. Every wound visible in the crime-scene photos and described in written accounts has been faithfully reproduced in *Phase 1*. The corners of the mouth have been slashed, almost ear to ear, and there's Perrault's "werewolf smile." Move along now, widdershins about the pinwheel, until we arrive at *Phase 5*. And here we find the taxidermied carcass of a large coyote that has been subjected to precisely the *same* mutilations as the body of Elizabeth Short, and the life casts of Eva. Its forelimbs have been arranged above the head, just as the Dahlia's were, though they never could have been posed that way in life. The beast lies supine, positioned in no way that seems especially natural for a coyote. It was not necessary to slash the corners of the mouth. And as for phases 2 through 4, one need only imagine any lycanthropic metamorphosis, the stepwise shifting from mangled woman to mangled canine, accomplished as any halfway decent horror-movie transmutation.

The face is only recognizable as Eva's in phases 1 and 2. I suppose I should consider this a mercy.

And at the end (which this will not be, but as another act of mercy, I will *pretend* it is) one question lingers foremost in my mind. Is this what Eva was seeking all along? Not enlightenment in the tutelage of her *bête noire*, but this grisly immortality, to be so reduced (or so elevated, depending on one's opinion of Perrault). To become a surrogate for that kneeling, red-capped girl in *Fecunda ratis*, and for a woman tortured and murdered decades before Eva was even conceived. To stumble, and descend, and finally lie there on her back, gazing upwards at the pale, jealous moon as the assembled beasts fall on her, and simply do what beasts have always done, and what they evermore will do.

The End

9

∽✺∽

There is a very famous poem by Matthew Arnold (1822–1888), "Dover Beach," that has always been a favorite of mine. I've read it aloud to myself many times, delighting in the interplay of words and metaphor. But, until this past week, it has never assumed a personal meaning for me. My own *private* meaning. It's only ever been pretty words written in a time when all the world was a different and rapidly changing place:

> *The Sea of Faith*
> *Was once, too, at the full, and round earth's shore*
> *Lay like the folds of a bright girdle furl'd.*
> *But now I only hear*
> *Its melancholy, long, withdrawing roar,*
> *Retreating, to the breath*
> *Of the night-wind, down the vast edges drear*
> *And naked shingles of the world.*

I've beheld the Sea of Faith, and now I'm left with no choice but to listen closely to the melancholy, long withdrawing roar, which is a siren's song on a fogbound night when waves pummel the naked shingles of the world.

Imp typed, "I'm free of the phantoms of Perrault and the Black Dahlia and the wolf who cried girl and the November Eva who never was and never came to me. I have locked them inside a story from which they can never escape to do me harm. I've exorcised them."

But I'm not unhaunted. I've already written on the permanence of haunting. I wrote, "Once Odysseus heard the sirens, I find it hard to believe he ever could have forgotten their song. He would have always been haunted by it all the rest of his life."

However, now I think I have crossed a threshold where my ghost story has ceased to be malicious twins. Now it wears a single face.

Imp typed, "This may, at least, make my ghost story, in some sense, comprehensible."

I have placed one Eva behind me. I have only July, and Caroline and Rosemary, and *The Drowning Girl* and Phillip George Salton-stall, "The Little Mermaid" and the Siren of Millville. That's quite enough ghosts for one madwoman.

> *But now I only hear*
> *Its melancholy, long, withdrawing roar,*
> *Retreating, to the breath*
> *Of the night-wind, down the vast edges drear*
> *And naked shingles of the world.*

I really should be out looking for a new job.

> *Wandering between two worlds, one dead*
> *The other powerless to be born,*
> *With nowhere yet to rest my head*
> *Like these, on earth I wait forlorn.*

All is changed utterly, the gyre still widens here in my night of first ages, and, in the end, I am left with a terrible beauty and a slouching beast. The monster is neither shackled nor is she conquered, and I gaze on her monstrous and free. And this, too, as my head races with Matthew Arnold, Yeats, Conrad, races and tangles, all wanting out at once. All wanting to be done writing of July Eva and my mermaid ghost story:

> *She steals to the window, and looks at the sand,*
> *And over the sand at the sea;*
> *And her eyes are set in a stare;*
> *And anon there breaks a sigh,*
> *And anon there drops a tear,*
> *From a sorrow-clouded eye,*
> *And a heart sorrow-laden,*
> *A long, long sigh;*
> *For the cold strange eyes of a little Mermaiden . . .*

It's been a strange day, but I'm going to try hard to relate it coherently, resorting to the sort of linear narrative that has so often now eluded me. I don't think in straight lines, neat number lines (0–9, 9–0), once upon a time and happily ever after, A–Z, whatever. But I'm going to try hard this time.

I spent the morning putting in applications at places that weren't hiring, but would be sooner or later. Bill gave me a good reference, and that surprised me, right? Sure, sure it did. But he said he understood it wasn't my fault, and he would hire me back if not for the owner, and he didn't want to see me long unemployed. I filled out applications at Utrecht on Wickenden Street, some other shops on Wickenden, shops on Thayer, at Wayland Square (including the Edge, though I know not one jot about being a barista). Ellen told me I should apply at Cellar Stories, so I did. I would love to work there. I would, though it seems unlikely. Altogether, I filled out fifteen applications. Maybe I'll be called back for an interview or two.

Abalyn and I arranged to meet at four o'clock p.m. downstairs at the Athenaeum. She said there was something she wanted to look up, which seemed strange to me, as she rarely seems to read anything but her digest-sized volumes of manga (which I confess make no sense to me, and always seemed very silly when I've tried to read them). She was seated at one of the long tables across from the tall portrait of George Washington. Her laptop was out and on, and she had her iPod and iPhone. She wasn't using any of them, but I suspect, for her, they're like Linus van Pelt's security blanket. Talismans against the unfriendly, intolerant, misunderstanding world. But she was reading a book. Not a very old book, and she closed it when I spoke to her. She closed it and looked up at me. The cellophane library cover glistened in the sunlight from the windows.

"Any luck with the job hunting?" she asked, and rubbed at her eyes.

"I don't know yet. Maybe. Probably not."

I sat down in the chair beside her and dropped my bag to the floor, one of Rosemary Anne's old shapeless bags. This one was pea-green corduroy.

"What about you? Did you find whatever it was you were looking for?"

She stared at the cover of the book a moment. It wasn't a very old book, and the cover read *The Lemming Cult: The Rise and Fall of the Open Door of Night* by William L. West. There was a PhD after the author's name. I turned away and stared at the shelves, instead. Being faced suddenly, unexpectedly, with this book, this particular book, Abalyn's discovery, I felt like I'd come suddenly upon a gruesome accident. No, that's not right. But I don't want to waste time finding a better analogy.

"I won't tell you, if you don't want to hear."

"I don't," I replied, still staring towards a shelf of plays and books on theater. "But what I don't know is worse than what I do." The unknown *thing* under the water, devouring and unseen, versus the banal danger of a hunted great white shark (*Carcharodon carcharias,* Smith, 1838; Greek, *karcharos,* meaning jagged, and *odous,* meaning tooth; kar-KAR-uh-don kar-KAR-ee-us).

"You're sure?"

"Please," I said, and maybe I whispered. But, in the library, my voice seemed very loud (even though, as I've noted, it can be a very noisy library).

I heard Abalyn open the book, but I didn't turn back to her. I stared at the tattered spines of antique editions and listened while she quietly read from Chapter 4:

" 'One of the more visible outspoken members of the cult was Eva Canning, a native of Newport, Rhode Island. Canning arrived in California in the late summer of 1981, having received a scholarship to attend UC Berkeley. As an undergraduate, she developed a strong interest in Mediterranean archaeology, and received her BS in anthropology in June 1985, afterwards remaining at Berkeley to work towards a PhD in sociocultural archaeology. During this time, she did fieldwork in Greece, Turkey, and on several Aegean islands. However, one of her two coadvisers was Jacova Angevine, and when Angevine left the university in 'eighty-eight, so did Canning. There are unsubstantiated rumors that the two had become lovers. Regardless, Canning would soon become one of Angevine's most trusted confidantes, and interviews with surviving members reveal that she was one of four women accorded the rank of High Priestess of the Open Door of Night. During the ceremonies at the Pierce Street temple in Monterey, Canning is said always to have been in attendance, and to have been among those responsible for the induction of new members.

Many journalists have extended Canning's role in the cult's

swift rise to prominence beyond recruitment. It's readily evident that it was through Canning's promotional efforts and acumen that the ODoN attracted so many so quickly. She not only took advantage of the nascent internet but spread the cult's doctrine via college campuses, the underground zine culture of the late eighties and early nineties, and numerous mentions appear in *Factsheet Five* from 1988 onwards. During this period, articles on ODoN, and two interviews with Canning, appear in zines in the US, UK, Canada, Australia, and Japan (for a summation, see Karaflogka, Anastasia, "Occult Discourse and the Efficacy of Zines," *Religion* 32 [2002]: 279–91). Following the events at Moss Landing, her suicide note (one of only four left behind) was printed in many of these homegrown publications.

While at Berkeley, Canning also arranged for the creation of the Usenet group alt.humanities.odon, which saw considerable traffic from 1988 to 1991. One can only imagine how much more damage Canning might have managed if she'd had the World Wide Web at her disposal.'"

Abalyn paused, and I didn't say anything for a moment. I say "a moment," but I don't know how long. And then I asked her, "Is that all?"

"No. That's not even the most important part. Do you want me to go on?"

"I do," I replied. "I want you to go on. You've begun this. You can't very well stop now."

And so she read a little more from Chapter 4:

" 'Before Eva Canning departed New England for California, she gave birth to an illegitimate daughter. The child was adopted by Canning's mother and father. I have chosen to omit her name here, as she's already suffered much unwanted and hurtful attention in connection to her mother's involvement with Jacova Angevine.' "

Abalyn stopped, and I could hear her turning a page or two.

Then she read, " 'Eva Canning's body was sent back East, and her badly mutilated and decomposed remains were duly cremated. Her ashes were strewn in the sea from high cliffs at the eastern edge of Aquidneck Island, near Salve Regina College, her mother's alma mater. However, there was also a modest memorial service at Middletown Cemetery in Newport. A headstone in the Canning family plot marks an empty grave.' "

Again, silence. I could hear footsteps overhead, and the voices of patrons and librarians. I glanced towards the staircase leading to the ground floor, polished oak and worn red carpeting.

"I want to go there," I said. "I need to go there, Abalyn. I have to see her grave for myself."

"It's too late to go today."

"Then we'll go tomorrow."

I don't have a membership to the Athenaeum, because I can't afford one. But I had several pages of *The Lemming Cult: The Rise and Fall of the Open Door of Night* by William L. West (New York: The Overlook Press, 1994) photocopied, so I'd have them for later, because of what Rosemary Anne said about remembering significant *things*.

As we left the library and stepped back out into the cold November evening, Abalyn asked if I was all right, and I lied and told her I was fine. "We need to stop by the market on the way home," I added.

And the next day, it snowed, and the next day, we went to Newport. Bah. Dah. Ba-ba.

Obituary from the *Newport Daily News* (April 11, 1991):

NEWPORT—EVA MAY CANNING

Age 30, of Lighthouse Avenue, Monterey, CA, drowned on April 4 at Moss Landing State Beach, Moss Landing, CA.

Born in Newport, RI, on October 30, 1960, she was the

daughter of Isadora (Snow) and the late Ellwood Arthur Canning.

Miss Canning received a bachelor of science in anthropology in June 1985 from the University of California, Berkeley.

Eva was working on a graduate degree in archaeology at the time of her death. She was widely traveled, especially in the eastern Mediterranean, and published several notable papers in prominent scientific journals. As a young girl, she had a passion for poetry, collecting seashells, and bird-watching.

She is survived by her daughter, E. L. Canning, and by her mother, and several aunts, uncles, and cousins.

Her funeral will be held on Monday, April 13, 1991, at 11 a.m. at the Memorial Funeral Home, 375 Broadway, Newport, with a funeral service at 12 p.m. in St. Spyridon's Greek Orthodox Church, Thames Street, Newport. Burial will be in Middletown Cemetery in Middletown.

Memorial donations may be made to St. Spyridon's Greek Orthodox Church, Endowment Fund, PO Box 427, Newport, RI 02840.

Eva Canning had a daughter. A daughter whose first initial is E. Why is her full name not given here? Anonymity, an effort to protect her from Eva's Open Door of Night connections and subsequent scandal? And who was the father? The daughter would have had to be born . . . when, while Eva was still in high school? Was the daughter raised by Eva's mother? Too many questions, and my head spins and lists with them. Abalyn found this obituary yesterday, and I have added it to my file labeled "Perishable Shippen; Eva Canning."

To say today has been unsettling doesn't do it justice by half. And, here, Imp types, "You've had stranger. Far stranger, India Morgan Phelps." And yes, I have. But it was strange, still, and unsettling. That's the word that keeps coming back to me. Unsettling. Doors have swung open, and doors have slammed shut. Truths (or, rather, facts) I had half convinced myself of have been cast into doubt all over again. One step backwards, as Caroline might have said.

Abalyn didn't want me to go, never mind she was the one who set this in motion by showing me that book and the obituary. "What good can possibly come of it?" she asked. "Whatever there is to know is here, right here in the obit." Then she pointed out that the toll across the Newport Bridge would be four dollars each way, going and coming back, and, still being unemployed, I shouldn't be throwing money away like that.

"I'll go alone," I told her. "If you won't go with me, I'm not afraid to go by myself. It's something I need to see, and I mean to go." I was standing at the window, looking down at Willow Street. Have I mentioned it snowed last night? No, I haven't. I was standing at the window looking down at the two inches or so of an early snowfall that had fallen the night before. The snowplow had just rumbled down the street, heaping mounds to either side, half-burying the sidewalks. The end of the drive was blocked now, and I'd have to shovel it before I could get the Honda out. I hate shoveling snow.

"India, it's already two o'clock," she said.

"That's not so late," I replied. "The roads should be clear, and I don't care what time it is."

She asked me to please at least call Dr. Ogilvy and tell her, and ask if she thought going to the cemetery was a bad idea. Abalyn said she'd go with me, if I called my psychiatrist and if Dr. Ogilvy didn't disapprove.

"She said I should find my own answers," I said. "She said I have to find my own answers. Dr. Ogilvy isn't my babysitter. She isn't my mother. I don't need her permission. I'm a grown woman."

"You are a fragile woman," Imp typed. "How long now since you cowered naked and filthy and delirious in a corner of your bedroom, raving about the wolf who cried girl on a snowy night in Connecticut?"

"Please," Abalyn pleaded. And after all she'd done for me, and all she'd lost on my account, I really couldn't tell her no. It's not as if her request were truly unreasonable. It's not like I could pretend it was.

"Fine," I said. "I'll call. But whatever she says, I'm going anyway."

"Just call her," Abalyn said. So, I called Dr. Ogilvy. I got lucky, and she had a few minutes between patients, so I didn't have to leave a message with the receptionist and wait around for her to call me back, which would have meant losing more daylight (and I will admit I didn't want to go to the graveyard after sunset; I don't like graveyards, and this one, I knew, was going to be lots worse than usual).

Dr. Ogilvy asked if I thought I was up to it. I told her yes, and she told me to go. She agreed it would be a good idea for Abalyn to accompany me. Abalyn grimaced at the news, but she'd been the one who struck the deal, and she didn't argue.

I drove. I drove slowly and carefully because of the snow. Abalyn smoked and blew smoke out her window, which she'd rolled down just a crack. We left Providence about three, left the city, and crossed the West Passage of the Narragansett Bay on the Jamestown Bridge. The water before us shimmered, blinding, in the sun, like mercury spilled on blue-gray slate. We crossed Conanicut Island, then up and over the Newport Bridge, with its pale green cables and guardrails, its two white lancet towers, the slate-and-mercury waters of the East Passage four hundred feet below us. I thought about seals, whales, sharks, how the bay had once been a series of river valleys that flooded fifteen thousand years ago when glaciers melted. Mostly, I tried not to think about what we'd find at the cemetery. We saw a bumper sticker on a car in front of us that read "A thesaurus is NOT a giant lizard." I laughed, but Abalyn didn't.

And then we were on Aquidneck Island. I skirted Newport, following the directions Abalyn had gotten from MapQuest. We took Miantonomi Avenue and Green End Avenue east to the intersection with Turner Road, and here I turned left, turned north. I passed homes and a nursery with dozens of low greenhouses. I also passed tennis courts, basketball courts, and a track field mostly buried beneath the snow. Then we'd reached the place where Turner intersects with Wyatt Road. The cemetery lay at the northeast corner of the crossroads, and I thought, they used to bury suicides at crossroads. The obituary gave the graveyard's name as Middletown Cemetery, but an incongruously cheerful blue and gold sign at the entrance called it Four Corners Cemetery.

Abalyn glared at the cemetery, and she said, "This is so fucking dumb. It's pointless, Imp." I didn't answer her.

And then *this* really happened. Abalyn was right there to see it. Just as we turned off Turner into the graveyard, a huge crow alighted on a headstone only a few feet from the driver's-side door. All those years ago, Caroline said, "If you're listening to a story, and a crow shows up like that, you can bet the storyteller is making the whole thing up." I didn't tell Abalyn what crows mean, and, truthfully, in this context, *I do not know.* But it really *did* happen.

The snow hadn't fallen as heavily on Aquidneck Island as in Providence, but the narrow chip-and-tar roads in the cemetery hadn't been cleared, so I had to drive very slowly. I knew how to find Eva Canning's grave, because I'd had Abalyn check a couple of genealogy websites before we left. She'd even found a diagram of the graveyard. Eva's grave was all the way back at the northern edge, where a low fieldstone wall separated the cemetery from a vineyard, gone brown with the season. The same fieldstone wall enclosed the entire graveyard.

Rhode Island has many picturesque, photogenic cemeteries. Four Corners isn't one of them. There are no trees, and most of the stones are the same weathered limestone and marble, few dating back before the late nineteenth century. I parked next to a huge mausoleum sort of thing. It was hardly more than an artificial hill, dirt heaped over a vacuity and fronted with granite blocks and a rusty iron door. There were patches of hay and dead turf on it, as though the caretakers were trying to get grass to grow. It was an ugly thing, and put me in mind of fairies, hollow hills, barrow dens, Tolkien, Mary Stewart. I switched off the car and looked at Abalyn.

"You don't have to get out," I said.

All she said was, "Yes, Imp, I do."

So we did. We both got out of the Honda. I stood by the car a moment, surveying the bleak cemetery. I glanced up at the sky, so blue and cloudless, so pale blue it was almost white, a wide carnivorous sky, as Rosemary Anne would have said. It wasn't anyplace I wanted to stay very long, and twilight wasn't far off. The shadows cast by the headstones were growing long. Abalyn lit another cigarette, and the cold wind took the smoke apart.

"Let's get this over with," she said.

It wasn't hard to find Abalyn Canning's marker. It was on the left (to the west) of the mausoleum barrow-den hill. It was set about twenty-five feet back from the road, surrounded by monuments bearing names like Cappucilli, Bowler, Hoxslii, Greer, Ashcroft, Haywood, Church, and, of course, other Cannings. It was a modest headstone carved from a brick-red granite, which distinguished it from its tiresome rows of gray-white neighbors. There was a garland of ivy carved at each upper corner. I read aloud what was written there, and then sat down on the snowy ground, already going spongy as the snow melted beneath that bright November sun.

"Fuck," Abalyn said, and she didn't say anything else until after we'd gotten back into the car. This is what was graven into the stone (I wrote it down, precisely):

CANNING

MOTHER

1960 EVA MAY CANNING 1991

DAUGHTER

1978 EVA LOUISE CANNING 2008

THEY THAT GO DOWN TO THE SEA

I said, "They were thirty years old when they died. They were both thirty. They were both Eva Canning." And Abalyn smoked her cigarette and said nothing at all. I read the epitaph aloud, "They that go down to the sea." And I heard a crow caw-cawing loudly somewhere very nearby. I'm not making that up, either. This is all as factual as it is true. "I don't know what it means," I said, and I sat on the soggy ground and cried for a while. My tears were like ice on my cheeks. Finally, Abalyn helped me up and led me back to the Honda. When we were safe inside, and I was behind the wheel, she asked, belatedly, if I was okay to drive. I told her yes. Yes, I can drive. I just want to be away from here. I just want to be far, far away from here and never, ever come back. I heard the crow again. Dusk was coming on fast.

"Then let's get moving," Abalyn said. "We can figure this shit out later. Here isn't the place to try."

I turned the key in the ignition. I retraced the path home: Turner to Green End to Miantonomi Avenue to the Newport Bridge, the East Passage, Conanicut Island, Jamestown, the West Passage, the Jamestown Bridge, Route 4 to I-95 back to Providence and the Armory and Willow Street.

But this I know. I made a list for Dr. Ogilvy, and the eighth item—"There was only one Eva Canning"—was a lie I'd told without meaning to. It was a mistaken epiphany that somehow has turned out wrong. I wrote *seven* truths that afternoon, not eight. Seven (7).

After dragging Abalyn off to the Middletown Cemetery (or Four Corners Cemetery), I wanted—no, needed—to give her something in return for that indulgence. And I gave her a secret, a secret so secret it scared me to admit it to myself, much less share it with another human being. Even with a woman whom I'd loved and still loved. This is the night after we go to Aquidneck Island, and after a dinner of bow-tie pasta with pesto and a green salad with vinaigrette dressing. It all tastes like paste to me. I ask her to come to the room where I paint, my studio. She looks uncertain at first. On the *qui vive,* as Caroline would have said.

"It will only take a few minutes," I said. "There's something I need you to see."

"Need or want?" she asks, and wipes at her mouth with a paper ~~toll~~ towel (I've never owned cloth napkins).

"Need," I reply, so she shrugs and nods and follows me to the room where I paint. I switch on the light. I say, "You didn't have to go with me today. You've been doing a lot of stuff you don't have to do."

"Imp, you don't owe me anything."

"It won't take but a moment," I tell her, deciding not to argue about the validity of unpaid debts. And then I went to an old wardrobe (found by the road, and I think it's from the 1920s, banged-up Art Nouveau, a cheap knockoff of something much more expensive).

"You don't need to do this again," she says, starting to sound exasperated, maybe at the borderlands of surly.

I don't say anything. I turn the small brass key that is always in the wardrobe's lock and open both doors. Inside are very many canvases, some stretched and stapled to wooden frames, others rolled and stacked like papyrus scrolls. The wardrobe breathes out the aromas of dust, oil paint, and cedar. I pull out the canvas nearest the front (one of the stretched, stapled ones) and hand it to Abalyn. She holds it a moment, staring down at the painting, then up at me, then back at the painting. I take another from the wardrobe, then another, and another, and another, until a dozen or more are scattered about on the floor or leaned against the walls.

"You did *all* these?" Abalyn asks, sounding like she won't believe me if I say I ~~id~~ did; I nod, not especially caring if she believes me or not. No, I do care. But I *want* not to care.

" 'The Mermaid of the Concrete ~~Sea~~ Ocean,' " she says. "The crippled woman and the painter . . . ," and trails off.

"I did these after I wrote the story."

"And after Eva," she almost whispers, and I say yes, after Eva Canning.

"I'm sorry," Abalyn says, and laughs a dry, hollow laugh. "I'm just a little freaked-out right now. You made up these paintings, that obsessed artist's paintings, and then, after Eva came, you actually *painted* his paintings?"

I nod, then sit down on the floor, holding the wardrobe key, and Abalyn (still holding the first canvas I took out) sits down in front of me.

"What happened with Eva, that inspired these?"

"Yeah, and the story I'd written. Before Eva came, I'd read a book about the shark that swam up Matawan Creek in New Jersey in 1916 and attacked three swimmers in the creek, miles and miles from the sea. Two of them died."

"That made you write a story about mermaids?"

"And what the painter found washed up at Atlantic City, and . . ." And I stop, because I don't think I can explain so that Abalyn will ever understand, and, besides, it's suddenly all sort of muddled together in my head. The chronology, I mean.

Abalyn's still holding the painting, my favorite of the lot—though part of me loathes them all—*Regarding the Shore from Whale Reef.* The painting hanging on the old woman's wall in the story. As I have written before, the mermaid has her back to the viewer. Buoyed by rough waves, she holds her arms outstretched to either side, her long hair floating around her like a dense tangle of kelp, and she gazes towards land and a whitewashed lighthouse perched on a granite promontory. It's the rugged slate and phyllite shore off Beavertail Point on Conanicut Island. I paid a fisherman twenty dollars to carry me out far enough for reference photos (and I got seasick). Also, I changed the name of Whale *Rock* to Whale *Reef.* I can't remember why.

In my short story, I wrote: "The viewer might be fooled into thinking this is only a painting of a woman swimming in the sea, as so little of her is showing above the waterline. She might be mistaken for a suicide, taking a final glimpse of the rugged strand before slipping below the surface. But, if one looks only a little closer, the patches of red-orange scales flecking her arms are unmistakable, and there are living creatures caught up in the snarls of her black hair: tiny crabs and brittle stars, the twisting shapes of strange oceanic worms and a gasping, wide-eyed fish of some sort, suffocating in the air."

"I thought maybe it would help," I say. Out on the street, a car horn honks three times. "Like you and Dr. Ogilvy thought writing 'Werewolf Smile' might help me."

"But . . . ," Abalyn started, then was silent for a second or two. "But that was *one story.* There must be, what? Thirty or forty of these?"

"Forty-seven," I say, "and a couple of sketch pads of studies I did beforehand. Sometimes, I've thought I should make a big pile in the backyard and burn them all. I've thought I should make a pyre. Maybe that would provide the catharsis painting them didn't." (Isn't that what Saltonstall did? And what did he *really* burn?)

"Forty-seven," Abalyn says, and laughs again, like she thinks I'm making the number up. Incredulous.

"You can count them if you want," I tell her.

"Imp, don't ever burn these. I don't care why you painted them. I don't care if that crazy bitch was in back of it." Her eyes wander across all those paintings; then she stares hard at me. "Just don't ever burn these. They're beautiful."

I don't make any promises. We sit there a long time, together and apart. I've seen people in love with art, and I think I'm watching Abalyn fall in love with my mermaid. It makes me want to burn them all the more.

Now, I have to tell the part of my ghost story about the mermaid, what happened after I tried to drown myself in the tub and Abalyn Armitage saved me and left me. I have to tell about the day that Eva Canning, the daughter of Eva Canning, came back for me, that day and all the days that followed, and how it ended.

10

There's always a siren, singing you to shipwreck. The harridans of *Sirenum scopuli*, three sharp rocks battered by Aegean waves, just off the coast of Capri. La Castelluccia, La Rotonda, Gallo Lungo. Or the Sirenuse archipelago, or Capo Peloro. Homer made them Harpies, the three winged women who sang deadly songs for Ulysses. Euripides and Eustathius and Servius and Virgil and so many others who put pen to paper to warn of sirens. Homer does not take care to name them (or was too wise to try), but some of these scholars did: Peisinoe, Aglaope, and Thelxiepeia, for example. Elsewhere (Spanish, Romanian, French, etc.), elsewhen, folklore makes of them mermaids: *Sirena*, *Sirène*, *Syrena*, *Sirenă*, and *Sereia* and on and on and on to lure sailors to shipwreck and drowning. Oh, and zoologists place manatees and dugongs and extinct Steller's sea cows (*Hydrodamalis gigas*) in the mammalian order Sirenia (Illiger, 1811), and herpetologists have placed certain legless salamanders in the genus *Siren*, in the family Sirenidae. They look like eels, but aren't. Aren't eels, I mean. I looked up the word for eel-shaped things: *anguilliform*. Neither manatees nor Sirenidae live as far north as the Blackstone River. Manatees and dugongs, some people say, are responsible for the stories of sirens, when sirens are said to be mermaids. Though manatees do not sing, at least not songs that men and women can hear. They're not amphibians. They're mammals who went back to the ocean, like whales, and dolphins, and Eva Canning. Whales sing pretty songs, and we can hear them plain as day.

My siren came from the Blackstone River in Massachusetts, a river with the same name as the street that runs past the hospital where my mother died. The Siren of Millville, Perishable Shippen, E. L. Canning, Eva Louise, daughter of Eva May, who walked into Monterey Bay off Moss Landing State Beach, California, when I was only four years old. Who followed a woman named Jacova Angevine into the sea, and who never walked back out again. The deep sea is eternal night, and Jacova Angevine opened that door for E. M. Canning, who obediently stepped through it, along with so many others. She left her illegitimate daughter (like Imp) to her own fate.

"That's enough rambling prologue, Imp. You're stalling again. You're still mired in *now*, and you've sat down to write about *then*."

That's true (and factual). I have sat down to make an end to this. To type the last of my ghost story there is to tell, or, at least, the last of the part from August 2008. One does not find closure, resolution. One is never unhaunted, no matter how much self-help happy-talk purveyors of pop psychology and motivational speaking ladle on. I know that. But at least I will not have to keep coming to the blue room with too many books and continue trying to make sense of my ghost story. I now understand it as well as ever I shall. When I'm done, I'll show it to Abalyn, and I'll show it to Dr. Ogilvy, and then I'll never show it to anyone else, not ever.

A siren came knocking at my door.

It was only a few days after I had lain down in a bathtub of icy water and tried to end an earwig by inhaling myself to oblivion.

Abalyn had gone away, and she'd taken all her things with her. I was alone. I was sitting on the sofa, where she sat so often with her laptop. I'd read the same paragraph of a novel several times. I can't recall what the novel was, and it hardly matters. There was a knock at the door. It wasn't a loud knocking. It was, I will say, almost a surreptitious knock, almost as if I weren't meant to hear it, though I was, of course. No one knocks meaning you not to hear, right? No one would ever do such a thing, as a knock at a door or window says "Here I am. Let me in."

I turned my head and stared at the door. My apartment door is painted the same blue as this room where I type. I waited, and in a few seconds, the surreptitious knock came again. Three raps against the wood. I had no idea who it might be. Abalyn had no reason to come back. Aunt Elaine never comes without calling. Likewise, my few friends all have instructions to always call before visiting. Perhaps, I thought, it was someone from upstairs or someone from downstairs. Perhaps it was Felicia, my landlady, or Gravy, her handyman. On the third surreptitious knock, I called out, "I'm coming." I stood up and walked to the door.

Before I opened it, I smelled the Blackstone River, exactly as it had smelled the day Abalyn and I drove up there, only to find nothing but a few footprints in the muddy bank. So, I knew who was behind the door. I breathed in silt and murky water and crayfish and carp and snakes and dragonflies, and so I knew precisely who had come calling. I said her name aloud, before I turned the knob.

I said, "Eva." And then I opened the door. My own Open Door of Night.

She stood on the landing in the same simple red sundress she'd been wearing that scalding day at Wayland Square, and that afternoon at the RISD Museum. She was barefoot, and her toenails were polished a silvery color that reminded me of nacre, which most people call mother-of-pearl. Rosemary Anne had mother-of-pearl earrings when I was a child, but she lost them before she went away to Butler Hospital and I've never found them. Eva stood before me, smiling. There was a bundle in her hands, something wrapped in butcher paper and tied up neat with twine.

"Your clothes," she said, holding out the package. "I had them cleaned." She didn't say hello. She offered me the package, and I took it from her.

"I knew you'd come," I said. "Even if I didn't know I knew, I knew all the same."

And she smiled like a shark, or like a barracuda might smile, and she said, "May I come in, India Morgan Phelps?"

I regarded her a moment, and then I said, "That day at the gallery, you told me the time for choice is behind us both. So, why are you bothering to ask?" And I thought of the stories that say vampires and other malevolent spirits have to be invited into your home. (Though hadn't I invited her once already?)

"I'm only being polite," she replied.

"But if I say no, you're not going to leave, are you?"

"No, Imp. We've come too far."

I very almost said, *"So remote from the night of first ages. . . . We are accustomed to look upon the shackled form of a conquered monster, but there—there you could look at a thing monstrous and free."* But I didn't. I didn't have the nerve, and I didn't think it would matter. There was no ward to drive her back, not from Joseph Conrad or Herman Melville or Matthew Arnold. Not from any holy book or infernal grimoire. I knew this, as surely as I knew the thing standing on my doorstep was alive and meant to enter, whether I wished it to or not.

But, to tell the truth, I desired nothing more.

"Yeah, you can come in," I said. "Where are my manners?"

"Well, you weren't expecting me."

"Of course I was," I told her, and she smiled again.

In a notebook, Leonardo da Vinci wrote, "The siren sings so sweetly, she lulls mariners to sleep. She boards ships and murders sleeping mariners." Translated into English, this is what he wrote. Those who wrote of the fairy Unseelie Court told of the *Each-Uisge* (ekh-ooshh-kya), the Kelpie, who haunted lakes and bays and rivers in Ireland and Scotland. It rose from the slime and the reeds, a *water horse*, and any foolish enough to ride were drowned and eaten. Except the liver. The *Each-Uisge* disdains the liver. I don't like liver, either.

Imp typed, "You're drifting again."

Sailing ships—clippers, dories, schooners, smacks, trawlers, gigantic cargo ships and toxic oil tankers, whaling ships—adrift on treacherous currents and storm winds, and they dash themselves to splinters on jagged headlands.

"Drifting," Imp typed. "Tiller hard to port. Hold to true north, if you're not to stray."

Eva Canning stepped across my threshold.

"Who are hearsed that die on the sea?"

She shut the door behind her, and the latch clicked loudly. She turned the dead bolt, and I found nothing the least bit strange about her doing it. Nothing strange at all about her locking me into my own apartment, with her. I understood she'd not come so far only to be interrupted by intruders. I imagine so many before me have drowned in the depths of her bottle-blue eyes. She's exactly, exactly, exactly as I remembered her from the July night by the Blackstone River, and from that day at the gallery. Her hair so long and the color of nothing at all, only the color of a place where no light has ever shone.

She turned away from the locked door. She turned towards me. She touched my cheek, and her skin felt like silk against mine. My skin felt like sandpaper compared with hers. This impression was so pronounced that I wanted to pull away and warn her not to cut herself. Her hand had not been fashioned to touch the likes of me. I think of stories I've read in books, tales of sharks brushing against swimmers, and how the denticles of sharkskin scrapes bare flesh raw. But here our roles are reversed, if only for this swift assemblage of instants. I am the author of abrasions, or I fear I will be.

But I draw no drop of blood from that silken hand.

"You hurt me," I say. "You put words in my mind, and I almost died to get them out again."

"I got your attention," she replies.

"You hurt Abalyn."

"Imp, she'd have been harmed far worse if she hadn't gone." And Eva quotes from *Hamlet*, " 'I must be cruel only to be kind. Thus bad begins and worse remains behind.' "

I know there will be no arguing with her. That lilting voice foolish Ulysses heard, that he ordered himself lashed to a mast that he might hear. Eva reduces any objection to bald-faced absurdity.

"You're a wicked thing. You're an abomination."

"I am as I am. As are you."

Those silken fingertips glide across my lips, and then across the bridge of my nose. I have never been touched with such perfect intimacy.

"You've come to kill me," I say very softly, and it surprises me that I don't sound afraid.

"I've done nothing of the sort," she replies, and that doesn't surprise me, either. What she says, I mean. It's easy to kill. It's easy to be a predator. A shark. A wolf. Not easy, no. People hunt wolves and sharks for no reason except the fact that they *are* sharks and wolves. I'm trying to say, I realize that whatever Eva Canning is, it's something far more subtle than a predator. She's come to feed, and maybe to devour, but not to kill. My face is being stroked by a beast that does not need to feed to devour.

"You let him see you. Saltonstall, I mean."

"I never said that."

"*The Drowning Girl*, you called it 'my painting.' "

"Did I?" she asks, and she smiles.

Her hand lingers at my left earlobe, and goose bumps speckle my arms. Her fingers brush through my hair.

"So, why are you here?"

"You stopped for me. No one else ever did," she says. "I've come to sing for you, because I owe you a kindness."

"Even if it's cruel."

"Even if," she says, and now her fingers are exploring the back of my neck. "And, in return, I will ask a small favor of you, Imp. But we'll talk about that later. Don't be afraid of me. You can't yet see it, but I've come to lead you out of the dark place where you've always lived. You can't glimpse it from here, but from *there*, you will." (Look upon the thing monstrous and free.)

She kissed me then, and I thought, *I've never been kissed before.*

(Oh. I've shifted tense, but then there is no proper tense in this Blakean land of dreams, this mnemonic labyrinth, past and present indistinguishable. *The past is the present, isn't it? It's the future, too.* Just like Mary Cavan Tyrone said.)

She kissed me. She is kissing me. Always, she will be kissing me. This is the way of hauntings, as I've said. Eva Canning, I think—I think I *only* thought this, but it seemed as though Eva Canning tasted like the sea. Taste, smell, sight, audition, the sensation of touch . . . they all blur just as time has blurred.

Her tongue enters my mouth, probing, and there's brief panic, because it's not so different from the day I tried to breathe underwater, the day I tried to inhale a tub filled with ice water. She is flowing into me. Only, this time, my body doesn't fight back. She is pouring down my throat, and I'm breathing her into me. But my lungs make no effort to resist the invasion.

This sounds like pornography. I read back over the page and it sounds like I'm writing pornography. It was never anything like that. My words aren't good enough. They're not equal to the task. I don't know how to communicate passion and longing, the wetness between my thighs, desire, that wish to have her within and around me, and not cheapen it. A woman struggles to describe demons, angels, and, being *only* a woman, she does their beauty and terror a disservice. I do Eva Canning, as she came to me, as I *saw* her, an abhorrent disservice.

> From childhood's hour I have not been
> As others were—I have not seen

Our lips parted, and the division brought greater despair by far even than the days I learned first of Rosemary's death, then of Caroline's, than the hour that Abalyn went away. I stumbled backwards and bumped against the arm of the sofa. I would have fallen, if it hadn't been there.

You really have no notion how delightful . . .

She stood between me and the door, and I was just beginning to see her, not as the mask to hide the *thing*, monstrous and free, a few inches of black water, and seeing her even clearer than that day at the museum. Her cheeks and shoulders shimmer, green-red-cyan iridescence, and only now does it occur to me she isn't wearing the sunglasses she wore that day at Wayland Square and that day at RISD, because her bottle-blue eyes are black, and I don't know why I ever mistook them for bottle-blue or any other color. Black is all colors, the absorption of all colors. No light escapes black. No light escapes the eyes of Eva Canning, when I still believe her the Siren of Millville.

"I will sing for you, ~~Winter~~ India Morgan," she said, smiling her frayed, sad, voracious, apologetic, sympathetic smile. That smile is etched evermore on the insides of my eyelids, and when I am dead, embalmed, and in my grave, I'll still see that smile. "I've come to sing for you, and to draw your song from you. And when we are done singing, you'll take me home, and I'll go down to my mother, who dreams of me each night."

The voyeur of utter destruction.

In hindsight.

The fortune from the fortune cookie I got the first time Abalyn and I ordered takeout: Don't stop now.

But I want to, because what's coming is as bad as those latest days off my meds, those last days spent in my corner or whispering madly into the typewriter until Abalyn used her key and found me. What's coming, it's that impossible to describe, I think, because it's that terrible, that beautiful, that derelict, and that private. But I'm so, so near The End. Don't stop now.

Much of what follows is confused, fuzzy. Especially the beginning of it. For one, I stopped taking my meds. And there was Eva, and whatever it meant that she'd crossed my threshold, and by that, I mean much more than she'd stepped across my doorsill. I mean very many things. I do recall that she called work and said she was a friend of mine, that I had an intestinal bug and would be out for a few days. I also remember that it was Eva who convinced me I'd be better off without my pills, because, after all, I had *her* now. And she said something like, "They would only blur your perceptions of me. They keep you from seeing what the gift of your insanity reveals, and what others never guess." At her bidding, I actually flushed it all down the toilet. The prescriptions. I sat at the toilet, emptying each bottle as she stood in the doorway, watching on approvingly. I flushed, and the swirling water stole my counterfeit sanity away.

She offered a hand, and helped me up off the floor. Though, truthfully, I wanted to stay there. The apartment was so awfully hot, and the tiles were cool beneath me. She pulled me to her, and then led me . . .

It'll be a lie if I settle for, "She pulled me to her, and then led me to bed." Though she did do that. But if I say that, and only that, it'll be a falsehood. It might be factual, but it wouldn't be true. "Take my hand, India. I'll show you how to fly." Fly, sing, swim. She led me to the bed, and she undressed me. She kissed me again. She kissed my mouth, and my breasts, and my sex. And then she led me into deepest winter, and to the Blackstone River. She took me into song, which became a far white country, until it became a painting, until it became the sea. But first, song was *only* song, and her lips only her lips.

Shoo, shoo, shoo la roo, shoo la rack shack, shoo la baba boo, When I find my sally bally bill come dibb-a-lin a boo shy lor-ree, Hush-a-bye, don't you cry, Go to sleepy little baby. When you wake, you shall have, All the pretty little horses. Blacks and bays, dapples and grays, Johnny's gone for a soldier. "Come home with me, little Matty Groves, come home with me tonight. Come home with me, little Matty Groves, and sleep with me till light." Johnny's gone for a soldier. They grew and grew in the old churchyard Till they could grow no higher At the end they formed, a true lover's knot And the rose grew round the briar. I am as brown as brown can be, And my eyes as black as sloe; I am as brisk as brisk can be, Johnny has gone for a soldier. "I put him in a tiny boat, And cast him out to sea, That he might sink or he might swim, But he'd never come back to me." And the only sound I hear, as it blows through the town, is the cry of the wind as it blows through the town, weave and spin, weave and spin. His ghost walked at midnight to the bedside of his Mar-i-Jane When he told her how dead he was; said she: "I'll go mad." "Since my love he is so dead," said she, "All joy on earth has fled for me." "I never more will happy be," and she went raving mad. Johnny has gone for a soldier. Twinki doodle dum, twinki doodle dum sang the bold fisherman. Shule, shule, shulagra, sure and sure and he loves me. Of thrupence a pound on the tea, of thrupence a pound on the tea. Siúl, Siúl, Siúl a ghrá Níl leigheas ar fáil ach leigheas an bháis Ó d'fhag tú mise is bocht mo chás Is go dté tú mo mhúirnín slán Way down yonder, down in the meadow There's a poor wee little lamby. The bees and the butterflies pickin' at its eyes, The poor wee thing cried for her mammy. Hush, little baby, don't say a word, o follow the whale; Where the icebergs do float And the stormy winds blaw, Where the land and the ocean Are covered wi' snaw. If that mockingbird don't sing, Mama's gonna buy you a diamond ring. Weave and spin, weave and spin, Johnny has gone for a soldier. He made a harp o her breast-bane, That he might play forever thereon. Johnny has gone for a soldier. Then three times 'round went our gallant ship, And three times 'round went she, And the third time that she went 'round She sank to the bottom of the sea. The boat capsized and four men were drowned, and we never caught that whale, Brave boys, And we never caught that whale. And a' the live-lang winter night The dead corp followed she. Weave and spin, weave and spin. I saw, I saw the light from heaven Come shining all around. I saw the light come shining. I saw the light come down. As slow our ship her foamy track Against the wind was cleaving, Shoo, shoo, shoo la roo shoo la rack shack, shoo la baba boo When I find my sally bally bill come dibb-a-lin a boo shy lor-ree, Johnny has gone for a soldier.

In those days that followed, all and every song was hers, and of her kind. She didn't ever tell me that. It was something I understood implicitly. It was an unspoken truth hung between us. Eva Canning laid me out on my bed, filleted me, and she buried her face between my thighs, and her tongue sang unspeakable songs into me.

They are too many to write them all down, so I settle for dread morsels. Most I can't recall, anyway, and, besides, I know now what I didn't know then. I've seen the grave in Middletown, and I know now my ghost story isn't the ghost story I thought it was, the one I set out to tell. My stories shape-shift like mermaids and werewolves. A lycanthropy of nouns, verbs, and adjectives, subjects and predicates, and so on and so forth.

She lapped between my legs, and filled me to bursting with music few have ever heard and lived. She made me Ulysses. She made me a lyre and a harp and flute. She played me (two meanings here). And songs are stories, and so she made of me a book, just as I became song. None of this means what it meant a few days ago, but I'm telling it as I *would* have told it before Abalyn went with me to Aquidneck Island. There will be time later for other revelations. *These* things are still true, and I think facts are patient things. Facts have all the time the universe allows.

I awoke one night, past midnight but long before dawn, and she was standing at the bedroom window, looking out on the house's stingy, weedy backyard, at the houses that face Wood Street, the sky, at everything you can see from that window. It's a depressing view, and I hardly ever open those curtains. Eva was naked, and her skin as iridescent as motor oil in a puddle. Even by the moonlight through the window, her skin shimmered.

"Did I dream—?" I began.

"You dreamed about me," she said.

"What are you looking at?" I asked, my voice filled with sleep and the taste of the dreams she'd given me, and the dreams that were still to come.

She looked over her shoulder at me, and she smiled. It was the saddest sort of smile. It was a smile that almost broke my heart. "Your heart is brittle, ~~Winter~~ India Morgan. Your heart's no more than a china shop, and all the world's that proverbial bull. Your heart's spun from molten glass.

"You should be asleep," she said.

"Something woke me," I replied. I asked her what she was looking at, and she turned to face the window again.

"Something woke me," she said.

I shut my eyes again, only wanting to sink back down to sleep, so tired, so happily, painfully worn from her ministrations and the songs and stories filling me alive. Then she said something more, and I'm not sure of what I heard. I'm only almost sure, which isn't at all the same as being sure, right?

I think Eva Canning said, "You're a ghost." But she wasn't speaking to me. What she was looking at was her reflection in the bedroom window, and I'm only almost sure that's what, whom, she was speaking to.

I choose this next song at random. This dream,

I believe I'll choose it, then one more.

Or two.

I'm painting a picture of days that are all but lost, and yet they are the most real and immediate days I've ever lived. I'm trying to recall those precious dreams and stories she sang and whispered across my lips and teeth and into my throat.

She knew hundreds of permutations of the story of how, in 1898, Phillip George Saltonstall came to paint *The Drowning Girl*. She told me most of them. She sang them to me. Some echoed his letter to Mary Farnum. Most didn't.

I remember this, whether I was dreaming or awake, or in that liminal space where she kept me most of the time. I sleepwalked through entire days.

I was in the forest at Rolling Dam on the Blackstone River, and it was deep into winter, and there'd been a heavy snowfall. I was naked as Eva had been standing at the bedroom window, but I wasn't cold. I didn't feel the cold at all. I was on the western shore, looking out across the dam, at all that water the color of pickled Spanish olives spilling over the convex top and crashing to the rocks below. The water above the dam was black, and who knows how deep, or what it hid. (And, writing this, I'm reminded of Natalie Wood trying to drown herself above a dam in *Splendor in the Grass*, and of Natalie Wood drowning in 1981 off the Isthmus of Catalina Island. She was afraid of drowning all her life, because, as a child, she almost did. Drown, I mean. Anyway, in *Splendor in the Grass*, the water above the dam was dark, too. But, in the movie, it was summer, not winter.)

The waters below Rolling Dam were rapids that roared and gurgled between snow-covered granite boulders. I walked down to the waterline, and saw that north of me, where the river bends sharply back to the west, it was frozen over, and the ice stretched away as far as I could see. A road of white laid between the boles and frosted limbs of paper birch, pines, maple boughs dappled with thousands of tiny red flowers despite the cold, oaks, willows, thick underbrush growths of rhododendron, hawthorn, greenbrier, wild grapes.

My breath didn't fog, and I suspected this was because I was dead, and so my body was almost as cold as the woods around me.

"What did you see there at the dam?" I type. "No lies. What did you see?"

I beg your pardon. I haven't lied yet.

There was a noise on my left, and I turned my head to see a doe watching me. She was so still I thought she might be dead, as well. Might be dead and taxidermied and left out here as a practical joke or a morbid bit of ornamentation. But then she blinked, and bolted, springing away into the trees. She should have made a great deal of noise, tearing through the forest like that, but she made no sound at all. Maybe she did, but the roar from the dam obscured it. The dam was so loud, like a wave always breaking and never withdrawing down the vast edges drear and naked shingles of the world. The doe went, her white tail a warning flash, but I thought I was alone. Except for crows cawing in the trees.

"Crows mean lies," Imp typed. "Don't forget that. Don't forget the plague doctors you never saw, the beak doctors."

Crows are not always lies. Sometimes, they're only hungry, rowdy, rude, punk crows perched in the bare branches of February trees. That's my soul up there. Sometimes, they're no more than that.

"Fine," Imp typed. "But after the doe, what did you see after the doe? When you looked across the Blackstone River above the dam, what did you see?"

I saw Jacova Angevine (I didn't know her name; I wouldn't learn her name for another two years and four months). I saw Jacova Angevine, leader of the Open Door of Night, the Prophet from Salinas, leading dozens and dozens of women and men into the river. They were all dressed in robes as white as the snow. None of them even tried to swim. They walked in, went down, and none of them came back up again. No air bubbles. It went on for a long time, and I was starting to think there'd be no end to that procession, when there was, and only one woman was left standing on the opposite shore. No, not a woman. A very young girl. She wasn't dressed in a white robe, but jeans and a sweater and a bright blue coat with a blue fur collar. She stood on the bank and peered into the tannin-stained river. It's only fifty yards or so across at Rolling Damn, and I could see her very clearly. She looked up, finally, and for an instant her eyes met mine. And then she turned and, like the doe, bolted into the forest.

"You're a ghost," she told her reflection.

I wanted to follow the girl, but I didn't dare enter that river, not with all those drowned men and women. I was certain they'd reach up and drag me down with them. Instead, I crouched in the snow, wild as any doe or bobcat or coyote. I crouched and watched the river. I pissed, and so I knew I must be alive, because I don't think dead women piss, do they? I huddled in the trees, beneath a cloudy Man Ray kind of sky almost as white as the snow. And, before the sun set, I began to feel the cold, and my body turned to ice. I was crystal, and the moon shone through me.

Imp types, "In 'Werewolf Smile,' you named yourself Winter."

We're sitting together in moonlight, and there are no lights on anywhere in the apartment. We're sitting together in front of the turntable and speakers, and I'm playing one of Rosemary Anne's records for Eva. She has told me she is always fascinated by the music she doesn't make, the music of man, the music above the sea, the music of the world above, though she's heard very little of it. So, I'm playing *Dreamboat Annie* for her, because I remember that's the one that Abalyn liked the most. Eva listens, and occasionally says something. The music is loud (she wants it that way), but I have no trouble at all hearing her words clearly above the guitars, the drums, the pianos and synthesizers, and the vocals.

I've just asked her, again, what she meant that day in the museum about *The Drowning Girl* being *her* painting. One song ends, another begins, and finally she says, "You see it, and are obsessed with it. But haven't you ever made it yours? Haven't you ever found yourself within it?"

I admitted I'd not.

She kissed me, and the music faded. In a few moments, I found myself standing on the riverbank again. This time ~~I was not Winter~~ it was not winter, but late summer, and the trees were a riot of green. There was very little I could see that was not one or another hue of green. But I noticed at once that I could only see a few feet in any direction. I couldn't see the sky, or very far along the bank to either side. I'd stepped into the cool, welcoming water, and when I look over my right shoulder, the space between the trees is impenetrable. There is above me no hint of the sky. It's not that I can't *see* the sky; it simply isn't there. And I understand then that I am not actually back at the river. Eva has kissed me, alchemical kiss, and now I am in the painting. No, I *am* the painting.

I inspect everything more closely, and there is about every surface—the river, the forest, the bark of the trees, the underbrush between them, even my own skin—there is about it all the unmistakable texture of linen stretched and framed. And this is when I feel the camel's hair brush and the oil paint dabbing tenderly, meticulously, at the space below my navel.

"You see?" Eva asks. And I am back with her in the moonlight. The record has ended, and the phonograph's pickup arm has automatically lifted and returned to the armrest. "It's as simple as that. Now it's your painting, too. It's only another way of singing."

It was a while before the disorientation passed, and I could speak. I said, "I wish there were something I could give you. You've given me so much."

She smiled, and kissed my cheek. "It's coming, love," she sighed. "Be patient. Soon enough now, it's coming."

As I've said above, there are countless other songs and stories Eva sang into me. Though, I see they're all variations on a theme. At most, distinguished one from another by disparities that seem far less important, less profound, to me now than they must have seemed then.

"You're a ghost," Eva told herself.

And she sang into me for days and days, nights and nights, making of me the vessel of a ghost's memories. She hid me, sequestered in her arms and my apartment, apart from all distraction, that I would have eyes and ears and touch and taste for her and her alone. I breathed her into me. I breathed in a ghost, insubstantial and ectoplasmic, a woman who believed herself a ghost, and a siren, and who was not a wolf and never had been. We spoke, somewhen in all that time, of Albert Perrault, and she said, "My mother . . . ," but then trailed off.

I wrote that I'd choose one story, and then another. But there are too many choices, and too little distinction. And I have. The girl standing at the riverbank, and then turning away. Not following the others into the river and so missing that chance forever. Not joining, so evermore apart. I can understand that. Caroline went in merciful hydrocarbon fumes, and Rosemary Anne, she's gone, too, and I am alone, in an exile of my own choosing, or of my own fear. I could join them, and, yet, I can't. I can't follow. Eva can't follow, but the sea has her heart and soul forever. "The Little Mermaid," and never "Little Red Riding Hood." Never Gévaudan. Always *The Drowning Girl,* and never Elizabeth Short. But I'm racing ahead of myself. Stop. Retrace your steps, Imp.

Eva didn't love me. I doubt she ever loved anyone. She loved the ocean. Trapped in a dark river in Massachusetts, she was only seeking her way home, the path flowing to the tide of a lover's arms. In "Werewolf Smile," I wrote of that fictionalized Eva, ". . . because I knew that she never *loved* any of them, any more than she loved me."

I've told about the river in winter, and becoming the painting, but I'm not going to write down all those story-songs, the mutable, unchanging permutations: a child on a merry-go-round, spinning round and round while her mother watched, and never getting anywhere at all; an emaciated creature with golden eyes and needle teeth lying hungry and watchful in the mud at the bottom of the deep water in back of Rolling Dam; the wrecks of ship after ship, seventeenth-, eighteenth-, nineteenth-century drownings; a beach leading down to the submarine Monterey Canyon, ninety-five miles long and out of soundings, almost twelve hundred feet deep; a beautiful, charismatic woman with an ancient idol of a god-thing she called Mother Hydra; an intricate mandala on the floor of a temple that had once been a warehouse, and the supplicants praying there for deliverance from terrestrial damnation; Phillip George Salton-stall climbing into the saddle; the rape of my mother by a man I have called Father; all those men and women marching into the sea; the hand of hurricane demons. See, Imp, they're all the same story, seen through the eyes of the ghost whom they haunt, and that ghost is Eva, and that ghost is me.

She showed me the face I needed to see, and that she needed me to see, to complete a circuit. It would end her haunting, even as it made mine worse. I couldn't have known this at the time, lost in her and off my meds.

There are no monsters. No werewolves. No sirens.

But she showed me her truest face, and it hardly matters whether it was ever factual.

The Siren of Millville writhed in her variegated coils upon my bed, the murdered, transformed soul of Perishable Shippen, who had surely perished, true to her name, even if she'd never existed. Eva writhed in the vermiform coils of eels and sea snakes, hagfish and lamprey. She fastened that ravenous, barbeled mouth about the folds of my labia, rasping teeth working at my clit. She writhed and coiled about me, wrapping me in a smothering, protective cocoon of slime, thick translucent mucus exuded from unseen glands or pores. Across her rib cage were drawn the gill slits of a shark, a deep row of four crimson slashes on either side of her torso, out of water and gasping, opening and closing, breathless but undying. Her breasts had vanished, leaving her chest flat except for those gills. I gazed into black eyes, eyes that were only black and nothing more, and they gazed into me.

She flowered, and bled me dry.

She took my voice, and filled me with song.

Unloving, she left me no choice but to love her.

Where there had been clean cotton sheets, there was a blanket of polyps, a hundred different species of sea anemones, the stinging embrace of their stinging tentacles planted there to keep us safe. We were immune to their neurotoxins, I understood instinctively, like the tiny clownfish that nest within anemones to escape the jaws of bigger fish are immune. To my eyes, the anemones were no different from a field of wildflowers. She flowered. And there were minute blue-ringed octopuses and sea snakes, nestled between those flowers, each sparing us its fatal bite. She called them all with melodies no mortal woman's throat may ever replicate. Crabs scuttled across my belly, and a razor rash of barnacles flecked my arms and legs. I questioned none of this. It was. It simply was. The room was filled with the darting, sinuous shadows of fish.

I came again and again and again.

Orgasm is too insufficient a word.

She held me tightly in arms the same bottle-blue as her eyes had once been, hands and webbed fingers and arms dappled with scales and photophores that glowed another shade of blue to illuminate the abyssal gloom of my bedroom, which must have sunk as deeply as anything has ever sunken. Her chitin claws drew welts on my breasts and face. Her lionfish spines impaled my heart and lungs.

She drew me down.

"Promise," she whispered with that lipless mouth. "Promise me, when we are done here."

And I did promise, barely half-understanding the pledge I'd made. I'd have promised her I'd fight my way through all the hells in which I'd never believed. I'd have promised her every remaining day of my life, had she asked.

"You are my savior," she whispered, coiling and uncoiling. "You are the end of my captivity."

"I love you," I told her.

"I'm wicked. Remember?"

"Then I love your wickedness, and I'll be wicked, too. I'll become an abomination."

"There's not an ounce of wickedness in you, India Morgan Phelps, and I'll not put it there."

"If you leave me," I said. "You leave me, I'll die," and I was trying so hard not to sob, but there were tears on my cheeks, tears instantly lost to the ocean filling my bedroom. "I'll drown if you ever leave me."

"No, Imp," she replied, her voice all kelp and bladderwrack. "You're not the girl who drowns. Not in this story you're writing. You're the girl who learns to swim."

"I want to believe you."

"Oh, ~~Winter~~ India, everything I've ever told you or ever will tell you is a lie, but *this*, this *one* thing is true." (I don't tell her I would one day write those words and put them in her mouth in a story titled "Werewolf Smile.")

She kissed me again, tasting all of brine, and her lips the lips of *l'Inconnue de la Seine*.

And then I began to sing. It was *my* song, and my song alone, never voiced since the dawn of time. It was everything I was, had been, might be. I swelled with song, and I sang.

"Like the fortune cookie said, 'Don't stop now,'" Imp typed. "You're almost at the end of it."

It's true. There's not that much more left to tell, though, possibly, what remains may be the most important part of the ghost story. I could draw it out, perhaps. There is so much more I haven't told, moments that transpired between myself and Eva Canning, and I could sit here and record all of them that I can remember. That would take many days more, many pages more. Even though there's not that much more left to tell. I have the time, I suppose. Still unemployed, I have quite a lot of time on my hands. So, yeah, I could draw it out, how I was seduced and romanced by my mermaid (who never was a wolf), my lover who would be a melusine, a daughter of Phorcys, the Siren of Millville trapped in the Blackstone River ages ago by a hurricane, who would be all these things and innumerable things more. In her way, and in *my* way, she bewitched me as surely as Circe, though her tinctures worked on my eyes and mind. The physical transformations she worked all upon herself.

Early one morning—and I cannot say how many days had passed since she'd crossed the threshold, since Abalyn had left, only that we'd remained in the apartment all that time. I had no need of food, or no need beyond whatever was already in the pantry and the fridge. So, early one morning in August I woke, and I was alone in the bed. The sheets were only sheets. All her anemones had melted away again. They came and went as they wished, or as she summoned and dismissed them. There were only the sheets, which smelled of sweat and sex and, so, faintly of the sea. I'd been dreaming of the day that Abalyn and I had gone to the river and seen nothing much at all, only in the dream, we did see something. I won't say what. What is not important. I woke from the dream, and lay blinking, immediately aware that Eva wasn't there beside me. I slept in her arms, or her in mine. We curled fetal as any unborn beast in one another's arms. We wrapped ourselves together as though all we were depended on those embraces.

"Eva?" I whispered, sleepily.

"Good morning, India Morgan," she said. She was at the bedroom window again, looking out at the sky, which was only just beginning to brighten. She wasn't naked this time. She'd put on her silky red dress, but was barefoot. The dawn light painted her pale face a muted shade of ginger. Ginger or butterscotch. The wolf Eva who never existed, she'd had butterscotch eyes. I considered that maybe the light came *from* within her, as much as it reflected *off* her. She stood very straight. She didn't look over her shoulder at me as she spoke. There was no iridescence remaining about her, and she only looked like any thin, pale woman. She was no longer unearthly, and I thought, *The spell is broken.* I thought, *Perhaps whatever happens from here on, it's my choice and my choice alone.*

This might have been true. Sometimes now, knowing what I know, I prefer to believe otherwise.

"You should put something on," she said, words soft as velvet. "I need you to take me to the sea today. We need to leave soon. I've put it off too long already."

I found no reason to doubt any of this. In every way, it seemed entirely sensible. I'd seen the sort of being she was, and borne witness to her magic, and of course she needed to be near the sea. I got up, found a cleanish pair of panties and mismatched socks (one argyle, one black and white stripes), cargo shorts, and a khaki tank top that Abalyn had left behind. I know now, and knew then, that I should have felt a pang of . . . something . . . seeing the tank top, but I didn't. I simply slipped it on.

I was tying my tennis shoes when she asked if I was hungry, if I needed breakfast before we left. I told her no, I wasn't hungry, though I was.

"Do you know Moonstone Beach?" she asked.

"Sure," I said. "Been there lots." In the summer, you can only walk a narrow strip of Moonstone Beach, because it used to be a nude beach, until 1989 or so when the US Fish and Wildlife people declared it a refuge for endangered piping plovers. From April to mid-September, you can't go where the plovers nest. They are tiny gray-white birds with black bands around their throats and between their eyes. They dash about the sand, pecking at whatever they eat, worms or bugs or whatever.

"Then we'll go to Moonstone Beach." And then she was talking about the January twelve winters before, when a tank barge and a tug both ran aground there. The barge spilled more than eight hundred thousand gallons of toxic heating oil into Block Island Sound and onto the beach. The name of the barge was *North Cape*, and the tug was named *Scandia*, and, during a storm, they'd run afoul of the rocks in the shallows just offshore. Both Trustom and Card ponds were contaminated by the spill—two salt ponds bordering the beach—and Moonstone was littered with the corpses of tens of millions of poisoned seabirds, lobsters, surf clams, and starfish. Anything that could be poisoned and was washed up onto the beach. People saved some of the birds. You can't save a poisoned lobster.

You really have no notion how delightful . . .

"It was a massacre," Eva said, and there was an unmistakable trace of bitterness in her voice. "She doesn't forget these things. Maybe people do. Maybe the birds come back and shellfish come back, and no one tells tourists what happened here. But the *sea* remembers. The memory of the sea encompasses eons."

I tell her how I found a trilobite fossil out on Conanicut Island when I was a kid. "It was sort of smooshed up, though, because the shale metamorphosed, got turned to slate . . . ," and then I realized I was prattling and trailed off.

"I sang for me," she said, and I sat on the bed, watching the butterscotch light on her face. "I sang you, and drew your song from you. I kept my promise."

"Do you think she's waiting?" I asked. "Your mother, I mean," and she didn't answer me. I wanted to tell her I loved her. I wanted to beg her to be with me forever, to strangle me in her bathypelagic reveries she'd only allowed me to briefly glimpse. I wanted to implore her to teach me metamorphosis, that I might coil and peer at the world through shark-black eyes. *Please teach me the witchcraft,* I thought, *so I can call the anemones and crabs, the octopuses and starfish. Stay and always be my sister, my lover, my teacher, my dissolution.* My thoughts were bright as the rising sun, and she heard them all. Or she only guessed.

"No," she whispered. "I've given as much as I may."

That's when I remembered my Moonstone dreams from July, dancing hand in hand to "The Lobster Quadrille" while Eva fiddled. But I kept them to myself. I went to the bathroom, brushed and flossed my teeth, used deodorant, and peed. My reflection, in the mirror on the medicine cabinet door, my reflection surprised me, but only a little. I'd lost weight, and my skin was sallow, and there were dark circles beneath my eyes.

Small price to pay, I silently told myself.

"I'm ready," I said, stepping back into the bedroom. Eva was still standing at the window. At last she turned away from the coming day. And I think, I almost am certain, that she said something about Aokigahara Jukai, but she was speaking so quietly, and I didn't ask her to repeat herself.

We left the house, left the city, and I took the Broad Street exit onto I-95 to South County. I had to find my sunglasses, the sun so bright on my left. The day was bright, the sky blue as blue ever is, no clouds at all. Eva found a radio station playing classical music, and . . .

"Don't stop now," Imp typed.

> *Full fadom five thy MOTHER lies,*
> *Of HER bones are Corrall made:*
> *Those are pearles that were HER eies*
> *Nothing of HER that doth fade,*
> *But doth suffer a Sea-change*
> *Into something rich, & strange:*

It takes us less than an hour to reach Moonstone Beach. I exit the interstate at . . . no, no sense in a blow-by-blow travelogue, is there? I left the interstate and drove south to the sea. I drove south, to the sea. The windows were down, and the air was sweet with the perfume of growing things. I drove, and we passed the picturesque rural pageant below I-95: the Kenyon Grist Mill (circa 1886, 1695) and fields of tall, dry cornstalks, forests and bracken and pastureland, fieldstone walls scabbed with moss and lichen, horses, and cows, and goats, trees so huge I imagine they must have been planted or taken root before the Revolutionary War, a handful of houses (some old and dignified, some new and shoddy), and a wide plot of Queen Anne's lace, their white flowers rustling lazily in the morning breeze. Ponds, and streams, and small bogs. A time or two, I wanted to pull the Honda over, to show Eva some thing or another. But I didn't. Back on Willow Street, she'd said, "We need to leave soon. I've put it off too long already."

She wouldn't want me to stop, so I didn't ask. I tried not to ask questions I already knew the answers to; Rosemary taught me not to do that.

By seven o'clock (I had to stop for gas, or we'd have gotten there sooner), we'd reached the sandy cul-de-sac, the turnaround at the end of Moonstone Beach Road. On one side, the west, the turn-around is flanked by Card Pond, and on the other side, the east, it's flanked by an impenetrable thicket, interlaced with stunted trees, and then Card Pond. I parked on the Card Pond side, and warned Eva to be careful of poison ivy when she got out, as it grows every-where near the beach. I didn't know whether or not she was allergic, but I'm awfully allergic to poison ivy. So cautioning her was reflex-ive. She hadn't worn shoes, after all. Eva smiled, opened the door, and got out of the car.

We stood there, with the car between us, for . . . for not too long. I spotted two swans on the pond and pointed them out to her. She nodded and said, "The dying swan, when years her temples pierce, In music-strains breathes out her life and verse. And, chant-ing her own dirge, tides on her wat'ry hearse."

Who are hearsed that die on the sea?

"Did you just make that up?" I asked.

"Hardly," she said, and laughed, but it was in no way an unkind or mocking laugh. "An English poet, Phineas Fletcher. He wrote it."

"Well, it's beautiful," I told her.

"Not as much as the swans," she replied.

"No," I agreed, "not that beautiful."

A gust of wind rippled the tea-colored surface of the pond, and one of the swans spread its wide wings.

"We shouldn't linger," she said then, and I followed her from the Honda down the trail of gray sand leading to the beach. We crossed the culvert that connects the two ponds. The tide was going out, so water was gurgling into Card Pond through the concrete pipe beneath us. There are only two or three lines of dunes dividing the salt ponds from the beach. The dunes were festooned with dog roses and the aforementioned poison ivy. That morning, there were the delicate pink and white dog roses in bloom, and still a few drooping scarlet rose hips that hadn't shriveled and dropped to the ground.

"Make it short," Imp typed. "We shouldn't linger."

I also type.

The air smelled of the sea, and of the dog roses. Beyond the dunes, Moonstone Beach is almost always very, very windy. The wind whipped madly through Eva's long hair. The wind was colder than I'd expected it to be, and I wished I'd brought a sweater. The air was so clear that morning, I could plainly make out the silhouette of Block Island, ten miles to the south. The beach was, as always, littered with seaweed and cobbles and pebbles: granite, slate, calcite, schist, and the opaque white moonstone for which the beach was named. The sea was calm, and only very low waves, ankle-high, rolled in and broke against the shoreline. The air was filled with herring gulls, a few of the larger black-backed gulls, and sleek cormorants streaking past.

No, Caroline. There were no crows, or ravens, or black birds of any sort.

Eva bent down and picked up a perfectly rounded moonstone, about the size of a chestnut, and she placed it in my hand, then closed my fingers around it.

"You can sing now, India Morgan Phelps," she said. "I wish your songs weren't going to cause you so much pain." And then she placed a hand on either side of my head and kissed me, and Eva tasted no different from any human woman I've ever kissed.

When our mouths parted, I said, "Let's go home."

Her bottle-blue eyes stared into my eyes. She didn't smile, and she didn't frown. I don't know a word for the expression that had settled over her face. Maybe the word is *calm*.

"No, Imp. That's not the way your ghost story ends," she said so softly I could hardly hear her voice over the wind. "That's not the way my ghost story ends, either."

And then the woman I knew as Eva Canning, daughter of Eva Canning, did what her mother had done seventeen years before. Eva turned away from me, and she walked into the sea. At first, the waves broke about her ankles, then about her thighs, soaking her red dress, red as rose hips. Then she swam a little ways. And then she was gone. I thought, *Love is watching someone die.*

I sat down on the beach and held the moonstone she'd given me. I sat there a long, long time, shivering and listening to the gulls.

BACK PAGES

NOVEMBER 27, 2010

"Whatever it was, or wasn't, it's done," I typed, "and you've written it down for me. You will always be haunted, but it's done. Thank you. You can go now."

Imp typed.

I typed.

JANUARY 18, 2011

Last night, I looked out the window and saw a red woman walking in the snow. I mean, she was wearing a red dress. But it wasn't her. Abalyn saw the woman, too, and it wasn't her. I think it's going to snow all winter.

JANUARY 27, 2011

I stumbled across this on the internet this morning. I wasn't looking for it. No, maybe I was. I still have my files, and I'll put the printout with everything else about Perrault. This much I will type:

[C]ertainly, far stranger things have been suggested regarding both his life and his works. And given the particulars of his short career, his involvement in the occult, and his penchant for cryptic affectations, it does not seem—to this author—so outlandish to ascribe to Albert Perrault a morbid sort of prescience or to believe that his presentation of *Last Drink Bird Head* upon the eve of his fatal motorcycle accident on the rue Cuvier was a carefully orchestrated move, designed to preserve his mystique *ad finem*. Indeed, it almost seems outlandish to believe otherwise.

As to the painting itself (currently on loan to the Musée national d'art moderne), *Last Drink Bird Head* is one of Perrault's largest and most thematically oblique canvases. After his disappointing experiments with sculpture and multimedia, it harks back to the paintings that heralded his ascent almost a decade ago. Here we have, once again, his "retro-expressionist-impressionist" vision and also a clear return to his earlier obsession with mythology.

A lone figure stands on a barren hilltop, silhouetted against a writhing night sky. However, this sky does not writhe with stars or moonlight, as in Van Gogh's *Starry Night*, but rather here the very *fabric* of the sky writhes. The

canvas itself seems to convulse. The blackness of a firma-
ment which might well reflect Perrault's conception of an
antipathetic cosmos, and might also be read as the projec-
tion of the painting's central figure and, by extension, the
artist's own psyche. There is but a single crimson dab of
light in all that black, contorted sky (recalling his earlier
Fecunda ratis), and it seems more like a baleful eye than any
ordinary celestial body. The distinctive shape and thickness
of the brushstrokes have rendered this sky a violent thing,
and I have found that it's difficult not to view the brushstrokes as the corridors of a sort of madman's maze, leading
round and round and, ultimately, nowhere at all.

And if the sky of *Last Drink Bird Head* could be said to
form a labyrinth, then the figure dominating the foreground
might fairly be construed as its inevitable "minotaur"—that
is, a malformed chimera trapped forever within its looping
confines. The figure has previously been described by one
prominent reviewer as representing the falcon-headed Egyptian sky god Horus (or Nekheny). Yet it seems clear to me
that Perrault's Bird Head avatar cannot accurately be described as "falcon-headed." Rather, the profile presented—a
small skull and long, slender, decurved bill—is more strongly
reminiscent of an ibis. This, then, brings to mind a different
Egyptian deity entirely—Thoth, scribe of the gods and in-
termediator between forces of good and evil.

In its left hand, the figure clutches a book, and on the
book's spine we may clearly discern three letters, presumably a portion of the title—LEV. I cannot help but note reports which surfaced shortly after Perrault's death that he'd
recently begun correspondence with a surviving member of
the late Jacova Angevine's Open Door of Night "suicide
cult," a woman referred to in his correspondence simply as

EMC. Since Angevine's infamous book, *Waking Leviathan*, is known to have been present in Albert Perrault's library . . .

Excerpt from *Gilded Thomas Art Review*

(Vol. 31, No. 7, Fall 2006; Minneapolis, MN)

This painting was not included in the exhibition at the Bell Gallery in 2008. I thought maybe I left before I saw it, as I left in such a state. But I consulted the gallery, and a catalog of the exhibition. The painting wasn't there. I assume it's still in France. But EMC, supposedly a survivor of the mass drownings off Moss Landing? Can there be any doubt who this correspondent was? He didn't know, did he? He didn't know.

February 7, 2011

And am I born to die
To lay this body down
And as my trembling spirit fly
Into a world unknown
A land of deepest shade
Unpierced by human thought
The dreary regions of the dead
Where all things are forgot

"IDUMEA," CHARLES WESLEY, 1793

FEBRUARY 10, 2011

Yesterday, at the Athenaeum, I was asked, "Are you still interested in Phillip Saltonstall?" By the librarian, I mean. The one who asked me two years ago if I knew some of his letters were at the John Hay Library.

"No," I said. But then I said, "Yes, I am," which made her look at me *that way*. But the expression passed quickly. She leaned close and whispered. It seemed conspiratorial, the whisper.

"Then you're not gonna believe this," she said. "You were especially interested in that one painting, right?"

"*The Drowning Girl*," I said, not wanting to say that at all, but what else could I have said?

She produced a very large book, the sort people call "coffee-table books." It was titled *Masters of Symbolism*. She opened it to pages 156–157, and there, on 156 (the left side), was *The Drowning Girl,* and on page 157, there was another of Saltonstall's paintings reproduced. Each filled almost an entire glossy page. The second painting is titled *Girl on a River*, and the book says it was painted in 1870, two years after *The Drowning Girl.* In most respects, the two are almost identical. But they are very, very different, and *Girl on a River*, at first I thought it was the more terrible of the two to see. At first, I almost gathered up my things and ran. After seeing it, I mean. The same girl stands in the same pool; more or less they are the same. Except the girl is not looking over her right shoulder, but is shown in left profile. She is gazing down at a black thing, almost like an immense serpent, half in and half out of the water. It's wrapped itself about her calves and seems to be slithering from the pool into the grass. She appears not the least bit alarmed. Curious, I think, maybe. Almost bemused. Abalyn would say that's a word that no one uses anymore, but she sort of looks that way, *bemused*. The thing looks slippery, and is absolutely black.

In 1897, Saltonstall wrote to Mary Farnum:

"It was then that a pitchy shape leapt up from the river. I know that is a vague description, but I can do no better. It was visible only for an instant, and it never coalesced into anything more distinct. Still, it left me with the disquieting impression that I'd beheld not any manner of fish, but possibly a great serpent, thick around as a telegraph pole and greater in size than any serpent I'd imagined lived anywhere outside the African or Amazonian tropics. Not a genuine serpent, but that's the nearest comparison I can draw, if I attempt to fashion of it anything more substantial than the shadows beneath the maples."

The man who wrote *Masters of Symbolism* referred to *Girl on a River* as a "lost painting." If it really *was* ever lost, then it was *found* three years ago, in the collection of the Hartnell College Gallery in Salinas, California. The author also notes that the painting was donated "by the estate of Theodore Angevine." Father of Jacova. Prophet from Salinas. Her father taught comparative literature, and he wrote mystery novels that I don't think were ever very popular.

Also, when I wrote of the figure in *The Drowning Girl*, I wrote, "Her long hair is almost the same shade of green as the water. . . ." That's not true. I knew it wasn't, but I said it anyway. The woman's hair is blonde. Yellow. Bright yellow, like sunflowers.

I'm not going to say anything about this to Abalyn. Lost paintings, daughters of mystery, mysteries and the pieces aren't ever going to stop falling into place. Or falling, anyway. One Eva, but two paintings.

FEBRUARY 11, 2011

FROM EDGAR ALLAN POE,
"THE DOOMED CITY (THE CITY IN THE SEA)," 1831:

Lo! Death hath rear'd HERself a throne
In a strange city, all alone,
Far down within the dim west—
And the good, and the bad, and the worst, and the best,
Have gone to their eternal rest.
There, shrines, and palaces, and towers
Are—not like anything of ours—
O! no—O! no—ours never loom
To heaven with that ungodly gloom!
Time-eaten towers that tremble not!

"In the mansions of Poseidon, She will prepare halls from coral and glass and the bones of whales. Palaces, shrines in a strange city. She will bring us home."

Jacova Angevine (1990)

MARCH 8, 2011

I saw Dr. Ogilvy today. She's pleased with my progress. She smiles at me the way that I know she really means the smile, that it isn't her "obligatory psychiatrist smile," but sincere and genuine:

"You know now that you'll never be sure what happened?" she asked.

"Yeah, I know now. I know that."

"And you can live with that."

I looked at a big sand dollar on one of her bookshelves, and then I said, "I can. I can live with that."

And that's when she smiled for me.

MARCH 18, 2011

We weave necessary fictions, and sometimes they save us. Our minds, our bodies. The siren taught me to sing, but she was a deceitful, manipulative ____, and she saw that I all but ~~helped~~ held the knife as she slit her wrists. So, I told myself another story, a pretty one where I helped a lost wolf who was actually a girl find herself and so become a wolf again. I laid one over the other, and made of myself a hero and not a fool. But my brain jangled and clamored, and I should have known it would never work.

April 7, 2011

By heaven, man, we are turned round and round in this world, like yonder windlass, and Fate is the handspike. And all the time, lo! that smiling sky, and this unsounded sea!

Herman Melville, *Moby-Dick* (1851)

April 10, 2011

I saw a red woman on the street today. She didn't turn and look at me.

April 10, 2011

It's a dream-kill-dream world in here.

April 20, 2011

Can one's mind, as I shall call it, affect one's body, as I shall call it? If so, that is *personal witchcraft*, or *internal witchcraft*. Can one's mind affect the bodies of other persons and other things outside?

If so, that is what I shall call *external witchcraft*.

Charles Fort, *Lo!* (1931)

Nothing about her is human except that she is *not* a wolf; it is as if the fur she thought she wore had melted into her skin and become part of it, although it does not exist.

Angela Carter, "Wolf-Alice" (1978)

JUNE 2, 2011

I went back to Moonstone Beach today. Abalyn went with me. I laid flowers on the water. I don't know if Eva liked flowers, but I cast onto the waves a wreath of ferns and primroses I'd woven. In the flower language of the Victorians, primroses meant "eternal love," though I know it's inappropriate, because I know that she never *loved* any of them, any more than she loved me. I'll say it's irony.

JUNE 4, 2011

Abalyn finished reading this manuscript yesterday. Well, more last night than yesterday. Afterwards, she stared at it a long time, and then she silently stared at me until I asked her to stop because it was making me nervous.

"It's sort of an amazing thing," she finally said.

"I should have written more about my painting," I replied, which made her stare at me again.

"Imp, what do you think those two short stories are about?" she asked.

"Oh," I said (or I said something like "oh"). "I was starting to think maybe they aren't actually part of the story. That maybe I ought take them out. The paintings, I mean."

Abalyn frowned. "You're wrong," she said. "If you tried, you couldn't be more wrong."

JUNE 10, 2011

One of Eva Canning's cousins, whose name is Jack Bowler, agreed to meet with me at his home in Jamestown. It's a dingy little sort of place, but he made me tea, and he was a pleasant man with too many cats. He's in his forties, and all his hair was gray. He collects nautical memorabilia, and his tiny house is filled with lobster pots, odds and ends from boats, framed photographs and paintings (prints) of whaling ships. I told him up front I was crazy, because I thought I should be honest. He peered at me a moment, and then he laughed and said, "Oh, what the hell ever." He smoked cigarette after cigarette, and didn't ask me if I minded. I didn't tell him that I did.

We talked for more than an hour, and many things were said, consequential and inconsequential. But I'm only going to put one part of it down.

I sipped my second cup of tea, and he said, "Yes, she was a child when her mother died. And she wasn't ever right after that. Maybe she wasn't ever right to start with. We weren't close, but my grandmother being her grandmother's sister, you hear things. She dropped out of school, finally, and wound up in the hospital twice." (Rhode Island Hospital, where I see Dr. Ogilvy; not Butler Hospital.) "I think she was about twenty, twenty-one, when she changed her name. Did it legal and everything."

A marmalade tom jumped into my lap and squinted at me, the way cats squint at interlopers whom they expect to at least have the courtesy to pet them or scratch behind their ears, having interloped and all. I petted him and he purred.

"She changed her name?"

"Yes, she did. Legally. She wasn't born Eva. That's not what her mother named her. Her mother didn't stick around long, but she was here long enough to name her. Child was christened Imogene down at the Central Baptist Church. Imogene May Canning. She changed it, like I said, not long after her mother died. She used to talk about going to California, to that place near Monterey where her mother and all those others died. But she never did."

I petted the marmalade tom in my lap, and didn't interrupt. I don't know what I would have said, anyway.

"Last time they put her in the hospital, someone found her naked at the side of the road somewhere up in Massachusetts. She was taken to the police, and they called her grandmother and brought her back to the hospital in Providence. She was sick. I mean, she'd gotten sick swimming in a river that winter. Bad case of pneumonia. They kept her for a few months, then let her out again. After that, I didn't hear much about her."

There was more talk, and more tea, and more cats.

He showed me the tooth of a sperm whale with a woman's portrait carved into it. He said he'd have more scrimshaw, only it's so expensive. He showed me a lump of ambergris he found at Mackerel Cove. He showed me the skull of a seal.

It was almost dark when I left, and I thanked him, and he said he wished he could have told me more. He asked if I wanted a cat, and I told him yes, but Abalyn's allergic.

JUNE 17, 2011

Went in the shop today (they're always glad to see me, even if I don't work there anymore). Spoke with Annunziata, who was on her break, and we went into the stockroom, and sat and talked a while. Mostly about . . . just mostly talked. But as I was about to leave, because she had to get back out front, she said something.

She said, "Strangest thing a couple of days ago. This lady came in, and, at first glance, she was a dead ringer for your old stalker."

I asked her what she meant by my "stalker."

And she stared at me a moment, first a blank expression, then confused; then she smiled and laughed.

"Blonde woman, right? Always wore sunglasses? Used to always ask about you when you weren't here?"

And I didn't miss a beat. I laughed. No, I pretended to laugh. I pretended to know what she was talking about.

"Wasn't her," Annunziata says. "Figured that out pretty quickly. But at first glance, you know."

I remember her now, from before Eva. My stalker.

Three questions, then:

How long was Eva Canning watching me? And why don't I remember her coming into the shop, when Annunziata insists we used to laugh about it, make jokes about my "stalker"?

And did Eva somehow know about my late-night drives?

No, four questions. Was *any* of it happenstance?

I think Annunziata saw that I was shaken, and when she rang me up she gave me her employee's discount, though she's not supposed to do that.

Jack Bowler said, "I mean, she'd gotten sick swimming in a river that winter."

"You know now that you'll never be sure what happened?" Dr. Ogilvy asked me.

"Yeah, I know now," I told her. "I know that."

I know that.

JUNE 21, 2011

Another pernicious meme, or only an urban legend dressed up to look like a haunting. Either way, I wish I'd known about it when I was writing about Aokigahara Jukai, and Seichō Matsumoto, and his novel.

In 1933, a Hungarian pianist, Rezső Seress, wrote a song he titled "Vége a világnak," which can be translated into English as "End of the World." A second set of lyrics was written by a Hungarian poet named László Jávor, and the song became known as "Szomorú vasárnap," or "Sad Sunday." The original lyrics mourn the destruction of Europe by World War II, and the second mourns the loss of a lover and makes a pledge to commit suicide, in hopes of a reunion in the afterlife. At least, I think that's how it all happened.

In 1941, retitled "Gloomy Sunday," the song became a hit for Billie Holiday. Holiday was nicknamed "Lady Day," though I don't know why. For many Christians, Lady Day is the Feast of the Annunciation of the Blessed Virgin, and I don't know why that would be Billie Holiday's nickname, right? Anyway, the song was a hit for her. But it all becomes very complicated, what happened with the song. With this maybe haunting. Online, I've found pages and pages devoted to "Gloomy Sunday," and I won't bother putting it all down here, just a few points.

By 1936, the song had become known as the "Hungarian Suicide Song," after it was blamed for a number of suicides (some say seventeen, but the number varies wildly). There are reports the song was banned in Hungary, but I can't find any evidence this really happened. There are claims that many more people committed suicide in America upon hearing the Billie Holiday version, maybe as many as two hundred. There are sources that claim the recording was banned from U.S. radio, but the claims are unsubstantiated. I read accounts of suicides found with the sheet music in pockets or gripped in dead hands or playing on gramophones.

Some sources claim Jávor's version was inspired by his real-life love for a former girlfriend, and that, after hearing the song, she took her life and left behind a two-word suicide note: "Gloomy Sunday." Again, this only seems to be a rumor. But it is a fact that Rezső Seress took his own life in 1968 by jumping from a building in Budapest; the fall didn't kill him, but in the hospital he was able to strangle himself with a piece of wire. I can't help but think of Rosemary Anne, restrained at 345 Blackstone Boulevard, but . . .

According to Michael Brooks' liner notes for *Lady Day—the Complete Billie Holiday on Columbia, 1933–1944,* " 'Gloomy Sunday' reached America in 1936 and, thanks to a brilliant publicity campaign, became known as 'The Hungarian Suicide Song.' Supposedly after hearing it, distraught lovers were hypnotized into heading straight out of the nearest open window, in much the same fashion as investors after October 1929; both stories are largely urban myths."

I cannot say what's true here, and what isn't. I can only note the similarity to Japan's "Suicide Forest," following the publication of a novel. I can only reiterate what I've said about hauntings being especially pernicious thought contagions.

See also Death Cab for Cutie's "I Will Follow You Into the Dark" (2006), which Abalyn played for me, and Blue Öyster Cult's "(Don't Fear) The Reaper" (1976; Rosemary had this album). Also, maybe, Roy Lichtenstein's *Drowning Girl* (1963), though eyes, not ears.

JUNE 29, 2011

A college student from Kingston found Eva's body, three days after she swam away from me. There wasn't much left. There was an article in the *Providence Journal*. She was identified by dental records. By her teeth. Sharks had been at her, said the coroner. Sharks and fish and crabs. Like the girl who dies in the beginning of *Jaws*. But the sharks didn't kill her, the coroner said. She drowned, and then sharks scavenged her body. A week later, a seven-foot shortfin mako shark (*Isurus oxyrinchus*) was caught down near Watch Hill. There was a woman's hand in its belly, and shreds of a red silk dress.

July 2, 2011

"Whatever it was, or wasn't, it's done," the girl named India Morgan Phelps typed, "and you've written it down. Your ghost story. Yes, you will always be haunted, but it's done. Thank you. You can go now."

Good night, Rosemary Anne.

Good night, Caroline.

Good night, Eva.

Abalyn says she's here to stay. She said she loves me. When she said it, there were no crows or ravens.

The End

AUTHOR'S NOTE

Never has a novel come easily to me, but never before has one come with such profound difficulty as did *The Drowning Girl: A Memoir.* I was sitting in the South Kingston Public Library (Peace Dale, RI) on August 8, 2009, reading a book on the Black Dahlia murder, when the germ of the story first began to take shape in my mind. Over the subsequent twenty-seven months (to paraphrase Kelly Link's marvelous observation), it shifted its shape many times. And it was not until the last day of October 2010, after numerous false starts and plotlines devised, then cast aside, that I found my way into the book. In the end, it was as simple as allowing Imp to speak in her own voice.

There are a great number of sources of inspiration I feel I should acknowledge—because this is what we do, writers and madwomen, take apart things and then put them back together again in other ways. Some of these inspirations are quoted or alluded to in the text; others are only echoed, implied, or paid homage. They include (but are not limited to) Lewis Carroll's *Alice's Adventures in Wonderland* (1865) and *Through the Looking-Glass, and What Alice Found There* (1871); the works of Charles Perrault, the Brothers Grimm, and Hans Christian Andersen; Radiohead's "There there (The Boney King of Nowhere)" (from *Hail to the Thief*, 2003); Anne Sexton's "With Mercy for the Greedy" (from *All My Pretty Ones*, 1962); Robert Frost's "Stopping by Woods on a Snowy Evening" (from *New Hampshire*, 1923); Poe's album *Haunted* (2000); Elia Kazan and William Inge's *Splendor in the Grass* (1961), and, by extension, William Wordsworth's poem "Ode: Intimations of Immortality from Recollections of Early Childhood" (*Poems, in Two Volumes*, 1807); David Tibet and Current 93's *Black Ships Ate the Sky* (2006); a number of paintings—William Bradford's *Arctic Sunset* (1874), Winslow Homer's *On a Lee Shore* (1900), Martin Johnson Heade's *Brazilian Forest* (1864) and *Salt Marshes of Newburyport, Massachusetts* (1875–1878), all from the collections of the Rhode Island School of Design; Dante Alighieri's *la Divina Commedia* (1308–1321); Peter Straub's *Ghost Story* (1979); Kelly Link's "Pretty Monsters" (2008); Death Cab for Cutie's "I Will Follow You Into the Dark" (from *Plans*, 2006); the music of R.E.M., especially "Find the River" (1992, which would have been quoted, herein, if lawyers didn't suck); Matthew Arnold's "Dover Beach" (from *New Poems*, 1867); Charles Wesley's "Idumea" (1793); Seichō Matsumoto's *Kuroi Jukai* (1960); Herman Melville's *Moby-Dick* (1851); Angela Carter's "Wolf-Alice," (1978); Charles Fort's *Lo!* (1931); Henry Francis Cary's translation of Dante's *la Divina Commedia* (1805–1814); and Edgar Allan Poe's "The Doomed City (The City in the Sea)" (1831, 1845). Also, various works by Virginia Woolf, Emily Dickinson, Joseph Conrad, T. S. Eliot, and Sir Ernest Henry Shackleton. As for the works and lives, the arts and letters, of Phillip George Saltonstall and Albert Perrault, those are entirely my own invention, with the help of Michael Zulli and Sonya Taaffe.

To a degree, the overall structure of the narrative was suggested by the late Henryk Górecki's Symphony No. 3, Op. 36 (*Symfonia pieśni żałosnych*, 1976), as conducted by David Zinman. Too, the influence of Neil Jordan and Danielle Dax, via *The Company of Wolves* (1984), should be fairly obvious, though I somehow was unaware of it until I'd finished the book. And the same can be said for another very obvious inspiration, Tim Buckley's "Song to the Siren" (1970, as reinterpreted by This Mortal Coil and Elizabeth Fraser on *It'll End in Tears*, [1984]).

I have many people to thank (names will be repeated), because without them, this novel genuinely would never have been written. First and foremost, Sonya Taaffe (above and beyond; and for granting me permission to use her "The Magdalene of Gévaudan") and Geoffrey H. Goodwin, who sat up with me on several occasions, long past midnight and almost until dawn, discussing where Imp's story might and might not be. I owe an especially great debt to a number of writers who, during a late-night, dawn-thirty impromptu "workshop" at ReaderCon 21, urged me on and provided many ideas that would become crucial to the shifting shape of the novel: Michael Cisco, Greer Gilman, Gemma Files, Erik Amundsen, and, again, Geoffrey H. Goodwin and Sonya Taaffe. My thanks to Peter Straub, for his brilliance and support, and to my agent, Merrilee Heifetz (Writers House), and editor, Anne Sowards, for their patience as I missed deadline after deadline, and still asked for more time. To Michele Alpern, who has restored my faith in copy editors. To my mother, Susan Ramey Cleveland, to Jeff VanderMeer, and everyone who loved *The Red Tree*. My thanks to Hilary Cerullo, MD, who calmed my mind so I could finally write again, and to Kristin Hersh—the Rat Girl—for showing me it was okay to *write* like I *think*. My gratitude to the staff of the Providence Athenaeum, the Harvard Museum of Natural History and the President and Fellows of Harvard College, the Rhode Island School of Design Museum, S. T. Joshi, Andrew Fuller, Andrew Migliore and the organizers of the 2010 H. P. Lovecraft Film Festival (Portland, OR), and to everyone in Boston, New York City, and Providence who has offered support, but are too numerous to name. Also, thanks to Elizabeth Bear, Holly Black, Dan Chaon, Brian Evanson, Neil Gaiman, Elizabeth

Hand, Kathe Koja, Bradford Morrow, Benjamin Percy, Peter Straub, Cathrynne M. Valente, and Jeff VanderMeer, who all read the book while it was still only a manuscript, and to Jacob Garbe and Casondra Brewster for words in perfect order, and to Melissa Bowman for a perfect analogy. And to Radiohead and Philip Ridley for letting me quote their songs. To Vince Locke for the illustrations that appear in this edition of the novel. My gratitude to Kyle Cassidy, for his vision, and to everyone else who helped us turn the book into photos and a Lilliputian film (Brian, Sarah, Dani, and Nicola). Again, all my love to Michael Zulli, who *became* my Saltonstall, and brought the man and his paintings into *this* world, with a sprig of nightshade and black serpentine. But, above all, thanks to my partner, Kathryn A. Pollnac, for putting up with my shit, and reading these words back to me again, and again, and again.

We're doing the impossible, and this makes us mighty.

AUTHOR'S BIOGRAPHY

Caitlín R. Kiernan is the author of nine novels, including *Daughter of Hounds*, *The Red Tree*, and *The Drowning Girl: A Memoir*. Her award-winning short fiction has been collected in several volumes, including *Tales of Pain and Wonder*; *To Charles Fort, with Love*; *Alabaster*; *The Ammonite Violin & Others*; *A is for Alien*; and the forthcoming *Confessions of a Five-Chambered Heart*. Two volumes of her erotica have been published, *Frog Toes and Tentacles* and *Tales from the Woeful Platypus*. In 2011, Subterranean Press published *Two Worlds and In Between: The Best of Caitlín R. Kiernan (Volume One)*. Volume Two will follow in 2014. She is a four-time nominee for the World Fantasy Award, a two-time nominee for the Shirley Jackson Award, and has been recognized by the James Tiptree, Jr. Award. Trained as a vertebrate paleontologist, she currently lives in Providence, Rhode Island. She's heard many sirens, and spoken with many wolves.